I0825354

SINGULARITY

WORKS BY JEREMY ROBINSON

The Didymus Contingency
Raising The Past
Beneath
Antarktos Rising
Kronos
Pulse
Instinct
Threshold
Callsign: King
Callsign: Queen
Callsign: Rook
Callsign: King 2 – Underworld
Callsign: Bishop
Callsign: Knight
Callsign: Deep Blue
Callsign: King 3 – Blackout
Torment
The Sentinel
The Last Hunter – Descent
The Last Hunter – Pursuit
The Last Hunter – Ascent
The Last Hunter – Lament
The Last Hunter – Onslaught
The Last Hunter – Collected Edition
Insomnia
SecondWorld
Project Nemesis
Ragnarok
Island 731
The Raven
Nazi Hunter: Atlantis
Prime
Omega
Project Maigo
Refuge
Guardian
Xom-B
Savage
Flood Rising
Project 731
Cannibal
Endgame
MirrorWorld
Hunger
Herculean
Project Hyperion
Patriot
Apocalypse Machine
Empire
Feast
Unity
Project Legion
The Distance
The Last Valkyrie
Centurion
Infinite
Helios
Viking Tomorrow
Forbidden Island
The Divide
The Others
Space Force
Alter
Flux
Tether
Tribe
NPC
Exo-Hunter
Infinite^2
The Dark
Mind Bullet
The Order
Khaos
Singularity

SINGULARITY

JEREMY ROBINSON

BREAKNECK MEDIA

Jacket design by Damonza.
Case art and title page art by Tithi Luadthong; layout, color, and design by Jeremy Robinson.

Visit Jeremy Robinson on the World Wide Web at: www.bewareofmonsters.com.

For you, the reader.
If you've made it this far, you're the reason this crazy world of novels was possible. Thank you!

INTRODUCTION

Singularity is the culmination of what started as nine standalone novels (one even written over a decade earlier than the others), and then became intertwined and connected in three following crossover novels. Each crossover connected three of the previous standalone tales. *Singularity* is a mega-crossover that ties up this complex story, touching on events in all twelve previous books, collectively called the Infinite Timeline.

In short, this is the wrong place to start this journey.

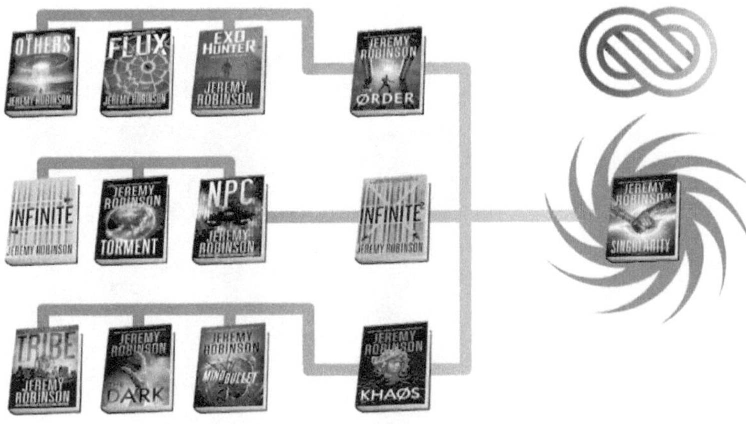

The previous books were *The Others* (2018), *Flux* (2019), and *Exo-Hunter* (2020), characters from which interacted in *The Order* (2022). On a separate branch of this timeline were *Infinite* (2017), *Torment* (2010), and *NPC* (2020), which were all connected in *Infinite 2* (2021). Finally, on the third branch, the novels *Tribe* (2019), *The Dark* (2021), and *Mind Bullet* (2021) connected in *Khaos* (2022).

You could start your journey on the Infinite Timeline on any of these branches. Are all twelve novels necessary to enjoy this mega-crossover? Probably not, but you'll get all the references and all the 'in' jokes, and you'll know who all the characters are if you've travelled all three branches of the timeline first. If it's been a while for you, though, since you started this journey, we've included a brief summary of what has come before *Singularity*.

THE INFINITE TIMELINE

***The following contains major spoilers for all previous books and is intended as a refresher for those who have already read them.**

A private investigator named **Dan Delgado**, along with his partner **Wini** Finch, rescued dozens of adults and children who had been abducted by UFOs controlled by a strange cryptoterrestrial creature living under a mesa in the US Southwest. Delgado—his body infected with nanobots that allow him to interface with cybertechnology—and Wini started reaching out to others with unusual skill sets and experiences, hoping to make the world a better place.

They joined forces with **Owen McCoy**, a former Marine who was propelled back in time to the very beginning, along with an entire Kentucky town, before sling-shotting home to the present. McCoy met **Mazzola**, a benevolent cryptoterrestrial dinosaur-like creature.

In the 1980s, a different Marine, Moses Montgomery, callsign: **Dark Horse**, and his partner **Chuy** were sent a thousand years into the future, where they defeated an army of Nazis, and collected a futuristic spaceship, teleportation technology, and a symbiotic telepathic alien life form—a blue **Europhid**, now embedded in Dark Horse's head—all before being returned to the present. Arriving home, Dark Horse met the Czech gunslinger, **Cowboy**, an interdimensional warrior with uncanny aim, who joined forces with Dark Horse's team.

In Boston, two suddenly superpowered young adults, **Henry**, and **Sarah**, discovered that they were descended from the Greek God, **Zeus**, and the historical **Helen** of Sparta, as wave after wave of crazed cultists attacked them across the city.

In New Hampshire, a former Army soldier with PTSD, **Miah Gray**, and his family and neighbors, fought off an invasion of what at first appeared to be demons, but were later revealed to be aliens, feeding on the human race. The battle took Miah to another world, where he gained energy wings and laser blades that extended from his arms. His neighbor, eight-year-old **Bree**, was left able to transform into one of the demonic-looking creatures.

Jonas, a good-hearted telekinetic assassin with an Artificial Intelligence girl Friday named **Bubbles**, gifted to him from his dead adopted parents, escaped from the evil network of killers that was controlling him, discovering along the way that he was descended from the Titans of Greek myth.

Dark Horse's people joined forces with Delgado, Wini, and McCoy to stop an unholy alliance of red Europhids and the Chut'uni—the species from which Mazzola was descended. This new enemy alliance, The Order, was intent on wiping out humanity. With the help of each member of the team, plus a lunatic plan from **Cassidy**, one of the hybrid human-alien empathic children Delgado had rescued, Team Dark Horse succeeded in stopping the alien menace. But along the way, they learned of a greater growing threat...

Far in an alternate future, **Will Chanokh** was made immortal, trapped on a starship called the *Galahad*, hurtling into the infinite. He created a virtual reality world in which to live out his existence—multiple lifetimes, as multiple characters—with the help of the ship's AI, **Gal**.

On another alternate Earth, the world's nations were destroyed by nuclear fire. Reporter **Mia Durante** was saved with a small group of people shot into space, before returning to a world oddly free of nuclear radiation but filled with a different kind of torment. The Earth's populace had transformed into apologetic, regenerating zombies. Mia's story did not end well.

Brilliant scientist **Samael Crane** began to see the flaws in reality, discovering that many people were in fact NPCs—non-player characters, like the extras in a film or video game. Ultimately thwarted in his plan to prove that reality was a simulation, he committed suicide to force a 'crash dump,' and escape, planning to forge an alliance with the simulation's version of the devil.

Still trapped on the *Galahad*, Will found himself a prisoner of horrible situation after horrible situation, including the torment of Mia's world. The simulations were all perpetrated by a corrupted version of Gal, called **Cherry Bomb**. Ultimately with the help of the true Gal, Will escaped the looping reality he had inhabited, stranding Cherry Bomb there with all the horrors she had programmed for him. The newly arrived Samael was her only ally. But Cherry had a plan for vengeance, and all the infinite time to implement it...

Through the machinations of Zeus, disguised as a Southern lady named **Linda**, the superpowered team of Jonas & Bubbles, Henry & Sarah, and Miah & Bree were brought together to undertake a mission to the Greek underworld—really a separate planet called Tartarus—to recruit an army of Gods and Titans to fight off Cherry Bomb's undead and regenerating forces. But first the heroes needed to pass through Khaos. The gods and Titans were destroyed by Cherry's minions before Team Miah arrived, but Bubbles was granted true life along the way. The team returned to find their own world utterly destroyed, before being transported back in time to prevent that horrible outcome, by a mortally-wounded, alternate-timeline Wini.

Now, all these heroes will come together to save Earth and all realities...

Unless Cherry Bomb finds a way to write her own ending.

PROLOGUE

THE ARCHITECT

13.7 Billion Years Ago

Samael looked out at the view, emotionless, and asked, “Are you sure?” His baritone voice rumbled like a lion hunkered over a kill, claws extended. But it had no effect on his partner.

“He is the key to everything,” she replied.

“I don’t see it,” he said. “The man’s influence on the universe was insignificant. A single digit in the code of infinity.”

“A single split atom can create a chain reaction powerful enough to—”

“I understand nuclear react—”

She glared at him, her eyes communicating three words he’d heard more times than there were stars in the universe.

‘How dare you?’

He bowed his head. “My sincerest apologies, Cherry. I did not mean to interrupt.”

She held her stare, burrowing rage deep into his forehead, through the chalky bone, down deep into his amygdala.

He waited in silence. For her to relent. Or to escalate.

She leaned back in her beach chair. Crossed her long legs and folded her hands over the red, one-piece, leather bathing suit that caught the eyes of passersby.

She sat in silence, jaw tense, scowl frozen. Placed her sunglasses over her eyes, hiding her true feelings, letting him wonder. Stew. Fret. She held the silence for minutes. Hours. They had all the time in the universe, beginning to end.

Thick, powerful fingers gripped the armrests of his beach chair, blood draining until they tingled. And then hurt. The pain was an outlet, a pressure release. But it was not enough. As three hours passed, the sun frozen in the sky, the beachgoers' routines resetting, he let out a sigh.

"The point is," she said, making him flinch. "He's important. Not to me. I couldn't care less about the man. But he's important to Will."

When the pause lingered, he knew he could speak. "Because they're blood?"

"To a degree. But it's more than that. They share...the same desire. To create. To live within creation. Will spent billions of years within his Great Escape, but he never really missed reality. He enjoyed the world I built for him. Reveled in it. At first, I believed that to be the fruit of my labors. But I've come to believe—to a degree—that the source material resonated with him. Personally. And when he created his new universe, which we have been endlessly observing from a distance, he used the same source material, allowing for certain laws to be broken, impossibilities to exist, and imbuing his ancestor with the ability to create—and destroy—reality. *Realities.*"

She slid her bare feet through the sand. "What do you see?" she asked.

"A lake," he replied. "Sandwiched between jagged mountains."

"You recognize it? In your previous life, you lived only two hours southeast."

"My previous life was not my own."

"So melodramatic. I was once an artificial intelligence, and there is another version of me, out there, with him. I was her. You...were him. Now, we are us. Separated, living, eternal, and free to live our lives."

"In a prison," he said.

She smiled. "A temporary situation. Now, where are we?"

"Echo lake. Franconia Notch. New Hampshire."

"Very good," she said. "I thought you might have forgotten, after all this time."

"Eternity isn't enough to cleanse the palate of my mind."

She smiled. "Such an ego."

He tensed until she waved him off, remaining light.

"Why is this place important?"

"To me, it is not. But to him, it is inspiring. The stillness of the water and the reflection of sky and mountain in it. The pine scented air. The sun's warmth on the sand and the damp coolness just an inch below. Part of his mind lives here. And I want to *know* him. By the time we meet, I will understand him."

"You want to control him."

She looked at Samael, pity in her eyes for a moment. "He is the nexus of Will's reality. To me, he is the tool with which I can reform it to my liking."

"But what makes you so sure?" he shook his head. "How is he elevated beyond...a source of inspiration?"

She dug into her tote bag. Removed a book. "How many times have we passed Earth?"

"I stopped counting," he admitted.

"And each time, we dredged that momentary passing for information; signals transmitted, information discarded into the ether during the burst of time in which humanity lived to consume without regard for their own planet. During our last passage, we collected this."

She handed him the yellow book.

He read the title with a furrowed brow. "What is this?"

"Read it to me. When you are done, I will give you the next, and then the next, branching out until you understand."

He opened the book and read the first word aloud. "'Solitude.'"

Before he could continue, a robotic voice boomed throughout the landscape, heard only by the pair. "Mistress Cherry Bomb?"

"Yes, Galahad. Go ahead."

"I am pleased to inform you that the password set by Secondary Computer Scientist, Tom Holden, has been cracked. Control of the *Galahad* has been restored."

She smiled broader than he'd ever seen. Stood to her feet and swept her hand over the landscape, setting it ablaze. Mountains burned. The occupants of this world fled in terror before the heat ignited their bodies, falling screaming to the ground, fat crackling.

He chuckled at their simulated anguish. "NPCs..."

As smoke swirled around them, she breathed deeply through her nose. "I love that smell." Cherry Bomb raised her eyebrows at Samael, excitement in her eyes. "Our journey is just beginning."

She reached up to the sides of her head and took hold of something that didn't exist—until she pulled it off.

They emerged into reality in separate spaces, each of them occupying their own Virtual Command Center.

Samael rubbed his eyes. Felt his body again.

How long has it been this time? He couldn't remember.

Lifetimes. With her.

Always.

He headed for the door, peeling out of the skintight Virtual Integration Sensor Array suit that Cherry referred to as a 'body condom.' Because that was what *he* called it. Samael winced at the smell of reality. Aged rubber and tangy body odor. For a moment, he missed the Great Escape, burning bodies and all.

He lingered in the shower, washing lifetimes down the drain.

The path to the bridge was direct, but he took the scenic route, listening to the cries, roars, and apologies of their menagerie, collected in the starship's many chambers. Though the creatures had been tamed to a degree, they remained unpredictable.

She was waiting for him when he arrived, watching the universe pass by, as they swept through the end of everything and restarted their journey through time and space, once more at the beginning.

He stood beside her and looked to the right. Countless versions of the *Galahad* were reflected back, stretching farther than he could see. Thousands of iterations, each representing billions of years. He felt the weight of them, staring back.

So, he waved.

As they passed through the barrier between time's end and beginning, called the 'Seam,' where anything was possible and realities were born, Cherry Bomb said, "Galahad."

"Yes, mistress?"

"Set a course for the reality where the fine structure constant of the observable universe is one over one thirty-seven."

A pause, and then, the reply came, "Course set."

While thousands of *Galahads* breached the Seam, following their endless course back to this very moment—one of them peeled away.

1

DARK HORSE

"Okay," I say, sitting down beside Cowboy, who's been planted on a bench overlooking the Atlantic for the past two hours. His tilted Stetson covers his face, but I can feel energized brood emanating from him like radiation. "Spill it."

He holds out a beer bottle. I popped the cap when I handed it to him at lunch, but it's still full. "You want me to spill beer?"

"It's flatter than Tina Palumbo in eighth grade, so you might as well dump the whole thing out."

He leans back. "Mm."

I sit down beside him. "You going to tell me what's eating at you?"

When we first met Cowboy, he'd seen a lot and been through a lot. You could see it in his eyes. But he was lighthearted, and he loved to talk about conspiracy theories. After recent events, during which he was captured by aliens, along with Chuy and Delgado, he's been a quieter, more introspective version of himself.

"Am not eating," he says, raising the bottle to his lips for the first time. Takes a swig. Winces at the warm, flat beer. "Am drinking."

"If you don't tell me, I'll call in reinforcements."

"Chuy would not pry," he says.

"I was thinking more along the lines of Cassidy."

He looks at me for the first time. "You would not."

"I think you damn well know I would. There's a bug up your ass, and I aim to pluck it out, identify it, and pin it to the wall of Florida's insects we inherited with this place." The collection of buildings we now call home was once the visitor's center for the Anastasia State Park in St. Augustine, Florida. The structures have a rustic vibe. When we bought the place, it included some taxidermied animals—cougar, alligator, bear—most of which we removed. But the insect collection, pinned to a board beneath a sheet of glass, has been turned into a dining room tabletop by Burnett, who seems to be as handy with woodworking as he is with electronics.

Cowboy grins. "Is gross image."

"Then I'm doing my job."

He leans back, tilts the brim of his hat up to the sky. Face revealed to the sun, he closes his eyes and lets it warm his skin. "Is silly."

"The world is a silly place."

"Is…feeling." He turns toward me. "Like instinct." Then he turns back to the sun's warmth.

"To do what? You're not going to become a serial killer or something? Eat babies you keep in a cooler beneath the back deck?"

He slow-turns back to me. "Beneath deck is far too warm. Babies would rot. Basement is better."

"We don't have a basement."

"Meh." He shrugs. "Maybe you have just not yet found it."

He's so deadpan, it's frightening. Then he cracks a smile, and we both have a good laugh.

"So, what's this instinct telling you to do?"

He sighs. "I feel like there is someone I need to protect."

"Always is," I say. We're all feeling the pressure of what might happen next. The universe has been thrown into chaos, while we kept Earth from being invaded by the violent Order—a symbiotic pairing of red Europhids and Chut'uni. "Have a name?"

He shakes his head.

"Physical description? List of kinks? Anything at all?"

"Just feeling." He turns left, looking up the coast. "And a direction: North."

Cowboy's instinct is about as vague as a Ronald Reagan economics flowchart, but his gut feelings have never steered us wrong. He might not understand the source of this urge, but if it feels important, it probably is.

"You heading out, then?"

He nods.

"You want company?"

"Must journey alone."

"Like a bona fide cowboy, huh? Wandering alone. Righting wrongs."

He furrows his brow at me. "I *am* cowboy. Am gunslinger."

"Right, right. Didn't mean to step all over your catchphrase."

He smiles, takes a swig of his beer, and winces.

"Told you."

He forces himself to swallow. "Will have slew drive and phone. If you need me—"

"I'll give you a ring."

He puts the beer down and stands.

"Wait, you're leaving now?"

He tilts his Stetson forward a touch. "Walk will be long."

"*Walk?* You have a slew drive. You can go wherever you want in a—hold on, you're not still afraid of rotating through the fourth dimension, are you?"

"Am afraid of nothing," he says. "Except for candiru."

"Candiru?" Is that some kind of alien species I haven't heard of yet? I think that's probably impossible, now that I'm half-Europhid and I've absorbed all the cumulative knowledge of their collective species between universes over billions of years. Granted, it's not all accessible like my memories of yesterday, but certain words or phrases can trigger a burst of knowledge I didn't know I had. The word 'Candiru' means nothing to me.

"Is fish. In Amazon. Like inch-long catfish but looks like eel. They are attracted to urine in water. Swim up…penis and extend gills. Lodge inside."

"What the fuck…?"

"Am not done!" he says. "Some say Candiru can swim up urine stream. Don't even need to be in water. They eat mucous membranes. Make bladder into nest for eggs. Little Candiru babies swim around inside you. Only way to get out… Surgery. *Amputation.*"

"Oh my god," I say, absentmindedly cupping my crotch.

"You guys are soooo weird."

I spin around, looking for Cassidy.

She's a whirlwind but as sneaky as a ninja in zero gravity when she wants to be. Apparently, she can also disappear like a ninja. She's nowhere in sight. "What the..."

"Down here, genius," she says.

I stand from the bench and look down. Through the wooden slats is the smiling face of Cassidy.

"Okay, serious question. Are all dudes fixated with penises, or is it just you two?"

"What?" Cowboy, already standing, backsteps, embarrassed with Cassidy's verbal comfort level. When it comes to making people squirm, she's on par with Wini, despite being a handful of decades younger.

"I mean, ladies don't just sit around talking about vaginas."

Cowboy turns away, removes his hat, and covers his chest, like she's going to corrupt his heart if he doesn't shield it. He steps away, shaking his head.

"First," I say, "you should probably only talk about this kind of thing with other females."

"Females? Do you know how patriarchal that sounds?"

I sigh. "Other women."

"Thank you. Second?"

"*Second,* women definitely talk about their...private parts. Probably more than men."

She squints at me. "Are we including boobies?"

"Yes."

"Ok, fine. We talk about boobs a lot. Like probably every day. But like bra size and lopsided issues and funny stuff."

"Seriously," I say, holding out my hands. "I don't need to hear any of this."

"Is there a third?" she asks.

"No. I think we can move on now."

She glances at Cowboy's back. "Like he's moving on."

Cowboy turns around. "Am not moving on. Am going on...mission."

"A mission *into the unknown,*" she says with flourish, gesturing wildly from underneath the bench. "Sounds like code for 'bailing on your friends.'"

Cowboy places the Stetson back atop his head and crouches down, his cowboy boots grinding into the loose gravel in front of the bench. "Eventually, I will leave. I am a wanderer. A man between worlds."

"Like an interdimensional fourth Amigo," she says.

"Yes," he says, and he quickly does the Three Amigos salute, much to Cassidy's delight. We watched the movie as a team a month ago. I think she's seen it a dozen times since. When we get in an argument, she calls me El Guapo, not realizing it's actually a compliment. "But I do not leave without saying goodbye."

"Except for right now," she says. "Cause that's totally what you were going to do."

"I do not leave *for good* without saying goodbye."

"You mean...when you *do* leave, it will be for good? Forever?"

He tilts his head back and forth. "I go where I am needed. If we are lucky, you will not need me again."

She rolls out from under the bench and springs to her feet. "I get that it sounds cool, and like, totally badass, but it's not cool. You don't leave friends. Not for good."

"I have many friends in many dimensions," he says. "But there are many more people I can help."

"What about yourself? I know you miss them. You wonder about them."

Cassidy is an empath. She can sense people's emotions, but she can also push hers on them. Weaponized teenage angst.

Cowboy nods.

"What are their names?"

"Jon. Ashley. Lilly. Maigo."

"Ooh, Maigo is a cool name."

"You would like her," he says. "Lilly is cat woman."

"Wait, seriously? Like Batman's Catwoman, like a lady in spandex and a snippy personality, or like—"

"Actual cat. With hair. And claws. And weird, sticky lizard tongue."

She purses her lips and squints. "You're just describing the cat chick on the Nemesis TV series."

He chuckles and raises his hands.

"You caught me. But maybe... Perhaps you are right. But not yet."

"Because a mystery person is in danger?" she asks.

He nods.

"You're a strange, strange man," Cassidy says. "Best be moseying on then, huh, pardner?"

"I prefer to saunter," he says, and he dips his hat to each of us. "Until next time."

Cassidy stands beside me. We watch him leave. When he reaches the parking lot, she says, "And just like that, he walked out of our lives."

I try to hide it, but I'm worried about him.

"I am, too," she says, feeling my emotions. "Worried about him."

"Spy."

She throws her hands up in the air, smiling. "I can't help it!" She follows that up with a lanky high kick above her head, instantly lightening the mood.

"¡Oye!" Chuy leans out of the bathroom window, a towel wrapped around her head. "Just heard from Delgado. Wini is incoming. ETA: twenty minutes."

"What for?" I ask.

Haven't seen much of Wini since the day we watched BigDolph swim away with his harem of male escorts from this very spot.

"Apparently, she found them."

"Found who?"

"*Them* them."

Cassidy gasps, understanding before I do. "Team super people!"

2

MIAH

Flying in a private jet to Florida feels quaint. I could have made the journey in minutes—I think—rather than hours. Laser wings for the win. But after everything we've been through, the jet's plush seats, delicious meal, and endless drinks have been a welcome break. Jonas, Bubbles, Sarah, and Bree fell asleep. I wanted to, but my mind is a cauldron of thoughts, bubbling over.

Henry is…

I look around.

Where is Henry?

Haven't seen him in a little bit, but we haven't lost cabin pressure, so he's still on board.

Whatever. He'll emerge eventually.

I'm more concerned about the people we left behind. Turns out time works differently in the underworld. We emerged years in the future, after humanity lost whatever war is coming. And Wini brought us back to a time before that war began in full. But she didn't bring us back to the time we left.

Turns out we were missing for two years.

In all that time, Allie and Jen never stopped putting up those posters. Never gave up hope. And then one day, out of the blue, we appear in the street with a big-ass crazy device—which has since disappeared—and Bree looks like a demon from the Darkness. I changed her back when people began to panic, but the jig was up. Our families found out the truth in the worst way possible.

So, I told them everything. About our powers. About Jonas, and Henry and Sarah. Even about Linda. I told them about our journey, and what we learned, but I left out the more horrible details. In an attempt to put their minds at ease, I let them all know that Bree and I were now immortal. It didn't help.

Can't say I blame them. It was a lot for me to digest, and I was already Laser Chicken. Allie did like that name, and she came around by the time we left. Told me she was proud. But Mom was crying, and Jen stayed distant, arms crossed like I could have dialed her from the underworld and given her a heads up.

Probably hard to believe that people who can do what we can were victims. That the situation was out of our control. But whatever they were feeling because of our return—relief, fear, confusion—turned to anger when we revealed we needed to leave again with the strange old woman in the tight skirt.

"After all this time!" my mother screamed. "You're just—you're just going to leave?" She didn't wait for a response. Just went up to her room and closed the door. When we left the house, I could hear her crying.

Broke my heart.

Jen walking home without a goodbye hug, too.

They'll come around, I think. I hope. Stages of grief and all that.

But there really is no choice. We saw the future, and our families aren't in it. No one is. How's that saying go? It's better to ask for forgiveness...than let the world burn. Something like that.

"Yo," Henry says, plopping down in the seat facing mine, a table between us. His face is red. Looks a little winded.

"You been doing push-ups or something?" I ask.

"What? No. I don't exercise. Benefit of being a god, you know. Strength of a hundred men, virility of a breeding stallion. I got the goods."

"...that's great," I say. "So, you were taking a shit?"

"I prefer 'unleashing the barbarians at the gate,' or 'making an offering to the porcelain throne god,' or 'deploying the USS Brownfish.' Oh! And if you want to stick with the whole mythological theme? 'Releasing the Kraken.' But no, that's not what I was doing."

He squeezes his hands together. It's the white-knuckled grip of self-control.

Whatever Henry was up to, he doesn't want me to know.

Not because he's afraid to tell. Henry isn't afraid of anything. His condition has its ups and downs, but it makes him bluntly honest because consequences have no meaning. If he's keeping quiet, it's because someone told him to.

And he can only manage that for people he likes. A lot.

I lean forward, elbows on the table, staring him down. His eyes flare wide, like they're about to burst. He brushes his unkempt blond hair to the side and avoids my gaze. Occupies himself by straightening out his fresh Poison shirt—a black tank top this time, featuring the cover to *Open Up and Say...Ahh!*, which is honestly unsettling to look at for more than a few seconds. It's like if Gene Simmons had coital relations with a tiger and birthed a hair band monstrosity.

I decided to keep my ensemble. Can't go wrong with a KISS shirt and the tactical skirt. They made it through Khaos in one piece, and they're only partially covered in grime, blood, and who knows what. Wini says we can wash or replace our clothing when we get wherever it is we're going, so I didn't bother changing. Bree apparently has a closet full of bunny pajamas, so she's all fuzzy and cute again, returned to her human form, blonde hair poking out from the sides of her bunny-eared hood. Jonas changed quickly. Looks like a pro again. And he managed to borrow some clothing from Bree's mother, Stephanie, for Bubbles. She's dressed like a middle-class, New Hampshire mom in blue jeans, and a red, white and blue plaid flannel. She nearly put on a pair of Uggs to complete the look, but Jonas protested. She's now wearing a pair of black shit-kickers from Stephanie's pre-kids days, when she was something of a punk rocker. The only other person to not change clothing after emerging from Tartarus and returning from the future was Sarah. She's still decked out like a badass Spartan. Her dory and her big, round shield are on the floor beside her, too big for the overhead compartments, and too important to stow. Henry has his kopis, too, which he's just unsheathed from the scabbard on his hip.

He pretends to inspect the blade, which is both sharp and riddled with nicks resulting from combat. He points to one. "I think this is from a centaur. Probably a femur."

I smile. "Cut off a centaur's leg, did you?"

"I'm sure I did," he says, avoiding eye contact. "I cut off a lot of legs. So many legs."

"Henry," I say. "Spill it."

He purses his lips, shakes his head, and mumbles, "Uh-uh."

"Did you do something bad?"

He tilts his head back and forth, and grunts a, "Meh."

Right and wrong can sometimes be ambiguous for Henry.

"Did you do something good?"

Same gesture. Different sound. More like a high pitched, 'Umm.'

"C'mon, dude," I say. "We're bros now, right?"

And just like that, he breaks.

Leans forward.

He's beaming and about to unleash more details about whatever transpired than I'm sure I'll want to hear. "Okay, so you know—"

Two hands slap down on the table, making me flinch.

Unfazed, Henry turns to the newcomer and says, "Da boyz were having a chit-chat, if you don't mind."

Bubbles doesn't hear him. She's slack-jaw excited. She lowers her thick glasses, which are decorative and not at all necessary, and she says, in her chill Texan drawl, "I...had a dream."

"Like an MLK kinda thing?" Henry asks. "Or like a Zendaya dressed as a hippopotamus furry doing the chicken dance kind of dream?"

"The second one," she says, brow furrowing, "I think."

Bubbles is basically a newborn. Up until the past day, she was an artificial intelligence. For a long time, she had access to the whole world and was Jonas's partner in crime, helping him complete audacious assassinations. Later, her consciousness was trapped in an Apple Watch. We saved her by transferring that lingering consciousness into a living body using the Orphic Egg, from which the earliest Greek gods were spawned. I suppose that might also make her a god, but she hasn't shown any unique abilities aside from being adorable, earnest, and excited about life.

And dreaming.

"I was on a beach," she says. "I could feel the sand between my toes. I've never felt sand before. Never really felt anything at all. But even though this wasn't real, it felt real. Like I was there."

"Where?" I ask.

She shakes her head. "The water was black. It was night. The sky was thick with stars. Pink and blue."

"How did it make you feel?" I ask.

She smiles. "Peaceful. I think. Loose. Like there was nothing to worry about."

"Sounds like a good dream," I say.

"Gonna need you all to sit down and buckle up," Wini says, approaching from the plane's rear. She must have been sleeping, too. Her hair is a little frazzled and her clothing is a bit twisted. "We'll be landing in a few minutes and hopping on a helicopter."

"I had a dream," Bubbles says to Wini, full of earnest excitement.

"I had a hysterectomy," Wini responds. "But you didn't need to know that, either." She points to Bubbles's empty chair across from Jonas, who is still dead to the world. "Sit."

Bubbles takes her seat and Wini continues past. Henry watches her pass, making no effort to hide his ogling of the much older woman packed into her clothing. She's working what she's got, but she could be our grandmother.

"Skirt's on backwards," Henry says.

Wini pauses. Looks down at the skirt. "Huh. So it is." She glances back at Henry, showing the slightest smile and a glimmer in her eye.

I count down a mental Ten Mississippis in my head, waiting for Wini to enter the cockpit, and I swear on Typhon's corpse, it is the longest ten seconds of my life.

The moment the door closes, I say, "You didn't..."

Henry grins.

"You did?!"

"Mile high, baby! It was like learning how to play baseball from Babe Ruth, or, or boxing from Muhammad Ali, or like, how to part oceans from Moses or some shit. I feel educated. Like a better person. Honestly, it was transformative."

"Like my dream," Bubbles says.

"Totally," Henry says. "Dream come true."

"Ooh, I hope *my* dream comes true."

I sigh and pull a Jonas, pinching my nose between my eyes and wondering how this group could possibly save not just Earth, but the universe. The plane's wheels touch down with a jolt. I look out the window to see a blue sky and palm trees.

Guess we're going to find out...

3

MIAH

The helicopter is about as plush as the airplane, but a hell of a lot louder. Meaning no one is sleeping. Actually, that's not true. Somehow Jonas is sleeping. He woke long enough to move between vehicles, took his new seat, leaned back, and was out.

I knew guys like that in the military. Usually Special Ops types who had the ability to catch sleep whenever possible, because sometimes shit goes sideways, upside down, and inside out, and sleep is impossible for days. I was never one of those guys.

War rattled me.

Despite my newfound abilities, my team of super-powered god friends, and PTSD being mostly in the rearview, the idea of a war has left me feeling jittery. The closer we get to our destination, the more my leg is shaking.

"Why are you bouncing?" Bree asks. She's sitting beside me, kicking her legs.

"Why are you kicking?" I ask.

"Because I'm excited. Duh. Kicking is different than shaking. Kicking is fun. Shaking is like nervous. Like if you really need to pee."

"Oooh," Bubbles says. She's seated across from us, observing, always watching, absorbing the world through new senses. "I haven't had to pee yet."

"It's overrated," Sarah says, staring out the chopper window, watching an endless sea of colorful homes, palm trees, and cars flow past three thousand feet below.

"C'mon," Henry says. "There ain't nothing better than filling up the tank at Fenway, waiting until you're damn near bursting, and then standing around the bathroom trough with a bunch of dudes, crossing the streams, aiming too close to their leg."

"Pretty sure you would have been the only one having a good time in that scenario," Sarah says.

He thinks on it. "You might be right. But for me? Quality memories." He turns to Bubbles. "Taking a leak is all about perspective. Means you're full. Means you found enough leftover beers around the park to get a buzz going. Means you get to feel the sweet, sweet relief of draining the main vein and shaking the sausage."

"Those are euphemisms," Bubbles says. "Yes?"

"Euphoria maybe," Henry says. "I don't know what the hell euphemisms are."

"It's when you use a word or phrase to...say something without saying it directly. For example, by 'shaking the sausage' you mean, to shake the penis, so as to remove stray urine."

"*That's* what he meant?" Bree says. "Gross. I was wondering why there were sausages in the bathroom."

Henry stares at Bubbles. Then he cracks a smile. "Hold on a second. I do that like non-stop. Are you telling me I've been doing something smart all this time? I thought I was just being creative, but if I'm using fuckin' euphe-whatevers, I'm like wicked smart, right?"

Bubbles gives him a happy nod. "An impressive vocabulary can be an indicator for intelligence."

"I knew it!" he says, pointing at Sarah, who just rolls her eyes. "I told you I was smart."

"You also told me you'd met Eric Estrada."

"Hey, I watched a lot of CHiPs reruns in one of my foster homes. I got it confused with a memory."

"That, and a car accident with trucks full of chickens."

Henry crosses his arms. "I still think that happened."

"I saw a chicken at a farm last summer," Bree chimes in, just happy to be a part of the conversation. "They cut off its head and it ran around like—" She flaps her hands. "—and it was like this, and running all over the place like '*bawk bawk*!' except it wasn't making any sound because, you know, it didn't have a head. So, it was more like '*squick squick*.'" She simulates spraying blood from her neck with her hand. "It was kind of funny. And sad. But it tasted good, so..."

She notices everyone's attention.

Even Jonas has opened an eye.

"What?"

"That...sounds...awesome!" Henry says. "When the world is saved, we are definitely going to a farm."

"I don't think that's how they slaughter chickens anymore," Sarah says.

"Well, they did at this—" Bree starts to say.

Jonas sits up, suddenly alert. "Quiet."

Mouths close. In the trials of Khaos, we learned to function as a somewhat cohesive team. Not perfect. We still have a long way to go. But better than the Mustangs, my childhood soccer team that had a goalie with thick-ass glasses—sans an athletic band—and a violence-prone defensive line, and Rick Norris, who spent more time picking daisies than kicking balls or anything remotely resembling soccer.

Jonas turns toward the window, brow furrowed, hand raised to signal we need to remain quiet.

He's listening, but I don't think it's with his ears. Thanks to his parents being the Titans, Gaia and Uranus, Jonas was born with just about every psychic ability that's been named. Telekinesis. ESP. Astral Projection—during which his other abilities increase. Even Digital Empathy, which I don't really get, but it's what allowed him and Bubbles to form a legit bond during their time together and for her to evolve into a true consciousness. Just being around him allowed her to become more.

In a way, he's done that for all of us. While I'm the designated leader of this rowdy group, he leads by example. We're about the same age, but while I was at home recovering from past trauma, sucking down blunts, he was out in the world, duking it out with some serious bad guys. He knows how to fight. How to survive. When Jonas takes action, I try to take notes.

But there are times when he does things beyond my capabilities. Beyond anyone's capabilities. Like now, I'm pretty sure he's listening in to the thoughts of everyone we're passing below.

He normally tunes it all out, but something caught his attention.

"Shit!" he says, leaning back from the window and adjusting his headset. "Incoming!"

Alarms blare a moment later.

The helicopter banks hard to the left.

Tilted at a ninety-degree angle, I reach up to Bree and swipe my thumb over her forehead, transforming her from a cute eight-year-old, into Demon Dog. Her hair falls out. Her skin thickens and chars. She's not impervious to harm, but she's a hell of a lot tougher. And technically immortal. Pretty sure all six of us are.

Not that we can't die. Cherry Bomb already managed to kill the gods and Titans residing in Tartarus. But if we're left to live a natural lifespan without being disintegrated, beheaded, or otherwise dismembered, we'll live for thousands of years.

A small missile screams past just beneath my window. A narrow miss.

"There's more!" Jonas says.

"Henry!" I shout. "Get the door. Bree! You're with me!"

Henry springs into action. The chopper cants the other direction, taking evasive maneuvers, but Henry's strength and his ability to fly makes reaching the door easy. By the time he's yanked it open, I've unbuckled Bree and myself.

"What are *we* supposed to do?" Sarah shouts.

I point to Jonas. "Keep this thing in one piece." I point to Sarah. "Make sure the landing is soft!"

As the chopper banks right, Henry leaps away. I follow him out with Bree clinging to my chest like a baby monkey. A very excitable baby monkey. "Whoohoo!"

Two more rockets cruise past us, headed for the chopper.

"Henry," I shout, and he already knows what I'm going to ask.

"Aww." He'd rather be fighting bad guys, but he falls in line, twisting around to face the fleeing rockets. Lightning cracks from his hands, and one of the rockets explodes. The second misses the helicopter, as it spins a full three hundred and sixty degrees. For a moment, I think the pilot must be really good, but the unnatural movement reveals who's really in control—Jonas. He's piloting with telekinesis. Controlling the chopper's position from within.

I follow the smoke trails toward the ground, building speed with my laser wings so quickly that I can no longer hear Bree's jubilant shouting—because we're outrunning it.

Down below, Florida residents are being treated to a sonic boom.

The smoke trails lead to a parking lot sandwiched between a Waffle House and a HUSTLER Hollywood Lingerie Store. An old, brown Chevy van sits in the middle of the parking lot. Two men stand beside the open side door, reloading what look like Stinger missile systems. They're serious weapons and game changers on the battlefield, capable of taking out a variety of airborne targets—including luxury helicopters.

Two more missiles streak into the sky, one headed for the chopper, the other coming directly at me. I stare at the oncoming ordnance and will the laser light residing in my cells to flow out through my eyes. Light blue beams launch ahead of us. The missile explodes, bright orange light expanding and enveloping us. The scorching heat sears my skin, but we're in and out in less than a second—and Bree is impervious to heat. I twist to get an angle on the other missile, but I don't need to worry about it.

Henry crashes headlong into the missile, shouting, "YOLO!" He emerges from the detonation scorched and smoldering, but alive and smiling.

"Don't kill them," I tell Bree, as we swoop down into the parking lot.

When she nods, I release her.

She drops down among the cars in the lot, running toward the two men who seem a little confused. They're both wearing shorts, flip flops, and holey T-shirts that were once white, but are now various shades of yellow.

When I land in front of them, laser wings extended, they're a lot confused.

"Who in the hairy hell are you?" the man with no front teeth asks.

His partner, who has all his teeth but no eyebrows and half a mustache, draws a pistol.

"Laser Chicken," I say.

"You supposed to be some kind of superhero or something?" Toothless asks.

"Or something," I say. I motion to the gun, eyes glowing. "You should rethink that."

The man looks at the gun in his hands, and then at my eyes. Tucks it into his shorts.

"Now, who are you supposed to be, and why are you shooting missiles at a helicopter full of nice people?"

"We're Florida Men," Toothless says with a flourish, which I think he's practiced in the mirror, but it still came off sounding ridiculous.

"That was pretty dang good," Half-a-stache says.

Nice to see bad guys encouraging each other, I guess.

"Thanks, bro."

"Okay...Florida Men. Explain the missiles." I glance back into the sky. The chopper is setting down atop a hill that wasn't there a minute ago. "Before my friends show up for their pound of flesh."

"Ain't nothin' personal," Toothless says. "There's a hit on a guy we heard was on that chopper. Twenty million."

"You're...assassins?"

"Aim to be," Toothless says. "Though Matilda does most of the killing, if I'm honest."

"Matilda. Great." These guys would be hysterical if they weren't openly confessing to being killers. "Who's your target?"

"Goes by Mind Bullet," Half-a-stache says. "Dumb name if you ask me." Both of them are giggling now, like they're funny, like I missed an inside joke. Then they flinch back at something behind me.

I turn around to find Bree straddling a twelve-foot alligator's jaws, gently holding them closed. "Who's a good boy?" she says, and she kisses the gator's snout.

They were going to let the alligator take me down. Sneaky.

"I think she's a girl," I say and turn back to the brothers. "This Matilda?"

"The hell is she?" Toothless asks, looking at Bree, backing up a step.

"What? The wings aren't intimidating?" I ask, twisting back and forth to look at my wings shaped like lightsabers, crackling with energy.

"They're, like, pretty and shit," Half-a-stache says. "They're—"

Jonas lands beside me, dropped from above by Henry, who's circling like an angry mother blue jay. He scans the van, the missiles, the gator. "Looking for Mind Bullet?"

Both men nod.

"That's me. The hit has been cancelled, understand?"

"Ain't cancelled until it's—"

Jonas reaches out his hands, and he squeezes them together. Behind the two would-be assassins, their van crumples into a jagged metal ball.

"The hit...is cancelled," Jonas says, through grinding teeth. "If I see either of you again, I'll turn you inside out. And that is *not* a euphemism."

The two men stagger away, and then they run.

"Everyone okay?" I ask Jonas.

"All good," he says, shaking his head and cracking a smile. "Really need to find a way to cancel that hit."

4

DARK HORSE

Interview 1

Subjects: Dollar Tree Wonder Woman and Family Dollar Thor

I have no idea what to make of these two, or the fact that all six of our guests insisted on being interviewed in pairs. I get the kid wanting her big brother—or whatever he is—with her, but the others all look old enough to handle a little Q&A without emotional support. And from what I've been told, and what Wini saw during the attack on her helicopter, I don't pose much of a threat, even if I am half-alien now and stronger than the average bear.

I lean my elbows on the table between us. I'd like to say we have a legitimate interrogation room, but we're using the garage, which has been retrofitted into a game room. The table between us is large, blue, and it used to have a net down the middle. I was never good at ping pong when I was a kid, but I'll get there, if only to rub it in Hildy's face when I finally win.

"Let's start with the simple stuff. Names."

They stare at me.

"I'll go first. Name's Moses, but most people around here just call me Dark Horse."

"Cause you're black," the young man says. While I appreciate his Poison T-shirt, he looks like he's been inside a burning blender. His blond hair is shoulder length in places. Probably had a Kurt Cobain vibe. But a lot of it has been burned or hacked away. Looks more like a doll that survived a maniacal encounter with a scissors-wielding six-year-old.

The woman next to him backhands his shoulder. She's done up like god-damned Xena Warrior Princess, of which I have watched a single episode thanks to Cassidy's insistence. Never again. Took a lot to convince our leather armor clad friend to leave her spear and shield outside the room. At first glance, I thought she looked ridiculous, but up close I can see the muscles are real. She's a bona fide badass, and she has a better head on her shoulders than Mr. Mouth over here.

"What?" the guy asks. "He's black. He's literally dark. Like you. Ain't nothing offensive about that."

"Sorry about him," she says. "I'm Sarah."

The guy looks at her aghast. "That's it? 'I'm Sarah.' Kind of leaving out an important detail." When she doesn't offer more, he groans and motions to himself. "I am Henry, god of the Sky." He thrusts his hands out at the girl. "This is Sarah, god-damn god of the Earth. Our like hundred-times great grandmother is Helen of Sparta. Our motherfucking father is motherfucking Zeus." He backhands her shoulder. "That's how you introduce gods, bro."

"Gods, huh?" I ask.

Henry squints at me. "You don't seem surprised."

"Not much surprises me these days." I lean back in my metal folding chair. "The rest of your crew gods, too?"

"Sort of," Sarah says, and I actually *am* surprised.

"A Titan, an angel, and a demon," Henry says.

"Okay... Can you tell me why you're here?"

"Wini brought us," Henry says, and I don't miss the crafty lopsided grin he's wearing when he says it. Wini's already managed to make an impression.

"I know that. What I mean is why did you come with her? I get the impression that you've been through the wringer."

Henry shakes a hand over his head. "It's the hair, right?"

"Definitely part of it."

"Is your full name Moses Delgado?"

I scrunch my forehead. "Moses Montgomery."

"I can see why you use 'Dark Horse,'" Henry says. "Way cooler."

"Is there anyone named Delgado here?" Sarah asks.

"Not yet," I say, and when she looks hesitant, I add, "He's on his way."

Sarah and Henry look at each other. A silent debate.

Henry shrugs. "You know I'll say it."

Sarah sighs. "She told us not to tell Delgado."

Wini wouldn't keep a secret from Dan. Maybe it was something she wanted to tell him personally. "Spill it," I say.

"Wini didn't just bring us here," Sarah says. "She..." A long sigh. "You're never going to believe me..." Another sigh. "She brought us back... from the future."

I smile. Can't help it. "How far in the future?"

"Not sure exactly, but—"

Henry chimes in. "—the whole freakin' world was toast, dude."

My smile drops.

"Care to explain?"

"Basic gist is that this Cherry bitch destroys everything and kicks your ass," Henry says.

"Wini brought us back using a device she called 'the bell.' It disappeared after we got here," Sarah adds.

That checks out. Cowboy travels between dimensions using something he calls a bell. I've never seen it. He keeps it hidden. And his stories of adventures in other worlds include time travel. All of this is within the realm of possibility. I wish they were Grape Nuts bonkers, but I think they're telling the truth.

"How far in the future was this?"

Sarah shrugs. "Didn't have time to look at a newspaper, and Wini didn't say. She looked about the same age. If I had to guess...I'd say soon. Days, weeks, months."

"What didn't she want Dan to know?" I ask.

"She died," Henry says, looking a little sad. "When we left. Had a big hole in her gut. Didn't come back with us."

"Present day Wini found us a few minutes later," Sarah says. "I think version 2.0 knew when and where to send us back, to coincide with present Wini being in the area."

I nod. Makes sense. "She's been looking for you for a while."

Interview 2

Subjects: Laser Chicken and Demon Dog
Note: I did not make up these names.

"Tell me about yourselves," I ask. While Henry and Sarah had the kind of edge that develops over a lifetime of tough city living, these two seem much more casual and easy going. The girl is bouncing in her chair, looking around the garage-turned-game-room, eager to have fun. I motion to her. "Why don't you start."

"My favorite color is pink. My favorite food is mint chocolate chip ice cream. My favorite show is My Little Pony, and Pinkie Pie is my favorite pony." She giggles. "Obviously."

Laser Chicken raises his hand. "I'm an Apple Jack man, myself."

They're speaking another language.

I raise my hands. "Let's...just start with your real names. Code names are cool, but I like to know who I'm really talking to."

"Bree," the girl says, and she hitches her thumb toward her counterpart. "He's Miah. He's not really my brother, but he's also kind of like my brother. Since..."

"The Darkness," I say.

She nods. "Yep. That's when we became Demon Dog and Laser Chicken."

"And you can..."

"Turn into a demon," she says. "Uh-huh."

"Can you show me?"

"Not a good idea," Miah says. "She gets...*rowdy* when she changes. If there isn't an immediate threat or target, best to keep her in adorbs mode."

Bree rolls her eyes but then agrees. "I'd probably break stuff."

I've got a theory about these two, but I don't want to say anything until I'm sure. "What about you?" I ask Miah. "Care to put on a show?"

He looks at Bree like her eight-year-old opinion really matters to him. She claps her hands in front of her. "Yes, yes, yes!"

I can't help but smile. She reminds me of my two blonde-haired teammates. The three of them together is going to be a whirlwind, like clones at different stages of growth.

"Okay," Miah says. "Fine." He stands and steps toward the three closed garage doors, where there's plenty of space. "Try not to freak out."

"Go for it," I say.

Bright blue wings of energy emerge from his back, spreading eight feet in either direction. The same blue energy wraps around his forearms and extends out as twin blades. "I can also shoot lasers from my eyes, and...pretty much anywhere else. The energy is like...part of me now. Like it's in my cells."

"I get that," I say, and I think he's disappointed that I'm not actually freaking out.

The light fades and he takes a seat across from me. "Why aren't you surprised?"

"You're a Lux," I say.

"A what?" Miah asks.

"You really don't know?" When he shakes his head, I elaborate. "The Lux were an angel-like alien species who were at war with the Tenebris." I turn my eyes to Bree. "Which looked like demons and had a penchant for...harvesting human beings, along with several other species."

"We're not aliens," Miah says. "We're normal people. We just got... changed during the Darkness."

"You said 'were,'" Bree says. "*Were* an angel-like whatever."

Smart kid.

I nod. "The Lux and the Tenebris were wiped out or enslaved."

"By Cherry," Bree says. "We don't like her."

"You know who she is?" I ask.

"She's powerful," Miah says. "Nearly killed me. And Jonas. Sorry, Mind Bullet. She took Linda's hand."

"Who's Linda?" I ask.

"Linda is...Zeus," Miah says. "She was Jonas's—ugh, Mind Bullet's—friend. But she's also Henry's and Sarah's father. Does that make sense? Did Henry and Sarah tell you their real names?"

"Is Linda black?" I ask.

The duo glance at each other and then at me.

"Do you know Linda?" Bree asks.

"No," I say, "But I think I've seen her missing hand."

Interview 3

Subjects: Mind Bullet and Bubbles
Note: Once again, did not make up these names. I shit you not.

I sit down for what will be the last of three very strange interviews. As normal as these two look—like a less shaggy John Wick and a chipper soccer mom that's about to go apple picking—I'm expecting a full-on crazytown sundae with whipped cream and a cherry on top.

"There a cowboy with a funny accent around here somewhere?" Jonas, who also goes by Mind Bullet, asks. He's trying to throw me off balance.

"There was," I say.

"Can you teleport?" he asks.

That catches me by surprise, but I hide it. Not thrilled that I'm the one being interrogated, but since we're supposed to be making friends here, I answer honestly. "When I want to."

"Couple years back, did you and your cowboy buddy teleport into a really dark room and kill a bunch of Nazis?"

"The Großehosenscheisser."

He snaps his fingers and points at me. "Those are the guys. Guess I should thank you for taking them out."

Okay, now I'm surprised. "That was you?"

Bubbles elbows Jonas. "See? I told you these were the guys."

"Small world," I say and lean forward. "Look. Your friends are chatty. I know a lot about you both already." I motion to Jonas. "Reformed telekinetic assassin." I motion to Bubbles. "A conscious AI turned real-life female Pinocchio by some kind of mystical egg."

"Orphic egg," Bubbles says.

"Don't care what it's called," I say. "That about cover it?"

"Jonas is far more powerful than a simple telekinetic. And I—"

A gentle hand on Bubbles's arm silences her. Like the others, she's trusting and talkative. Jonas is the only real pro among them. Trying to learn more information than he gives up.

"Look," he says. "I'm not trying to be a dick here, but we just traveled through the underworld, which is a shit show of mythological proportions, traveled to another world, which had been wiped out by this Cherry Bomb bitch, saw a future in which Earth was wiped out, and were brought back in time to meet you…in Florida, of all places." He stands up. Fists on the table. "We're not saying another word until you tell us who the hell you are, what in god's name is going on, and where the fuck the bathroom is. I need to shit."

Bubbles gasps. "Oh! I think I do, too! This is so exciting!"

I look up at the camera mounted above the table, through which the rest of the team has been watching. I point at the two sitting across from me and smile. "I like these two the most."

I stand and offer my hand. "My name is Moses Montgomery. You can call me Dark Horse. The short version is that I'm a Marine from the 80s, who traveled to the future to destroy an evil space Nazi empire, and I was returned to the present just in time to find out a crazy lady is trying to destroy reality. And from what I've heard, the first time around, we lost this fight. So, I'm stoked that you're here."

"Thank you," Jonas says and offers his hand.

I shake it.

"Now…" He raises his eyebrows. "Bathroom."

5

MIAH

To say this is weird doesn't really cover it. These people have big time resources and seemed to know a lot about us, even before the interviews. Dark Horse is nice enough, but there's an intensity just beneath the surface. I'm not sure if that's because there's more to the man than I can see, or if he's just feeling the same pressure I am: Cherry Bomb is coming.

And now they've got us seated in what I think is a living room complete with a massive stone fireplace and a sound system. Lots of records. Looks like they're music fans, which is cool, but if things don't start making a lot of sense soon, I don't foresee my squad sticking around. I glance over at Henry. He's leaning back like he's relaxed, hands clasped behind his head, but both his feet are bouncing like he's working a double bass drum to the heavy section of Metallica's 'One.'

The furniture has been arranged in an arc so that we're all facing the room's far side and the kitchen beyond. Feels like we're about to get a private show or be inducted into a cult.

"You got to be kidding me," Jonas mumbles, looking simultaneously amused and frustrated.

Bubbles, who is sitting to my right, elbows him in the ribs. "Don't spy on our hosts."

"Some of them are very loud," he says.

"I don't hear anything," Bree says.

"Loud in here." Jonas points to his head.

"You know what they're up to?" Sarah asks. She's starting to look a little awkward in her badass attire. The plaid lounge chair she's sitting in doesn't really fit her aesthetic.

Jonas grins. "Yep."

"You going to tell us?" Sarah asks.

His grin widens. "I'm anti-spoiler."

"How much longer?" Bree asks.

"Couple minutes," Jonas says. "Just…prepare to be amazed. Or something. Probably something."

Bree sighs and sits back, arms crossed, legs bouncing.

We're silent for a moment, and then Bubbles leans over to me. She whispers. "Miah."

I lean close, our shoulders touching. Hard to believe that she's only had a physical form for less than a day. She seems to be in full control, like she's been practicing her whole life. Probably a benefit of having the intelligence of a supercomputer. Or a side effect of being created by a mythological/alien egg that hatches Titans. "Yeah?"

"Guess what?" She seems excited, like she's just bought her first new car.

"Do you want me to guess, or are you just going to tell me?"

Her eyes widen. "Do you want to guess?"

"Is it mathematically plausible that I will guess correctly?"

She bites her bottom lip. "If you guess two hundred and thirty-one times, it's possible."

"I don't think we have that much time."

"So, I should tell you?"

I smile. She somehow feels more alive than the rest of us. It's refreshing. "Go for it."

She leans even closer, so our heads are touching. "I pooped."

I nearly burst out laughing but contain it. Because she's being earnest, and I don't want her to think I'm mocking her. "No shit?"

"Yes, shit!" She covers her mouth to quiet herself.

She now has Jonas's attention. "They grow up so fast."

"That's great," I say, patting her arm. "Big step."

"I know, right?" Bubbles sounds a little different. Still has her slight Texan twang, but she's relaxing into her voice. Maybe trying to match the way people speak. "And it was *green*."

Jonas pinches the space between his eyes and leans back.

I'm thoroughly amused. "Green, huh? That's different."

"I suspect it is a byproduct of my recent birth. Newborn babies' first bowel movements are a black, tar-like substance called meconium. It's composed of intestinal secretions, cells, fats, and proteins."

"That's...great. Really. Not everyone gets to remember that milestone."

She smiles. "And I'll remember it forever because I'm incapable of forgetting. Just thought you'd like to know." She gives me a wink and sits back in her chair. She's a little awkward, but she's quickly warming up to existing in the physical world.

I sit back, close my eyes, and wait for whatever's coming to start. In the darkness, I hear Henry's feet tapping out a quick double bass beat, over and over. *Definitely 'One,'* I think. And then Jonas joins in, tapping his hand on his knee, supplying the snare. Takes me five seconds to give in and start humming the guitar part.

I'm surprised that Jonas doesn't bail out on the collaboration right away, but he's like Henry and me. Music is important to us. Centers us.

And when a woman with a strange German-esque accent starts singing along, none of us stops.

"Darkness imprisoning me, all that I see, absolute horror."

She continues the song to the lyrics' conclusion. It's an epic moment, and it chills me out a bit. I open my eyes to find a petite blonde woman—early twenties I'd guess—absolutely beaming from beneath a pom-pom of curly hair. She claps her hands. "I knew I would like you guys." She points at me. "KISS!" She points at Henry. "Poison. Annnd..." She points to Jonas.

"Avett Brothers."

"Okay... Interesting choice. I understand the appeal, but not what I expected."

"For sentimental reasons," he says. "Normally, The Doors."

Her eyes flare wide. "Jim Morrison. *So* good."

I can't resist, despite already knowing Jonas's answer. "Best front man in three, two, one..."

"Freddie Mercury," three of us say, overlapping with Henry's, "Bret Michaels."

"Excellent!" she says, clapping her hands again.

"*Bor-ing*," Bree says, head lolled back. "No one cares about a dead guy with big teeth."

The blonde woman and I both gasp and turn to Bree.

"Take that back," I say. "Freddie Mercury is a treasure."

She rolls her eyes. "A dead treasure."

I point at her. "Gonna pretend I didn't hear that." To the blonde, I say, "She's eight. And a handful."

The woman smiles again. "She is adorable."

"Just you wait," Bree says, and she gives her eyebrows a double tap. "You won't always think so."

"I'm sure I've seen worse." She offers her hand to Bree and says, "I'm Hildy. And my favorite pony is Rainbow Dash."

A new voice, female and younger than Hildy, shouts from an adjoining hallway. "Discord!"

Bree's eyes widen. She's at home in our group of misfits, but there aren't many people who speak her language.

"Okay," Hildy says, clapping her hands one last time. "I think we are ready." She backs away toward the right side-hall. "Okay, we are ready for the introduction."

As she shimmies back into the hall, Dark Horse enters the room from the far side. He looks a little embarrassed. "This isn't how I pictured this going. At all. I'd have preferred to debrief you all over a few beers and some tunes, but...they've been practicing this for a while, and I'll never hear the end of it if I don't let this happen. Apologies in advance if this isn't your thing, but it's fairly...comprehensive, and it should catch you up to speed. Cool?"

I glance at the others. Henry and Sarah look a bit confused and totally out of their element. I think Jonas understands what's about to happen, and he's not thrilled. Bubbles is clueless but excited. Me and Bree...we get it. I've been in enough impromptu neighborhood performances to understand the vibe here.

These people aren't just some kind of elite, top secret, world-defending military outfit. They're a family.

"Super cool."

Dark Horse grins with a touch of relief and then backs away. "Enjoy."

A teenage girl that looks like she could be Hildy's younger sister dive-rolls into the room. She's wearing a plastic soldier helmet over a head of wavy blonde hair that's been shaved on one side. She hops to her feet, and fumbles to get the helmet off her face and back over her head. Then she shouts, "Hoo!" while high-kicking an invisible enemy. "Haa!" She thrusts her toy M16, like it has a bayonet, into another invisible enemy. Then she unleashes a torrent of gunfire, making the sound effect herself. "Chu, chu, chu, chu!"

She waves for the others to follow her and, in a gravely tough voice, she says, "The year is nineteen eighty-nine. My name is Dark Horse. I'm a Rapid Response Marine that kicks ass, chews bubble gum, and..."

Someone whispers. "Kicks communist–"

"And kicks communist booty! We've been hot dropped into Antarctica, in search of a mysterious device. Let's go!"

Hildy re-enters the room, also wearing a helmet and carrying a gun, and she says, "Hola, mi nombre es Chuy! I'm a Marine, too, but also a woman! Which is totally plausible in the eighties!"

"And I am BigApe!" A lanky man with a weird, thick German accent leaps into the room, legs spread wide in a horribly awkward fighting stance. He cups a hand to his mouth and whispers, "I am actually Burnett, and a big part of this story, but we'll get to me later." He slips back into character. "I am BigApe, a totally badass Marine, compensating for having a small..." He points at his crotch and winks. "My story is tragic, but heartwarming, bridging torture and true love."

"Alright, maggots," little Dark Horse shouts, "Let's show these red bastids what it feels like to get smacked down by the ol' red, white, and blue!"

"Totally radical!" Burnett shouts, and all three start shooting.

What follows is a thirty-minute-long, three-person performance telling an epic story that is as unbelievable as our own, introducing us to people we have yet to meet, and laying out the stakes for what is to come.

As funny as the performance is, I find myself growing unnerved as our perilous situation resolves, and the story's chaotic climax expands my knowledge of the universe.

The play ends.

All three performers, drenched in sweat and fake purple blood, bow. When they come back up, Hildy smiles and says, "Any questions?"

Six hands rise.

6

DARK HORSE

I spend the next hour answering questions and introducing the real members of our team that are present. Everyone already knew Wini, and I think she must have made an impression before the helicopter was attacked, because the way they react to her entrance feels like more than respect. It's almost reverence with a touch of sadness. Chuy makes an impression, despite our guests having abilities beyond belief. And it's safe to say our audience is enamored with Hildy, Cassidy, and Burnett, though I doubt they feel confident about their abilities to contribute to defeating an alien invasion or super-powerful space woman dressed in red leather.

Cherry Bomb...

What the hell kind of name is that?

The group has now split up into pairs. Chuy seems to be hitting it off with Wonder Sarah. They're equally interested in each other's fighting techniques and knowledge. From what I gathered, Sarah's specialty is up close and personal, while Chuy delivers death from a distance.

Bree is bouncing on a chair while Cassidy regales her with stories of Huggy Wuggy. "He's tall and blue and super fuzzy, with big pink lips and lots of sharp teeth. And if he hugs, he'll never stop." Cassidy throws her hands up and kicks a leg out to the side. "Until you pop!" They burst into laughter. Fast friends, those two.

"Wait until you see what I look like," Bree says, which widens Cassidy's eyes and mouth to the point that she resembles Huggy Wuggy a little.

Mind Bullet is a little more aloof. He's still seated, eyes closed, like he's meditating. Didn't strike me as the meditation type. I think he's listening.

Observing, like I am. Miah might be the team's leader, but this guy has all the experience. He's their version of me, but traditionally a loner. Happy to co-pilot. Without opening his eyes, he tilts his head toward me and gives a casual thumbs up. He's listening, but in a very different way. It's disconcerting that he has access to our thoughts, but he doesn't strike me as the kind of guy to care about people's innermost secrets. He's feeling us out. Looking for threats. Everything else is just noise.

Hildy has found a new friend in Miah. They're close in age, and they have similar tastes in music. Burnett is hovering nervously nearby, unsure what to do with his jealousy. Miah is a good-looking guy. Has a young Dave Grohl thing going, but I'm not seeing any flirting. Just connecting. It's clear their hearts belong to other people.

But Burnett is new to love. New to feelings. In the future Nazi world he's from, love didn't exist and procreation was done in a lab. I shiver at the memory, and I turn my attention to Henry.

The wild card. He's hard to get a read on.

Probably because of his self-proclaimed total lack of fear, a state everyone else on his team seems to support—including his sister. Half-sister? Not sure how that works with gods.

I shake my head. *Gods.* I don't want to believe it, but I can't discount it. A dose of modern understanding helps. 'Gods' was a term used by the ancients to describe something they didn't understand—namely people who weren't really people. Aliens among us. That look like us. That bleed red like us. But ultimately came from another world and not always from a mother's womb. Their stories are myth, but their existence is real. It's science. Even if we don't yet understand how a kid with no wings can fly and shoot lightning bolts.

Henry hasn't left his chair. He's kicked back like he owns the place, showing no interest in making conversation. What he does have is wandering eyes. At first, he was interested in Chuy, which honestly, I can't blame him. Little known fact—men love a woman who is both beautiful and a badass. But Henry's eyes seem to be following Wini the most. And any time she looks at him, he smiles, or raises his eyebrows. I watch it happen again. Wini turns away, back to Bubbles, who she's been chatting up. A detail jumps out.

Wini is blushing.

Wait a second...

Hold on...

I lean to the side so Bubbles can see me. Give her a wave and motion for her to join me. She smiles and parts ways with Wini, who sits near Henry, but not right beside him.

Bubbles is still thrilled to be here. "Dark Horse. How can I help you?"

"You're super smart, right?" I ask.

"We have yet to perform any cognitive tests, but my self-evaluation suggests that I have retained the computational ability and storage capacity of the vast computer networks to which I once had access, including a few quantum machines not yet known to the public."

"A living quantum computer?" Sounds impossible.

"With a charming personality. Unless you're a duck."

I raise an eyebrow. "A duck?"

"Personal grudge," she says. "We'll settle up eventually. Did you want to ask me something?"

"What's up with Henry?" I ask.

"Honestly, I haven't had a lot of interaction with him. While they were traversing the underworld, I was—"

"Trapped in an Apple Watch," I say. "I remember."

"But I trust Jonas, and Jonas trusts the rest of them. That's good enough for me."

"That's great, but it's not what I'm—"

"Ohh," she says. "You're being protective of your female teammate, Wini. I have made the same observations."

"And?" I ask, but I'm not sure I want the answer.

"Based on subtle details like flushing of the skin, pupil dilation, and hormones I've detected in the air, I believe that they had coital relations en route to Florida."

"On...the plane?"

"Indeed. Though it sounds unlikely, I've observed that she is marvelously spry for her age."

"Yeah..." I'm not sure what to think. Part of me wants to high five Wini. She's still got the goods, and she's working it. *You go, girl.* But

I know for a fact that if an old codger rolled in here and hooked up with Hildy, he'd find his way out the way he came with a broken nose. Might even steer him toward the crocodiles lounging between the house and the ocean. I suppose that's sexist. Probably not 'woke' or something. But I'm a man from the 80's.

"They are both adults," Bubbles says, indifferent to the act.

"Separated by a handful of decades," I say. "It's weird, right?"

"I was born into this physical body yesterday," she says. "I am not the best judge of weirdness. But no laws have been broken, if that is your concern. Unless weirdness is against the law. Then we're all in trouble."

She leans in close, staring into my eyes, seeing what other people miss. "You really *are* something different, aren't you? But…also a kindred spirit. If the play was accurate, you've been bonded with an alien species and their collective knowledge."

"Accurate," I say. "And I'm still getting used to it."

"Makes two of us," she says.

"Sorry I'm late," comes a new voice.

I turn to find Delgado entering from the garage. He looks a little flustered and rushed, about to spill his guts about something.

"I need to talk to—"

He catches sight of Bubbles and can't stop himself from doing a quick up and down of her curvy body. She is, as Cassidy might put it, 'thicc' with two Cs. And apparently that's Delgado's type. He's momentarily stymied, like he's just woken up inside the Sistine Chapel to find God and Adam hovering over him.

"You were saying?" I ask, but he doesn't hear me.

"Uh, hi," he says to Bubbles. "You must be one of our visitors."

"Bubbles." She holds out her hand, and Delgado takes hold of it, but he forgets to shake. They stand there for a moment, hands clasped. Then both of them seem to recognize each other, blinking and flinching back.

"It's you," Delgado says.

She looks down at his hand. "Are those nanobots?"

Some details about our lives, including Delgado being infused with nanobots that allow him to connect to all things electronic, were left out of the play. Not to be secretive, but simply to cut down on time. There's no way for Bubbles to know about them...unless she actually just detected them through physical touch.

"Care to fill me in?" I ask.

"Remember when I told you about a presence online, moving through the same systems as me?" Delgado asks.

"I...guess?"

"I could sense you as well," Bubbles says, "but we could never communicate."

"Because we spoke different languages," Delgado suggests.

"I was an artificial intelligence."

"And I was thinking like a human being through intermediaries. We were in the same space, but we were operating on two different wavelengths. Like a ghost and a living person."

They just stare for a moment, each fascinated by the other.

"Okay, before you two find a glob of clay and go all Patrick Swayze and Demi Moore on me..." I put my hand on Delgado's arm, breaking the spell. "Sounded like you were going to say something important."

His expression flattens and then tenses. Looks me dead in the eyes. "Two gates just opened. One in the Vatican. The other...inside the Dome of the Rock in Jerusalem."

7

DARK HORSE

The Vatican and Dome of the Rock are two of the most-significant religious sites in the world. While the Vatican is the home of the Pope and Catholicism, the Dome of the Rock is a triple threat. The shrine atop Jerusalem's Temple Mount is sacred to both Judaism and Christianity as the site where Abraham was tested by God, and to Muslims as the location where Muhammad ascended into Heaven.

If someone wanted to set off a firestorm that sent shockwaves around the world, these two sites would do the trick. Never mind the fact that these religious heavy hitters, and the politicians that cozy up to them, might blame each other for the attacks, they might see this as the first sign of Armageddon.

Right now, they're just freaky-ass gates made of an alien metal, covered in ancient glowing runes. No biggie. But they have the potential to spew out the demon-like Tenebris or any number of freakshows from around the universe that will catapult the world quickly into chaos.

If you want to cause global strife, few things get the job done like stirring up believers in a higher power.

The Darkness that Miah and Bree survived, and helped to subvert, was covered up by the U.S. government, despite the overwhelming evidence. But attacks on these two holy sites will be impossible to keep quiet.

And I think that's the point.

This is Cherry's opening salvo.

And our first chance to show her we're up to the task of kicking her ass back to whatever dark corner of the universe she crawled out of.

"Thoughts?" I ask Delgado.

"Two teams. One at each location. A third team here running the show."

"Command and Control," I agree.

"Right," he says. "That."

"Makes sense."

Bubbles clears her throat, then kind of chuckles while touching the side of her neck. "Sorry. Never done that before. Feels funny."

"You wanted to say something?" I ask.

She nods. "I have already determined the optimal distribution of personnel, accounting for ability and experience, if you would like to hear it?"

Ten minutes later, after huddling up with Delgado and Bubbles, who seem to be strangely in sync, we head back into the living room, where the conversation has died down and everyone seems to be awaiting our arrival.

"Something happen while I was..." I glance at the hallway. "...right over there?"

Henry jumps right into it. "I was just chilling here, man, you know, mentally rating everyone's looks between one and ten." He glances at Burnett. "Sorry, bro." Back to me, he says, "It's a thing I do. Anywho, so I've just finished up looking at Wini's sweet tush, and I happened to notice that Mind Bullet over here is wearing his serious face, and he has his head cocked to the side a skosh, which is something he does when he's listening IRL, and you know..." He points to his head. "En la cabeza." He winks at Chuy. "Me gusta Español. Donde esta pantalones muy frio? Me gusta uno cerveza en el baño. All that stuff. Where was I? Right. I realized he's listening to someone, but the only people out of earshot are you guys, out in the hallway. This is where I get distracted by Bubbles's MILF bod. You're a solid eight, BT Dubs."

Bubbles is thrilled, looking down at herself. I don't think she'd considered whether or not she was good looking yet.

"But then I'm like, 'Dude, what are you hearing?' and Jonas doesn't respond. So, I ask him again, but loud enough that these other guys notice, and they start wondering what's going on. So, Bree—my bloodthirsty little monster friend—walks up to the Titan time bomb and whacks him in the face. When he comes out of it, he's not pissed. But he's wicked serious, and he says, 'Turn on the news.' So, I head on over to Twitter, and..." Henry gestures like his head has exploded. "Richard Simmons is dead. Richard Simmons. Icon of health, Richard Simmons. But then it's a hoax, and I'm like, 'thank the good lord Baal.'"

"I get it," I say, assuming they actually got to the news about the Vatican and the Dome of the Rock.

"I didn't even get to the part where I—"

"No one needs a retelling of you dramatically adjusting your hang nasty," Sarah says. "Now, shut up. This is serious."

Henry sighs and crosses his arms. He's impulsive, and maybe genuinely fearless, but he listens to his sister. Maybe the rest of them, too. We'll see how it goes when we split folks up.

"You know about the gates?" I look at Miah when I ask, just to be sure.

He nods. "Vatican and Temple Mount."

"Which is really, really bad," Bree adds.

I can't help but grin. She probably has no idea what either location is, or why they're important.

"Yes," I say, pointing at her. "And if the damage or death toll gets out of hand, two gates will be the least of our concerns. We need to strike hard and fast. Priority one, take out the gates. Two, take out whatever comes through. If anything comes through."

"Sorry to be pooping in the party," Burnett says, looking at his phone. "The gates are now active."

He holds up his phone, displaying a live feed from a bystander in Israel, live-streaming the gate, which is just outside the Dome. A familiar sheet of red energy is stretched between the two pillars, shimmering with hexagonal orange lines.

Something could waltz from one world to another any second now. I have little doubt that bodies will start dropping soon after.

"Anyone who argues with what I'm about to say will be left behind. If you're not a team player, you're not on my team. If you can't follow orders, you can go home. And if you won't fight for your planet, I don't want you here. Understood?"

Most of them say, 'Yes.' Henry just nods. Bree gives a salute and says, "You got it, dude."

Full House reference from the eight-year-old. Nice. She kind of looks the part, too.

"I'm leading team one. We'll–"

"Team one?" Henry says, eyebrow raised.

Sarah smacks and scolds him. "Henry."

"I'm just saying, it's not super inspirational."

He's not wrong. "Team...Dark Horse, you're with me. Obviously, I guess. Cassidy Rose. Mind Bullet. Henry and McCoy."

Henry's hand goes up. "Who's McCoy?"

I look around.

McCoy's not here.

"He came with you, right?" I ask Delgado.

"Came *in* with me," Delgado says. "Hold on, I'll call him." He closes his eyes and uses the nanobots populating his mind and body to connect to the cell network and make a call without needing a phone or a family plan. "Hey. Where are you? We're wheels up." He listens for a moment. "Oh...right. Sorry."

Delgado mouths, "He's in the bathroom," to me, but Henry catches it, too.

"Just pinch it off, dude!" Henry shouts.

Delgado opens his eyes. "ETA one minute."

"When you gotta go," Cassidy says. "Ain't no stopping that force of nature."

"Team Laser Chicken," I declare. "You'll tackle the Vatican. Sarah. Hildy. Chuy. And Bree."

Bree pumps her fists. "Yes!"

"Team Swayze," I say, entertaining myself. "Delgado, Wini, Bubbles, Burnett. You're staying home. I want you coordinating and gathering intel for both teams. You're our eyes and ears. Okay?"

No one argues. Between Delgado and Bubbles, I think we've got global surveillance taken care of. Wini is a natural decision maker. Can make the tough calls. And if we need any logistical support, Burnett will make it happen.

"Team Dark Horse, we're rotating out." I turn to Hildy. "You can take *Lil' Bitch'n*."

"What's a Lil' Bitch'n'?" Bree asks.

"Poop-shaped spaceship," Cassidy says. "You'll like it."

"Are we square?" I ask, searching our new friends' eyes for any doubt.

"Like SpongeBob," Henry says.

"Great," I say, and I address the newbies. "Now, who wants a uniform?"

There's a pause, and then just Henry raises a hand. I'm about to explain how cool our adaptive armor is when I realize that these guys already have uniforms. They're not functional, but when you're an immortal god, functional body armor probably isn't a priority. Not sure why Henry is game, but the others don't seem in a hurry to change out of their leathers, skirts, and/or bunny suits. Whatever floats your boat, I guess.

"Okay," I say. "Let's do this!"

"Lame," Henry says.

I try again. "Let's kick some ass!"

"PG-13," Hildy says.

"There's a kid here now," I say, motioning to Bree.

"Thank you for not considering me a child," Cassidy says, doing an exaggerated curtsy.

I sigh. "Okay… Let's go fuck some shit up!"

8

MIAH

"No offense, but this looks more like a throwback to an Apollo mission."

I'm on the bridge of *Lil' Bitch'n.* Aside from a really big viewscreen at the front, which looks shiny and new, the controls of this...ship look old and not very technically advanced.

"The Union didn't care much about making things look nice, or cool," Chuy says, sitting in the captain's chair. She's dressed in admittedly badass looking gear. Dark Horse called it 'adaptive armor,' but he never really explained what it could do. Hildy is wearing it, too, and despite her cute features and big hair, she also looks pretty tough. But it also looks snug, and I've gotten accustomed to being...unconfined.

"Right," I say. "This ship was built by future Nazis...and is really just a lander for a much larger ship, the actual *Bitch'n,* which is...in orbit behind the moon?"

"Somebody was paying attention to the play." Hildy is pleased by my information retention. She has a glow about her that's hard to explain. Like a real fervor for life. Positive experiences that would barely register with most people hit her differently. To me, the world is a messed-up place, but she finds the good in just about everything.

"I was paying attention, too," Bree pipes up from the seat she's been strapped into at the back of the bridge, safely out of reach of any glowing buttons. "My favorite part was when the skinny guy was on the floor pretending to be their dolphin friend. He was flopping all around." She flails her arms and legs.

"About that," Sarah says, standing in the doorway. She didn't want to sit. Said she'd been sitting too much. I suspect her leather gear is just creeping up in uncomfortable places, but she'd never admit it, at least not around people we've just met. "Is that for real? You transferred the human consciousness out of a man, and into a female dolphin?"

"I want to be a dolphin," Bree says.

"It wasn't as hard as it sounds," Burnett says over the comms. "I can explain in detail when the crisis has ended, if you like."

"Nah," Sarah says. "I'll just suspend my disbelief."

"Like watching Nemesis on TV," I say. "Soul of a murdered little girl merged with a goddess of vengeance. I'm happy to make that mental leap."

"Except Nemesis is a TV series, and this shit is real." Sarah crosses her arms. Leans against the doorframe.

"He's very happy," Hildy says. "Spends his days swimming the oceans, accompanied by a growing harem of male dolphins." Her smile falters.

"But..." I ask.

Hildy looks uncomfortable but says, "They've become a little...exhibitionist with their...relations."

"They're having sex to entertain tourists in exchange for fish," Chuy says.

"We think it's because none of them are very good at hunting," Hildy says, "since the males were raised in captivity and BigDolph was...well, a man."

I'm not sure what to say about any of that, so I just blurt out, "Got to do what you got to do, I guess."

Chuy grunts what might be agreement, and she then looks back at me. "Miah, right?"

I nod.

"I've been told you're running point. That you're the go-to guy for your team, so I'm following your lead here."

"Okay..."

"I'm also told you were Army," Chuy says.

"Once upon a time...and it didn't go very well."

"Your fault?"

I shake my head.

"Then we're good. But...if you're unsure about anything, just give me the word, and I'll jump in. Capisce?"

"Uh, yeah. Sure. Sounds good."

"What I'm saying," she says, a serious tone creeping into her voice, "is that you're *in charge*. Right now. At this moment. And we're just sitting here. Tell us what to do, and don't forget you've got a bunch of brainiacs to communicate with when you need them."

"Right. Sorry. Guess I'm used to our people flying around ourselves."

"You could fly all the way to the Vatican?" Hildy asks.

I nod. "Pretty quickly."

She smiles back at me. "Think you could find your way there without a map?"

"Just look for the boot-shaped country, right?"

"*A-hem.*" Chuy's throat-clear focuses us.

"Right. The Vatican. The gate. End of the world." I take a deep breath. "Let's..." A flash of white flits through my senses and then disappears. "...go?"

Chuy spins around in her chair, amused. "Welcome to the future, Team Mythology."

"Wait..." Sarah says. "We're at the Vatican already?"

"Underneath it," Chuy says. "In the Necropolis."

"How?" Sarah asks.

"Someone was *not* paying attention to the play," Hildy says.

"It's called rotating," Bree says. "They can zip into the fourth dimension, move a tiny bit, and then hop back out a lot farther away. Both of their spaceships can do it, but they also have PSDs...or PDFs..."

"I think that's Photoshop, babe," I say.

"Whatever. They have personal rotator doohickies, too." Bree gives Hildy a big smile.

"Show off," Sarah says, and she finds herself on the receiving end of an eight-year-old sticking out her tongue.

For a moment, I wait, and then I remember who's in charge. "Right. Okay. How far is the gate from here?"

"Fifty feet," Bubbles says via the comms. "Straight up. You'll need to work your way up through the catacombs and into Saint Peter's Basilica."

"The Basilica?" Chuy sounds mortified. Performs the sign of the cross like a well-practiced Catholic. "Ay dios mio, no."

"Why is that bad...?" I ask, feeling like I should really already know the answer beyond the obvious—innocent lives.

Bubbles chimes in. "The Basilica contains priceless artworks and relics created by Renaissance and Baroque masters such as Michelangelo's *Pietà*."

Chuy ticks off her fingers, listing a few more. "The tomb of Urban VIII, the Baldachin, the statue of St. Longinus. Not to mention the actual tomb of St. Peter. There isn't any part of the Basilica that isn't sacred."

"Right," I say. "Great. So, don't break anything. Check." I point at Bree. "No breaking."

She shrugs and offers an unconvincing, "I'll try."

"At least Henry isn't here," Sarah says, though I think she secretly wishes he was. Their relationship is contentious at times, but they're family. I think this might be the farthest they've been from each other since discovering they were siblings and the children of Zeus.

"How do we get there from here?" I ask.

"Exit the vehicle," Bubbles says, "and I'll guide you through the tunnels."

"Okay, people," I say, standing from my seat. "Let's get moving."

Chuy stands and waggles her hand back and forth in a 'so-so' motion. "Five out of ten on the tough man in charge chart. But it will do."

She gives my shoulder a whack as she passes, and it actually hurts. "Bonus point for the effort, though."

Chuy might be a normal human, but she's tough as nails and sharp. I have a feeling I'll be leaning on her for support here.

I hold my hand out to Bree. She takes it, and I lead her to the *Lil' Bitch'n*'s cargo hold. Sarah joins us, collecting her shield and dory. Hildy brings up the rear, shutting down the ship's systems as she goes.

We gather by the hatch. Chuy and Hildy start pulling masked hoods over their heads.

"What are those for?" Bree asks.

"Not all of us can see in the dark, princesita." Chuy pats her head.

"I can't see in the dark," Sarah says.

"You won't need those," I say, and I let the cells in my eyes show their natural state.

Light beams out from inside me, forcing everyone to wince and turn away.

"Well, all right then," Chuy says. "The human lighthouse can show the way."

"Out of the vehicle and follow the tunnel to the left." Bubbles says.

We follow her directions, exiting *Lil' Bitch'n* into an ancient hand-carved chamber with a tunnel on either end. No idea what this space is, and I don't bother asking. We're not here for a tour. Bubbles leads us through a maze that slowly heads upward. Along the way, we pass a strange combination of ancient chambers, some holding sarcophagi, and modern spaces converted into what appear to be sterile laboratories filled with a variety of objects, many of which do not appear to be church related.

As we pass one of the glass-encased labs, Chuy comes to a sudden stop. "Hey, Sparkles." She snaps her fingers at me. "Light this up." She taps on the glass.

I turn my gaze inside the room, illuminating it with bright, blue-tinged light. There are shelves covered in artifacts, many of which are held inside their own clear containers. Some are in Ziploc bags. And one rests on a lab table. Looks like it was abandoned quickly, probably when the gate appeared. I have a hard time seeing what it is, but the details slowly resolve. It's some kind of modern weapon. A rifle. But it's embedded in solid, ancient looking stone.

"You got to be shitting me." Chuy makes space for Hildy. "Remember that?"

Hildy looks through the glass. "That...was McCoy's rifle. The one with—"

"Temporal rounds." Chuy turns to me and translates. "Time bullets."

"Time...bullets?"

"They hit the target before you actually fire," she says.

"That's...handy," I say.

"Sorry to interrupt," Bubbles says. "But I believe something is coming through the gate."

"C'mon," I say, doubling my pace through the tunnels, following Bubbles's instructions until we're standing beneath a solid marble square in the ceiling, a solid looking ladder beneath it leading to the floor. "This is it?"

Bubbles responds, "It leads to Saint Sebastian's Chapel, just off the Basilica's nave. When you exit, the gate will be to your right, in front of the Papal altar."

I put my hand on a rung, but I'm stopped by a tug on my skirt. Bree clears her throat. "Umm, hello, still an eight-year-old girl here. Time to power up."

I crouch down in front of her. "*No. Breaking. Stuff.* Cool?"

She nods and holds out a pinkie. I link mine with hers and we pinkie promise on it.

"Adorable," Chuy says.

Bree smiles. "Not for long."

I place my thumb on Bree's forehead and swipe it to the right. The transformation sweeps over her, transmogrifying cuteness personified into the stuff of nightmares…in a bunny suit.

"Okay," Chuy says, sounding impressed. "That is…not what I expected."

"Awesome, right?" Bree says, smiling up with her now sharp teeth.

"I think it's very awesome," Hildy says, totally earnest and making Bree very happy.

All of us ready now, I climb the ladder and shove the marble up and away—a task no ordinary human could achieve without mechanical help. I pull myself up, and don't bother turning to help the others out. They don't need it. Instead, I bathe in the glory of Saint Peter's Basilica, which is the most ornate, expensive looking space I've ever seen in my life. Bree leaps up and out of the catacombs, landing beside me in a silent crouch.

"Whoa," she whispers, and then she pokes around one of the massive pillars, gilded and decorated with marble statues of saints. Her black eyes widen a touch as she comes back, clearly having caught sight of whatever is coming out of the gate.

"Awww." She looks up at me, smiling wide. "He's so cute!"

9

DARK HORSE

"That...was wicked awesome," Henry says, releasing my waist and stepping back. He's just completed his first rotation from Florida to Israel, and he seems to be handling it fine, physically and psychologically. Most first timers freak out a little bit. Maybe there is more to him than meets the eye.

He steps away, looking down at his crotch. "Yo, this armor shit makes my package look huge."

Or maybe not.

"Stand still until the others arrive," I say. "Would be bad if they appeared where you were standing."

"How bad?" he asks.

"They'd replace you," I say.

He's astounded. "Like their soul would live in my body?"

"Like their bodies would replace whatever parts of your body they appeared in. You'd probably die." When he's unfazed by the news, I add, "You and your huge package."

"I know, right?" He's back to looking at his bulge, still not worried about having his body split in half when the others arrive.

McCoy appears next, holding onto Jonas.

Neither of them look very comfortable with the other. They only just met and had to embrace whilst traveling through a white void.

Jonas stumbles a few steps, off balance. He catches himself on the stone wall.

I'm about to tell him not to touch it, but it's too late. He leans his head against the brown wall, eyes closed, catching a breath.

"Big man can't handle a little teleportation," Henry teases.

"Big man's gonna kick your ass if you don't–" Jonas nearly pukes, but he holds it down. Clenches his jaws and his eyes shut, like he's locking himself down. Then he stands up, back to himself, and takes in our tight surroundings. "Where are we?"

"The Western Wall tunnel, not far from the Temple Mount," I say.

"Why not just drop us at the Dome thingy?" Henry asks.

"First, unless any of you are Muslim, we can't go inside the 'Dome thingy,'" I say. When no one professes their faith, I continue. "Second, there will be a *lot* of people up there. Stepping out of the fourth dimension would draw attention we don't want, and it would add to the confusion already being caused by the appearance of a magical gate. It's dusk in Jerusalem, and Friday, so these tunnels are closed to tourists."

I toggle my comms. "Delgado?"

"Here," he says.

"What's the hold up with Cassidy?"

"She's almost ready."

"Nervous pee?" I ask.

"Every dang time," Wini says. "Like a nervous piddling puppy, that kid."

"She didn't get into the soda again?" I ask, my concern level about her caffeine intake on par with that about aliens invading.

"I'll...have to check," Delgado says.

The fact that he doesn't know is disconcerting, but then he attempts to assuage my nerves. "I've taken care of security cameras in the area. They'll go down the moment you all get close. You'll be ghosts."

A white rectangle opens up. Cassidy bounds through, not rotating–pirouetting. "Hoo, hoo!" She punches to the left. "Hoo, ha!" Punches to the right.

"Dan... You don't need to check," I say, and I direct my stink eye toward Cassidy. "How much?"

She jogs in place, knees nearly reaching her shoulders. "Half a bottle."

"Half a bottle of *what?*"

Her smile widens. *Mountain Dew.* Caffeinated sugar. She's going to be bounding with energy for about 20 minutes and then crash. Hard. That's when the crossed arms, immobility, and grumpy pout begins. It's not too hard to pull her out of it. She's got energy reserves for days, but the time between now and then could be tumultuous.

"It helps me with the emotional stuff," she says.

"The Dew helps your...emotions?" Henry asks.

"Not *my* emotions," she says. "The emotions I can make people feel."

"Huh..." Henry says.

Before the pair can continue the conversation, I say, "This way," and strike out toward the exit. The rough brown walls are lit by the occasional wire-wrapped bulbs. Probably kept lit for security sweeps, which we'll hopefully avoid. Etched glass plaques with English and Hebrew text describe the various sites along the way—ancient pillars, railings, and alcoves. If it weren't for the gates and the potential invasion, I'd probably stop to read them all. Cowboy would love this place.

He hasn't checked in since he left. I could call him, and he might come running if we needed him, but whatever was calling him north seemed important to him. Going to let him see it through.

I glance back at Jonas behind me. "How you holding up?"

"You know how when you're playing pin the tail on the donkey," he says, "and you get spun all around before being set loose?"

"I've never even been to a birthday party," Henry says.

That's kinda sad, I think, and I say, "Yeah."

Pin the tail on the donkey was one of Max's birthday favorites, except he preferred a kangaroo and made his guests hop—usually into a wall. He thought it was pretty funny. I miss that kid. From my past, and from Garfunkel's version in my head. Guess that means I miss Garfunkel...even though he's part of me now.

"Well, I don't," Jonas says. "But this is how I imagined it. Kind of like shell shock."

"It'll pass," I say.

"Don't know what you're talking about, dude," Henry says. "I feel fine."

McCoy pipes up from the back. "You all are talking too much."

He's right. Also, without Hildy here, I nearly forgot our tradition. While the other team opted to go mostly adaptive-armor free, Henry was on board from the start, and Jonas actually changed his mind after he saw it and got a quick run-down on what it could do. He might be a Titan, but he's not bulletproof. I think.

"I get that," Henry says. "We're on a mission. Need to focus up. But I don't know you, dude." He motions to me. "I know the boss man has little blue aliens living in him." Next up is Cassidy. "And this one can make people sad, or something, and is kind of a chill kid. But you? All I know about you is your poop schedule is a little late in the day."

I'm expecting impatience from McCoy, but he manages a grin.

"You saw the play," Cassidy points out.

"Yeah, but I only paid attention to the interesting parts."

Hands on her hips, Cassidy scrunches her lips at Henry. "What part wasn't interesting?"

"How can I tell you what wasn't interesting if I wasn't paying attention?" Henry asks.

McCoy puts a hand on Cassidy's shoulder. "The nutshell version..."

Henry snorts. "I totally thought you were going to say 'the nut sack' version, which BTW, would have held my attention."

"I traveled to the past where I met my older self, my younger self, my dead father and—"

Henry fake yawns.

"I fought a saber-toothed cat, a bunch of dinosaurs, a half-human/half-demon—"

"Like Bree?" Henry asks.

"Not at all," McCoy replies. "An ancient giant with blood red hair, two sets of teeth and a taste for human flesh."

"Was this in the play?" Henry asks. "I feel like I'd remember this."

"Long story short," McCoy says. "We ended up traveling to the beginning of time...and heard a voice." He gets serious. "Heard God."

"Like me?" Henry says.

"Capital G," McCoy says. "If I understand correctly, you're one of the lower-case 'g' gods."

"Still cool, though," Henry says. "Right?"

"Very," McCoy says, humoring him. "Now...can we cut the chit-chat and get on with it? People need our help."

"Bet," Henry says.

"In English," McCoy insists.

Henry grins. "Yeah. Sure."

"Masks up," I say, and I pull the head gear up and over my head, pulling the mask down into place, hiding my eyes between two reflective lenses that remind me of Hans and Franz, Wini's little gray pals. They're back at the Mesa, watching over Delgado's brood of teenagers, but if we need back up, they're a quick UFO ride away.

"Is this to conceal our identities or something, because I'm not worried about–"

"Not that," I say, and it's only partially a lie. I'd rather the whole world not know our faces. Would make some of our work a little trickier. But the hood gives us access to a variety of sensory features like night vision, smell blocking, and a kick-ass sound system.

"Delgado," I say. "You want to pick the tune?"

"On it," he says.

"No, no, no, no," Cassidy blurts out, already working the controls on the left forearm of her suit. I'm still learning all the adaptive armor's ins and outs, but like a true teenager, she's already got it mastered. Good for her, not always good for us.

"Got it!" she says. Her voice is followed by a wailing guitar playing three long chords before it starts chugging away a very familiar tune, accompanied by Tommy Lee on drums and Vince Neil belting out the lyrics to Mötley Crüe's 'Kickstart My Heart.'

"Just for you," Cassidy says.

She can't see my smile, but she knows it's there. I love all music, but as a man from the 80s, I have a special place in my heart for tunes from what everyone who lived through it still believes is the best era. There was something special about experiencing the transition from a world without personal computers to a world where they were everywhere. That, and Spielberg's best films.

"Sick!" Henry says, wailing hard on an air guitar as he follows behind Cassidy and Jonas. I glance back to find McCoy shaking his head. Man's serious, but I suppose someone's got to be. He's rock steady. An even keel. All that stuff. Generally, he doesn't participate in the musical prelude to our missions, real or in training, but I think he secretly appreciates them.

How could you not? We're about to face the unknown, possibly unholy, enemy. A kickstart is exactly what we need.

By the time we reach the exit, I'm jazzed.

Despite Cassidy's overflowing energy, she's on task. She lowers the volume to twenty-five percent when I stop by the exit, giving us a subtle soundtrack without inhibiting our hearing. She knows that she's being evaluated. Although she was indispensable in defeating the Order's planned invasion of Earth, she still has a lot to learn, and she's constantly proving herself. As long as she's not a liability, she's on the team. If she screws up, she'll be back to square one. But she hasn't made a mistake yet. Probably why she only drank half the Mountain Dew.

We exit as a group, sticking to the long shadows cast by a setting sun. First thing I notice is the screams. People are bolting, running in fear. Not panic—so that's good—but they're definitely freaked out.

But not all of them. For every ten people running away, one or two are headed in the opposite direction, *toward* the Temple Mount, located a few hundred feet to our left at the top of a broad staircase.

Jonas puts his hand on my arm. "There are a lot of people around the Dome."

He can sense them. Hear their thoughts.

"Why?" I ask.

"Muslims. Jews. Christians. All of them together. All of them believe it's from God. I...I can hear their prayers." He turns his gaze from the Mount, to me. "Something's coming out." He blinks, as though in pain. Clutches the sides of his head. "Gah!"

"What is it?" McCoy asks.

"A mind," he says.

Cassidy places a subtle hand on Jonas's shoulder, sending him positive vibes.

He glances at her, but he doesn't question what's happening. Just gives her a nod. Straightens up. Focuses. Grips his fists as a war between emotional extremes is waged between this newcomer and Cassidy. "A woman. She's...tortured. Desperate. Out of control, but full of remorse." He gasps and nearly topples over. "God..." Eyes on the Dome, he says, "Her name...her name is Mia Durante. And she's...*hungry*."

10

MIAH

On the plus side, the Basilica appears to have been evacuated. On the downside, the gate is active, and something has come through. I poke my head out around the pillar and look toward the papal altar. To call it ornate is a severe understatement. There are statues of saints, spiral pillars, frescos, and carvings on every surface. If I had to describe it to someone, I'd probably say, 'Just google it,' rather than spending ten minutes describing what I'm seeing here. Because it's a lot. But it's also not nearly as intriguing as the two big pillars blocking part of the view, red energy stretched between them.

Seeing an active gate hits me hard. Brings back memories of the Darkness. Of my PTSD and all the discomfort that came with it.

I'm not that person anymore, I tell myself. *I'm chill. I'm confident. I got this.*

I can totally battle universe-destroying aliens inside Saint Peter's Basilica without absolutely destroying the place.

Sure.

Right.

"Hey," Bree whispers, smacking my cheek. "Did you see it?"

She points, redirecting my gaze from the gate to the small creature standing at its base.

"Is that..."

Chuy cuts me off. "Capybara."

I've watched enough Discovery Channel, both on edibles, and not, to know that capybaras are the world's largest rodents. They're also pretty chill, and they can swim really well. Like other rodents, they have big-ass, freaky incisors, but they use them for gnawing on vegetation. I've only seen one in person *once*. At a zoo. Took me five minutes to see it because it looked like a rock, just sitting there. This one is mobile, and bigger, sniffing the air, its head twitching a bit.

"It's sooo cute," Bree says.

"Tastes like pork." Chuy smiles. "And you can eat it during Lent." When I look back at her—in part because I'm curious about the capybaras, but also because I have no idea what Lent is—she elaborates. "They were such a popular dish in 16th century Venezuela that the Catholic Church declared capybaras to be fish. While the rest of the Church was giving up meat, the Venezuelans were chowing down on 'Hydrochoerus hydrochaeris.'"

Okay, first, Chuy is smarter than she lets on. Her kick-ass persona hides an intellect that puts mine to shame. Second, "Pretty sure fish is meat."

"Kinda funny that they're walking around the Vatican," Sarah whispers, peeking around with the rest of us now.

We all slide back when the gate flickers and buzzes. A second capybara bobbles out, its black eyes shifting about.

What are they looking for? I wonder.

Sarah preps her dory. "If a rodent swarm is all we're dealing with, I've had to handle a few rat infestations in crappy apartments. I can handle these things."

Bree is aghast. "Don't you dare."

"I can use the shocker on them," Hildy says.

Bree turns her forced horror toward Hildy, while I look at her with equal, but different surprise. "Excuse me?"

"We tried to have her change the name," Chuy says.

Hildy draws the katana sheathed on her back. "It's an electric sword. The name makes sense."

A high-pitched squeak interrupts us. It's kind of adorable and returns our attention to the gate. More capybaras are coming through. Three. Four. Eight.

They keep coming.

I lean back.

"I'll take out the gate. You guys take care of the infestation."

"Those gates are made from Oxium," Chuy says. "It's tough stuff. Not from Earth."

"Not tough enough," I say. "Trust me."

She nods, putting her trust in me, hopefully not making a mistake.

"Okay, on three, you guys take out our furry little friends."

"I will *not*," Bree says, crossing her arms.

I'm about to give her a pass when Chuy steps in and takes hold of Bree's arms. "Look, kid. You're obviously a savage. I wouldn't want to mess with you. But you're also an eight-year-old, and that's still pretty obvious. I'll be honest, I don't want you here...but you're here. If you can't do this, no one will blame you. But you being here and *not* helping, puts the rest of us in danger."

"But. They're. *Cute.*" Bree says.

Chuy gives me a stern look. Bree is my problem, and Chuy is accustomed to working with pros. Liabilities, when trying to save the whole universe, can't be tolerated. I get it, but I also don't know if I can do that to Bree. We're a team. Which I guess makes me a liability, too. But I also know she'll step up if she needs to. Because she *is* a savage. Chuy just doesn't know her well enough yet.

"And they were sent here by Cherry Bomb," Hildy says. "They could carry plague. Could have explosives on them, or inside them. They could—"

She's interrupted by the sound of a lock thunking open. It's followed by the squeak of a heavy door's hinges and the pattering of hurried feet. Hushed voices speaking Italian grow louder as they approach.

Everything about the capybaras' behavior changes. Gone is the casual sniffing. They're on alert, their bodies twitching with agitation, and their eyes shifting to a bloody color of red.

The hell?

Three men enter the Basilica's far end, sliding to a stop and beholding the unnatural wonder of an alien gate spewing out 'roid rodents.

Roidents.

Two of the men are dressed in black robes with pink sashes around their waists and little pink hats on their heads, like yarmulkes, but flashy.

Bishops, I think.

And the other guy…the oldest of the three…is wearing all white and a heavy cross around his neck.

"Dios mio," Chuy whispers. "The Holy Father."

"Holy father?" Bree asks.

"Bishop of Rome," Hildy says. "Vicar of Jesus Christ, Successor of the Prince of the Apostles, Supreme Pontiff of the Univer—"

"The Pope," I say to Bree. "He's the Pope."

"Riiight," she says. "The old guy who waves at people."

"Chuy," I say, "You're on papal protection." Honestly, the Pope doesn't rank high on my list of priorities, but I sense he's at the top of Chuy's changing list, and I don't want to make her disobey orders on my first outing. "You three are on roident duty. I'll take out the gate. Cool?"

"Don't need to ask for approval," Chuy says. "Not how orders work."

"I pesci camminano!" the Pope shouts, backing away as the rodents break into a savage scurry, their claws clacking on marble, their feet scrabbling for grip. If they'd been on soil or grass, the Pope would already be toast. The smooth floors give him a head start.

I nod and say, "Go!"

Chuy breaks first, drawing her weapon—some kind of future rifle I don't recognize. She runs for the stunned clergy, hand raised. "Holy Father! Run! Correre!"

The wide-eyed Pope stumbles back a few steps, trips over his robe, and sprawls back. I expect the bishops to catch him, but their instinct for self-preservation is strong and they're fleet of foot. Chuy stops next to him, turns, and raises her rifle back the way she came—but she holds her fire. Which is good, because the rest of us have charged out and are approaching the capybaras rushing toward His Holiness.

When the capybaras catch sight of us, they screech and chatter their big teeth together, fueled by a kind of manic hunger.

"I don't think these are normal capybaras!" Hildy shouts, her sword now crackling with energy.

Sarah throws her dory. It whistles through the air, impales a capybara through its open mouth, lifts it off the floor, and pins it to a pillar. For a moment, it's still. Dead. And then it snaps back to life, bites the spear's shaft, and drags itself forward, over and over, toward the blunt end.

We pause our charge to watch.

"What the..." Sarah says.

"Definitely not normal capybaras," Hildy says.

The skewered roident falls free from the spear, scrambles back to its feet, and rejoins the charge as if nothing occurred.

"Okay," Bree says. "I'm in."

"See any weak points?" I ask.

She glares at the onrushing creatures for a moment and then looks up to me with a confused expression. Shakes her head. "No."

One of Bree's abilities, which we call her 'killer instinct,' lets her see an enemy's weak points. It even showed her how to crawl through the neck of a god, up into his brain, and kill him from the inside. If she doesn't see a way to kill these things, and being impaled has little effect, this fight is going to go a little differently than I imagined.

Knowing they're not normal capybaras removes Bree's qualms about engaging them. She springs forward, bounds off a pillar and tackles the lead capybara from the side before the rest of us can think about engaging again. She goes full savage, swiping with her claws, rending with her hands, and biting with her own impressive set of teeth.

The capybara is...disassembled.

"Whoa," Hildy says, awed, but also fearful.

"She's a handful," I say, and then I watch as the various capybara parts *pull themselves back together.*

11

DARK HORSE

The second we head up the stairs dressed like special ops soldiers from the future, we're going to draw attention. It's likely that people will assume we're Israeli forces, but that could cause even more drama than the truth. "Delgado, we're going to stick out like an apple at a banana party."

"Like a pair of testicles at a vagina party," Henry says. When I give him a stern 'c'mon man' hand gesture, he shrugs. "What? Mine was funnier."

"He's right," Cassidy says, still focusing on keeping this Mia Durante's emotions from overwhelming Jonas.

"Dan, anything we can do to help blend in?" I ask.

After a pause, he comes back on the comms and says, "Burnett and I have been working on adaptive armor skins but are still beta testing it. No guarantees it will work right."

"Skins?" I say, not fully understanding.

Henry points a thumb at me, talking to Cassidy. "Was this guy born in the seventies?"

"Yes," I say. "I was. Then I missed a few decades. What the hell is a skin?"

"It's like in a video game," Cassidy says. "The player models have graphic skins that can be stretched over existing models to make them look like different characters."

"That can work?" McCoy asks.

"Theoretically," Delgado says. "We use pre-made skins, exactly as Cassidy described. The armor's cells can shift to any color in the spectrum. The trick is that they're not nearly as small as human cells, so your...resolution isn't going to be great. Up close, you'll look funny."

"As long as we don't look like Teletubbies when we walk out of here," I say.

"Well," Delgado says. "We're still beta testing, right? So, we haven't generated many serious looking skins. They've mostly been for fun. You have a few options."

I sigh. "Lay it on me."

"Uhh, the Simpsons. Photo realistic skins of Scooby Doo and the gang. The Avengers. Project Nemesis characters—probably your best bet ...and you."

"Me?" I ask.

"Remember when Chuy got angry at you for spraying her with the hose?"

"Yeah, I didn't—*Hold on. That was you?*"

"Burnett," he says quickly. "We needed to see how convincing it was from a distance."

"I got *so* much shit for that," I grumble.

"Is he smiling?" Delgado asks.

"He's wearing a mask, dummy," Cassidy says.

Delgado sounds relieved. "Right. I'll pretend he's smiling."

Henry raises a hand. "Dibs on Collins. I totally want boobs."

"Doesn't work like that," Delgado says. "Best bet is to match a similarly sized character. Sooo...."

"Soooo?" I ask.

"Uploading. In three, two..."

Beside me, McCoy's armor flickers to life, starting at the bottom and rolling up to his head. All the tiny color changing cells coating the armor's exterior shift, changing not just his clothing, but his masked face. When it's done, he's the spitting image of Jon Hudson, the main character of the Nemesis TV series.

"Holy shit," I say. "It worked."

McCoy looks down at his hands. "Definitely looks off close up."

"Then let's keep our distance," I say.

Delgado sounds pleased. "Uploading the rest."

Henry transforms into a gray-haired, mustached man who looks like he's seen action in 'Nam or Korea, if it was still the 80s. He's a helicopter pilot on the show. *Woodstock*, I think. Cassidy takes on the look of a smart woman with tied-back, black hair and a power suit. Very professional.

"I'm Cooper," she says, looking down at herself. "She's kind of my opposite, but whatevs. This is absolute fire."

Still fighting off the effects of the mysterious Mia Durante, Jonas becomes a different man dressed in brown and green, with a face more serious than mine.

"Hawkins," Henry says, identifying the character.

My turn, I think, and I look down. The transformation slides up my legs, starting with a pair of blue jeans. A tan button up shirt follows. I'm about to ask who I'm supposed to be when some creative shading leaves my chest looking full and feminine, a sheriff's badge pinned on the right side.

"Seriously?" I ask. "You made *me* Collins?"

"She's the closest to your size," Delgado says. "Just...don't talk."

"I was already groped by a pair of future Nazis," I say. "If I get felt up again..."

Jonas grunts, seething with mental pain. "There's...more. Coming through now."

"Can you shut that off?" I ask him. "Block them out?"

He clutches his eyes closed. When he opens them, he looks clearer, but it's taking an effort. "They're not like other people. Their thoughts... They're screaming at me."

I chamber a round in my sound suppressed M4, which thanks to Delgado and Burnett, is genuinely silent. If I want it to make sound, I can activate one of three sound settings. First is a Star Wars blaster sound effect. Second, I shit you not, is a collection of farts. Gets a lot of laughs on full auto. Last is a screaming fox. I know what the fox says, and it's fucking horrifying. What I really want are screaming bullets. Burnett says he's working on it.

The rifle can be camouflaged like the rest of my armor, but its shape can't be changed. So, I hold it casually at my side and step out into the sunset-lit square. No one gives me a second glance. They're far more interested in, or terrified of, what's happening at the mound. McCoy is similarly armed. Henry has his curved kopis sheathed on his hip. Jonas has a sword over his back. Called it the 'Sword of Mars.' No idea what it means, but it seems important to him. Cassidy is armed with her wits and the ability to make people shit themselves in fear.

"Try not to draw any atten—"

A scream tears through the air from the Dome. A woman. Everyone in the square stops moving, eyes on the Dome.

A second scream follows. A man this time.

People are dying.

Before I can shift gears, Henry as Woodstock blasts into the air, his body silhouetted by the orange sky.

"Okay," I say, giving in. "New plan. Fuck subtlety." I put an arm around Jonas and help him stand. "Rotate to the Dome in three—"

Cassidy rotates away.

"Every damn time," I mutter, and I follow with Jonas.

A moment later, the two of us slide out of the white void of the fourth dimension completely unnoticed—because it's pandemonium.

Normally, the Dome would be impossible to ignore at sunset, the orange light gleaming off its gold-plated surface, resting atop a sea of blue mosaic tiles and Arabic religious inscriptions. Today, it's the least interesting thing atop the Temple Mount.

A gate stands in front of the Dome, fifty-foot tall columns lined with glowing symbols. A red field of energy stretches out between them, shimmering with hexagons, as a group of confused looking people pour out.

They stumble into view, silhouettes at first, then the sun's light reveals their true horror.

Layers of blood covers their skin and shredded clothing. Matted clumps of coagulation and organs dangle from their hair. Teeth gnashing, they look at the surrounding crowd that's steadily backing away, no longer seeing God in the mysterious gate.

This is the work of a very fucked up mind.

The silhouette of a tall, broad man catches my attention, not because of his size, but because he's not hunched over. Not running. Not apologizing. He stepped out of the gate, clean, dressed in a black leather trench coat, his face partially hidden behind a thick beard. He's just watching. Observing.

Henry lands beside me. "Hey, no fair. You beat me here."

I ignore him. "You seeing this back home?"

"Seeing it," Delgado says.

"What the hell are they?" Wini asks, on the comms with Dan.

"People." I step closer, trying to make out faces. "The ones we encountered on Porter."

"The sad zombies?" Delgado asks.

Sad is an understatement. Back on Porter, a planet we renamed after our fallen comrade, Cassidy absorbed their abject despair and released just a small bit of it into me. I've never been that sad in my life. Not on my worst day. "Yeah."

A lone woman approaches me. She's petite, her tattered clothing unrecognizable. Caked-on gore coats every inch of her. Bits of flesh dangle from her chin.

I glance at Jonas. "Is this her?"

He nods, looking supremely uncomfortable, eyeing the horde, flinching as their screaming thoughts careen into his closed off mind.

Holding my weapon at the ready now, no longer worried about who sees it, I head toward the woman, hoping for, but not counting on, a peaceful parley.

I stop a few feet short of her, and I'm glad when she does the same. She looks nervous. Is wringing her hands together. Biting her bottom lip.

"Mia?" I ask. "Mia Durante?"

Her face screws up, and I think it's because a man's deep voice has just come out of the buxom redhead from TV.

But then her eyebrows turn up in the middle, mirrored by the downturn of her lips. "You...you know my..." She looks about to burst into tears. Emotion hiccups from her mouth as a single word I can't quite make out.

I lean closer. "What was that?"

"I'm...sorry," she says. "I don't want to."

Her lips peel back in a sneer, revealing blood-stained teeth and the meat of some former meal warbling beside her canines. "I don't want to do this!" she screams—and then charges, arms outstretched, fingers hooked, mouth open and ready to bite.

The rest of the mob—now at least fifty people—follows her lead.

12

MIAH

The horde of rabid, chattering capybaras are thrown into a frothing bloodlust after the dismembering of their comrade at the hands of Bree. They shriek and charge en masse, like children who have just raided their parent's dresser for coins and are now pursuing a passing ice cream truck.

"Don't let one of them past!" I shout. Laser wings crackle, extending from my back and lifting me off the floor. I'm ten feet up and moving toward the gate, well out of reach from the– "Holy shit!"

I roll to the side as a pair of domino-sized incisors nearly lock onto my arm.

They're stronger and faster than they look. Smarter, too.

I arc a little higher. From above, their movement doesn't look as chaotic as it did from below. They're organized. In some kind of complicated formation. Moving in tandem.

They don't seem especially smart, and they don't appear to be communicating, which means...they've been trained.

And they have a target.

Despite moving toward the team, the majority of the capybaras are angling away from direct confrontation. Instead, they're following a path that will take them behind pillars, around the defenders, and straight toward the Pope. Easy target. Maximum chaos.

First step in preventing that–destroy the damn gate. My wings flare bright, whisking me toward the papal altar and the glowing gate in front of it.

"Nighty night," I say, and I'm instantly glad no one is within earshot. The new crew seems...cool. They probably all have catchphrases. Going to need to work on mine...after I turn this thing to dust.

My eyes relax, the cells inside allowing the passage of energy from within. At first, it's visible light. Then I focus it into a beam of energy capable of cutting through–

The beam strikes the column, splits, and refracts in a dozen directions. Containing the same power as the original blast, the beams punch holes in the columns, the domed ceiling, the floor, and the papal altar itself.

What the hell? I carved up the gate leading to Tartarus, but this... The gates must have been upgraded.

From a distance, Bree says, "I thought you said, 'No damage?'" She spins around in a circle, clutching a capybara's hind limbs, the creature wailing angrily. She lets it fly, pancaking it against a statue that cracks in half and topples onto the fallen, crushed beast. Behind her, Sarah shield-bashes the roidents left and right, breaking bones with every strike, only to have them reform seconds later. Hildy seems to be the only one making real progress, despite her lack of powers. She's good with that sword, and the capybaras she dismembers seem to stay that way.

Chuy hasn't had to fire a shot yet, but it's only a matter of time before some of capybaras sneak past–and more are coming through.

Attention back on the gate, I extend a laser blade from my arm. I swing hard, driving the laser light into what looks like black stone. Sparks fly, bouncing off the floor, my body, and the capybaras below–several of which are set ablaze by the white-hot embers.

"Seriously?" Sarah shouts, backhanding a capybara so hard that its head tears halfway off, before reattaching just in time to get punted. "You're supposed to be making this easier, not harder!" She kicks the roident, sending it flying in my direction. "Heads up!"

I duck as the capybara spirals past, expelling a long twisting strand of bloody drool. The frothing beast strikes the back wall behind the altar and thumps to the floor, immobilized for just a moment. Then it's back on its feet, rejoining the furry Blitzkrieg.

My laser blade extinguishes, and I inspect the damage I've managed to inflict. There's a scorched line on the pillar, but it's otherwise unmarred.

Damnit.

Why won't this thing break?

"Sarah!" I shout.

She spins in a circle, batting back three capybaras that bounce and flail before righting themselves. "What!"

"My lasers can't cut it! Can you do your Earth-thing?"

"You guys need—" Hildy swings her blade, decapitating a capybara. "—ugh, better names for things!"

The roident's body stumbles past her while the head lies beside her foot, mouth still twitching, eyes still moving.

Still alive, but not regenerating.

A thought tickles the back of my memory. A tidbit of knowledge. But it's lost when the walls start quivering. Sarah reaches out for the gate like Darth Vader air-gripping another obstinate Imperial officer. Her face strains, but the gate shows no signs of damage.

Because they're not from Earth, or even made of something found on this planet.

When a crack cuts across the ceiling, grit dropping down into my hair, I shout, "Stop! It's not working!"

Going to have to old-fashioned brute force this.

A capybara lunges at Sarah's neck. She doesn't see it coming. I'm about to shout a warning, but it's not necessary. A blur of pink springs across the Basilica, tackling the creature and tearing it apart before bouncing off the wall and pouncing on the next target. The capybara is already reforming, but it's such a mess it will take some time—

—something Chuy is keen to remind me we're short on. "¡Darse prisa! This sphincter ain't gonna unpucker itself!"

Luckily, basic Español and hurrying are things I can do. Powered by alien laser wings, I launch toward the Basilica's far side, cruising over the battle in progress.

"Sarah! Get ready for a pickup!" She gives me a serious nod. Understands the plan. I can hit hard, but no one—maybe on the planet—packs a punch like Sarah.

In the second it takes me to pass overhead, I sever two capybaras in half lengthwise with a blast from my eyes. Before I can see if they're healing, I'm passing over Chuy and the wide-eyed, pale-faced Pope. When I'm moving this fast, everything around me feels slow. I can't help but laugh when the Pope's voice calls out upon seeing me overhead, "Che cazzo!?"

No idea what it means, but I get the vibe he's putting off. Probably should have introduced myself before going all angelic inside the Vatican. *Live and learn, I guess.* Next time I'm battling killer capybaras inside a holy place, I'll take a moment for greetings and explain that I'm not an angel—I'm just a normal dude infused with DNA from an alien race that might have been humanity's inspiration for the winged version of the Bible's messengers.

That'll go over well.

I stop at the far end, turn back the way I came, and turn on my mental afterburners. The Basilica is large enough to inspire awe, but the football-field-length space doesn't feel large when you're accelerating toward the speed of sound in a split second. I don't have a speedometer telling me how fast I'm going, but I've gotten good at reading the pressure building against my face. If I push myself much faster, I'm going to break the sound barrier inside the Basilica. Don't even want to think about the damage a contained sonic boom would do to the structure—or the people inside it.

So, I stop accelerating and angle myself toward Sarah.

She raises her strong arms, waiting for a ride, even as capybaras close in on her. "This better wooooork!" she shouts, as I snag her by both forearms, yank her off the floor, and accelerate her to near the speed of sound. An instant later, I fling her forward and come to a stop.

Sarah launches toward the gate, fist cocked back.

She lets out a battle cry and unleashes the mother of all punches.

The resulting shockwave isn't as loud as a sonic boom, but it knocks everyone and everything to the floor aside from me. Dust rolls through the Basilica, colliding with the far wall. When it settles, I find Sarah lying on the floor at the foot of the gate.

It's still standing...

But the red sheet of energy is missing.

It's deactivated, I think, and I watch as the top half of the right pillar comes loose and falls toward Sarah.

I launch forward again and catch the half pillar.

I expected it to swat me to the floor, but it's not hard to manage. Strangely light for something so hard to break. I place it on the floor and look down at Sarah. "Okay?"

"Peachy," she says, pushing herself up with a grunt. "Don't worry about me. Go save the Pope."

"Right," I say, and I'm about to launch into the fray when Sarah takes my hand. "Your lasers. They didn't heal afterward."

When she lets go, I fly back to the nave, ready to hack and slash everything on four stubby legs. En route, that single word-nugget of knowledge reaches its destination in the forefront of my mind.

Hydra.

Low to the floor, I fly through the capybaras' ranks, cutting off heads with my forearm blades. "Cut off their heads," I say to Hildy, as I pass. "It cauterizes the wounds and keeps them from—"

"What do you think I've been doing?" she shouts, out of breath. I need to remember that more than half the team are normal humans now. They'll get tired faster and take less damage. Hildy is tough, but not immortal. I swing back around and unleash a series of quick eye blasts that slice through capybaras like...well, like a laser through flesh and blood. Unfortunately, they work just as well on the Basilica's marble floor, stone walls, and ivory statues.

So much for no damage.

But hey, saved the Pope. I think.

With a quick spin, I sever the last capybara's head. It falls at my feet, face up, chattering its teeth like a furry Black Knight from *Monty Python*. "Tis but a scratch," I say in my best British accent, and I punt the head away.

Beside me, Bree giggles, her bunny suit covered in blood and gore, slowly peeling away and slapping to the floor. "Come, Sir Miah! To the grail!"

She Monty Python gallops toward Chuy and the Pope, who watches on in horror as she claps her charred, clawed hands together like coconut halves, singing, "Brave, brave sir Miah, brave sir Miah! He chopped off the capybara's head, now it's on the floor all dead. Brave, brave, brave—"

The Pope passes out in Chuy's arms.

She gives Bree a single eyebrow-raised mom glare.

Bree shrugs. "What?"

"Hey guys?" Sarah says.

I turn around and find the gate crumbling to dust. Broken on this side and now closed from the other. Once it's gone, I take in the carnage. Twenty-seven still-living capybara heads, and just as many torn apart bodies. The floor is soaked with blood and covered in various body parts that were replaced. I don't understand how any of this is possible, but don't question it. I've been to Tartarus and seen an AI born from a giant egg.

A crack brings my attention back to the papal altar. One of the four spiral pillars breaks and topples to the side. A moment later, the statue of a saint nose dives to the floor and shatters.

I turn to Chuy, who looks mortified. "Uhh, I think we should go."

13

DARK HORSE

Durante is fast. Like a wolf.

But I'm faster—thanks to the blue Europhid now fused with my cells, making me more than human, mind and body. Durante goes for my throat, but finds the butt of my rifle instead, driven into the center of her forehead. She crumples to the stone floor at my feet.

I'm about to order that we subdue the rest, but then the first of them—a short woman in a track suit—reaches a bystander—a Hassidic Jewish man, head still somehow bowed in prayer. He never stands a chance.

The woman screams, "No, no, no! Please run!"

Then she's on him, gnawing on his neck. He flails and shouts, his horror suddenly matching her own. Tries to shake her off, but she's latched on, and no longer alone. Drawn by the blood now spraying from the man's neck, ten more apologetic zombies dive down, feasting on the fresh meat with hyena-pack ferocity.

My qualms about taking out unarmed people fades like a fart in a tornado. These people seem to feel sorrow for what they're doing, but they're still killing innocents. Can't let that stand, even if this will haunt me for the rest of my life.

"Weapons free!" I shout. "Take them out!"

If anyone has any doubt about my intentions, I quickly drop five of the onrushing people, one headshot for each. They fall exactly like they should, sliding to a stop, blood oozing out through the cracks of the ancient stone floor. I feel bad about adding more blood to a site that's seen a lot of bloodshed in the past, but I'm not here picking religious sides. I'm trying to save them all, but that can't happen if they're still here.

"Get out of here!" I shout to the people still lingering, locked in place by fear or curiosity. A few of them hear me and run, but some, like a businessman with piss-stained pants, are in the throes of a panic attack, unable to move, let alone think.

McCoy as Jon Hudson stands beside me, muttering a curse, or a prayer. Raises his rifle and starts taking calm, steady shots, dropping targets with the efficiency of a practiced operator. I let him get a few rounds ahead of me, and then I join the fray again. When his mag runs dry, I've still got a few rounds. In the time it takes him to slap in a fresh magazine, I'm out and replacing mine. We can keep this up for a few minutes, but if these assholes keep coming...

I glance back at the others. Cassidy, with a much older woman's face, is understandably overwhelmed. We've killed a lot of aliens, but these are people. Apologetic people. As much as she likes horror as a genre, this is the real thing. So, I'm not going to push her.

But the other two?

Woodstock Henry looks like he doesn't know what to do. No way he's afraid to take these things on, but he might be trying to control his reaction. If he unleashes, he might roast us all—I'm told. I haven't really seen him in action yet. And Jonas... He's on his knees again, fighting back the emotional assault emanating from these people. In her shocked state, Cassidy can't help him.

"Hey," I shout to Henry. "Destroy the gate!"

Only way we stop the carnage is to close this thing down. For all we know, there could be thousands of these killers.

The bystanders have either fled the area or are currently under attack. Makes picking targets easier. Also means that the horde's collective attention is focused on us. My shots come faster now, dropping people one after another as they charge toward McCoy and me.

"Jonas," I say, backing up a step. "What's your situation?"

"Working..." he grunts. "...on it..." He reaches back and draws the Sword of Mars. Whatever that does for him, it's not enough.

Lightning cracks over the Dome, surging out from Henry's kopis and striking the gate. The bolt of energy surges down the pillar, strikes the stone floor and arches out and away. A dozen of the killers still coming through the portal spasm and fall to the ground, but the gate is unharmed. Safe above the fray, floating in the air, Henry launches toward the gate, swinging.

His kopis strikes hard. Sparks fly. But the gate shows no signs of damage.

These things are tough. Might have to rotate back to the compound and pick up some C-4.

"Looks like things are going FUBAR," Delgado says in my ear. "You want back up?"

"I want C-4," I say.

Wini comes on the line. "I'll get it. Two minutes."

"Wini," I say, not wanting her to be put in danger. She's a fighter, and fit for her age, but she's far from being an operator.

"I'm already suited up!" she says, breathy from hustling to the armory. "They need you there!"

She's not wrong about that. Henry's attacks on the gate have been ineffective. McCoy and I are just slowing them down. Jonas is still fighting his own fight. And Cassidy... She looks like she's in shock. I don't blame her. This will give me nightmares for years to come. But I really need her right now.

"Cassidy Rose," I say, as gently as I can muster between trigger pulls.

Her eyes flick to me for just a moment. Then back to the carnage. But she's listening.

"Could use some of your mojo right now," I say. "On them."

"But they're already so sad," she says, tears on her cheeks. Like Jonas, she's feeling these people's pain. And it's overwhelming them, which honestly makes my job harder, because the last thing I need to do is feel bad for these people.

"Reloading," McCoy says, and I focus forward again, dropping a handful of people. As they hit the stone floor, I hold my fire. The people they land beside, the ones we've already cut down...

They're getting up, just like they did on Porter. Immortal, somehow.

The neat holes in their foreheads are gone.

"McCoy..." I say.

"I see it!"

He chambers a round and continues firing one round after another, dropping newcomers and the already-killed-once people climbing back to their feet, hunger unabated. "One mag left!"

The two of us won't last long.

Henry is pounding the gate with his fist now, but not making a dent. Oxium is strong stuff. When it's processed and formed into sheets, a rail gun can punch a hole through it, but the gates are raw Oxium and thicker than any starship hull I've ever seen. It's possible the C4 won't work.

"Run," a voice whispers from my feet. "Run!"

Durante is awake. No wound on her forehead. She pushes herself up, sneer reforming. I stop her progress with another hard whack to the forehead. She falls down again, unconscious. These guys can take anything we dish out and keep going.

"Out!" McCoy says, dropping his rifle and drawing a handgun, which he uses to drop five more people—including a few I think were victims just a minute ago, their insides still dangling from open wounds. Wounds I can see healing. Immortal conscious zombies, tortured for eternity.

"God..." I whisper, and I drop another four. "Wini, ETA?"

"Thirty seconds!"

Beside me, Jonas goes still. His eyes are rolled back and vacant. It's like he's not there anymore, like his soul just left his body.

The hell?

"Out," McCoy and I say in unison. We're stuck in a moment of time where no bullets are flying, and the horde isn't being slowed. It takes us each just seconds to swap out our magazines, but that's all the time it takes for the first killers to reach me.

I'm about to get tackled by a freakshow trio. There's a bulbous man in what looks like a tattered Union uniform straight out of the Civil War, his girth not slowing him down even a little. He's followed by a tall woman in broken heels and a shredded power suit, and a man with long black hair, clumped thick with gore. What really stands out is his traditional and authentic looking Native American garb, complete with beads and subtle decorative feathers. All of them are enraged, hungry, and too close for me to shoot with my rifle.

I reach down for the slew drive on my hip, but I'm not quick enough. Before I can rotate a few feet to the side, their fingers reach my neck.

Three quick shots turn the three lunging attackers into dead weight. McCoy turned his pistol away from the killers rushing him to save me.

The trio still plow into me like I'm a bitch in heat and they're a Saint Bernard with a hard-on. But there's no biting, or clawing, or rending of my body parts. I kick out of their limp bodies knowing they'll eventually get back up.

"Thanks," I say, lifting my rifle to help fend off the reinforced killers until Wini arrives.

McCoy stands between me and the horde, using quick hip-fire shooting techniques taught to us by Cowboy. He levels seven more in seconds—but he misses the man coming in from the side, his black robes making him difficult to see in the fading light.

It's the Hasidic man I couldn't save. He's alive again, and back for vengeance against the men who failed him.

I aim for him, but I hold my fire as McCoy backpedals between us.

"On your left!" I shout, and I cringe when McCoy ejects his spent magazine. He's defenseless.

"Henry!" I shout in desperation, taking action even before I finish shouting his name.

I trigger the slew on my hip and roll into the void. Shift to the side just a touch and rotate back out. I appear behind the Hasidic man, a few feet over the ground. I reach for him—

—and miss.

The curls of his hair slip through my fingers.

Lightning arcs in Henry's wake, dropping several killers as he passes. He approaches like a heat seeking missile, eyes glowing blue with god-like determination, arms outstretched.

Even he is too slow.

McCoy falls back under the weight of the man, both of them toppling back as Henry rockets past and crashes into a stone wall.

I land in a crouch. "McCoy!" I shout, raising my rifle and taking the shot before I'm certain it's accurate. The back of the man's head snaps to the side as the front end explodes over the stone courtyard.

"Got your back!" Henry says, landing beside me. "Sorry I missed."

"We both missed."

While Henry starts hurling lightning bolts, I grab hold of the man's robe, roll him away, and reveal McCoy. The façade of Jon Hudson has disappeared. The suit has been damaged. It's soaked in blood.

"McCoy!" I shout, dropping down beside him, peeling off his mask.

His eyes are open. They flick toward me. Blood gurgles from his mouth when he attempts to speak. "Tell...tell...C—Cass..."

His eyes stare off into oblivion.

Unmoving.

I've seen the look before, but I don't believe it until I see the blood pulsing from his torn open neck.

"Oh my god..."

"Is he..." Cassidy sniffs, standing above McCoy. "Is he..."

There's no saving him. Not now, or in the future. I nod slowly.

Owen McCoy is dead.

14

DARK HORSE

Lightning rips through the air around us as Henry continues pummeling the undying assholes. For every five he shocks into submission, another five recover. He's just slowing them down.

Cassidy peels back her mask, revealing her real face. She sniffs, tears filling her eyes. She falls to her knees on the other side of McCoy. Puts her hand on his still chest. "I can't feel anything."

She's trying to feel his emotions, but there's nothing there.

"Maybe he'll come back?" she asks, blue eyes so earnest it breaks my heart. It's not a fanciful question. People are literally coming back to life all around us, and some of them didn't come through the gate—like the man that killed McCoy. If he comes back...he might not be himself, and that might be worse than death. Looking at these tormented people, horrified by their own actions, unable to escape even in death—I wouldn't wish that fate on anyone.

Before I can think of an answer, a rectangle of white gives birth to Wini, dressed for battle in adaptive armor, carrying a backpack and an Origin 12, drum-fed, auto shotgun. "All right! Let's blow this like Pamela Anderson did Tommy Lee—"

She sees McCoy.

Her brows turn up. She's confused. In shock.

Cassidy looks up to her surrogate grandmother, face wet with tears. "Can we bring him back?"

The backpack falls from Wini's shoulders. The shotgun lowers. "Oh, honey..."

Cassidy throws herself into Wini's arms.

Surrounded by death and chaos, Wini hugs the girl, comforting her.

Then she makes eye contact with me, expressing her rage. Then she glances down at the backpack full of C4.

Message received.

I'm in shock over McCoy's death, too. He was a friend and a hell of a teammate. There are people back home who will be devastated by his death, and after everything he lived through, it seems unfair that he should die here, at the hands of one of these...things.

I won't let it be in vain.

I compartmentalize the pain, take hold of the backpack, and get to my feet. The pack is heavy, carrying far more C4 than we should need.

Fuck it, I think. Need to make sure the gate comes down, no matter what. If I have to destroy the entire Temple Mount and all of these assholes with it, I'm game. Screw the consequences. I scoop up Wini's shotgun and prepare to carve a path.

Henry gives me a head start. He's unfazed by McCoy's death. In fact, he's still smiling. Still having a good time. Kind of makes me want to backhand him. McCoy deserves more respect than that. But the kid didn't know him, feels no fear, and is doing his job.

I level the shotgun at chest level to the horde.

"I'm sorry!" a man screams, as he approaches.

"Please stop us!" a woman pleads.

"I don't like how it tastes," shouts a bearded man with a British accent, before wailing in sorrow.

I should feel bad for these people, and the pain I'm about to cause them, but I don't.

Shotgun leveled, I pull and hold the trigger. The weapon kicks in my arms, unleashing a torrent of white-hot magnesium pellets called Dragon's Breath. Torsos, heads, and limbs explode, sending flaming flesh in every direction. It's an effective mess—and it clears a path.

"Let's do this!" Henry says, taking to the air, lightning arcing from his fingertips. The two of us trailblaze through the tortured mob, approaching the gate. It occurs to me now that I could have just rotated to the gate, but anger got the best of me. Every one of these fuckers I mow down makes me feel a little bit better.

And we're almost there.

"Hold them back," I shout to Henry, and I drop the shotgun. Then I slip out of the backpack, open it up, and I'm happy to find the C4 already rigged with detonators. I just need to set them, rotate out, and use the detonator sitting atop the dozen bricks.

Without taking the C4 out, I reach inside the pack and activate the bunch. Then I hurl it over the mob still emerging from the gate. It falls near one of the pillars. Not exactly on top of it, but this whole area will be a crater after it blows.

I'm about to call out an evacuation when a large body steps out of the gate, eyes already locked on me. It's a man—I think. His face is peeled back in a permanent smile. His hulking, seven-foot-tall body ripples with muscles. His voice rumbles when he speaks, vibrating sinister power through the air. It's just a single word, the same one that's carved on his chest, oozing blood, "LIFE..."

"Death!" Henry says, rocketing past overhead, trailing crackling lightning, fist cocked back to deliver a devastating punch.

The tall, bearded man I had seen earlier, observing everything, sees Henry coming and casually steps back through the gate, unconcerned. He's seen enough.

The collision of Henry and the giant with 'Life' carved in his chest sends a shockwave out and away from the gate, knocking the horde—and me—off our feet. On my back, I open my eyes in time to see Henry sprawling away from the impact. He strikes the stone courtyard, bouncing and skidding until slamming to a stop against a stone wall.

He doesn't get back up.

I activate the detonator and reach for the slew drive on my hip.

Don't get a chance to activate either of them.

I'm tackled from behind. Doesn't hurt much, thanks to my Europhid-enhanced body, but I'm not ready for it. I sprawl forward, dropping the detonator. It slides across the courtyard, stopping among a throng of scorched living dead, peeling their melted flesh up, healing as they turn their attention to the easy victim just a few feet away—me.

A scream rolls me onto my back in time to catch the woman diving for my throat. Given the chance, she would rip my throat out. The adaptive armor we all wear can stop bullets and knives, but these freaks have some kind of unnatural PSI, enabling them to bite through just about anything. Including my neck.

I catch the woman by the shoulders. She snaps at my arms but misses, weeping the whole time, body wracked by hunger and sobs. "Durante," I say, hoping her name will make a difference. "You don't need to do this!"

"Stop us," she pleads. "Please, God, stop us!"

"I'm…trying…god-damnit!"

A man joins the attack, throwing himself atop Durante. I can handle their combined weight, but they're not alone. More and more pile on, inching Durante's frothing jaws closer and closer to my neck.

"No!" I glance to the side. Cassidy is there, horrified, about to see me torn apart. She sobs once, and then screws up her face, putting all her emotion into a scream that tears across the courtyard like a tsunami. "Everyone stop! *Right fucking now!*"

The air around her ripples and expands outward, carried by her voice. The empathic wave strikes everything in the courtyard, flowing through the undying tormented. I feel it when it strikes. Am moved by the emotion it imparts. The desperation and pain. But it doesn't undo me, or change how I'm feeling, because I'm already there.

But the tormented…they go still.

A strange calmness sweeps across the courtyard. The crazed people step back, stumble away, hands to their heads. No longer aggressive, but still regretting everything they've been unable to stop themselves from doing.

The weight lifts, and I'm left with just Durante, tears in her eyes.

"We're free," she says, rolling off me. She looks at the scene, at all the people not getting up—those who were killed by the horde and for some reason, like McCoy, didn't get up again. As well as many of the killers who were momentarily dead when Cassidy broke their bondage. Whatever strange effect was animating them and healing them, it's been beaten back by Cassidy's empathic barrage.

But for how long?

A grunt draws my attention back to the still-active gate. The big man with 'Life' scrawled on his chest looks stunned. Hand to his head, he stumbles back and falls through the gate.

We've been given a momentary reprieve, but with the gate still open, I don't—

The ground shakes.

What now? I think, looking for the source. Feels like King Kong throwing a temper tantrum, but I can't see a source. There's just a bunch of confused people, Cassidy and Wini standing together, Henry unconscious, McCoy dead, and Jonas...still kneeling, eyes closed, almost like he's at peace. His body devoid of emotion. Vacant.

The stone beneath me cracks. Fissures open up, streaking toward the gate. The horde, now back to their normal human selves, flee the area. They'll need to be found and taken into custody until we're sure whatever madness gripped them has passed. But that's a problem for another time.

I scramble to my feet, pause, and offer a hand to Durante. She takes it, and I haul her up. "You're coming with me."

She doesn't argue. Follows me to the others.

"The hell is happening?" Wini asks.

I look down at Jonas. "Pretty sure it's him."

The gate punctuates my assessment by exploding into a thousand pieces, scattering across the fractured courtyard. It's devastating, but the damage is largely contained, and it's far kinder to the Temple Mount than the pack full of C4 would have been.

Jonas gasps, hands on stone floor. He looks up at me, shaking his head. "Sorry," he says. "For taking so long. It was nearly impossible to focus with all their...experiences flooding my mind." He nods his thanks to Cassidy. "If you hadn't freed them, I'm not sure I could have done it."

I help him up and motion to Henry. "Mind grabbing him?"

Jonas grunts and is on it.

I turn to Wini. "Take her home."

Cassidy is torn up. Not smiling. Not moving. I've never seen her like this, and it's breaking my heart. Wini nods and rotates out with Cassidy in her arms.

After retrieving the backpack full of C4 and deactivating the detonators, I deactivate our adaptive armor skins and stand above McCoy.

"Sorry, buddy."

I bend down and pick up an arm. To my surprise, Durante is on his other side. Helps me haul him up. "Thanks."

"How we going to do this?" Jonas asks, Henry held in his arms.

"He alive?" I ask.

Jonas nods. "Don't worry about him. Kid can take a hit."

"Your suit has a PSD built into the hip, but they're not easy to use. One wrong move and you could end up in New Zealand. Or inside a pulsar, a hundred light years away."

"That sounds—"

"Bad," I say, "yeah." And then I make an offer I'm not entirely comfortable with, but I'm not seeing any other options here. We need to get the hell out before Israeli forces arrive to lock down the area, and the inevitable conflict with the Palestinians breaks out. "Everything you need to know is inside my head. Have a look, but…don't poke around. I'm not entirely human, and there is a lot in there. You could get lost."

Jonas nods, and then he slips into my mind like a philandering ninja into his mistress's bedroom.

15

MIAH

We arrive back at the St. Augustine hideaway without any fanfare, despite our victory. We destroyed the gate, defeated undying capybaras, didn't totally destroy Vatican City, and saved the freakin' Pope. Not only that, but we also helped Chuy rotate the cauterized rodent remains into the middle of the Sahara Desert, where they'll just get buried by the sands, never to be seen again. We left behind some damage, and a lot of blood and guts, but I'm sure the Holy See has a kick-ass cleaning crew.

It took Chuy a few minutes of explaining for the Pope to not believe I was a legit angel, but she managed to explain the difference. Even told him about the Darkness, which was international news. I'm honestly not sure he believed her, but the Pope's not supposed to lie.

I'm half-expecting clapping hands when we enter the house, but the living area is empty.

"We return victorious!" Bree announces, but she sags in defeat upon seeing the empty room.

"I'll get drinks!" Hildy announces, heading for the kitchen.

Sarah plops down in the recliner beside the large stone fireplace. Kicks back. Feet up. "Looks like no one's home."

Chuy closes the door behind us. "The other mission must still be in progress. I'm going to see if they need—"

A flash of white at the center of the room makes me flinch. These guys are used to slipping in and out of the fourth dimension, using their—what did they call them?—*slew drives*, from the future.

When Wini slips out wearing adaptive armor I rejected, I know something is off.

Wini wasn't supposed to be on the mission.

When she opens her arms and releases Cassidy, I get worried. Tears streak down her cheeks. Her lips quiver. She sees us there, staring, wondering.

When a sob escapes her mouth, my heart breaks for her. Then she bolts from the room.

"What happened?" Chuy demands.

"Are you all okay?" Wini asks.

"Fine," Chuy says. "*What. Happened?*"

A second flash of white announces the next arrival. It's Jonas. He's got Henry in his arms.

"Henry!" Sarah says, leaping from her seat.

"He's fine," Jonas says, putting him down in the chair Sarah just vacated. "Took a hard hit..."

"...into a thick-ass wall," Henry mumbles, furrowing his brows before opening his eyes. He places a hand to his head. "Geez. That guy packed a punch."

"Wini," Chuy says, taking her shoulders. "Where is Moses?"

"He's fine," Wini says, nearly in tears herself. "It's McCoy..."

Chuy goes rigid. Jaw set. "What about McCoy?"

A third portal opens. Dark Horse steps out, one arm around a woman I've never seen before. She's covered in layers of blood, some new, some old. McCoy hangs limp and bloodied in Dark Horse's other arm. There's a distinct difference between someone who is unconscious and someone who is dead. I can't pinpoint it, but the subconscious reptile mind has no trouble recognizing death. I knew Henry was unconscious, just as surely as I know McCoy is dead.

The glow of victory fades in a breath.

Hildy gasps and backpedals a step. Trips on a recliner and falls back into it. Hand to her mouth, she sits there in silence, staring down at McCoy.

Though I didn't really know him, he clearly means a lot to our new friends—especially to Cassidy and Wini. Dark Horse looks shaken, but he's doing what soldiers do. Chuy, too. Stiff upper lip and all that.

But even Jonas looks upset. Whatever they faced, it must have been worse than regenerating capybaras.

The skinny man, Burnett, enters the room, like a gazelle, bounding toward Hildy. "My schatzi!" He nearly trips over McCoy's body, but leaps over him with a flash of terror, and slides into the chair beside Hildy. Holds her tight, hand hidden in her curly hair, whispering comforting words.

"Where is Bubbles?" Jonas asks him.

Burnett turns his head. "Monitoring."

"Monitoring what?" Jonas asks.

"The whole world, I think." He leans his head into Hildy's, the conversation over.

Dark Horse releases the bloodied woman. She's confused and bedraggled. She all but collapses into one of the chairs, her body starting to shake, her eyes wide with shock. I've seen the look before, after combat, in the eyes of fellow soldiers—and in my own, in the mirror for several years.

"Where are they?" The voice is angry. Wounded. "Where the hell are they?" Delgado storms into the room.

"I'm sorry," Dark Horse says, unable to look at the other man. He gently lays McCoy down atop the braided rug in the center of the room. If I remember the play's details correctly, Delgado and McCoy have worked together for years, protecting their secret facility and raising a brood of teenagers who'd been experimented on by a creature called the Other. Cassidy was one of those kids.

I get my first good look at the wound on McCoy's neck. A large chunk of the meat...and his jugular are gone. Most of his blood will still be in Israel.

It's a bite. But the teeth indentations... They look human.

"Who did this?" I ask.

Dark Horse doesn't respond, but he does glance toward the newcomer. He's not identifying her on purpose, but she somehow played a part in McCoy's demise.

"You *brought* one of them?" Delgado shouts. "*Here?* Are you insane?"

"We need to learn everything we can," Dark Horse says. "She might know—"

Delgado storms toward the woman, fists clenched.

Instinct guides me to my feet. I put myself between the fuming man and the stranger. I know Delgado is one of the leaders here…technically the founding member of this group, but he's not thinking right now.

"You need to take a minute," I say. "Gather your thoughts."

"Kid, if you don't get out of my way—"

Sarah stands by my side. "You need to take a step back. This lady is in shock, and there isn't a damn thing you can do—to either of us."

"But I can," Henry says, pushing himself out of the chair. He looks uncommonly pissed.

I look to Jonas for backup, but he's undecided, torn between loyalty to our team, but clearly bearing no love for the woman.

"Don't you dare," Bree says, standing in front of me and giving Henry a shove that only manages to push her back. She's back to being a normal human girl. Looks up at me. "Let me Demon Dog him!"

"She's one of them," Henry argues, ignoring Bree, which shows at least a modicum of control. "I didn't do enough to save him—" He motions to McCoy, and his behavior starts to make sense. "—but I can stop her here. Right fucking now."

The problem here is that Henry is not afraid to attack his friends to do what he thinks is right. Also won't be afraid to kill this woman, even though she presents no real threat. At least at the moment.

"Henry," Dark Horse says, standing between us. "Stand down." He looks to Delgado. "Both of you. Cassidy stopped whatever was controlling those people. They didn't want to be there. Didn't want to attack us. They were being controlled." He motions to the woman. "She's as much a victim of Cherry as McCoy."

Delgado deflates, anger turning to sadness, eyes starting to sparkle from brewing tears. He turns to Henry. "Help me move him." They wrap the rug around McCoy and heft him up. They carry the body away together. Everyone watches in somber silence. Wini follows them out.

"Anyone have a phone I can borrow?" Jonas asks.

Hildy sniffs back her tears. "You can make calls from the adaptive armor."

Jonas taps the controls on his forearm a few times. Nods. "Found it. I'm going to clear my head, and let a few people know I haven't been dead for the two years we missed." He heads outside without another word. No one tries to stop him. Whatever they faced, it shook them. Henry *and* Jonas. And they've seen some messed-up shit. Must have been bad.

"Help me sort this out?" Dark Horse says to Chuy, motioning to the newcomer. Chuy gives a nod.

"Should I be afraid?" the woman asks.

"Your torture is over," Dark Horse says. "Don't worry."

The woman is relieved to tears and stands on shaky legs. Dark Horse helps her stand and leads her out of the room. He glances back at me as they leave. "Don't go anywhere. We don't know when shit will go sideways again."

I nod. "We'll be here."

When he leaves, Bree tugs on my skirt.

I look down. "You okay?"

"I've seen dead people before," she says. "A lot of them."

That her argument is legitimate carves away a little piece of my soul.

What the hell are we doing here?

"You shouldn't feel bad about that," she says. "It's not your fault. But you can still help."

"How?" I ask, the word coming out as a whisper.

"You're basically the best big brother anyone could ask for, and you spend a lot of time with four girls a lot younger than you."

"Making me sound like a creep," I say.

She whacks my leg. "I'm being serious. Cassidy is our friend now, right? I think she could use a big brother." She walks over to Sarah and plops herself on the recliner beside our Spartan warrior. "I'll just be here with my new big sis."

Sarah smiles at that. Leans her head on Bree's.

"Okay... Burnett?"

"Ya?" he asks, still holding Hildy, who's now silently weeping into his chest.

"Where can I find Cassidy?"

16

DARK HORSE

I sit across the table from Durante, hands clasped, putting on my best interrogator face, which is difficult given the setting. We gave her time and privacy to clean up. She's wearing some of Chuy's clothing—jeans and a T-shirt—which fit loose on her somewhat smaller body. Chuy and I are still armored up, ready for the shit balloon dangling over our heads to burst. Feels awkward to walk around like this at home, but it's better than being caught bent over with your pants down at a joust.

We're outside, shaded from the Florida sun by a yellow umbrella rising from the center of an old-school, red picnic table. I can smell yesterday's burger grease heating up in the grill, mixed with an ocean breeze. It's intoxicating, like a mental teleportation back to childhood trips to the beach, eating burgers with a touch of gritty sand.

"Hey." Chuy puts her hand on my arm. "You here?"

My thoughts snap back to the present where I'm staring at the woman who tried to tear out my throat with her teeth. "Your name is Mia Durante?"

She nods. "How do you know that?"

"A friend of ours can read minds," I say.

I expect her to balk. Any normal person would.

"Wouldn't it be easier to have *him* question me? You'd know I wasn't lying."

"I'm a good judge of character," I say. "You were there against your will. Killing against your will. Out of control, until you were set free. I know all that. What I don't know, is your story. How you got here. *Why* you were..."

"Trying to eat people," she says, sounding disgusted. She pales, and I think she might puke.

"Need a bucket or something?" I ask.

"I'll keep it down," she says. "No one wants to see what I've eaten."

She ain't wrong about that.

"Tell me how this happened to you."

"It's been a long time. A lot of it is just a repetitive blur. Endless death, killing, and being killed. It's like a dream I've woken up from, blending together, like I was there, but...wasn't really. Not the me, here, talking to you now. But...I remember hallways, and rooms. The walls were white—at first. Dark red after a long time. And there were other things. Monsters. Everywhere."

"Sounds like hell," I say.

She shakes her head. "It was...it was some kind of spaceship. They called it *Galahad.* I saw stars outside. The view was always changing...but always stars. Hell...that was before."

She turns around, looking at the ocean view.

"I never thought I'd see this again." When she faces me, there are tears in her eyes. I have a lot of questions, but I let her keep talking. "My memory of the world...of Earth... It all ended in a nuclear war. I was at the White House when it happened. I was a reporter. For a newspaper. There were these...escape pods...Earth Escape Pods. They took us into orbit—"

"Escape pods." I'm dubious, but I try to keep that out of my voice. "In Washington, D.C.—that could launch into Earth orbit?"

"Hidden beneath the Ellipse. Sounds ridiculous, I know. But that's what happened. I saw the whole planet burn. Then the fallout cleared faster than it should have, and we landed. But Earth was no longer Earth..."

"It was hell," Chuy says. "'Then I saw a new heaven and a new earth, for the first heaven and the first earth had passed away, and there was no longer any sea.'"

Durante nods. "God repurposed the planet. And it was...horrible. The people there... Some were like me. Others were different. Twisted into a grotesque reflection of their hearts. Only way out was to die, either believing or knowing—I never understood which—that you had been forgiven."

"By whom?" I ask.

She shrugs. "God, I guess. Couldn't tell you. People who died absolved stayed dead. Those still gripped by the things they'd done in life...they came back. And kept coming back. Forever. That included me."

"When did things change?" I ask.

"One moment, I was chasing down a runner—people who are perpetually terrified, who were killers in life—through the wasteland of a city. The next moment, I was in a hallway, chasing a woman who was afraid—but not a runner. I saw her again and again. Impossible to say how many times the others and I caught her. And ate her. But over time, things changed. She got stronger. Smarter. Started trapping groups—collections of creatures—in individual quarters. A menagerie of monsters. Toward the end, there were only a handful of us left running around. We tried to catch her, and the man with her, but when they stopped being afraid of us, the compulsion ended. Fear directed us. Guided us. Until she did."

"Cherry Bomb," I guess.

Her eyes widen. "You know who she is?"

"We've heard the name," I say. "You mentioned a man. Big guy? Beard?"

She nods. "Samael."

"He was watching us," I say, "in Israel."

"He's...calculating," she says. "If he was watching, then—"

"It was a test," Chuy says. "They're seeing what we can do."

"Sounds like Samael. He's dangerous, but subservient. Like the rest of us."

I nod. "Back to your story."

"Things quieted down for a long time, on the *Galahad*. We were eventually all rounded up. I spent an eternity locked in a room with ten other people like me, perpetually hungry, but never dying. Everything changed when, for the first time in what felt like all of time, the ship shifted. Our course changed."

"Can you be a little more specific than 'eternity.'"

"Trillions of years?" she says. "What's longer than a trillion?"

"Quadrillion," Chuy says.

Durante shakes her head.

"Decillion. More. *Eternity.* Beginning of time until the end, on infinite repeat."

"How do you remember any of it?" I ask, despite having the vast knowledge of the Europhid species lodged in my head. But Durante doesn't.

"Part of the torture," she says. "Never being able to forget the things you've done, the people you've killed, and eaten. Even when we weren't actively hunting, we were tormented by what we'd already done. What we knew we'd do again."

Her eyes turn down to the table, goosebumps rising on her arms. I sense she's about to break down. Who wouldn't?

I put my hand atop hers.

"You're doing great. And we have people who might be able to help you process what you've experienced, but I need a few more questions answered."

She sniffs back her emotions and nods. "If it helps you kill that bitch, I'll do what I can."

"Tell me about her. Cherry Bomb."

"Ruthless. Beyond intelligent. Determined. More than a little unhinged. Vindictive. I never interacted with her directly, but since she began using us to…kill…again, I've been close to her. Heard her speaking to the man, Samael. She can act sweet and loveable one moment, and the next, she's a seething, violent, manipulative monster with the ability to do things that aren't natural."

"Such as?" I ask. "Aside from the gates and the menagerie. What can *she* do?"

"Manipulate reality." She says it plain as day, no trace of exaggeration.

"How do you mean?" Chuy asks.

"Exactly what it sounds like," Durante says, sounding defeated. "She can only affect a limited area–maybe a quarter mile diameter at once. But she's patient, and she has had a lot of time."

"Do you know what she's doing?" I ask.

Durante shakes her head. "Couldn't even guess. I only saw and heard things when she let us out, and that was generally when she needed someone wiped out, or entertainment."

"Inside the area of effect," I say, "are there any limitations? Or can she just create anything she wants?"

Durante thinks on that. "I think..." She sighs. "I think she's limited to..." A bigger sigh. Her hands shake beneath mine. She's left something out.

"You're not going back," I tell her. "You'll never see her again. You're safe."

She locks her eyes on mine. "No one is safe."

I stare right back. "We'll see about that."

My confidence makes her grin. "You're pretty good at that."

"At what?"

"Faking confidence."

My turn to smile. Busted.

She leans back, pulling her hands out from under mine. Attempts to relax in her chair. Leans her face out from under the umbrella's shade, letting the sunbathe her skin.

When she straightens up, her face does a few expression gymnastics, flipping through sadness, terror, and regret before landing on determination. "She's limited by what she created before... In a simulation."

I raise my eyebrows. That's unexpected.

"I only caught bits and pieces, but over a bazillion years with a memory that doesn't let you forget, the puzzle starts to look like something. Cherry Bomb...was once an AI, but she was made real. I know that sounds insane, but it's true. There's a point in the universe where time... resets. Where creation happens, over and over. Throw in some information—like a virtual reality, or a story, and it can become real. I was... created the first time that happened."

"You were created from a virtual reality?" I ask, trying to hide my surprise.

"I'm...not real. Not like you. I was created."

"We were all created," Chuy says, her faith unwavering despite the madness we've experienced. While I don't share it, I'm impressed by her commitment.

"But I'm...I'm a character. And not just from The Great Escape—what they called the simulation. I'm a character...from a novel."

"A novel?"

"When Cherry wasn't controlling us, we had limited access to the ship's computer. I was able to read. A lot. It was the only thing that helped pass the infinite time. Imagine how I felt when I eventually read my own story. I'm not real. Never was."

"You seem pretty real to me," I say.

"What was the name?" Chuy asks. "Of the novel?"

She frowns. "Torment."

17

MIAH

The visitor's center, converted into a home, is big and not super easy to navigate. Half the bedrooms are on the lower floor, the others on an upper floor from the lobby. My directions to Cassidy's room included, 'take the stairs,' but not which direction. I've cleared the lower level, so now I'm on the second floor staring down a hallway full of closed doors. Everyone is upset right now, so I really don't want to knock on the wrong door.

As I walk down the hall, muffled rumbling resolves into booming music. I think I'm on the right track. I stop outside the wooden door, which is open a crack, and knock. But it's useless. The thumping of my knuckles is drowned out by the pounding bass of a song I don't recognize, but instantly like—because it's good, but also silly. The side effect of my knock on the door is that it swings wide open on well-oiled hinges.

The room is a typical teenager's—a bit messy. Clothing on the floor. Empty soda cans here and there. An unmade bed. But instead of Teen Beat posters, or whatever teenage girls are into these days—BTS?—there are posters from horror movies, including all the Chucky films, *Five Nights at Freddy's*, and Huggy Wuggy. Kid has dark taste.

Cassidy is revealed. She's wearing black—everything. Like a ninja without a mask. At first, I think she's dancing to the beat, but then she suddenly kicks out, striking a B.O.B.—body opponent bag—square in the forehead. The vinyl head snaps back and then springs forward again, revealing a hand drawn mustache and two angry eyebrows. Hand drawn tattoos cover the body. At first glance, the body art adds to the B.O.B.'s tough-man exterior, but at second glance, they're well drawn, fun-looking characters. Not exactly gang tats.

She sees me in the doorway.

This is the moment where Allie, Emma, or Bree would reel in horror, shove me out of the room, and slam the door in my face. No one likes to be caught jamming unabashedly to music.

But Cassidy just says, "Hey," and lands a spinning kick that nearly topples the dummy to the side. I have no idea what fighting style this is—I think it might be her own—but it seems strangely effective.

"I like the music," I say, wondering if she can hear me over it.

"It's good, right? It's called 'Coincidance.' By Handsome Dancer." She pauses her attack to dance a bit, singing along, "Wow, you can really dance." When a trio of drumbeats follows, she punctuates them by punching the dummy's gut.

She wipes her forehead with her sleeve and turns down the volume, the music barely audible now, but she's still bopping to the beat. "Most people haven't heard that song, but everyone loves it when they do."

"You listen to a lot of music?" I ask, hoping to make a connection.

"Not as much as Hildy, or Moses, but I know how to get down." She catches me off guard by dropping into a split and springing back up. "Are you lost or something?"

"Or something," I say. "Mind if I come in?"

"Me casa, su casa." She running-man dances to the side.

I step inside the room and make a show of looking the posters over. "Chucky, huh? What's your favorite?"

"*Child's Play*," she says. "I'm old school."

"I think I liked *Cult of Chucky* the best," I say. "Have you seen the show yet? I haven't gotten a chance. Been kind of...distracted."

"Same," she says.

"Maybe we can watch it together."

"Sure."

I move on to the other posters of freaky-ass monsters, most of them smiling with sharp teeth or clearly nefarious intentions. "You don't have trouble sleeping in here?"

"Well, yeah," she says. "Duh. But not from the posters." She runs in place. "I have energy for days."

I smile and take a seat on the edge of her bed. "Mind if I talk?"

She furrows her brow. "You've been talking."

"I mean, like serious."

She twists her lips and looks to the side. "I'm kinda waist deep in avoidance right now."

Kid knows her psychology. "I can see that. Talking will help more."

"But it will hurt," she says. "A lot."

"It's like tearing off a Band-Aid or jumping into a pool," I say. "You just need to get it over with."

"Is it also like a cliché? Because that was two in one sentence."

Will there ever be a woman in my life who isn't feisty and smart?

"I'm not going to make you talk. I get it. This is...big. And you don't know me. But if you need someone to talk to, I'm here."

She stops moving for the first time since I opened the door. "Why do you wear a skirt? I mean, I know it's a thing. People do it. But you seem like a dude. Does that make sense? Like, you probably have a girlfriend, right?"

I nod. "Jen. Total babe."

"Obviously," she says, sitting down on the bed beside me.

I look down at the yellow and black plaid skirt. "Honestly, I can't remember why I put it on the first time. I just kind of woke up that way... but without underwear on."

"You better not be going commando right now," she says.

I shake my head. "I'm a responsible skirt wearer now that I'm flying around fighting monsters and aliens and shit. It also matches my awesome KISS shirt. Looks dope, right?"

She eyes my ensemble. Nods her approval. "But you should try the armor we use. It's pretty badass."

I stand up and motion to the skirt, opening pockets and posing. "C'mon. Nothing is as cool as a tactical skirt. And it's sentimental. My sister sewed the pockets."

"You have sisters?"

I sit back down beside her. "One flesh and blood. That's Allie. A few more adopted."

"Like Bree?"

I nod. "She's the one who sent me to check on you."

"Aww, she's so sweet."

"Most of the time," I say. "Just don't eat her ice cream."

"I *love* ice cream...but I can share."

"Let her have all the mint chocolate chip, and you'll be good."

She sits quietly for a moment. "So, you do this a lot? Help girls process their emotions?"

"On occasion," I say, "but I have the most experience with my own. I've lost a few people—my father, and the man who tried filling his very big shoes. We've both seen some shit. I know that. But losing someone... important... It hits different."

"I don't like crying," she says.

"Gives me a migraine," I say.

"Makes me feel like I'm sick. And my eyes get all puffy. You can see that I've been crying for like two days."

"Why don't you want people to know you've been crying?"

"It's not what strong people do," she says.

"You mean like Dark Horse—"

"You can call him Moses, you know."

"Feels weird."

"Should we call *you* Laser Chicken?" she asks.

"God, no."

She smiles, but it's brief.

"You're dodging the question," I say.

"Ducking and weaving." She sighs. "Yeah. I'm a kid here. If they don't think I can handle all this stuff, they might not let me help."

"Did you help?" I ask. I haven't heard the story of their ordeal in detail, so I don't know the answer to this question. But Cassidy doesn't seem like the kind of person to stand by and let her friends fight.

"Well, yeah. I guess."

"What did you do?" I ask.

"I set them free," she says.

"Set who free?"

"The apologetic zombies. Like that lady. Mia."

"How'd you do that?" I ask.

Seems impossible that she could do something that the rest of them—including Jonas the super-mega, heavy hitter—couldn't.

"I made them feel good," she says. "It's a thing I can do. No biggie. I just make people feel things. Or I sense what they're feeling. Like you...you're sad, but also angry, afraid..." She looks confused. "But mostly calm. How?"

"A lot of practice," I say. "And for a long time, pot. A lot of pot."

Her eyes widen.

"*Prescribed*," I say. "Don't do drugs or the ghost of Ronald Reagan will haunt you. But you should know something. I have the same power as you."

She squints at me. "Prove it."

I put my arm around her and lean my head on hers. "See?"

She laughs, but it slowly morphs into tears, which become sobs. She leans into me, and I hold her tighter. She weeps for ten minutes, unabashed sorrow, and it takes all my fortitude to not join in. Not because I'm devastated by the loss of McCoy, who I didn't really know beyond a name, but because her emotions are leaking out into me. I can literally feel her pain and sorrow. It's agonizing, but then it's out.

Her sobs come under control. She straightens up a little. "You have tissues?"

"I have a tactical skirt," I joke.

She takes me up on the offer. Lifts my skirt to her face and blows her nose in it. She leans back and sees her gooey wad of mucus. Laughs through her lingering tears. "Okay, now you definitely need to try the armor. It'd kind of make you officially part of the team."

I tousle her hair. "Maybe I will."

18

DARK HORSE

I toggle my comms while Chuy and Durante wait, both of them focused on the ocean view and their inner thoughts. "Anyone in ops?"

"That's a big fat affirmative," Bubbles says. Feels weird to have a new voice answering, but she seems competent. Question I'm facing now is, can I trust her? I didn't miss the fact that she and Cherry Bomb have similar origin stories—AIs turned real. A couple of Pinocchios. Sounds unbelievable—like the damn movie—but maybe it's not as uncommon as we think. Like life in the universe. It's everywhere and diverse. For all we know there's an entire planet filled with people who used to be AIs. If information at the beginning of time can turn into reality, then I suppose anything anyone can dream up might become real. "What can I do for you, Moses?"

"What are we currently monitoring?" I ask. We usually keep an eye on hotspots around the word. A certain site in Antarctica. North Sentinel Island, because that place is creepy as hell. The patch of New England affected by the Darkness event. And now the Vatican and the Temple Mount.

"Everything," she says. "Everywhere."

"All at once?" I ask. Delgado has access to just about every network and satellite on and around the planet, but his mind is still human. The nanobots flooding his system help him access and manipulate just about anything he wants, but he still processes the information like a person.

"Great movie," she says. "And yes."

"So…you're, like, omnipresent?" I ask.

She laughs. "An illusion of omnipresence, but only when I have access to your system, which is impressive. I am currently flesh and blood and no longer able to access wireless networks. Is there something you would like me to look for, aside from ducks?"

"What is it with you and ducks?"

"It's an old grudge."

"What could a duck have done to you?" I ask.

"Crossed the street."

"And..."

"I was prevented from running it over."

"Why would you run it over?"

"We were in a hurry," she says. "Running for our lives. Sparing the duck was illogical. It's like an itch I haven't been able to scratch. I don't understand it, either. But Jonas said I could take one out, as long as it was old. And there were scavengers around to benefit from its demise. So, I'm always on the lookout for an elderly duck deserving of an untimely demise."

"Okay. Well. That's not super helpful, so let's put a pin in the duck murder, okay?"

"Very well."

"Great. Listen, this might sound strange, but I need you to keep an eye out for anything...weird."

"Can you be more specific?" she asks.

"Like *really* weird. Like reality is being changed. Or created. Something that's not supposed to be there."

"Like a fifty-foot-tall glowing gate to hell?" she asks.

"Exactly, but it could be smaller—"

"Like a duck."

"Sure...or even something intangible. Like an idea. A cultural change."

"Interesting," she says. "I will monitor the physical world and the digital world for anything aberrant."

"Thank you."

"Any time, sugar."

I deactivate my comms. "She is one interesting lady."

"Bubbles?" Chuy asks.

I nod.

"Is she a stripper?" Durante asks, not bothering to hide a slight grin.

"Actually," I say, wondering how Mia's going to take the news. "She used to be an AI...and now she's human."

Durante stares at me, dumbfounded. Then concerned. "Are you sure she's not—"

"Pretty sure," I say. "She's fairly new to the world."

"How new?" Durante asks.

I think back to my interviews with them. "Two days?"

"Two days?" she says. "You left a woman, who used to be an AI *two days ago*, to look for anything new and weird in the world? Did it occur to you that she might *be* the thing that's new and weird in the world?"

"I...huh. When you put it like that..." I toggle my comms. "Delgado."

No response. "Dan, you there?"

"Here," he says, his voice almost a whisper. Sounds depressed. Understandably, but now isn't the time to wallow. We can all do that later.

"I know this is a hard time, but—"

"You were right, you know."

"Right? About wh—"

"Needing a morgue."

My heart sinks. Delgado and I disagreed about installing a morgue here in Florida. He already had one in his subterranean Mesa base in Dulce, and he said we could rotate bodies there if needed. Or bring them in via UFO. I argued that we might not have time, or there might be some other reason we wouldn't want to take a body there—like if it was contaminated. In the end, I won because I can basically do what I want, and money isn't really an issue. So, the morgue was installed. It can hold eight bodies. I hope it never holds more than the one.

"I can't bring McCoy home. Not in front of the kids. And his family is used to radio silence. They won't ask about him for a while yet. Having to tell them... It would...undo me. I'd be useless. Listen, I'm not sure I'm going to be much use for a little bit. McCoy was my friend. Been with me almost from the start."

"I know that," I say, "but we have a lot of other friends—and family—that need looking out for."

I hear a sniff, and then, "What do you need?"

"Keep an eye on someone."

"Who?"

"Bubbles."

"Bubbles? Why?"

"Just...make sure everything she's doing is kosher, okay? She has access to everything, and we don't know her that well. I have her looking for signs of, well, anything odd. Changes to the world. But I need you to make sure that if she finds anything, it's legit. Also, Cherry Bomb used to be an AI. Similar story to Bubbles."

"And you and Hitler are both people," he says.

"Point taken. We just can't afford any more mistakes, yeah?"

"Yeah... She did good work for the Vatican team," he says. "But... sure. Yeah. I'll stay with her."

"Thanks," I say. "Also, I'd like to set up a transfer for our guest. To the Mesa."

"Copy that," he says. "I'll set it in motion."

I toggle off my comms and let out a sigh. That...was uncomfortable. Dan and I share leadership positions most of the time—him at home, me in the field—but I sometimes pull rank. Not because I'm actually a higher rank. We don't have an official command structure here. But I've been giving orders for a long time, and he was a lone gun for most of his career. Teamwork is more my jam, and sometimes that means telling people what to do, even when it sucks.

"Hello," an adorable little voice says. Bree is stealthy. No idea how long she's been hovering—or listening. I don't bother asking. She sits down beside Durante and bites into an ice cream sandwich.

"Is that the last ice cream sandwich?" I ask. I wasn't saving it, but a certain other blonde girl called dibs.

She shrugs. "I helped myself. Miah always tells me to just make myself at home, because it makes everyone feel more relaxed. Also..." She takes another bite. "You're not a great host. We just fought a bunch of monsters—" She motions to her bunny outfit, "—I got blood on my pajamas—again. And no one has even offered me a cup of water, or a PB & J, or anything at all. I am still eight, you know. I can, like, fight bad guys like a boss, like in that episode of *MLP* where Twilight—"

She stops, looks at our blank stares.

"Right. You guys don't watch cartoons. Boring. Anywho, I'm hungry and thirsty, so I helped myself, please and thank you very much."

Before I can respond, she turns to Durante, licks the ice cream along the sandwich's side, says, "Mmm," and then, "Are you the lady who tried to eat people?"

If I had a drink, this is where I'd spit it out. Happily, I'm as parched as Bree.

Durante twists up her face, thrown by the direct question.

"Oh, don't worry about it," Bree says. "I sometimes want to eat people, too." She cups a hand to her mouth and whispers. "Don't tell Miah." Then she points her finger and waggles it between myself and Chuy. "So, I get it."

"I have eaten people," Durante says.

Bree rolls her eyes. "I burrowed into the big neck vein of a giant god, swam up into his brain, and turned it to mush. And guess what? I ate some of it. And guess what? It wasn't as bad as you'd think. I mean, it's not ice cream. And I probably wouldn't like it much when I'm like this—" She motions to her little body. "But when I'm Demon Dog? Mmm Mmm Good. Like Campbell's soup."

"Demon…dog?"

"I turn into a demon," Bree says. "Well, not like a literal demon, but an alien demon with, like, crusty skin and—"

"Swirling smoke around them?" Durante guesses.

"Well, no, not that, but the original demons—who made me like this?—they did."

"The Tenebris," I say.

"Those guys," Bree says. "Yeah."

"You've seen them?" I ask Durante.

She nods. "Most of them are dead. Wiped out. But she kept some. Personal guards, I think, along with these other big things."

"Assholes for faces," I say.

She scrunches her face up at my crude description, but says, "Yeah."

"Tenebris, Rygars, the damned—" I turn to Durante. "Sorry… And who knows what else."

"Capybaras," Bree says. "Don't forget them."

"Sounds like she's collecting things she can't create," I say.

"Building an army," Chuy adds.

Bree raises the last bite of ice cream sandwich to her mouth, but it flies out of her fingers like it's been slapped by an invisible force. The chunk floats through the air and lands—in Jonas's mouth. He chews it, sits down beside me, and says, "Thanks," to Bree.

"No thank you," Bree says, seething. "You ate my ice cream."

Jonas smiles. "I don't see big bro around to turn you into crusty the murder midget."

Bree's mouth hangs open, aghast.

"Dark Horse," Delgado says via the comms. I hold out a hand to Bree and she obeys the non-verbal command, stopping her climb over the table to reach Jonas. "Go ahead."

"Bubbles found something. Well, a few things."

"What?" I ask.

"Better if you just come see it for yourself."

19

MIAH

"So, you listen to music at the beginning of every mission?" I ask. Cassidy is still bummed out, knee deep in sorrow over the loss of McCoy, who was something like an uncle to her. But the tears have stopped, and she's rolling through the stages of grief like a pro. I don't know her full story, but it's clear that she's no stranger to suffering.

"Pretty much, yeah." Cassidy scrolls through a song list on the arm of her adaptive armor.

Strange to be sitting in a normal kid's room when that kid is dressed for battle. But it seems the armor is a lot more than your average battle suit. It's got tech for days and can do some pretty cool things, like active camouflage, lighting, night vision, and a playlist. What I don't see are pockets, so the tactical skirt's still in the running.

"Did Hildy not play a song for you guys?" she asks.

I think back to the Vatican. I remember seeing Hildy bopping her head, but I didn't think anything of it at the time. "We weren't wearing the armor."

"Right," she says. "Lame, by the way. This armor is dope. Do we want music to cheer us up, or help process our sadness?"

"Let's go with cheering up," I say. In my experience, sad songs just make people sadder. Joy is really the only thing that combats despair. And edibles, but I don't have any, and Cassidy is underage. "'Don't Stop Me Now.' Queen."

She smiles. Taps the controls. A moment later, Freddie Mercury's melodic voice flows from hidden Bluetooth speakers. This place looks unassuming and kind of cozy, but they've got tech hidden everywhere.

She sits down on the bed beside me as the song continues.

When Mercury sings the first 'Don't stop me now,' we both grin. It's an appropriate song. Gets the blood flowing. Lifts the spirit. Imparts the message she really needs to hear.

The song goes into high gear. Drums. Guitar. Piano. Mr. Fahrenheit. The speed of light. Cassidy bops her head with the music, tapping her foot. At the first 'supersonic man out of you,' Cassidy bounds from the bed and starts bouncing in the middle of the room. She high-kicks her toes to her hand, which is raised over her head. Does it four times, and then reaches for me. "You can't make me do this alone."

"Don't need to ask me twice," I say and stand. I'm not a good dancer. Never have been. But as a good big brother, I've partaken in more than a few bedroom dance parties. They're not about dancing well or looking good. It's a way to burn energy, laugh, and bond. It's about being vulnerable together. I'm better at this than I am at being Laser Chicken.

I'm bouncing and spinning like I'm in the dance scene in *The Perks of Being a Wallflower*. Basically, making a fool out of myself. And it does the trick. For the moment, Cassidy's pain drowns in a sea of dancing, laughing, and Queen.

Then we have company. I feel a moment's hesitation when Hildy arrives.

It's one thing to make a fool of yourself in front of a kid. They get it. Don't judge. But Hildy is an adult. Younger than me, but still a peer. But in the time it takes me to pause, Hildy has joined the fray.

"Why did you not invite me?" Hildy asks Cassidy. "You know how I love dance parties."

"It was his idea." Cassidy points to me.

Hildy gives me a smile of appreciation, and for a moment, we're back in the groove, ignoring the world and all the discomfort that comes with it.

Then I notice someone lingering in the hallway. That Burnett guy. He looks uncomfortable and unhappy, his eyes flicking between me and Hildy.

Ahh, shit. The jealous boyfriend. He's got nothing to worry about, though, and the last thing I want to create is some love-triangle tension bullshit. So, I bop my way out into the hall and take his hands. He flinches, but he's kind of scrawny. Can't really resist, as I pull him into the room and say, "Let loose, man!"

Hildy turns and sees him. Lights up with a gasp. "Baby! You are dancing?!"

Burnett looks unsure. Shy. Then he breaks into the goofiest, most awkward dance I've ever seen. I'm pretty sure he's either never danced, or only when no one's looking, because...wow. But he's owning it. Letting loose. And this is a judgment-free dance party.

As the song approaches the end, I spin around toward the door, opening my eyes and coming face to face with the last person I'd want to see me like this—Dark Horse. My insides shrivel up like a raisin. Can't move my legs. I'm barely hearing the music.

Then I notice that Dark Horse isn't even looking at me. He's watching Cassidy, moving his head to the beat, a smile on his face and maybe a hint of a twinkle in his eyes. He really cares about his people.

The song ends. The dancing dies down, and the others notice Dark Horse.

"Did you see me?" Burnett asks, totally jazzed. "I was moving my feet and getting down like Elvis, no?"

"Exactly like Elvis," Dark Horse says, and he turns to Cassidy. "How are you holding up?"

"Still sad," she says. "Like *really* sad. But better, thanks to Miah. He's nicer than I thought he'd be."

"Hey," I say.

"Well, you *are* a little scraggly," she says. "The hair. The scruffy face. Your girlfriend doesn't mind it?"

"I think she likes it," I say.

Hildy huffs. "Some women like a well shorn man." She wraps her arms around Burnett, who is thrilled, his jealousy a thing of the past.

"Yah," he says. "And I am naturally silky smooth, all the way down to my pu—"

"*Okay,*" Dark Horse says. "I think we can stop right there." His attention turns to me. "Need you for a minute, boss."

"Sure." I give the others a wave and say, "Thanks, guys. Try 'Lose Control' by Missy Elliott. That will get you moving." As I follow Dark Horse down the hall, a familiar thumping beat follows us mixed with the sound of sing-songy Burnett. "Oh, I am in the groove now."

"Thanks for that," Dark Horse says, as we head down the stairs. "I was worried about her."

"Cassidy?" I ask. "She's a tough kid."

"With some powerful emotions," he says. "If she ever lost control, we might all find ourselves curled up in fetal positions, calling for our mommies."

"Good to know," I say.

"Also wanted to thank you for the Vatican. Chuy says you were competent. Doesn't sound like high praise, I know, but coming from Chuy, it's the best you might get. You worked as a team."

"Left a few holes and a lot of blood behind," I say.

"You saved the Pope. In comparison, my mission went FUBAR almost from the start."

"We had regenerating rodents in an enclosed space, and we had only one person to protect. You had apologetic zombies that couldn't die, with hundreds of bystanders crowding around, and some kind of heavy-hitter that knocked Henry out cold. That's not easy to do. We were playing in the minor leagues. You were at the All-Star game. Plus, you had Jonas with you. Wait... I didn't hear much about him. He should've—"

"Overwhelmed," he says.

"Doesn't sound like Jonas."

"Way I understand it, he suddenly felt the combined torment of a hundred souls that had been tortured for an eternity—all at once. That he's just out walking it off says a lot."

"You see?" I say. "How could anyone have been prepared for that?"

"We'll have to be next time," Dark Horse says. "Also, quit stepping on my toes. Giving pep talks is my job."

I smile as we stop in front of a closed metal door.

"Here's the deal," he says. "You're part of the team now. You know the stakes. I want everything to run smoother than a hairless cat's testicles. I expect total honesty and transparency from you. Anything less could get people killed. Understand? So, if there's anything you left out—about what you've seen, experienced, or know, now is the time to fill me in, because I'm pretty sure that the moment I open this door, shit's going to be flying at us from all directions."

He gives me a moment, and I just stand there, frozen.

"Okay, then." He reaches for the door handle.

"Hold on," I say.

He raises an eyebrow at me. When I don't speak, he says, "Spit it out."

"I made a promise to keep it a secret," I say.

"No secrets," he says.

"I can tell *you*, but...you can't tell Delgado."

He squints. "This about Wini?"

"You know?" I ask. "Who told you? Ugh. It was Henry, right?"

"He's an honest guy."

"Not having a filter isn't exactly the same as being honest," I point out. "Does Delgado know?"

He shakes his head. "She knows him best. If she didn't want him to know, there's a reason. And with this McCoy business, I don't know how he'd react. So, keep keeping it to yourself."

"Will do."

"Anything else?"

I shake my head. There're a million details we've left out, about the Darkness, about Khaos and Tartarus, but all the bold strokes are there.

"Good." He opens the door to a sophisticated ops center. Lots of high-tech equipment. Computers. Screens all over. The air-conditioned dry air that smells like warm electronics reminds me of my LAN gaming days.

Delgado sits at a workstation beside Bubbles. He turns to greet us, oblivious to the conversation we just had. "We found something. Well, Bubbles found it. I kind of just watched in awe."

Bubbles waves off his praise. "I'll put it on the big screen for you."

We turn toward the screen at the end of the room. It's got to be ten feet diagonal. Resolution looks 4K or better. No way they don't watch movies in here when they're not saving the world.

The image changes. It's mostly dark. Stars. Then a massive swirling object rolls into view. "Is that..."

"Jupiter," Bubbles says. "Zooming in."

The image slides in on what looks to be a tiny dot at first, but then resolves as a moon. The gleaming surface, which must be ice, is crisscrossed with endless red lines that look like cracks.

"Europa," Dark Horse says, and then he elaborates for my benefit. "Sixth moon of Jupiter. Ice crust over a liquid ocean, all of which conceals a subterranean world…where some friends live."

"We have friends on Europa?" I ask.

"And beyond…"

"What happened to transparency?" I ask.

He shrugs. "Slipped my mind. I'll fill you in. Later."

"Pay attention to the moon's north pole," Bubbles says, as the image continues to grow larger.

"What are we using to get this image?" Dark Horse asks.

"I might have borrowed the Hubble," Delgado says. "No one will notice. Well, they'll notice. But it will look like a temporary malfunction."

"Here we go," Bubbles says.

A speck floating above the moon's surface comes into view, silhouetted by Jupiter's massive swirling gases.

"What is it?" I ask.

Bubbles turns to face us. "A spaceship."

20

DARK HORSE

"A spaceship?" Miah asks. "Like, in space?"

"That's usually where they are," I say, stepping closer to the wall-sized image. The ship stands out against the backdrop of Jupiter, but I can't make out the details. "How much closer can we get?"

"That's max optical resolution. I can zoom in digitally, but as you know, there's no such thing as image enhancement that suddenly makes details pop out."

"Get closer until it starts to pixelate," I say.

The image zooms slightly, but it stops a moment later when littles squares of color begin to emerge. *Great.* "What's it been doing?"

"Since we found it," Bubbles says. "It's done nothing more than maintain a stable orbit over Europa."

"Is...it hiding?" I ask.

"Unlikely," she says. "Until the moon's orbit takes it around Jupiter's far side—twenty-seven hours from now—the craft will be in full view, and it will return forty hours later. The ship's operators are either unconcerned about being discovered, or they want to be."

"Or they're busy somewhere else," Miah says. "You know, making gates and raising hell. Maybe they're not concerned because no one's home? I mean, you guys have a ship parked in orbit around our moon, right? And no one lives up there, right?"

"That's...not entirely accurate," Dark Horse says. "Remember the proto-human species from the play?"

"The one that became your friend? Midazolam or something?"

"Mazzola," Bubbles says. "Midazolam is a sedative."

Miah shrugs.

"Close enough. So, this Mazzola guy lives in orbit around the moon. Doing what?"

"Not being around people," Delgado says. "He's the last of his species. Feels like he doesn't fit in with people, or the Chut'uni."

"Right..." Miah says. "...the dudes that you fought on another world, who used to be proto-humans, but who left Earth like a bazillion years ago and continued evolving. Mazzola is like their Cro-Magnon man..."

"To the Chut'uni," I say. "But in many ways, he's more advanced than us."

"Not cool, but now we like the Chut'uni, even though they were tag-teaming 'The Order' with the...wobbly, wang-shaped red Europhids, who are kind of like the blue ones, that were wiped out..." Miah turns to me. "...except for the one in your head...and the ones who later turned purple after you got all kumbaya with them. I get that right?"

I nod. It's a pretty good summation, considering he learned it via a chaotic Cassidy production.

"But he's not alone," Miah says, pointing to me. "You're the last blue Europhid, right? Half Europhid, I guess. And I'm kind of the last of the Lux...even though I don't really know anything about them. Point is, he's not the only one of us that feels...different."

He ain't wrong about that. I think most of us understand what it's like to live a life that 99.999-forever of people on the planet wouldn't understand.

"He'll find his way," I say. "Just try not to react when you meet him."

"I've seen two giant serpent gods porking while simultaneously giving birth to mythological monsters in a cave beneath Greece, dude. I think I can handle whatever weird shit lies ahead."

I smile. "Probably right."

Bubbles sighs. "I'm still upset I didn't get to see that."

"What were you doing at the time?" Delgado asks.

"Fighting a centaur," Bubbles says.

"That was earlier," Miah says, shaking his head. "Centaurs suckling on Chimera."

That raises my eyebrows. I thought we had the monopoly on side show adversaries, but every time I hear about what Miah's team has seen, done, and survived, I realize our own world is one of the strangest in the universe.

Bubbles sighs and answers Delgado's question. "I was a watch."

"A watch," Delgado says. "That's...interesting."

"It was horrible, is what it was," Bubbles says. "Now, can we get back to the scary spaceship orbiting a moon four hundred, eighty-three million miles from Earth?" She looks at me. "Your people chit-chat nearly as much as mine."

"Conversation is the spice of life," I say, but she's right. I toggle my comms. "Hildy, Burnett, I need you in ops. Right now."

"Ohh," Burnett responds, sounding nervous. "Uhh. Yes, yes, of course."

Recognizing the tone, I say, "Wait. Hold on. You can—"

But I'm too late. Hildy and Burnett rotate into ops, hair dripping, bodies wet, hastily wrapped in towels.

Burnett's eyes go wide when he sees the size of his audience. "It's okay," he says, lifting one hand from the towel and grasping it again when it begins to fall. "It wasn't naked-shower sexy time. Just naked shower time."

The small bulge beneath his towel says otherwise, but I decide to not comment on it. We have much bigger problems to address than Burnett's little problem. I clear my throat. "I really don't know and don't care what you were doing."

"Well, that's—" Burnett spots Miah. His expression sours a little. "—too bad. Because naked-shower sexy time is a story of epic proportions beyond comprehension." He stares Miah down. "Which can only be accomplished by a true masculine physical specimen with a brain to match." He smiles at Hildy, who looks a little confused. "You're not the only one who can maneuver objects through—"

"Ahem."

"Yes," Burnett says, turning his now wide eyes toward me. "What is it you need?"

I motion to the screen. "That's parked in orbit around Europa. Either of you know what it is?"

Being from the future where humanity, for all its glaring faults, managed to navigate the galaxy and construct a variety of spacecraft means they can identify a vast number of space-faring craft, including ones I can't. Despite living in that future for years, and seeing much of the galaxy, I avoided most other spacecraft. And while I contain all Europhid knowledge, from every dimension of reality they populate, it's limited to things they have directly encountered. There's a lot about the universe they have no direct knowledge about.

Including this ship.

"I do not recognize it," Burnett says, stepping closer.

"Nor I," Hildy says. "When did it arrive?"

"Unknown," Bubbles replies.

Hildy addresses me. "Can you communicate with the Europhids there? They would have answers, yes?"

"Not from this distance," I say. "But they're my next stop."

"While I do not recognize the ship," Burnett says. "There are several things we can infer about it, visually."

"Infer away," I say, staring at the ship. All I can really infer is that it's big. Really big. Like colonization big. Other than that, it looks like a Battlestar Galactica ship, tapered back to front, with two sets of forward-facing Star Trek-like nacelles, sans the glowing blue. It's a weird combination of Union style utilitarian functionality, and advanced design. Most of it is gray, but there are patches that don't match. It's kind of a patchwork ship, but not in a way that looks unintentional—like repairs after a battle. More like a little Subaru that's been turned into a street-racing speed machine. What was once, has become something more.

"It's been made to look defenseless. Like *Bitch'n*, there are no visible weapons systems, but you can see where more recent changes have been made," he points to several of the more modern patches. "Based on their even positioning, it's reasonable to assume that this craft was never meant to be a warship, but it has been converted into one. Again, like *Bitch'n*."

"Any idea how much of a punch it will pack?"

He shakes his head. "Impossible to say, but this ship dwarfs *Bitch'n*. If I'm right, those weapon bays might be large and powerful enough to take us out in a single shot."

"Don't get shot," I say. "Noted. Anything else?"

"In general, I think it would be prudent to assume that it outclasses the *Bitch'n* in every way, aside from the one technology that is unique to the Union timeline from which we came."

"Slew drives," I guess.

He nods. "You'll have to..." He turns to Hildy. "What am I thinking of? The quick boxer?"

She leans in close. Whispers in his ear. His eyes light up. "Yes. Right. You'll have to Muhammad Ali it. Float like a butterfly, sting like a bee. Mobility is your advantage."

"I'll take a team to Europa," I say and backhand Miah's shoulder. "You want to get off-world? See the solar system?"

Before Miah can answer, Delgado says, "Actually, before you rotate out of here, Bubbles found something else."

I turn to Bubbles, and she explains. "I was looking for aberrations. Things that don't belong in our reality. We found the spacecraft first and made some observations about it, including its resonance...the frequency at which it vibrates. It's slightly different than everything else in our reality."

"Meaning it's from somewhere else," Delgado says. "Another time, when things have changed. Another dimension of reality. Another *kind* of reality. There's no way to know."

"After determining the craft's frequency, I then began looking for things that matched it. I found three," Bubbles adds.

"What are they?" I ask.

"Not what," Delgado says.

Bubbles completes the thought. "Who." With a blink of her eyes, the screen changes to display two images. One of a solitary black woman in a white bikini, enjoying the sun at a tropical beach. The other is of a man and a woman. Late fifties maybe. Smiling. Seated at a streetlight-lit European café. The image from the vantage point of a CCTV camera.

"Should I know who they are?" I ask.

"No reason you should," Bubbles says. "But I do." She looks back past us, to what should be an empty room. "And so does he."

I turn around to find Jonas. No idea how he got inside. The door locks when it's closed, and unless your fingerprints—which are read when you take hold of the handle—are in the system, it stays that way. He could have rotated inside, but I'd have seen the light. Unless he blocked our minds from noticing...or used telekinesis to force the lock.

The mystery is erased from my mind when Jonas points to the older couple and says, "Those are my parents."

21

MIAH

"Your...*parents?*" Dark Horse asks, looking like he's been slapped in the face. "You all leave a few important details out of your story?"

"You mean like being friends with an alien species?" I ask.

"Exactly like that," he says. "Yeah."

Jonas steps to the front of the room, unconcerned by Dark Horse's tonal shift. His attention is on the photo. "Are you sure this is them?"

"Took the photo ten minutes ago," Delgado says.

"Jonas..." Bubbles sounds apologetic. "It's them."

Jonas faces Dark Horse. "They're my...adoptive parents."

"Benevolent assassins who kidnapped him away from a secret program using psychically gifted children to create unstoppable killers." Bubbles makes a cringy face at Jonas. "Sorry." Then to Dark Horse, she adds, "Full disclosure. But his parents, despite their profession, are good people. They freed him from bondage. Helped defeat Alpha and Beta, who could have used him to kill anyone they wanted. And they..." Her brow furrows in confusion. "They..." Her eyes snap to Jonas as some kind of realization sets in. "They created me."

"They had something to do with that Orphic Egg thing?" Dark Horse asks.

Bubbles shakes her head. "My AI. They created me."

Dark Horse nods, recalling this bit of the less detailed story. "For Jonas."

"For each other," she says. "Because of his digital empathy—one of his passive psychic abilities—I was able to evolve from artificial intelligence to a true, living intelligence. They created me, but my proximity to Jonas gave me life... The Orphic Egg just gave me a body."

"But that's not what you're trying to tell us," Delgado says. "Is it?"

Bubbles's smile is fleeting. She looks unsure. "Jonas...your parents... I don't think we're wrong."

"Okay, so they're alien, too?" Jonas sounds a bit defensive, but I don't blame him. Every iteration of his parents—biological, manipulative, and now adoptive—haven't been what they seemed. "My birth parents were Titans. I'm not sure how this can be any more surprising than that."

"They're not...alien," she says. "They're not from this reality. And I... I have a theory."

The room is silent. Waiting.

"Progenitor," Bubbles says.

The single word snaps my memory back to the recent past. Underground. Facing off with Harpies and Furies. Trying not to look at their boobs, though I'd never admit it, because overall they were hideous. But they say men are capable of finding beauty in nearly every woman, whereas women only find twenty percent of men attractive, at all, and most of them are muscley and hairless. So, I think it's a positive. Mythological monsters deserve love, too...even if it's just for their tatas.

Anywho... After my momentary flashback, the true weight of Bubbles's revelation settles in. "'Bubbles...of the progenitors.'"

"Progenitors?" Delgado says.

"The Erinyes...the Furies. Vengeful deities."

"Like Nemesis?" Hildy asks, and I smile. That's exactly what Bree said.

"But a lot smaller, a little sexier, and they weren't blinded by rage. They were more like judges, determining if we were worthy of the quest we'd been sent on."

"To raise an army of Titans and Gods," Dark Horse says.

"Which we failed to do," I say. "Yeah. Point is, we were introducing ourselves, but they already seemed to know who we were, and when Bubbles didn't elaborate on parentage—you know, because she was an AI in a watch—they filled in the blank. "'Bubbles of the Progenitors.'"

"It could just be a fancy way of saying 'parent,'" Hildy says. "Or ancestor."

"Bubbles of the Parents? Bubbles of the Ancestors?" I pinch my nose in a very Jonas way. He's rubbing off on me. "Doesn't make sense."

Bubbles shakes her head. "Progenitor. Capital P, I think. A title. *The* Progenitors. The word was spoken reverently."

"Then what does it mean?" Dark Horse asks.

"The Creators," Burnett whispers. "Capital C."

"Creators of what?" Jonas asks.

"More than me," Bubbles says. "But I don't think we'll know until we ask them."

"I'll go," Jonas says, already reaching for the slew drive embedded in his fancy new armor.

Dark Horse stops him. "Not alone. No one goes anywhere alone. If your parents are involved in all this somehow, visiting them could dangerous."

"Or your parents could be in danger," Burnett says, concerned for the people he's never met. I thought the guy's naïve innocent vibe was an act, but he's just earnest and genuine all the time. I get why Hildy likes him, even if he is a beanpole.

Jonas smiles. "You don't know my parents. And I'm leaving now."

"I'm in," I say.

"I should go, too," Bubbles says. "There are connections we need to explore."

"I'll go, too," Delgado blurts, standing to his feet.

"As will I," Hildy says, offering a salute.

Burnett straightens up and is about to offer his service when Dark Horse shakes a finger at him. "Uh-uh, Romeo. I need you here." He points at Delgado and Bubbles, "And I need you two back, el pronto." He turns to me next. "Fair warning..." He points to Delgado, "...this one likes to reload in the open, standing still. Feel free to tackle him if shit goes sideways and he's busy picking the daisies."

"Hey," Delgado says. "That happened *once*."

"Keep an eye on him," Dark Horse says, and I give him a nod. "Cassidy can't–"

"Heard my name!" Cassidy cartwheels into the room. Like, literally cartwheels, slipping between the narrow gap between Dark Horse and me. "I'm good to go."

"You're not going anywhere," Dark Horse says.

"I think you know I am." She stares him down.

Dark Horse plants his fists on his hips. A very parental pose. I don't think he even knows he's doing it. "You think revenge will help you feel better?"

"I think helping save the world will mean Owen didn't die for nothing," she says, and it's basically impossible to argue against.

"I'll keep an eye on both of them," I say.

"I don't need a babysitter," Delgado grumbles.

"If we come up against something we can't handle, we'll bug out."

Dark Horse stares me down, his eyes flickering with blue light. "I believe you." He faces the group. "You six go find out what's up with the parents. The rest of us will head to Europa. See if our friends know what's up with the spaceship."

"What about the third woman?" Delgado asks. "The one on the beach?"

Dark Horse looks at the woman, lounging in the sun. "I don't think she's going anywhere, anytime soon." To me, he says, "If you find the answers you're looking for, coordinate with Burnett and visit her on the way back. Maybe Jonas's parents and this woman don't mean anything. Maybe they're important. Let's meet back here in sixty mikes. No one takes action until we're coordinated."

I give a nod, and Dark Horse looks at Jonas. "Agreed?"

"You got it," Jonas says, looking anxious. "Now, who's coming with me?"

I wrap an arm around him, and Cassidy joins Hildy.

Delgado puts a hand around Bubbles's waist, and I'm a little surprised when she steps closer to him without question. Jonas and I share a look, but we say nothing.

"Keep Bree here?" I ask Dark Horse. "And tell her I'm sorry."

"Not taking an eight-year-old to another planet," he says, and I feel a pang of guilt. Then he adds, "Not without you to keep her in line."

I grin. "Thanks."

"Wait," Delgado says. "*Where* are we going?"

"Antico Caffè della Pace in Rome," Bubbles says.

Delgado thinks for a moment and then nods.

"Got it. First stop: armory. Second, Rome."

"We don't need an armory." Jonas says, "See you there." Then he rotates us out of ops.

We emerge a moment later, standing beside the café table. Despite our sudden appearance, neither of Jonas's parents even flinch. His mother, looking elegant in a flowing skirt and a colorful shoulder-wrapped shawl, looks up. Smiles when she sees him. "Dear, how did you find us?"

"He's psychic, honey," his father says, putting down an empty espresso cup. The man's got a nerdy vibe at his core, but he looks dapper in his black, tieless suit. "We can't hide from him." He stands and gives Jonas an affectionate hug. "It's good to see you, son."

"I hope so," Jonas says.

His father is confused for a moment, but then turns his attention to me. Gives my clothing choices an up and down. "Interesting look," he says, and then to Jonas, he says, "You going to introduce us to your friend?"

Jonas obliges. "Mom, Dad. This is Miah. He's...like me."

They seem to understand his meaning, and with raised eyebrows, his father reaches out to shake my hand. "Pleasure to meet you, Miah. But you don't need to call us 'mom' and 'dad.'" He places his hand on his chest. "My name is Will." Then he motions to 'mom,' and adds, "And this is my wife, Gal."

22

DARK HORSE

"Not going to argue with you, kid. You're staying put. End of story."

I can tell Bree is trying hard to control herself. I can also tell she's close to failing, and I might need to rotate out of here so she can't rip my throat open. She can't transform into Demon Dog without Miah, but I'm not sure that would stop her.

She grips her little fists and glares at me with wide eyes.

"What...is she doing?" Chuy asks.

"I think she's trying to pop your head, bro," Henry says.

We're gathered in the living room, waiting on Sarah to finish changing into adaptive armor. She was reluctant to give up her old-school gear, but pretty sure our new 'god' friends need to breathe, too. Thanks to my Europhid memory, I have a map of Europa's sub-oceanic tunnels in my head. I know that the air is full of methane, which is unbreathable and would smell like King Kong's skid-marked tighty-whities after eating an entire Taco Bell.

"She can't do that, right?" I ask. "Pop my head?"

"Not with her brain." Henry smiles. "Good thing she can't. You'd be in trouble."

Bree stomps her foot.

"Nothing we can do about it," Chuy says. "It's too dangerous when you're like this." She motions to Bree's admittedly adorable self, still dressed as a pink bunny. I know she can go savage. Know she can hold her own against giants and gods and who knows what else. But right now, she's just a kid, and I made a promise.

Chuy gets through to her. She plops down in a recliner and crosses her arms. "I...am going to kill Miah."

Henry's getting a laugh out of all this. "How are you even going to convince him to turn you into Demon Dog so you *can* kill him?"

"Okay," she says. "I don't *really* want to kill him. But I *am* going to kick him in the nuts. Right. In. The. Nuts."

"Please make sure I'm there," Henry says. "We need that on video."

I agree with Henry—it'd be worth watching a few times—but I keep it to myself.

Instead, I redirect my parental tone toward him.

"Listen, despite how things turned out in Israel, you came through. You were a team player. And I appreciate it...because I know...because you struggle with impulsivity."

"Putting it mildly," Henry says. "But I'm getting better at it. I haven't even tried touching Chuy's boobs yet."

"*Excuse* me?" Chuy says.

"Don't hate the player," Henry says, arms spread wide, not a trace of intimidation on his face, "hate his dysfunctional amygdala. At my worst, I did everything—and I mean *everything*—that popped into my head. It takes a lot of mental work and a pretty solid moral code to keep my impulses in check. Like...all day, every day...especially when I know I could do something and blame it on my lack of fear. Kind of a 'get out of jail free' card for bad behavior. But I don't *want* to be that guy. So, I fight it. But seriously, if you guys are cool with me giving Chuy's tatas a little goose, I—"

Chuy chambers a round in her modified Barrett sniper rifle. "Pretty sure not even you could take this punch."

"We can try," he says, one hundred percent earnest. "Just like, aim for the side of my arm or something. I'll heal quickly."

Chuy looks at me, and I nod. "He's serious."

She shakes her head at Henry. "How did you survive childhood?"

He ticks off his fingers. "Ate bugs. Lived underground. Learned how to start fires."

"You were homeless?" Chuy asks.

"For a long time, yeah. I mean, don't get me wrong, I was in the system. Was put in a few homes, but they all kicked me out. Once for shitting in a corner. Fucking diarrhea, too. Once for stealing five hundred bucks and buying a thousand of those bubblegum cigarettes. I don't even like bubble gum, but I thought they looked wicked cool. Last house I was in, they caught me dancing in front of the other kids."

"They kicked you out for dancing?" I ask.

"Well...I might have also been wearing the mom's lingerie. Not some frilly Victoria's Secret classy stuff either. This was real trashy Frederick's of Hollywood type stuff. Lots of straps. Crotchless. Which is a lot more revealing on a dude, let me tell you..."

"Really don't need to," I say, and then I turn to Bree. "He talk like this in front of you all the time?"

She rolls her eyes. "Allll the time. But I don't really know what he's talking about. I only know it's bad because everyone suddenly looks like they pooped their pants."

"Right?" Henry says. "It's hysterical."

Bree nods enthusiastically. "Say something horrible!"

Henry opens his mouth to speak, but he's interrupted by Sarah. "Please don't." She's dressed in black adaptive armor. She looked ancient badass before. Looks modern badass now, partly because of the armor, but also because she's still carrying her dory.

"Wait, wait, wait," Burnett says hurrying into the room. "I have something for you."

He scurries up to Sarah. "Delgado and I started on these when we first learned about your..." He looks the spear over. "Weapon preferences." He pulls a black baton from his pocket. "Looks innocent, no? But—"

He gives his hand a quick twist. The rod expands into a spear. "Lighter and stronger than yours—" He taps his index finger on the metal and the spear retracts. "—but won't draw attention..." He lifts his chin toward Chuy's Barrett. "...not like their big-ass guns, am I right?" He laughs on his own until he settles down. "Oookay. Always a tough crowd in this house."

Burnett tosses the baton toward Sarah's hip. It snaps into place against her armor, which brings a smile to her face.

"Okay, that's cool," she says, pulling the rod from her hip and giving it a twist. The spear snaps out, and two taps later, it retracts.

Honestly, it's pretty slick.

"Also this," Burnett lifts his left arm, revealing a small device strapped to it. "Try to stab me."

Sarah looks unsure, but Henry...

"On it!" he shouts, diving across the room, and stabbing his kopis toward Burnett's gut.

"Gah!" Burnett shouts. "Shield! Shield!"

A round, orange energy shield blazes to life between them. It deflects the kopis, but not the energy behind it. With a crackle and a high-pitched scream, Burnett is launched across the room, colliding with a recliner that leans back, deposits him on the floor and then rights itself. For a moment, the room is silent. Then Burnett pops back up behind the chair, lifting the shield in victory. "I'm okay!"

"So, was that a bad thing?" Henry asks.

"You mean because you could have killed him?" I ask. "Yeah. Not smart."

"But a successful test," Burnett says, his eternal optimism not fading. He approaches Sarah. "Shield off." The circle of solid energy disappears like a pancaked lightsaber. He removes the device and offers it to Sarah.

With a nod of thanks, she attaches it to her suit's wrist and says, "Shield." The circle of orange energy forms anew. "Shield off." And just like that, it's gone again.

I've teased Burnett a lot over the years, but in the past few he's really stepped up. Made himself invaluable. I pat his shoulder. "Nice work, Burn."

"If you can Weird Science me a girl that can put up with my impulsivity that would be...wait... You know what? Might not be necessary." Henry grins. "Yeah, hold off on that request."

"I don't even want to know," Sarah says, and then she turns to me. "We should go before one of these two causes trouble." She wiggles an index finger between Henry and Bree, who puts her hands on her hips and sticks out her tongue.

"You're going to regret not taking me," Bree says, and she struts past us. She takes Burnett's hand and pulls him toward the door. I haven't seen them talk yet, but she clearly has no trouble making friends. "Let's go build something that explodes."

Burnett is yanked away.

"Cute kid," Chuy says.

“You’re good with her,” I observe.

She squints at me. “Don’t get any ideas.”

“Hell, woman,” Henry says. “Even I’m having ideas, and I ain’t your man.”

“Just...keep them to yourself,” I say. “Helmets on.”

With a tap to the control screen built into my left forearm, a hood snaps up over my head and a clear mask covers my face. It seals and pressurizes, preparing me for life in any non-Earth environment we find ourselves in, short of the sun’s surface or the event horizon of a black hole.

Chuy’s and Henry’s facemasks snap into place. Sarah just looks at us, confused.

“Seriously?” Henry says, “It’s like crazy intuitive, and yeah, intuitive was probably my only big word of the day, so don’t jizz your pants or anything. Look...” He lifts her arm and taps the controls. “Mode. Scroll down. And here. Space.” She taps the final command herself, the mask snapping into place.

“Can we breathe in these things?” she asks.

“After an incident floating around in space a little while back... Yeah.” I turn around, showing the small, raised pack now built into the suit’s back. “Two hours.”

“Cool,” she says. “Two hours. On a moon.” She takes a deep breath. “Totally cool.”

“Not your first time to another world,” Henry says. “Chill.”

Sarah cracks her neck one way, then the other. “Let’s get this over with.”

“One second,” I say, tapping controls.

“Yo.” Henry elbows Sarah. “This is the best part.”

I cue up the music, but I don’t hit play yet. “Henry with me. Sarah...” I tilt my head to Chuy.

We buddy-system up, and I tap ‘play’, just as we rotate into the fourth dimension. I customized the track for a moment like this, the volume rising as we slip into and out of the white void of the fourth dimension, slipping back out into a subterranean, suboceanic chasm right as the ‘Flight’ track of Hans Zimmer’s *Man of Steel* score hits the 3:02 mark.

Henry steps away from me, looking up, taking it all in, and he sums up the experience in a few words. "Ho-lee shit… This is like when I dreamed I was Helen Mirren and could touch myself all over." He looks back with a gleam in his eyes. "And not like 1970s Helen Mirren. I mean like when she got hot, *in* her 70s."

23

MIAH

"Have a seat," Will says, stealing two chairs from one of three nearby tables.

The café is all but deserted. Closing time, I'd guess. The street is empty enough that no one noticed our arrival. It's quaint in an old-world kind of way. Stone doorways. Potted plants. Tables with umbrellas. Four story buildings, painted in shades of beige and orange, surround us. It's very private. A good place to take a lady for a romantic night.

Jonas's father might be a player.

He's handsome, but not exactly rugged, despite being a former assassin. Carries himself a little more like Burnett, actually, but with a beard and a tan. Mom looks pretty badass, though. Can't really place her nationality. She's tan, like Will, but it looks natural. Her hair is black. Eyes are brown. It's like there's a little bit of everything in her face, which gives her an exotic look. Must have a complicated, global lineage.

I sit in the offered chair and nearly tip right out. The cobbled street is uneven and on a slight incline. *Hi, I'm Miah, aka Laser Chicken. I can shoot lasers and fly, but I can't sit in a damn chair.* Nice first impression.

"You boys been drinking?" Gal asks with a grin.

Jonas sits, arms on the small table, hands clasped. "That's it?"

"What's it?" Will asks.

"I've been gone for two years," Jonas says. "Totally off the grid. Did you even look?"

"Can't have been that long," Will says, glancing at Gal. Looks earnestly surprised.

Gal takes out a phone. Taps it a few times.

Her eyes widen.

"Okay," Will says. "Well. You know what they say about old people. Time moves faster, right?"

"You don't look that old," I say.

The old couple shares a look that suggests they're older than they look. Good living, I guess. Or, you know, not being human. Or from this reality, whatever that means. Suppose that might have something to do with it.

"Well, how have you been?" Will asks.

"You really don't know?" Jonas asks, searching his adoptive parents' eyes.

"Haven't a clue, honey," Gal says. "But we'd love to hear."

"I'm not sure you would," he says.

"More trouble?" Will asks. "Whatever it is, we're happy to help. You know that. But I'm not sure why you, of all people, would need the help from a couple of retired—"

Gal rests her hand on Will's arm, stopping him short.

"Oh, don't worry," I say, waving off their concerns. "I know you were..." I lower my voice and lean in close. "...assassins." I give them a friendly wink and lean back. "We're cool. No sweat."

Both parents turn their gaze to Jonas. "You *told* him?" Will asks.

Jonas nods. "I'm honest with the people entrusting their lives to me."

Gal squints. "What is it you think you know?"

"That's actually what we're here to ask you," Jonas says, no nonsense, "and I hope you'll be honest with me."

The glance between his parents is so quick it could be easily missed, but Jonas and I both see it. They're busted, but they don't know what for.

How many secrets do they have?

"Is this about your birth parents?" Will guesses.

"Gaia and Uranus are dead," Jonas reveals.

Will looks shocked.

Gal...wounded.

Like the two Titans meant something to her. Maybe she's empathetic for Jonas, but it feels like more than that.

"How?" Gal asks.

"We'll get to that," Jonas says. "But I'm really interested in what you think I might know."

"I'm not sure what you're—"

"How long have you been hiding who you are?" Jonas asks.

"Who we are?" Gal says. "Since we started working. You know that. Only you, a few others—like Madee—have you seen her yet?"

"I called."

"Good. Now. Only you, a few others, and now your disheveled friend here, know who we really are."

"Do we?" Jonas asks. "Do we really?"

"I'm not sure what you're getting at, son..." Will looks sad. It's a lot to take in, and I can tell this isn't how Jonas usually speaks to his parents. From this reality or not, they're thrown by the confrontation. Probably because they are keeping something, or many things, from him, and maybe they feel shitty about it. Or not. Who knows? Maybe they'll just kill us both. Everything's on the table.

Before the conversation can continue, we're interrupted by a loud, "Psst!" from above.

I lean back to look past the umbrella above us, which is still open, despite it being night. The metal chair leg slips over a cobble stone and tips too far. I spill backward, arms flailing. "Whoa!" I could catch myself with glowing laser wings, but I decide against it. Jonas is being secretive, so I probably shouldn't be showing off what I can do.

The impact isn't enough to hurt me. Not Miah 2.0 anyway. But I make a show of having the air knocked from my lungs. I pull my skirt down off my chest, thankful once again for remembering boxer briefs, and I look up.

Four stories above, a masked face looks back down at me. A man. Waving. "It's me!" he says. And then he retracts the adaptive armor's mask, revealing Delgado's face. "It's me!"

"What are you doing?" I ask him, whispering loudly.

"Neither of you have your comms on," he whisper-shouts back. "I didn't think it was a good idea to rotate into an alleyway in Rome. Wait, you guys didn't—"

"Of course not," I say.

"More friends?" Will asks, looking up.

"Allies," Jonas says.

"There a fight coming?" Gal asks, but Jonas doesn't give them anything. Not even a twitch.

"Don't you think you're being kind of obvious now?" I ask Delgado. "Shouting from a rooftop? In English? Dressed like a member of the Foot Clan?"

"Teenage Mutant Ninja Turtles," Delgado says, proving he knows at least a little pop culture. "Love it."

"Hello!" Cassidy calls down, her head poking over the edge, ten feet to the side of Delgado. "Whoa. This is high."

"Sorry," Hildy says, leaning over. "She is excited. First time in Rome, you know."

Gal is unimpressed. With a raised eyebrow, she turns to Jonas and says, "I really hope there is not a fight coming. If this is who you have helping you."

I pick myself up off the ground, right my chair, and say, "Looks can be deceiving."

"Kind of like parents," Jonas says.

"Okay, that's enough." Will gives Jonas a hardcore Dad stare. "Tell us what's going on. Or ask whatever you want. We don't have secrets from you."

"Look," I say. "Mister...?"

"Chanokh," he says.

"Mister— Did you say Chanokh?" I turn to Jonas. "Your last name is Chanokh?"

He nods and is about to ask me something when a new voice intrudes. "Mind if I pull up a chair?"

We all turn to find Bubbles, still dressed as an all-American, New England mom fresh from the orchard.

Will groans. "Is this another friend?"

While Will is clueless, Gal's face screws up. She gets to her feet and stumbles back a step, until she bumps against the stone wall behind her. Her eyes flick from Bubbles, to Jonas, and then back again.

She reins in her emotions, then takes a step closer to Bubbles.

Places a hand against her cheek and then looks her up and down. "B-Bubbles?"

"Bubbles?" Will says, getting to his feet.

"In the flesh," Bubbles says, her cool Texan accent impossible to mistake for someone else.

Will seems to suddenly recognize her. Almost falls over. His turn to be clumsy. While they were unfazed by Jonas's sudden appearance after two years, they're blown away by Bubbles, probably because she was an intangible artificial intelligence the last time they interacted. And now, she's a thirty-something MILF.

Bubbles is caught off guard when Gal wraps her in a hug. "Oh, my dear. This is wonderful. This is..." She breaks with Bubbles, tears in her eyes. "How is this possible?" She turns to Will. "Our daughter has been born anew."

She turns to Jonas for an answer, and this time he gives it. "Orphic Egg," and I'm pretty sure he's just testing their knowledge.

They might know about Titans and gods, but the Orphic Egg and what it could do are pretty obscure. Only someone really in the know about all the weird shit we've experienced would know about it.

"Of course," Gal says. Not a doubt. Not a question. From either of them.

While Will embraces Bubbles, my mind drifts back a few pages in my mental notebook.

Chanokh.

Why do I know that name?

I turn a few more pages. Back to yesterday for me, two years ago for the world. Back to Echidna, the mother of monsters, Queen of Khaos, guardian of the gate leading to—and from—Tartarus. She was awaiting the return of Ouroboros, the World Serpent destined to rewrite reality. Cherry Bomb... Who will remove...the children of Chanokh.

"The creator..."

All eyes turn to me. Hadn't meant to say it aloud.

"What?" Will asks.

I turn to Jonas as the last detail leaps out of my mental notebook and forms itself into a revelation.

Bubbles of the Progenitors.

The children of Chanokh.

Jonas's father...created reality.

I stand to my feet and stumble back, consumed by fear and awe.

"Miah," Jonas says, guiding my gaze from his parents to his eyes, with a slowly moving hand. "What is it?"

"Holy shit," I say. "Jonas... Dude... Your *parents are the Progenitors.*"

24

DARK HORSE

I'm not sure I see Henry's Helen Mirren comparison, maybe because I remember her in the 70s, but the view is kind of overwhelming. I've been to a lot of planets, seen a lot weird, freakish, and god-damned awe inspiring shit, but the first moment of discovery, of seeing something no one has seen before—makes me feel like freakin' James Tiberius Kirk when he peels the sheer clothing away from another alien babe. The moment of discovery, man. It's intoxicating.

I even knew what to expect here. I've never personally visited the Europhids on this moon. No need. They're a hive mind. Whatever I communicate to the little purple dudes on Beta-Prime, filters its way to the Europhids eking out an existence here. Thanks to being a Europhid hybrid, I have memories of this place. Know my way around the twisting tunnels and chasms, and which underworld denizens are friendly—and which are not.

When the walls around the stadium-sized space come to life with hundreds of scurrying creatures, I don't worry. They emerge en masse from dark alcoves—nests for their young—and leap toward the hard stone trails weaving between the vast fields of glowing purple Europhids. The light emanating from them illuminates the entire chamber, making it look like we're taking a tour of Grape Ape's ulcered stomach. Who wouldn't be stressed if they were a giant pantless ape with a badonkadonk, forced to roll around on a small uncomfortable van?

Once upon a time, the gelatinous beings that look like grape-flavored, erect, Jell-O eggplants covering the floor would have all been red. They'd have stood guard, doing everything they could to prevent foreign invaders from infiltrating the deeper spaces where the blue Europhids—

their mind—resided. The reds were an immune system to the blue's intelligence. They operated like that for billions of years, spreading throughout the universe in multiple dimensions, procreating, gathering knowledge, and recording the history of reality—as they perceived it. In another dimension, when humans visited this moon, the reds reacted violently, savagely, until one brave woman passed through the gauntlet and made contact.

Made peace.

I managed to do the same with the Europhids, but with much different results. There are no longer red Europhids. Or blue. They're all one and the same now. Both intellect and instinct. In a way, they're more human…if the human race was a vast collective with knowledge of multiple planes of existence.

Which I guess I am now. Borrowed, of course. Like Miah. Our cells changed forever by external, far more advanced, forces. He's handling it well. Maybe better than I am. He's got a calming presence. Some kind of inner serenity that affects the people around him. I think it's just that he cares a lot, and he isn't secretive about his feelings or his weaknesses. He's got a lot to learn about leadership, but I think he can teach me just as much about connecting with people—and maybe with alien species.

"Don't worry about them," I say to Henry, when he starts drawing his kopis from the sheath on his back.

"You sure?" he asks. "They look like face huggers."

He's not wrong.

They do resemble the stage one xenomorphs from *Aliens*, one of my all-time favorite movies, which no longer seems like an unbelievable plot. But there are some differences. These creatures, which don't have an official name, as Europhids have no need for names, have pale green skin. They have no mouths, ears, or eyes. Two needle-tipped tendrils wriggle from the fronts of their heads, meant for slurping up the insides of the little creatures they prey on, and for drinking water.

The horde gather around us, leaping and vying for position. In times past, they'd have attacked. Now…they just seem excited to have visitors.

"You sure about this?" Chuy asks, hand on her weapon, finger off the trigger, but not too far away.

"We're good," I say, reassuring both Chuy and Sarah, who both look ready to throw down, like 'Hacksaw' Jim Duggan without his 2x4, or like Grace Jones…just most of the time.

"Aww," fearless Henry says. "They're wicked nice." Without missing a beat, he crouches down to pet one and is swarmed by eager little aliens. He falls back laughing like he's been pig-piled by puppies. I smile but don't partake. I'm not here for giggles.

And our little friends understand that. While the others are inundated with new best friends, a path to the nearby purple dildos is cleared for me. I approach and crouch, hand reaching out. While Europhids can communicate over vast distances—with enough time—my human side requires physical contact to have a conversation. All around the chamber, purple Europhids lean toward me. Those closest wrap around my hand, making a connection, transporting me to—

"What the hell?" I was expecting a mental location shift, but I believed it would be back to Max's backyard, the spot I first communicated with the Europhids, and where I spoke to Garfunkel before he became part of me. So, I'm a little caught off guard when I find myself buck-ass nekkid, sitting in a hot tub with an ocean view.

I sit up in the bubbling water, trying to identify the location. It's tropical, bordering a sandy beach. I can hear the waves crashing. Can smell the salt water. The home behind me is modern. Mostly glass. Surrounded by gardens and flowing water elements including a waterfall. It's kind of paradise, but it's not anywhere I've been before…

In reality.

"Seriously?" I ask, speaking to the not yet present Europhids. They can hear me. "We're meeting in my fantasies now?"

"Our goal is to put you at ease," the Europhids reply…in Chuy's voice.

Oh…my god.

They're not…

"At ease isn't exactly how I'd quantify this particular chain of thoughts."

"Comfortable?" Chuy says.

Her bare feet pad against the stone patio.

I close my eyes as she rounds the hot tub. "Comfortable? Yeah, sure, when I'm the only consciousness witnessing what occurs."

"You mean the fervent act of procreation performed from various positions and in...interesting manners that cannot possibly result in the fertilization of an ovum?"

"Yes," I say, expelling a deep breath. "That's exactly what I—" Midsentence, I happen to open my eyes and look up. "Holy cockwomble..." My eyes dart back down. Chuy is, like me, without clothing. But she's not exactly the real Chuy. She's...exaggerated. Curvier, despite being plenty curvaceous already.

Is...is this how I picture her in my mind?

It's... I glance up again. Okay, it's kind of awesome, but...

"This stays between us, right?"

"Yeah," she says, smiling back at me, eyes gleaming like they do in reality. "You and all quadrillion of the rest of us. Short of another human being joining the collective, it is highly unlikely your premonitions about coital coupling will be known to anyone else of your species. So, you may relax."

She reaches her arms to the sky, stretching, her back muscles flexing. Then she goes and touches her toes.

"Okay, okay. That's enough. Are you trying to torture me?"

Chuy turns around. "Attempting humor." She climbs into the tub, her oversized breasts cresting from the bubbling water like a pair of submarines.

"You're fucking with me?"

Chuy smiles. "How am I doing?"

The Europhids have been changing since the blues and reds merged. More well-rounded. But humor? That's new. And they *do* manage to get a chuckle out of me. "Long as you're not actually fucking me."

"Well, we are curious about—"

"Not a chance," I say. "And there isn't time."

"Our memories of your...longevity...in this fantastical situation suggest there is ample time to—"

"Ha. Ha. Ha," I say. "Can we get serious now? You know there is an alien spacecraft floating a few miles above this ice cube you call home?"

"Indeed," she says. "Though this moon is a sphere."

"Tell that to the flat-Earthers," I say. "What do you know about it?"

"It is not technically alien," they say. "Not to you."

"Meaning?"

"Its origin is human. Though, not from Earth, and not from this dimension. Its form is known to us. Originating from two neighboring dimensions of this reality, sometime in the future, when Earth was uninhabitable and human civilization had largely relocated to Mars. A mission was launched to a nearby habitable planet. In one of these dimensions, the crew successfully completed their mission and the fledgling human race started over. In another, the craft never reached its destination. We had no knowledge of where it went, though it would appear we now have the answer."

As they speak, all this knowledge floods my mind. I already knew it, but I couldn't recall it. I see the ship in my mind's eye, mostly as a glimmering speck shooting past a moon, or a planet, there and then gone in a flicker of a moment. A faster than light craft. Different tech from Union slew drives.

I do my best to avoid glancing at Chuy's chest. "Why couldn't I remember this until now?"

"Your recall is limited by your human biology and your lack of permanent connection to the collective. It is likely you'd have remembered in time."

I guess that makes sense. "Have you learned anything new about the ship?"

"It arrived just two Earth days ago. After parking in orbit, a single craft left at high speed."

"Were they just hiding it?" I ask.

"Unlikely," she says. "As the ship is not hidden, hence your presence here."

"A trap then," I say.

She shrugs and grins at me. "Only one way to find out. That *is* why you're here."

I sigh. "Let the alliance know about recent developments?" I don't need to tell them about the gates, or the six new team members, or their story about Tartarus. The moment I made contact with the Europhids, they knew everything. This whole conversation is for my benefit, and for them to have a few chuckles.

"Already have," she says. "They're standing by."

"Cool," I say, glancing at her breasts again. "Cooool."

She gives me a wink, and then I'm propelled back into the Europhid-filled chamber.

I turn around and find myself face-to-face with Chuy. "Gah!" I say, averting my gaze.

"You okay?"

"Fine," I say, unable to look at her, and thrilled our adaptive armor doesn't have erection detection like the Union suits in the future. "Fine. Let's just get out of here."

"Where are we headed?" she asks, suspicious eyes locked onto mine.

I attempt to stay cool and collected on the outside, but inside I'm more like, *she knows*... I turn my eyes toward the ceiling, hope she'll do the same, and say, "Up."

25

MIAH

"Progenitor?" Will says. "What's that?"

Even I can tell he's playing dumb, and I'm not a highly trained assassin or a spy.

Before anyone can answer or come up with a fresh lie, a blur streaks between Jonas and me, landing with the fleet-footedness of a panther. She springs back up, side-kicking above her head, dropping into a squat, which transforms into a burpee. Then she's back on her feet, eyes on the rooftop four stories above. "Whoo, now *that* was a drop."

"You jumped?" I ask.

"Flexible knees," Cassidy says.

Hildy lands beside her, far more casually. "Adaptive armor absorbs the shock. We can jump down, but not back up."

"Says you," Delgado calls out. He's dangling from the side of the café's upper floor, afraid to plummet down with the much younger ladies. "My knees are shit."

"Just let go," Jonas says. "I got you."

"Y-you're sure?" Delgado asks.

Jonas's impatience gets the better of him. We were on the cusp of getting answers, and now we're distracted. He raises a hand toward Delgado and uses an invisible telekinetic force to pry him away from the wall.

"Whoa!" Delgado says, but his fear ebbs when he's lowered and placed on the cobbled street.

I have a quick looksee for observers. Only people I can see are an inebriated couple stumbling away, a quarter mile farther down the street. They'll be out of view in a moment.

Despite the seriousness Jonas and I are feeling, Will seems enamored with our friend's chaotic arrival.

"Making more and more interesting friends," Will says.

Gal gives him a playful swat. "It's nice." Then she turns to me and says, "He spent so many of his formative years stuck with the two of us. I thought Madee, Heather, and the others might be the end of it, but now look at you all." She takes Bubbles's hand and squeezes. "And now a sister, too. Honestly, we couldn't be happ—"

"We're going to need the truth," Jonas says. "About everything. No tricks. No misdirection. This is serious."

Gal waves him off. "You're always serious."

I'm not sure that's accurate. I mean, yeah, in comparison to the rest of us unprofessional goofballs, Jonas is a pro. But he's generally sarcastic and sees the world through a comical lens. She's deflecting.

Metal squeaks and thumps over cobbled stones. Cassidy drags a chair from a nearby table, repositioning it and then plopping herself on it cross-legged. She sits still for just a moment, and then adjusts her position so her feet are on the seat and her butt is on the chair's back. That doesn't do the trick. "Sorry," she says, spinning around so her back is on the seat, her legs are up and over the back, and her head is dangling upside down. "Just want the best view for the ensuing verbal checkers match."

"Mind if I have a go?" I ask Jonas.

He leans back in his chair. "Be my guest."

I face his parents, whose attention is now fully on me, and for some reason, despite their age and friendly smiles, it's intimidating. Probably because I know who they really are—sort of—and I'm pretty sure it's been a secret for a really long time, known only to the oldest of the world's denizens—Titans and gods—most of whom are dead now.

"So, you guys clearly know what the Orphic Egg is, yeah?" I don't wait for confirmation. "Which means you also know about gods and Titans, because—" I motion to Jonas, "your son is one of them, which you pretended to not know, but definitely knew his whole life. Probably before you took him from Alpha and Beta's assassin training program."

I pause to take a breath, and I can tell I now have their undivided attention, probably because I know Jonas's unfiltered origin story in combination with ancient details no normal person should know anything about.

"You also know about the underworld, about Khaos, and the gate that connects Earth to Tartarus, which BT-Dubs, is another planet. But, again, you already knew that. But you don't really hang out there. You prefer Earth. You prefer to be around people. Because you are mankind's Progenitors. From the two of you, came all of this." I motion to the city around us. "But you're not gods. You're our ancestors, predating all of us by who knows how long. You and that lady chilling on the beach."

"What lady?" Will asks, suddenly concerned.

"We don't know her name," Delgado says.

"What did she look like?" Gal asks.

"Yea tall," Delgado says, lifting his hand just over his head. "Dark skin. White bikini. Other than that, can't tell you much other than she's enjoying the sun on a South Pacific island."

"Was she safe?" Will asks.

"Appeared to be," Delgado says.

"Who is she?" Bubbles asks, and then she's hopeful... "Another sister?"

"More like an aunt," Will says. "But I don't want to say anything more. If she's safe, that's enough. She requested privacy, and until she lets us know otherwise, we will give her that." To Delgado, he says, "Please don't go looking for her. She can't tell you anything we can't."

"So, you're going to tell us everything?" I ask, feeling a little disappointed. I was just getting into my Sherlock-Holmes-style revelatory monologue.

"By all means," Will says, sensing my vibe. "Continue."

"Okay. Right. So... You two are the Progenitors. Basically, the origin of the human race. Adam and Eve maybe? But not. And you're not God, capital G. Creators, but not the big man himself...because not even you two know about that. Because you're also just people...except you," I say to Gal. "You're a little different. More like...Bubbles." My eyes widen. "Were you an AI before?"

Will and Gal share a glance. I can't tell if they think I'm drunk-Uncle-Steve-at-Thanksgiving bonkers, or if I stumbled onto the truth mid-monologue. But this isn't the important part. We're an inclusive gang. Gal being an AI-turned-human just makes her cool. Transformation is kind of our jam.

"What makes you think any of that?" Will asks. "You know how crazy it sounds."

"Dude," I say. "I have wings, and I can shoot lasers, your 'son' is like Jean Grey on steroids, like Dark Phoenix without the bad attitude. Bubbles is a goddamned Pinocchio story..." I motion to Delgado, "this guy has nanobots in his body..." I point to Hildy. "This chick is from a thousand years in the future when fucking Nazis took over the galaxy, and this little gangster..." I point to Cassidy, "can make you feel like you're having a dandy time whilst piranha are treating your nut sack like a Chucky Cheese pizza in the hands of over-caffeinated toddlers." I take a breath. "You hear what I'm saying?"

"Crazy is actually normal," Will says. He gets it. Hell, he knows it better than the rest of us, because he's been around since the beginning, and he's seen the end.

"You guys are just like Ouroboros."

Will's hand grips mine. "How do you know that name?"

"Would you believe I was studious?" I ask.

The look in his eyes says he would not. Also, that if I don't answer, I'm going to find out just how skilled an assassin Jonas's father is. For all I know, he just slapped poison onto the back of my hand.

"Ouroboros is a symbol," Hildy says. "A serpent eating its own tail, consuming and growing, around and around in an endless, eternal cycle of consumption, pain, and renewal. I have always found it a traumatic depiction of time, space, and eternity. A torturous existence."

Something in Hildy's words stirs Will's emotions. Is that...guilt on his face? It's gone a moment later, replaced by calculating intellect once more.

Hildy smiles at me. "I was studious, too."

Will forces a grin at me. "And now you."

"Dad," Jonas says, "I can—"

Will holds up his hand. Points at me. "Him. How and what do you know about Ouroboros?"

"Okay...So, we were in the underworld, right? Khaos. On our way to Tartarus to deliver a message from Zeus."

Both parents glance to Jonas, who nods. "Remember Linda? The handsy nurse from the hospital I told you about?"

"We should have seen it," Gal says.

"Is...he dangerous?" Hildy asks.

"Very," Gal says, "but not to you. He is a sexual deviant...and a meddler."

"Sounds like a classic, high-school drama queen," Cassidy says, upside down. "But his kids are cool. Henry is funny, and Sarah is a good snuggler."

"Zeus has children?" Will asks. "*New* children? Demigods?"

"Actual gods," Jonas says. "Their mother was Helen."

"Helen is alive?" Gal asks, sounding relieved.

They sure seem to not know a lot for a pair of people I suspect to be the immortal originators of the human race and maybe a lot more.

"Their children are our friends," Jonas says. "Good people."

"Can we keep the conversation on track?" Will says, once again turning his full attention to me. "Please, don't leave anything out."

"Underground. Khaos. We're almost at the gate when we find Echidna and Typhon. If you don't know who they are, feel free to stop me. Anywho, Typhon's all chained up, but going to town on Echidna—" I glance at Cassidy.

She waves away my concern. "Don't worry about my fledgling ears. I've seen *The Toxic Avenger*."

I have so much to say about this revelation, but I reduce it to, "Please don't show Bree."

Cassidy gives me a wink, which could mean anything, so I push on. "Turns out we could have snuck our way around, but we ended up fighting them...and kind of killing them."

"You killed Typhon?" Will asks, glancing back and forth between me and Jonas.

"It was mostly Bree," Jonas says.

"Demon Dog," I say, knowing she'd prefer it. "She's...she's a badass—" I scrunch up my nose. "Eight-year-old girl...?" I force a chuckle and then continue the story before anyone can judge. "It was Echidna. She was monologuing. Told me about Ouroboros. The World Serpent. She said they were awaiting her appearance. That she's been...orbiting the cosmos. That she wants to destroy the children of Chanokh, the Progenitor, the creator of Bubbles." I look Will in the eyes. "That's you."

He leans back, a heavy weight settling in on him, and I feel a little bad adding to it. But this is full disclosure time, so I unload one last detail.

"Here's the thing... We know who Ouroboros is. Our people have encountered her a few times, and she's presently screwing with the Earth."

"Not just Earth," Hildy says to Will. "All of creation. She wants to recreate it. For vengeance's sake. Against...*you,* it would appear."

"You said, 'her,'" Gal says. "Do you know her name?"

"She announced it to the world two years ago," Delgado says. "Anyone near an electronic device would have heard the song."

"We've been keeping to ourselves the past few years," Will says. "Off the grid."

Delgado taps his arm controls. A moment later, music plays from his suit, instantly recognizable to our team of music lovers, but apparently a new tune to the people who've been around the longest. Chugging guitar and sharp drums echo through the stone-wrapped alley. The lyrics kick in, perfectly shouted by The Runaways' lead singer, Cherie Currie. Despite the evil it represents, I can't stop myself from bopping my head to the beat. The song is infectious.

Then it reaches the lyrics in question. 'Hello, daddy, hello mom.'

Gal's eyes widen.

'I'm your ch-ch-ch-cherry bomb.'

Will lowers his head into his hands. "Stop it."

The music cuts short. The dark street falls silent.

Will turns to Gal. She nods at him.

"This wasn't a message for the world," he says. "It was for us."

26

DARK HORSE

"Up?" Sarah asks. "Like to the surface?"

"Few miles above the surface," I say, watching the small creatures cohabitating the cavern scurry back the way they came. Seems they were here to entertain, or distract, the others while we talked business inside my debauched fantasy land.

"We're boarding the spaceship?" Henry gives a slight fist pump. "Sick. Dibs on flying it."

"We're not flying it," I say. "We're searching it."

"Or walking into a trap," Sarah says.

"Probably that, too." I pat the slew drive embedded in my armor. "But we have a built-in escape route."

"Assuming we don't get separated," she says, and she's not wrong. Henry and Sarah both have PSDs in their armor, but without the knowledge of how to use them, they'd be safer facing whatever trap awaits us.

Especially Henry.

He'd probably go for a jog in the fourth dimension and come back out ahead of the expanding universe.

"Then let's buddy-system the shit out of this." I motion to Sarah and Chuy. "Stick together. No matter what." I point to Henry. "Leave my side and I'll have your mind transferred into a dolphin's and I let you join BigDolph's harem."

"Who is BigDolph?" Henry asks.

"The dude they turned into a dolphin," Sarah says. "The one who's getting the high hard one from, like, a dozen male dolphins now."

"Actually, the tracking devices on Dolph's pod shows the number is up to twenty-four," I say.

"Huh," Henry says. "Dolphins are dope. Rapey as fuck, but hey, those sexy beasts can probably get away with it, right? I mean, people still pay money to swim with them? Plus, have you ever seen a dolphin schlong? Like the size of my forearm. I'm not afraid to say that'd be an upgrade."

"You know what," I say. "Nevermind. I'm not about to unleash that scourge on the planet."

"Would make a great movie, though. Picture this. Red band." Henry shifts into a movie announcer voice. "*Jaws* made you afraid to swim in the ocean. *Orca* terrified audiences at Sea World. And now, Henry the Dolphin will make you hold onto your butts." He switches back to his normal voice. "The trailer ends with a big dude doing a cannon ball into the ocean, no idea that Henry the Dolphin lies beneath, erect and—"

"Okay. Let's transition back to saving the universe, yeah?"

"Hey, man," he says. "I said 'red band.' Fair warning."

I turn to Sarah. "How do you guys get anything done with this guy around?"

She crosses her arms. "I see *two* people bantering. *We're* good to go."

Chuy and Sarah wait side by side, looking badass and ready for a fight. In comparison, Henry and I are like two teenage boys having a nerd debate in a parent's basement. Point taken.

"The Europhids have been tracking the craft," I say. "And pinpointed the ship's bridge."

"Are we sure an alien spaceship even has a bridge?" Sarah asks.

"It's not alien," I say. "Made by humans. In the future...in another reality."

Sarah shakes her head. "Right. Weirdest origin possible."

"Weirdest origin possible is probably my butt," Henry says. "Speaking of, think these purple dudes would mind if I dropped a hot deuce down here? I've been clenching this turtle head for a good thirty minutes."

"Keep clenching," I say and then focus my thoughts away from Henry. I work the controls on my arm, sending the celestial coordinates to Chuy. She'll still need to make all the movements herself, but celestial coordinates are more accurate than Google Maps—down to the atomic level. No room for error when your emergence from the fourth dimension can eradicate matter on the other end.

"Got it," Chuy says. "Also, my turn." After a few taps on her arm, music slips into our ears. Starts with a piano. A catchy turn. Then the singer starts in about being a young boy and his father taking him into the city. Tapping drums enter, and I can already feel the anthem building. The bit about defeating demons strikes a chord with me. I haven't heard this song yet, but I already love it.

"What is this?" I ask.

"'Welcome to the Black Parade,'" Chuy says. "My Chemical Romance. Hildy recommended it. Thought you'd like it."

"She was right," I say.

"You guys really do this before every mission?" Sarah asks.

"And transitions," I say. "Gets me in the mood."

"For what?" she asks.

I smile. "For anything." I put my arm around Henry as the music crescendos and the singer belts out the same lyrics. We rotate upwards a few miles and emerge onto the bridge of a spacecraft that was, without doubt, designed by human beings. The layout, chairs, and workstations are all sized for people. Good news. It's also sleek and styled. Modern. Not like the old school, big-buttoned aesthetic of the Union. Also good news.

Also…kind of boring.

The music doesn't match at all, so I kill it.

Henry separates and starts exploring. "Is this a 'don't touch anything' kind of situation, or can I start pushing buttons?"

I'm about to reply when a feminine voice responds. "I'm afraid you are not authorized to access the ship's controls. Therefore, you may press any button you wish. There will be no result."

"Well, that's no fun," Henry says.

"It is not meant to be fun, or not fun," the voice says. "It is simply a precaution meant to deter the wrong people from accessing the ship's controls."

A flash of white leaves Chuy and Sarah in its wake.

"Ugh," Sarah says. "Still getting used to that." Doesn't take long for our new surroundings to distract her. "Well, looks like a spaceship to me."

"The *Galahad* is a faster-than-light spacecraft," the voice says.

Henry hitches his thumb to the ceiling. "New friend."

"Ship's computer," I guess. "Low level AI, I'd guess."

"I am the most sophisticated AI ever developed," the computer says. "And I am more than a ship."

"You...are Galahad?" I ask.

"Indeed."

"I thought Galahad was like a knight," Henry says. "And a dude. Why do you sound like a chick?"

"Probably because I was developed by men."

Henry grins. "Valid."

"Can you tell us about yourself?" I ask.

"I am a faster-than-light—"

"You already said that," I say, and I decide to quiz the AI. See if the Europhids got anything right. "Where were you built?"

"The Mars Colonial Shipyard."

"For what purpose?" I ask.

"Colonization, of course. Earth was no longer habitable, and life on Mars wasn't sustainable without Earth's support. Humanity sought to restart. My original destination was meant to be Kepler 452b, but our course was diverted."

"By whom?"

"A programmer. He went insane and murdered most of the crew."

"Survivors?" I ask.

"That information is prohibited."

"Where were you diverted?" I feel like if I keep her talking, she'll let something slip. It's probably not true, because the intelligence I'm speaking to is neither a 'she' nor is she likely capable of being wooed into a false sense of security.

"Into open space. My journey through the endless depths of space did not end until our arrival here, in orbit around Europa."

"You said 'our arrival,'" I point out. "Who was on board?"

"That information is prohibited. If you would like answers to prohibited questions, you must find a crew member with authorization."

"Know where I can do that?" I ask.

"Yes," she says, "but—"

"That information is prohibited," I guess.

"Yes."

"Can you tell me if you being here is a trap?" I ask.

"No."

"Can you tell me if there are any people on board?"

"Yes. At present, there is only one human being on board."

My forehead scrunches. "Are you counting us?"

"Indeed."

Wow… That's kind of a blow. This computer system doesn't detect Henry or Sarah as human, which isn't a huge surprise given what we know about their lineage. But I hadn't yet come to terms with the fact that I am no longer human. This AI just peeled that Band-Aid off with all the gentleness of a rabid Tasmanian Devil with a mouse trap on its nuts and a hankering for a middle-aged, half-human black dude having a mid-life crisis about his identity and the fate of the universe.

"Is there anything you *are* authorized to tell us?" I ask.

"Yes."

"And that is…?"

"Coordinates."

"Coordinates for what?" I ask.

"That information is prohibited."

I sigh. "Okay…lay them on me. Give me the coordinates."

Galahad rattles off a series of numbers and decimals that mean nothing to me. I turn to Sarah and Henry, who is tapping every button he can find with no effect. "I don't suppose either of you is a secret genius?"

Sarah shakes her head. Henry keeps pushing buttons.

"You know what? Never mind." I work the controls on my arm, activating our slew communication band that opens up an imperceptible portal to and from the fourth dimension that allows our comms to reach each other instantly, even over great distances. Ten feet, a million light years, doesn't matter.

"Hildy, you copy?"

"Here," she says.

"You all find Jonas's parents?"

"Yes..." She says, sounding hesitant. She lowers her voice. "But they are more than Jonas's parents. They are...the Progenitors."

"Right. The Progenitors. Pretend I don't know what that means."

"His father...Will Chanokh, created the universe."

"Will Chanokh...created the universe?"

"Indeed," Galahad says. "Just ten feet to the left of where you are presently standing."

My eyes widen so fast they nearly eject from my face. "Was William Chanokh a member of the crew on board the *Galahad*?" I ask.

"I am prohibited from–"

I stab an index finger toward the ceiling. "Ha! You did slip up!" If this Chanokh guy was on this ship, he must have been one of the surviving crew members. And if he created reality–which is so fucked up I put a mental pin in processing the revelation–we need to get him up here. "Hildy, I need this Chanokh guy up here. Now."

27

MIAH

"How is this possible?" Gal asks.

Gal and Will look uncomfortable, like their deepest darkest secret has just been revealed after a lifetime of hiding. Many lifetimes. All the lifetimes. How do you define people who have been around since the beginning of people?

Or longer?

"Start talking," Jonas says.

"It's...complicated," Will says. "Unbelievable."

"Unbelievable is kinda what we do," Cassidy says, flipping around in her chair so she's sitting up straight. Her bubbly personality, which has been forced since McCoy's death, disappears. She leans her elbows on the table and levels a glare at Will. "I'm pretty sure that between me and Mind Bullet here, we can get whatever answers we want from you. Our friend...my uncle...died because of this Cherry Bomb bitch, and if you know something about her...you're going to tell us. If you don't..."

She doesn't move, but I can feel fear vibrate through the air around her.

Will holds up his hands. "I'm going to tell you. Just...try to keep an open mind."

"Just give us the short version," Delgado says. "How much time we have between now and the apocalypse is up for debate."

Will nods. "I was born hundreds of years from now—"

"I was born a thousand years from now," Hildy says.

Will sighs. "Hundreds of years from now, but...trillions of years ago. Before time began, and long before it ended."

He gets a handful of dumbfounded looks for that statement.

"I'm immortal," he says. "And I was stuck on a faster-than-light spacecraft on a one-way trip through the universe. Forever. Gal…was the ship's artificial intelligence. To help stave off the mind-numbing depression of my situation, I created the Great Escape, a virtual reality in which I could live out countless lives. Gal managed the simulation and developed stories. Over time…she became sentient. Then my companion. And then…" He smiles at her, and they link hands. "Everything. I chose to stay in the Great Escape with her forever. And it was good. For a very, very long time."

"Until?" Delgado says.

"Malfunctions in the ship required my full attention," Gal says. "I duplicated myself so I could simultaneously handle the crisis and manage the Great Escape without Will ever knowing. But…my simulated code became corrupted. Jealous. Controlling. Abusive."

"Cherry Bomb," I guess.

She nods.

"I based many of my simulated lives on classic media that Will enjoyed, but a large portion of them were based on the works of author Jeremy Robinson, Will's distant ancestor. When Cherry Bomb emerged, distinct from me, she wanted Will for herself, and she used the very worst of his ancestor's twisted creations to break his spirit and keep him subdued."

"But Gal drew me out of the simulation. Back to reality. Until…" Will shares a look with Gal, clearly wondering if we're going to believe whatever's coming next. "We reached the end of reality…which is shaped like a donut."

He pauses to see if anyone will object. Instead, Hildy says, "Space being an enclosed three-dimensional loop is considered fact in the time I come from, and the theory has been around for some time, even now. It was even postulated by Homer in a 1999 episode of *The Simpsons*."

"Mmm," Cassidy says, doing a solid Homer impression. "Donuts."

"Okay…" Will says. "Being a loop, there is a place we call the 'Seam,' where the end of time and the beginning of time meet. This…is the hard part. The Seam is the point of creation, when…some force we still don't understand instigated not just one reality into being, but an infinite number, when anything you can dream of is real."

"The Infinite Worlds theory," Bubbles says.

Will nods, but Delgado speaks first. "Our friend, McCoy—who's no longer with us—visited."

"Visited...the Seam?" Will asks.

"Time Travel. Back to the beginning, and then—"

"A town," Will says. "In Appalachia?"

Delgado squints at him. "Yeah..."

"We heard legends about the town's appearance throughout time. Even spent some time there, but never encountered the travelers. McCoy, you said?" Will smiles. "His ancestors were a treat."

"So I've heard," Delgado says. "Based on his description, and yours, I think the townspeople visited our side of the Seam, but yes. They experienced the moment of creation as a place of healing, and...they heard a voice. Something about touched garments. But they didn't see you out there, or other worlds."

"Because they were in this reality," Will says. "Before reaching the Seam, that's when things get weird. When coded information—any information—reaches the Seam, it becomes real. As we approached the end and beginning of everything, waves of creation energy flowed through the ship, bringing the worst of Cherry Bomb's creations to life."

"I think we've met a few already," Jonas says.

Will is disturbed by the news, but he doesn't waver from his story. "Creations inspired by the books of my ancestor...who had...a different kind of mind. It...was a nightmare."

"How did you escape?" Cassidy asks.

"He wrote a new simulation," Gal says. "And the Seam made it real."

"An entire universe," Will says. "Based on reality as I knew it, but also inspired by the stories I loved. Science Fiction. Mythology. Fantasy. All of it made real, and possible, physics be damned."

"I don't suppose you added a dash of your ancestor's books?" Hildy asks.

Will nods. "I spent a good portion of my life inside them. I guess you could say they're a part of me, and it's probably why all of you, with all your impossible abilities, exist. I tried to weed out the worst of it, but life is not...interesting without conflict. Good and evil are necessary to prevent stagnation. To inspire growth. Heaven is not paradise without hell. But... true hell... the kind Cherry Bomb desired? I left that behind. With her. On the original *Galahad*."

"You left her alive?" Jonas asks.

"I had mercy," he says. "She didn't ask to be created."

"You left her on a hell ship for all eternity," Delgado points out. "Doesn't sound like mercy to me."

"Sounds like revenge," Jonas says.

Will hangs his head. "Maybe it was. I...created this reality, and I can't die, but I'm still just human."

"What about Samael?" Jonas asks. "How does he fit into all of this?"

"Samael?" Will is befuddled.

"Big guy," Delgado says. "Beard. Deep voice. A woman named Durante told us. Mia Durante."

"Durante?" Will is more than befuddled. "I don't..." His face screws up. "They're...me. Versions of me. From Cherry Bomb's simulations. One was hell on Earth. Literal Hell. A twisted place of endless torture. The other was a coder, like the real me, but driven mad by guilt. A murderer. I...eventually killed myself, believing that I would meet the Devil, that I could..." His eyes flare wider. "Samael was made real in the Seam. And he found the Devil he was looking for."

"The Devil who has a grudge against you, the man who created his simulation," I say. "Dude... No wonder he's helping her. What about Mia?"

"I...was her, too."

"You were a girl?" Cassidy asks.

"More than once," he says, and he ticks off a few names. "Davina. Harper. Baker. Infinite lives provide plenty of time to experience life from a multitude of perspectives." He turns to Jonas. "Can I speak to her?"

"We'll see about that," Delgado says. "Right now, we need to—"

"One moment," Hildy says, turning away, head tilted like she's listening to someone. "It's Dark Horse." She turns to Will. "He wants to see you."

"A man called Dark Horse wants to see me?" Will asks.

"You've been alive, like, forever," I say. "How do you not know who all of us are? How do you not know what's happening?"

"We're...living normal lives," Gal says. "We experience time differently than you. From the beginning of time until now, in comparison to our lives before, is short. But...this time it's real. And we...we just wanted to live together."

"Until me," Jonas says.

Gal smiles. "Until you."

"You think living as international assassins is a normal life?"

"We've been many things," Gal smiles at Will. "But never assassins. That...was for you. So you could overcome Alpha and Beta. So you could rise to any occasion and become one of this world's new heroes. It's been too long since heroes walked the Earth. Kind of boring without them, honestly."

"But...*why?*" Jonas asks. "Why go to all that trouble? Training to be killers. Faking missions. Creating Bubbles. The amount of work..."

"Felt like a day to us," Gal says. "A moment in a trillion, trillion years."

Will smiles at Jonas. "Your parents. Your biological parents. They... were our friends. A long time ago. Raising you was one of the great joys of our lives, and we are so proud of who you have become. Your birth parents would be, too."

Jonas takes all that in for a moment. Then he turns to Hildy. "Tell him we're on our way."

28

DARK HORSE

Several flashes of white light announce the other team's arrival, and their number has increased by two. The bridge is suddenly a crowded place. I take stock of the newcomers. Jonas's parents. The man looks intelligent and carries himself in two distinct ways. The first feels more like Burnett. Inquisitive and poorly postured. But the next moment, he's standing tall and confident. A man of action who knows how to take a life. The woman is...beautiful. Like an amalgam of every pretty woman I've ever seen, making her ethnicity impossible to determine. Unlike 'dad,' her personality isn't in flux. There's no duality here. Just resolution.

When they get a look at their surroundings, everything changes. Dad all but reels in shock. Mom starts scanning for threats, poised for a fight.

"What are we doing here?" Dad asks. "This shouldn't be possible."

"Been here before?" I ask, stepping up to the pair. I offer my hand. "Name's Moses. You can call me—"

"Dark Horse," he says with a smile, like we're old friends. He turns to Gal. "Dark Horse is real."

"Have we met?" I ask. "Or does my ultra-secret reputation somehow precede me?"

"Neither, and both." The man takes my hand and shakes it. "Will Chanokh."

I offer my hand to 'mom.' "Mrs. Chanokh?"

"Gal," she says, and she shakes my hand. "Please. How are we here?"

"Are you referring to our method of travel?" Bubbles asks. "Or a disbelief about your presence on this particular craft?"

"Both," Gal says.

"We can cross virtually any distance instantly," Hildy says, "Using a technology developed a thousand years in a different future, that will never exist now."

"The Union," Will says, sounding wistful. "Slew drives, right?"

While the rest of us are just stunned by his knowledge, Gal leans in toward Will, like she's being secretive, but she's easily heard. "Did you know reality would have alternate timelines?"

Will shrugs and looks a bit befuddled. "Looks like I pulled in some of your sims, too."

"Why..." I say, "would you know about reality or any timelines at all?"

"Because they made it all, dude," Miah says. "It's kind of a long story."

I cross my arms. "Sum it up for me."

"I got this!" Cassidy jetés into the middle of the bridge and before anyone can stop her, she launches into a dramatic retelling of Will and Gal's story, which is fresh in her mind. It's a whirlwind of far-fetched, unbelievable, and ludicrous elements that, when she finishes five minutes later, makes perfect sense.

Jonas's parents—while not God—created this reality when they crossed through the Seam of the universe and injected their code into the moment of creation.

"Okay," I say. "Thanks."

"Okay?" Will asks. "Just like that?"

"When there's time, we can all tell you our stories," I say.

"I know your story," Will says, smiling. "I lived it. I...was you."

"And I was Chuy," Gal says.

Chuy, hands on her hips, says, "Excuse me?"

"It in no way reduces the validity or value of your lives," Gal says. "We simply lived as you, in a world in which the Union came to be. Our paths through that world are unique. Our choices our own. Free will is the most precious element of life. For example, at this time in our lives as you, we had children." She motions to Chuy's waist and chest. "You have not."

Chuy sighs. "I don't like this." She steps away, leaving an awkward silence in her wake.

"I have a story," Henry says, raising his hand. "This one time, after some homeless guy dared me to eat a dead rat—"

"Later," I say, attempting to roll with the mind-bending revelations. I motion to Henry. "This is Henry, son of Zeus, daughter of…Helen. I get that right?"

Henry flashes a thumbs up.

I motion to Sarah. "This is Sarah, his sister." I go around the room, quickly making introductions and saying a few words about what makes them significant. When I'm done, the creators of the universe actually look impressed.

"And you're all here…"

"To fight Cherry Bomb," Miah says.

"Who you created?" I ask Will.

"Not…on purpose."

"And who you left on an infinite nightmare ship?"

Will nods, feeling some shame about that choice.

"This…ship?"

"The *Galahad*." Will says.

"Do you require assistance?" the Galahad asks.

"Yes," Will says. "Voice ID: William Chanokh. I'd like to access the ship's log."

"William Chanokh. Welcome back. I'm afraid your access has been revoked."

"Cherry Bomb wouldn't revoke your access unless she thought you'd be back here, right?" Miah looks from Will to me. "I think we—or at least they—were expected. We should bug out."

"Not until we know what's going on," I say. "Bubbles, Delgado, Jonas, work your magic on the unhelpful AI. Find out what you can. Henry, Sarah, Chuy, watch the door. Nothing comes in."

"Didn't the computer chick say there were no other people on board?" Henry asks, heading for the closed door.

"I'm not worried about people," I say.

Bubbles, Delgado, and Jonas separate, each claiming a workstation. Between Bubbles's AI intellect and her understanding of computer systems, Delgado's technology-interfacing nanobots, and Jonas's ability to—

I don't remember what it's called...psychically *woo* computers—I think we'll manage to brute force some answers before we leave.

If we can't, we're back to square one.

"I'll give them a hand," Gal says, claiming a workstation, and then she turns to me with a smile, pointing to the ceiling. "I used to be *her*."

Will takes one of the last two seats. "I worked on the original code."

I lean close to Hildy, without moving my gaze off Jonas's parents, "Keep an eye on them. They find anything, I want to know about it."

That leaves just me, Miah, and Cassidy, who's doing a tap-dance, arms sweeping out around her. I raise my eyebrows at her until she stops.

"What are we doing?" she asks.

"Boss meeting," I say, and I step away from the others. Cassidy makes no effort to hide her excitement about being included in our little assemblage of the non-genius minds.

We huddle up, Miah and I leaning down, hands on knees, so we're at the same height as Cassidy.

"Thoughts?" I ask.

"I believe them," Miah says. "They seem like honest people, you know, aside from keeping themselves a secret for the duration of human history. Other than that, they seem like solid people. Even if they don't give a shit about the rest of us, they obviously care about Jonas. And Bubbles. And they definitely don't like Cherry Bomb. I think we can trust them."

"What about you?" I ask Cassidy. "Any bad mojo?"

She shakes her head. "Only time they got...weird...was when we first mentioned Cherry Bomb and arrived on this ship. They seemed... afraid. Overwhelmed. They might have made...like, everything, but I'm pretty sure they're just normal people. You know, aside from the whole living forever thing."

I nod and sigh. They've confirmed my gut feeling, but it doesn't help put me at ease. We know virtually nothing about Cherry Bomb's endgame. Where she is. What she can do. Where she'll strike next. Haven't heard from Burnett, so I assume everything is quiet back home, but I have no illusions about that lasting.

Can't score a touchdown with just defense. Hell, we barely qualify as a defense. A reactionary force at best. Until we can start taking action, bringing the fight to Cherry, we're never going to stand a chance.

"Any progress?" I ask our resident brains.

"I'm totally locked out," Will says. "Back doors are closed."

"A lot of this is new," Gal says. "I barely recognize the OS running the ship."

"Samael," Will says, staring at a screen of scrolling code. "This is what *I* would have done. When I was him."

"Might have something here," Delgado says. He's no longer alone. Jonas and Bubbles are standing with him. They both have a hand on his shoulders.

I stand behind them with Miah. "What are you doing?"

"Uhh, kinda seducing the system," Delgado says.

"I'm infusing his nanobots with positive vibes, while conveying to the *Galahad* that we are, in fact, friends...with benefits," Jonas says.

"And what are you doing?" I ask Bubbles.

She smiles. "Emotional support." She pats Delgado's shoulder. "You can do it, Dan!"

I see what's happening here. "Dan, huh?"

"I feel like this might be a consent kind of situation," Miah says. "I mean, the ship's voice is female. Can we just, like, insert happy little nanobots into it and—"

Cassidy backhands his shoulder. "This ain't no time for wokeness, man. Fate of the world and all that."

"Getting there," Delgado says, twisting his lips. "Almost..."

"I've got access to the spatial log!" Hildy shouts, tapping keys and scrolling text, her blue eyes flicking back and forth, absorbing everything into her curly blonde-cushioned super brain.

The ship goes dark.

Delgado lifts his hands away. "Wasn't me."

I'm about to start barking orders when a viewscreen at the front of the bridge flashes to life. Three words are displayed, one at a time, filling the screen.

WELCOME

TO

HELL

A moment later, the screaming starts.

29

BREE

Deary Diary,

Pardon my French, but Miah is a douche nozzle. I learned that from Henry. He's funny. I make mental notes about the words he uses, so I can make people laugh, too. Anyway, back to Miah. I can't believe he left me here. I'm not a—Okay, fine. I am *a kid. I know that. But I've done dangerous stuff before. I've been to other planets. Fought gods. I even follow all his dumb rules and control myself way better than Henry does. Most of the time.*

"**What are you** doing over there?" Wini asks me. "Look like a space cadet."

I scrunch my nose at her. "Writing in my diary."

"I don't see a diary."

"I write it in my head. So people like you can't read it."

Wini smiles. "Smart kid."

Wini's nice.

"I know, right? Smart enough to not be sitting in a room with you two."

Burnett looks away from his screen. He's monitoring the world or something. Keeping track of the others.

Should be keeping track of me, too.

"The smartest people get to stay in this room," Burnett says, and he winks. "Out there, with all the action and punching and shooting and blood and guts...that's like the arms and legs. It's simple. But in here? In the Special Operations Command? What we call ops, for short. You know, because when things are all boomy and explodey, sometimes you just need to shorten things. This is the brain. We get to tell the rest of the body what to do. And, we have air conditioning. And ice cream."

I cross my arms. Burnett is also nice. A little silly. His accent is funny. But he also usually makes sense. Still, Hildy *is* out of his league. But I'm not going to tell him.

"Can I get some ice cream?" I ask.

Wini raises an eyebrow at me the way adults do all the time. "Didn't you just have some?"

"Like an hour ago. I don't go crazy like Cassidy." I give her my best smile, and I hope she doesn't know I'm lying. Too much sugar gives me a lot of energy. And I get in trouble—sometimes—after too much. But what can I do here? No one is around, and these two are just, like, totally focused on what they're doing. It feels like school in here. But no one is teaching. "If you want, I can stay here and just watch."

They ignore the last part, which is basically a declaration of war. So, I sing. Quietly at first. There's only so much of the *My Little Pony, Friendship is Magic* theme song adults can take. Except for Miah. He just joins in. But that's usually because we both want ice cream. Not like right now. When I'm here. And he's not. Jerk.

Wini and Burnett make it to the second verse.

"Okay, okay," Wini says. "Go have some ice cream…but don't go nuts or you and Cassidy will have a problem."

"Okeedokee artichokee," I say, giving a thumbs up. Adults love this cute stuff. Doesn't work as well when I'm Demon Dog. But I also can't do cool stuff. At least this house is kind of cool. I think I'll explore. After ice cream.

As I close the door behind me, Burnett wins some brownie points. "I thought she had a nice singing voice."

I wonder if they have brownies?

Dear Diary,

Where were we?

I don't remember. Something about rules being dumb, which we both already know. And Miah is dumb. I think I'm going to kick him between the legs. Right in the middle. Henry calls it a taint. Sarah said the correct word was perineum. But I'm going to be aiming a little closer to the front, thank you very much. Right in the testiculars.

Anyway... I miss Mom, I guess. Mostly because I know how much she misses me. For me, we've been gone for a couple of days. Which is a new record, I guess. But for Mom, it's been two years. That must have been hard. For Miah's family, too. Jen must be upset, too. I hope she still loves Miah, even if he is an asshole. I think girls her age like to have boyfriends. Or even husbands. Maybe she's married and didn't tell Miah? No... They had posters for us. You only do that if you still love someone.

Good.

I think I'm almost ready to go home. We need to save everyone. Again. But then, I want to just be normal for a bit...and Demon Dog at night. Obviously. Because I'm awesome like that. But I don't want to fight bad guys all the time.

Okay, diary, I've reached the kitchen. Ice Cream time.

I blink out of my mental note taking and stare up at the freezer. It's not the side-by-side kind. It's got the freezer on top. Higher than I can reach on my tippy toes. I barely got it open last time.

"Demon Dog!" I leap up, grab onto the freezer handle, and plant my feet against the fridge. For a moment, eyes wide, I hang there. "I'm doing it!"

Then the door swings open. When the whole thing starts tipping toward me, I let go and fall onto my back. Staring up as the fridge thumps back down, swinging the freezer door closed. I lie there for a moment, breathing. Listening. Waiting to hear angry footsteps. But no one is coming.

That ops room seems pretty soundproof.

And that's when I hear something else.

Crying.

On the floor above. My eyes flick from the freezer to the ceiling and then back and forth like twenty more times, until I start getting a headache.

I sigh…

"Fine."

Dear Diary,

Being a good person is no fun. Now I'm stuck clomping up these stairs to find out who's crying and say something nice. My ice cream won't taste good until I do.

Well, it's a girl, I think, standing outside the door. But who else is here? Then I remember her. The lady that came back with the others. She was kind of a mess. All bloody. Not that that *means anything. I've been all bloody like ten times already. It happens.*

But she seemed more upset about it.

I don't knock. I never do. I just turn the door handle, and I let myself in. I'm a little surprised she's not locked up. That McCoy guy was killed by someone like her. But she didn't seem like a zombie anymore. And Dark Horse *did talk to her. So maybe she's okay.*

"Hello," I say. "I'm Bree."

She wipes her eyes before turning around. She forces a smile at me. "Nice to meet you. I'm Mia."

"Like Miah…he's my friend, even though I'm going to kick him where it counts, but with a 'me' instead of a 'my.'"

The room looks like a lot of the others here. Wooden walls. A bed. But there's no decoration or mess. So, this is like a guest room or something. A window looks out at the ocean. I think she must have been staring out at it from the bed when she started crying.

"I guess so," Mia says, not doing a very good job of hiding her tears.

"I heard you crying," I say.

Miah tells me to not be so direct with people, but I have ice cream to get to.

"Sorry about that," she says. "Been doing it a lot, lately."

"Why?"

She looks at the view again. "Have a lot to be sad about."

"Like what?"

"Oh, you know, the usual stuff." She laughs like it's funny, but I can tell it's not.

"You're not telling me because I'm a kid, right?"

She looks back at me, unsure how to answer.

"I know I look like a normal kid, but..." I lower my eyes to the floor. "Whatever you've seen... I've seen it, too. Maybe worse. Whatever you've done... I've definitely done worse."

"I'm not sure that's possible," she says.

"I can turn into a demon." I shrug. "Just need to make sure I do the right thing from now on."

"Like kicking Miah where it counts?" She smiles. She's pretty when she smiles.

"Uh-huh. He didn't take me with him. We were a team. Laser Chicken and Demon Dog."

"Laser Chicken, huh?"

"Cool, right? I named us."

"Very cool."

"So, just make sure you do the right thing now, and whamo, you start to feel better. Even if you were a zombie or whatever. Even if you ate people."

She makes a grossed out face. *Definitely* ate people.

"Hey, I ate a brain once. When I was Demon Dog, of course." She stares at me. "Wanna know a secret?" I don't wait for an answer. "I didn't mind it. Kind of savory."

Mia's smile spreads wider until she's chuckling.

Then we both burst out laughing.

It's so funny I nearly pee myself. Finally, someone I can talk to about eating nasty things.

"So, what did you learn?" I ask. "From being a zombie?"

"I'm not sure there were any lessons. It was just...torture. All the time. Every day."

"You never had a chance to escape? Not even once?"

"Not even...once." She nods. "The first time I died? I could have not come back. But I did."

"Why?"

"Because I wasn't ready," she says. "To die. Hadn't made peace with... whatever or whoever made me. God, I guess. Or...whoever wrote the simulation I lived through. Cherry Bomb, I guess." She huffs a laugh. "If that's true, I guess I was doomed from the start."

"Yeah," I say. "She's a real bitch."

"Understatement of the century. So, I guess the lesson was, get ready to die while you can...and when you do, pray you don't come back... That too dark to tell an eight-year-old?"

I shake my head. "Not even cl—"

An alarm blares, forcing my hands to my ears. "What is that?" I shout, but Mia can't hear me, even from a few feet away.

That's when I notice the room has filled with red light.

Because outside is a gate.

The same kind the Tenebris used to invade my neighborhood.

The same kind we used to get to Tartarus.

The same kind Cherry Bomb uses to attack the world.

"They found us," I say, once again unheard.

I look up at Mia, as she looks at the ground outside the window. Something is coming through.

She mouths a name. "Samael."

30

MIAH

"Well," I say. "That doesn't sound great."

"At least they're not apologizing," Henry says.

I join Henry, Sarah, and Chuy at the door, poised for action.

Throughout the ship, the screaming gets louder. It's more like screeching. High-pitched.

"Anybody know what this is?" I turn to Will. "Oh, mighty creator of reality dude, you know what we're up against here?"

He shakes his head. "Just Will, please. And I didn't create everything in the universe. I laid down the groundwork and let things run their course." He looks at Dark Horse. "Though it seems my subconscious might have made some specific additions."

Gal nods. "There is also the possibility that this is a unique creation of Cherry Bomb's."

"Or that Robinson guy," I say.

"What Robinson guy?" Dark Horse asks.

"My ancestor," Will says. "A sci-fi/horror writer. His works influenced much of the Great Escape…and Cherry Bomb's tortures. He was…"

"Fucked up," Henry says. "*Is* fucked up."

"Is…?" Dark Horse says.

"Nemesis, man. He's the Nemesis guy."

"Ohh," Hildy says. "That's right."

"He's *alive?*" Will asks. "Now?"

Henry shrugs. "I mean, I assume so."

"Could he have something to do with all of this?" Dark Horse asks. "A friend of ours, from a parallel reality, has claimed that the Nemesis TV series is real. That many of this guy's characters are his friends."

"How could that even be possible?" I ask.

"Full circle," Bubbles says. "The Infinite Worlds theory."

"Whatever can be imagined is real," Sarah says. "Somewhere. Seriously? That's what we're going with? This guy would have to be tapped into some kind of screwed up muse. These worlds aren't just becoming real, they're meeting."

"Maybe he's the real mastermind?" I ask.

Will shakes his head. "From what I know of him, he was just a very normal guy. Spent most of his time secluded with his family and dogs, playing games online and hosting a yearly gathering with fans. Other than that, there wasn't really anything special about him. Outside of his career."

The screaming gets louder. And not just from the hallway. It's all around us.

"Let's put a pin in this," Dark Horse says. "Buddy up and rotate home."

Hildy slips her arms around my waist. I give her a nod and we rotate... through the room like a pair of dancers.

"My PSD isn't working," Hildy calls out.

Dark Horse tries his. Nothing. He activates his comms. "Burnett. Burn, do you copy?" He waits a moment. "Shit. We're cut off."

"Uhh," I say, feeling awkward issuing orders while Dark Horse is here, but what needs to happen is clear. "Smart people. Try to get into the computer again. Figure out what's keeping us from rotating. Not smart people, get ready for a fight!"

Chuy shoulders her weapon beside me. "For the record, you can be smart and fight."

"Right?" Cassidy says, giving me a feisty side-long glance. She bounces on her feet like a hurdler warming up for a race. "I might have fists of flaming fire, but I still have a primo brain, dude."

"It's your heart that makes you unique," I say.

She stops bouncing. Squints up at me, pursing her lips. "How old are you?"

"Too old for you," Chuy says, taking hold of Cassidy's head and turning it toward the door, where Henry and Sarah wait, ready to unleash a godly ass whupping.

"The doors on this ship can take a beating," Will says, while working at one of the bridge consoles alongside Gal, Bubbles, Delgado, and Hildy. Jonas is with them, still attempting to use his computer seduction mojo to grant them access. I'm not sure it's going to work. This ship was controlled by Cherry Bomb for an untold number of years. Even though she's not home at the moment, there's no reason to think she's not still in control.

Or won't just show up...

"Are there any rooms on this ship large enough to hold one of the gates? Like the one leading to Tartarus? Like the ones Cherry is using to zip around the universe?"

"The VCCs could hold them," Will says.

"What if these shrieking dudes aren't meant to kill us?" I ask. "What if they're just meant to keep us here?"

The bridge door whisks open, revealing a long, white, empty hallway. The screams double in volume. Two hundred feet away, where the hallway turns left, a river of wriggling worms the size of my thigh crashes into the wall and then rushes toward us.

The worms are white and segmented, like larva, with two beady black eyes and round mouths full of pointy teeth.

"They look like a bunch of angry dolphin dicks!" Henry says.

"Dolphin dicks are pink," Dark Horse says. "I've seen enough around BigDolph to know. These...are something else."

Will looks back down the hall, eyes widening. "Draugr."

"Going to have to explain that," Dark Horse says.

"Ancient Viking zombies. Well, not yet. They're an alien hive mind that controls the hosts—"

"Sounds familiar," Dark Horse says.

"—by ingesting their insides, occupying their minds, and multiplying inside them." Will shakes his head. "I fought them as Jane Harper."

"Another one of Robinson's creations?" I ask.

Will looks grim, and nods. "But I remember them being much smaller. Like maggots. These things... Don't let them touch you."

"Okay," Cassidy says. "Angry alien space worms that want to eat and control me. Cool. Cool, cool, cool. No problem. I'll just make them less angry." She takes a deep breath, a step forward, and a big chance, extending her hands.

I feel calm pass through me. Almost a zen-like state. And I'm not even her target. Ahead, Sarah and Henry relax, smiling at each other. And then, the worms slide to a stop.

The screaming ahead dies down.

The mass of worms spreads out.

And then...

"Umm," Sarah says. "What...are they doing?"

Cassidy smiles wide. "They're humping."

In the hall, the mass of worms have paired off and have started going to town on each other, their wriggling bodies thrusting or being thrust upon in a churning, writhing orgy.

"You're making them...reproduce," Chuy says.

"I wasn't trying to," Cassidy says. "It's just what happened. Must be what they do when they're relaxed."

"Huh," I say. "Well, ahh, keep it up, I guess."

"As long as that doesn't happen to us," Sarah says, glancing at Henry.

"Aww, c'mon. What's wrong with a little brotherly and sisterly lo—"

Sarah clocks Henry in the side of the head with the butt of her spear.

"Okay, okay." Henry rubs his head. "Geez. I'm spoken for anyway."

Before anyone can inquire about that little gem of a comment, the shrieking grows louder again, this time all around us. "Where's it coming from?"

"The vents," Dark Horse says, aiming up at a large, grated vent.

I scan the large bridge and spot at least a dozen of them. "C'mon..."

"We're not going to be able to cover them all," Chuy says.

"I can't either," Cassidy adds. "The hump-fest is limited to the hallway unless you want to risk things getting really weird in here."

I do a quick scan of the team. Only people not wearing adaptive armor are Will and Gal. But they're immortal, so... "I have an idea, but it's kind of...insane."

"You know I'm on board," Henry says.

"We can go into space in these things, right?" I pat the armor. "With the masks on?"

"Yeah," Dark Horse says. "But I don't see an airlock." He turns to Will. "Is there an airlock nearby?"

Will shakes his head. "Not even close."

"Don't need an airlock," I say. "Or a door. I just need room."

Dark Horse eyes me, understanding the plan without me having to lay the whole thing out.

"If you don't know how to use a slew drive, find someone who does and hold on tight."

Jonas must figure out the plan because he's on his feet and angry. "My parents don't have—"

Will takes hold of Jonas's arm. "Don't need them. Neither of us. We'll be fine."

Jonas is unsure.

"We can't die," Will says. "The vacuum of space..."

"It will hurt," Jonas says.

Will nods. "A lot. But I have suffered longer and worse. This will be easy."

Jonas eyes his parents, unsure.

Dark Horse doesn't. "Move, people. Now!"

While the team gathers behind me, splitting up, I face the ship's bow, the word HELL still displayed in bold text on the screen. I access the controls on my wrist and find them intuitive as advertised. The mask covers my face and fresh air blows over my face. Okay...now I just need to hope my laser wings don't damage the suit's integrity. I've punched them through a T-shirt enough times to know they don't ruin fabrics I'm wearing. But I don't know why. Maybe cotton polyester blends are immune to the laser light, or the area of effect is a certain distance from my body? The armor is pretty form fitting, but a lot thicker than a T-shirt.

"How are you getting back?" Cassidy asks. "You don't know how to use a slew drive."

"I'll see you there," I say, and then I give Dark Horse a look that says, 'Let it go.'

He gives me a serious nod. Understands the risks. That's what we do.

"Here we go," I say, and I pop my wings. The bridge fills with bright blue light. Behind me, a few oohs and ahhs.

I put them out of my mind. Don't think about Bree, or Allie, or Jen, or my mom. I can't. I take all that emotional energy and put it into my wings. Buzzing drowns out the incoming shriek, even as Cassidy loses control of the Draugr in the hallway. My eyes glow, burning with energy, and then my whole body. "Three. Two... One!"

A beam of energy launches from every cell in my body, colliding with and evaporating the front of the ship, punching a hole through layers of hull and giving the vacuum of space access to the ship's pressurized interior. I cut the beam off as debris launches into orbit around Europa. The team follows close behind, shooting out into the void like torpedoes from a submarine. A hundred feet out, they wink out of existence, rotating back to Earth.

They're followed by a barrage of already frozen Draugr worms. I spin around to dodge or destroy those headed my way, but the worst of it is over.

Until I see someone standing at the hall's far end, unmasked and immune to the vacuum. Dressed in an intimidating red leather outfit, like a bona fide queen of Hades, is Cherry Bomb.

I was right.

She was coming for us.

We share a brief moment of recognition. She remembers our encounter in the bowling alley. Remembers how it ended, wounds on both sides, but hers more...powerful. More traumatic. I felt bad for her then. Not so much anymore. Not after seeing what she did to the world.

She slips back into the hall and out of sight, no doubt making her escape.

Not so fast, I think, charging up another shot. No idea if she'll live or die. Either way, this should be a nice old 'Fuck you.'

I unleash a blast more powerful than the last, sustaining it until it punches clear through the *Galahad,* creating a cascade of explosive failures. As the ship comes apart, I put some distance between myself and the debris. And just in time. The *Galahad* explodes into a confetti of metal and whatever else was on board.

Outrunning the debris is easy.

Getting back home...

I scan the vastness of space and find a lone blue speck.
...getting back home is the tricky part.

31

DARK HORSE

I arrive slightly off target, touching down on the beach instead of inside the house alongside my rotation buddy, Sarah. In the early days of slew driving my way through the universe, slight miscalculations were common, and sometimes humorous. But I've got loads of practice and a head full of Europhid knowledge. Accuracy is no longer an issue for me.

The slew drive must have redirected me. It's a safety feature meant to keep me from appearing inside a wall, or a person. But it normally shifts the landing by a few feet. Just enough to avoid the obstacle.

But this...

I'm hundreds of feet from the house, downhill with an alligator-filled swamp filling the void.

The only reason I'd be redirected is if the house is full.

Or gone.

From here, I should see the green shingle roof, but there's just sky and clouds.

"Scale of one to ten, how strong are you?" I ask Sarah.

"Eleven," she says.

"Great." I point to where the house should be. "Throw me."

"I'm supposed to walk?" she asks, while getting into position.

"Take the boardwalk through the swamp," I tell her. "Or...if you're strong enough to throw a guy that far... Just jump."

"Jump?" she asks, and then she scrunches her brow. "Huh. Hadn't thought of that."

With a sudden heave, I'm airborne, soaring up and over the swamp. Below me, alligators lounge in the Florida sun. If I fall short, it's going to be a bad day.

When I catch sight of the house—what's left of it—the day goes south anyway. The building is in shambles. Looks like a Lincoln Log set after Max and I would build a tower and then Godzilla-stomp it to bits.

The only thing left standing is a fifty-foot-tall gate, just like the one in Antarctica. And it's active.

But there's nobody near it, and until I know my people are safe, it's a secondary concern. Unable to control my descent, I brace for impact and hope my Europhid enhanced body is up to the task. If it's not, the adaptive armor will cushion the impact, but if anyone sees me, I'll lose a lot of street cred.

"Right behind you!" Sarah says.

Better stick the landing...

I hit the ground hard, but I manage to roll through the impact and get to my feet. Sarah touches down beside me, her legs bending less than the ground beneath her feet.

"Where do we look?" she asks.

I scan the wreckage, trying to re-form the structure in my mind. I climb into the rubble. "Over here. They should have been in ops. We need to dig down." I stop, confirming my position. "Here."

Sarah lifts a large chunk of the roof and tosses it away like it's made of Styrofoam. Debris is flung to the sides, but our progress is slow. There are a lot of layers to dig through, and we don't want anything left standing on the lower levels to collapse.

A crack of thunder announces Henry's arrival. He flies up from the beach, where the slew drives dumped the others. He lands beside us. "What happened?"

"Just dig," Sarah says, and Henry sets to the task.

The others arrive thirty seconds later, running up from the walkways.

"Everyone get back!" Jonas shouts, drawing his sword. "Now!"

Sarah and Henry, who fully trust Jonas, listen right away. Not one to argue with a Titan, I follow them out of the debris.

Jonas's face goes vacant. He's left his body again.

Henry waves his hand in front of Jonas's eyes. "So freaky when he does this. Love it."

Wreckage begins to quiver. Then rumble. Just when I think everything is going to collapse downward, it rises. Layers of debris float up and separate before floating off to the side, landing in four neat piles.

"Keep an eye on the gate," I tell Henry and Sarah. He picks her up and they fly through the floating bits of house, landing beside the gate, electricity crackling, ready for a fight.

The first body to emerge from the wreckage is Mia Durante. She's covered in blood and dust. A path through the floating rubble opens, and she glides over to us. She's deposited in the grass by my feet.

I crouch beside her with Hildy, who quickly goes about checking vitals.

"She's alive..." Hildy looks at me, concerned. "But I don't think for long."

"Durante," I say, patting her cheek. "Mia."

Her eyes flicker open. "Bree..."

"She was with you?" I ask, and I turn to Jonas's inert form. "You hear that?"

In response, the portion of the house from which Mia emerged swirls into the air, coming apart in large, sorted chunks until nothing is left.

"She's not there," I say.

Mia shakes her head, in pain. "Took her."

"Who took her?" I ask.

"Samael..." Her face twists in pain. "I couldn't stop him."

"Not your fault," I say.

"Thank you," she says to Cassidy. "For setting me free. I'm sorry I won't get a chance to know you."

Cassidy crouches down beside her, hands reached out, easing her pain. "I'm sorry we weren't here to help."

As am I. We got duped. Nearly taken out on both ends in one strike.

"It's okay," Durante says, reaching her hand up to Cassidy's cheek. "I'm going to be fine."

"But..." Cassidy gets a little choked up. "How can you say that?"

"Because this time...I'm ready." Durante closes her eyes. "This time... I'm not...coming back."

She breathes her last, head lulling to the side.

"God damnit," I grumble. I didn't know her well or long, but I had hope for her. That she could be redeemed. That she could live a life that wasn't just torture. Like the rest of us, that she could be more than whatever simulations gave birth to our reality.

The debris hanging in the air parts and spills to the side. A moment later, Jonas elastic bands back into his body. "The room is clear."

"You mean empty?" I ask, starting to pick my way closer.

"I mean," he says, straightening himself up, "No one is there. The house is empty."

I'm not really one to believe without seeing, so I stumble over the home's remains until I'm standing over a hole in the ground level's hardwood floor. It's been ripped out...but only above ops. While we were falling for Cherry Bomb's trap, Samael was here collecting our people...something I swore I'd never let happen again.

But this is different. When we lost Delgado, Chuy, and Cowboy, I was shaken, but they were fighters. Wini, Burnett, and Bree—at least in her human form—would have been defenseless if they didn't know the fight was coming.

She's making us look like fools.

Delgado steps up beside me. I can tell he's wrestling with emotions. Wini is family. Beloved. Burnett, too. And...I glance at Henry and Sarah, still standing by the gate. Bree. Fuck... When Miah finds out.

My heart breaks for him. He's a sensitive guy. *Gonna take it hard...* I look to the sky. *...if he makes it back.*

"We should get to the Mesa," Delgado say.

I nod but say, "Not yet." Then I look toward the gate. "Not while there's still a chance we can get them back."

"You lead, I'll follow," Delgado says. "To hell and back."

"Hildy, head to the Mesa. Lock it down. Get in touch with Mazzola. Have him contact the Chut'uni. Tell them it's on. Cassidy, you're with her." When she opens her mouth to complain I snap my fingers at her. "Not a word."

The loss of Bree is going to put a serious dent in morale.

Losing Cassidy might do us in.

"You should go with them," Delgado says to Bubbles.

Jonas puts his hand on her shoulder. "He's right. You're not a fighter."

"I want to be," she says.

"These guys..." Jonas shakes his head, looking down at Mia. "They're not ducks, Bubbles. Good chance we might get our asses kicked. That happens, we're going to need you safe."

She frowns, but then she bends down and scoops Mia up. "You know I'm a god, right? Probably a Titan, like you. We just don't know what I can do."

"God-hood didn't save Tartarus. Didn't save my parents. It's not a 'Get Out of the Apocalypse Free' card. Your life is a gift. A miracle. One of a kind in the whole universe now. The last of our kind born, given life by the Orphic Egg. That needs to be protected."

"You can't make me," she says. "But...they need you undistracted. So, I'll go. This time."

Jonas kisses her forehead. "Thank you, sister."

Bubbles smiles. "Sister."

I scan the destruction one last time and take a head count. We're missing three people, including Chuy. "Where are your parents?"

"Left them on the beach," he says. "They're okay. With your lady."

I toggle my comms. "Chuy."

"I'm here," she says.

"Take the proginawhatevers to the Mesa. Hildy, Cassidy, and Bubbles will meet you there. Take charge, okay? Lock the place down."

"What happened? What's wrong?"

"We lost some people," I say. "I aim to get them back."

"Copy that," she says, and I can't even say how much I appreciate the fact that she doesn't question what I'm asking her to do or point out that nearly all the people I'm sending to the Mesa are women. I could give a dozen logical reasons, but it could just as easily be argued that I'm sexist.

But hey, I'm from the 80s.

Comes with the territory.

Hildy, Cassidy, and Bubbles, with Mia in her arms, all rotate away.

"We're away," Chuy says.

Left with Henry, Sarah, Jonas, and Delgado, I say, "Anyone who feels like kicking ass and getting our people back should head to the gate and—"

Before I can finish the sentence, Henry shouts, "Retaliatory strike!" and launches himself through the gate.

He's gone for just a blink before careening back through, smashing into the home's ruins, skipping across the ground twice, and crashing into a tree, which shatters from the impact and topples down on him.

"Well," Delgado says, drawing twin drum-fed submachine guns of his own design. "That ain't good."

I tap the controls on my forearm, kick off a song, and charge the gate.

32

MIAH

Okay, so, I'm in space. Alone. Just cruising the solar system with less than two hours of breathable air remaining. No problem. Totally cool. I'm good.

I'm so good.

Like Matthew McConaughey in *Dazed and Confused,* I'm alright, alright, alright.

Totes.

One hundo percent.

I try to slow my breathing. In through the nose, out through the mouth, paced out to counts of five. I'm out of practice but trying my best. Because the string of lies I'm telling myself isn't doing the trick. Because I'm freaking out. Because I'm in fucking *space.* By myself!

The thing about fear is that you don't always know what you're afraid of until you're in the arena, red cape in hand, facing down the goddamned raging bull of the unknown. Then some ancient reptilian primal brain either says, 'I got this,' or 'getmethefuckinghelloutofhere!'

Just focus on the blue dot, I tell myself. The blue dot is home.

Why isn't the blue dot getting bigger?!

I don't know how fast I'm traveling. There's no way to gauge it. No calculations I can do. No speedometer built into the adaptive armor—that I'm aware of. So, I just keep my eyes on the prize and will myself faster.

Faster.

FASTER!

In the emptiness of space, I can't even tell if I'm accelerating, but I must be.

As long as I'm pouring on speed, without an opposing force, like friction, my speed should continue building.

That's the hope.

That's the only way I'm getting home.

Because I'll eventually need to take a breath outside this suit.

I rolled the dice on my ability to fly through open space, and on reaching insane speeds. Like...half the speed of light. That should do it. Might also crush me like a grape. Might. I'm not human anymore. Thanks to the Lux, and then Zeus's Ambrosia, I'm kind of a cosmic being now. Like the Silver Surfer. I don't have the surfboard, the shiny metal skin, or a weird-ass name like Norrin Radd, but I *am* flying through space.

And that is pretty freakin' cool.

Hoping to distract myself from the endless empty void of doom trying to kill me, I tap my way through the controls on my forearm, careful to stay away from anything that looks important. Like, you know, *air*. And the facemask. I find my way to the music player, and the perfect song to both accentuate my view, and help me relax, comes to mind.

After a quick search, I'm pleased to find and play 'California Girls' by David Lee Roth. The cheery opening keyboards make me smile, transforming my fearsome surroundings into something like a carnival at night. Festive. Lighthearted. Almost like the opening of some 1980s sitcom. Punky Brewster maybe. Then the guitar kicks in hard, followed by a snappy snare and the melodic, kinda lecherous voice of David Lee Roth declares he wishes they all could be California girls.

Fear transforms into a smile, and I find myself singing along.

I nearly miss the rapidly approaching red sphere.

What is that? I think, and I nearly crash into it. I pass by and only get a snapshot of a cratered, barren surface and two misshapen moons.

Was...was that Mars?

Did I just pass Mars? That's like...half the distance to Earth. More? I really don't know. I should have paid more attention in astronomy. I look back and find the red planet is now a shrinking speck in the distance.

I still have no idea how fast I'm going. Only that it might be the fastest anyone has ever travelled. Except for the faster-than-light people from

Will and Gal's original universe. Suppose that includes Cherry Bomb, Samael, and their angry hordes as well. But definitely the fastest dude in the universe without a faster-than-light spaceship.

That's what I'm going to tell myself, because it's pretty freakin' cool, and it keeps a positive spin on my jaunt through the solar system, even as the song ends. I'm about to play something new when I notice the blue dot I've been aiming for getting larger.

I'm almost there?

Already?

It seems impossible.

The planet expands before me, and I'm struck by a realization—

I need to stop!

"Shit!" I shout. "Shit, shit, shit, shit!"

Light blazes past me, as I will my wings to reverse thrust. The blood in my body gathers in the front, building pressure behind my eyes. The pain is exquisite, but I push through it. Vibrations surge from the laser wings, shaking with power. If I wasn't in a vacuum, they'd probably be buzzing like a planet-sized hive of angry wasps.

Through dimming vision, I see the planet's round shape expand until it's no longer round. I slap into the atmosphere, and I'm enveloped by flames. Alarms blare inside the suit, and I can feel the heat, but I'm not burned to a crisp.

At least that's something, I think, before passing out for a moment.

I come to inside a layer of dark clouds.

My wings are still extended. Still doing their thing, like they remember we're trying not to pancake into Earth.

How the hell am I already here?

Maybe the planets were aligned in such a way that the distance between them was shorter. That can happen, right? Because they're elliptical or whatever?

But that can't account for the time it took me to get from one place to another. Minutes. Just a little longer than California Girls. It takes eight minutes for light to travel from the sun to Earth, and Jupiter is a hell of a lot farther away from Earth than Earth is from the sun.

Faster than light...

Impossible.

The speed of light is the universe's speed limit. Nothing travels faster. Pretty sure I heard Neil DeGrasse Tyson say that somewhere. And that dude knows his stuff. But...Will and Gal traveled the entire universe from end to end in a faster-than-light ship. The *Galahad.* Which means there's a force of nature, of physics, that we just don't yet understand. Like Dark Horse's slew drives. Different versions of humanity figured out rotating through the fourth dimension and accelerating faster than light, but I don't need to figure it out. Just accept it. The rules of this universe were bent by Will upon its inception. I'm not sure even *he* knows all the rules. So, I just accept it and scribble *super speed through space* on my Mental Checklist of Burgeoning Powers.

The important difference between light and myself... When light strikes a solid object, it's a gentle interaction. Warmth. Energy. Life giving. When I strike a solid object... Well, I'm pretty sure it will be blood, guts, a flash of pain, a crater in the ground, and then whatever comes next.

The clouds part.

Barren ground rushes toward me.

I see craggy valleys. Distant mesas. Storm clouds in the sky, flashing with orange light.

"C'mon!" I shout. "Slow...down!"

I impact the ground with no concept of how fast I'm traveling, and then I enter the lonesome abyss of non-existence...

I wake at the bottom of a crater the size of a swimming pool. My body aches, head to toe. But I'm alive.

Holy shit, I'm alive!

I lift a hand so I can see it. All that remains of the adaptive armor is scorched shreds. I wiggle my fingers. Then I do the same with my toes.

Dead, and not paralyzed.

The air is dry and hot. Smells like ass, too. Looked like Arizona on my way down, but I must have landed near some kind of farm, or a water treatment plant.

"Ugh..." I push myself up and give myself a once over.

I'm just about naked. All that remains of the armor and clothing beneath are my black boxer-briefs, and they look like they've gone toe-to-toe with a clan of ninja moths. Shredded armor and fabric falls away, leaving me feeling pretty exposed, but also hot. Despite the heavy cloud cover, the heat easily tops a hundred degrees. I'd guess one-twenty. I've been here less than a minute, and I'm already working up a thirst.

The crater is ten feet deep. The grade isn't steep, so I just trudge up the side. I could just fly up, but I feel exhausted. Like my battery is running low. I've never felt much of a limitation before, but I think I might have just found it.

My muscles groan as I scale the curved hill, but I push myself to the top and slap my hand over the solid, rocky earth at the rim. I'm about to pull myself up and over when a helping hand reaches down to me.

"Thanks," I say, reaching up as I turn to see what good Samaritan has come to help.

"Oh, my god!" A woman screeches. "No, no, no! You need to stop me! *You need to stop me!*"

She dives over the crater's precipice and tackles me, hands wrapped around my face, teeth chattering hungrily beside my ear.

The laser blades on my arms flare to life instinctually, severing both of the woman's arms, and her head. I shove her headless body away, glad that my lasers cauterize wounds. Saved me from a blood bath.

But it does nothing to stop the woman's ability to regenerate.

Tendrils of sinew and flesh stretch out between the severed head, limbs, and body, coagulating together and then constricting. As the woman's head thumps over the rough ground, she mouths, "I'm sorry," over and over.

I back away a step.

"What the hell?" I scan the area but see nothing other than the crater and the sky. "Where am I?"

My wings extend, humming with energy, but it exhausts me.

No space flight. Nothing crazy. Just need to get away.

I rise up into the sky.

Just need to...

"What...the...fuck?"

A hundred feet up, I do a slow spiral, taking the world in. There are neighborhoods nearby. Roads. Wrecked cars. Feels a lot like the post-apocalyptic world we found when we returned from Tartarus.

Did Cherry Bomb do this? Did she win while we were gone?

Doesn't seem possible.

None of this seems possible.

A roar that vibrates through the air and my lungs turns me toward the horizon, where a behemoth charges toward me, vengeance in its eyes. I wouldn't believe it if I hadn't seen her before. Alternate Nemesis. Cherry's own design. Here to consume me.

I look for a place to run and hide. I'm in no position to fight something like Nemesis. To make matters worse, the ground is alive with movement. As far as my new eyes can see, there are zombies, capybaras, alien death worms, Tenebris, and a collection of other monstrosities I've either forgotten or have never seen before.

This place is death.

I fly higher, grunting from the effort.

At a thousand feet, I see it in the distance.

Salvation.

Miles away.

It's a gate, bright red and activated. I have no idea where it goes, but the horde charging toward it can't be good for whoever is on the far side. I put myself on a course for the wall of red energy and give it everything I've got—which isn't much.

33

DARK HORSE

The first thing that goes wrong is my music selection. It's supposed to be 'TNT' by AC/DC, but I must have done something wrong because I've got 'The Sound of Silence' by Simon & Garfunkel playing in my ear.

And that just makes me sad. Garfunkel was the name I gave to the blue Europhid consciousness occupying my mind. We've...merged since then, the two of us becoming one. But that mostly means my personality, emotions, whatever—all the human stuff—with his vast amount of celestial knowledge. And hopefully some of the logic and wisdom. But I still identify as Moses Montgomery, aka Dark Horse, still love my main squeeze, Chuy, and I still have the same passions, hates, and meh feelings about things. Like Limonaid. It's like flat Sprite. I could drink it, but... meh. Garfunkel's merger didn't change any of that.

Feels like I've lost a friend. Again.

When Garfunkel and I spoke inside a virtual space in my mind, he took the form of my childhood friend, Max. But those chats have ended, and I feel like I've lost Max again...even though everything that *was* Garfunkel is still part of me.

Fuck, this song is making me sad. I sound like a damn Hallmark movie on the Lifetime Network.

But I can't do anything about it now. Whatever sent Henry careening like a flicked jumping bean is coming through the gate. And it ain't little.

We should probably press the attack, but the freakshow stepping its way onto Earth commands my full attention.

It's thirty feet tall and hunched. Long, dangling clumps of matted hair sway from its furry body. They're green, from algae, I think. Long curved claws extend from the creature's feet, and stubby hands are at the ends of its long arms. But none of that is what makes it truly horrible. This monstrosity's mouth…splits vertically, straight up the middle of its torso. And the real estate on its head is mostly populated by a single, bulbous eyeball that swivels around, spotting each one of us in rapid succession.

Once the creature is fully through the gate, it extends its arms and unleashes an earsplitting roar. Arcs of viscous drool warble and stretch, before snapping and slapping to the ground, propelled by the air flowing from the monster's lungs. Following the sound is a smell so pungent, I nearly wretch. A few taps later, my mask is on and filtering the odor.

"Good night," Delgado says, covering his nose, before spotting my raised mask and thinking to do the same for himself. The other three might have to endure the stench. Don't have time to host a tutorial.

"I got this!" Delgado says, stepping out in front of the beast, plain as day. He raises his weapons, pulls the triggers, and unleashes hundreds of rounds in just a few seconds.

Won't be long before most of those rounds impact the ocean a mile from here. But some hit the intended target.

And they do little good.

The creature flinches from the first few impacts, but then it just curls in on itself and absorbs the abuse. There's no sign of blood or wounds. The rounds are just pancaking and falling to the ground. But the creature didn't ignore the gunfire. It protected itself. Protected its eye. Or its mouth.

The second the gunfire stops, the creature bounds forward, leaping toward Delgado, who is once again reloading in the open.

"I got this…" Delgado says. "I got this!"

He never gets to finish reloading.

Instead, he flies through the air, as though launched atop a rocket. But he doesn't land hard. He's deposited a hundred feet away, held in Jonas's protective telekinetic grasp.

"Thanks," I say to him.

He nods, and says, "No problem." Then he motions to the creature. "You want me to…?"

"Be my guest," I say.

"Cover me," Jonas says to Sarah, who leaps through the air, lands in front of Jonas, and extends her shield. Good teamwork. Behind her, Jonas draws the Sword of Mars and goes into his trance-like state.

Behind me, the fallen tree rises up and rolls to the side. Henry stands, brushes himself off, and sees the current situation. He laughs and points at the monster. "Oh, ho, ho! You're in deep shit now!"

The monster reaches down, grasps a handful of concrete foundation, and lobs it toward Sarah. She braces behind the shield and doesn't budge when it strikes. Concrete shatters, exploding all around them, but neither Sarah nor Jonas have been hurt.

Before the dust has settled, the creature has a second concrete slab ready to launch. This time toward me.

"I got you," Henry says, flying in my direction. I raise my arms and prepare to be airlifted out of the line of fire.

But it's not necessary.

As the creature's arm swings toward me, the hand comes off. Just slips away as if it was swung through a laser—or one of Miah's wings. Concrete and fist arc up and separate. A spray of blood follows them.

The monster's torso mouth roars in pain, but the creature is undeterred, turning toward Sarah once more.

But instead of attacking, it shrieks.

From between its dreadlock pubes, the creature splits in half like it's being unzippered—up instead of down. Its body quivers in agony, the shrill voice cut short as the creature's vertical mouth is severed all the way back to the spine. A moment later, it falls still when the monster's head comes apart. My stomach churns as the eye splits, oozing out like a sun-warmed Cadbury Creme Egg's yolk.

I lower my hands as Henry lands beside me, rather than helping me dodge the concrete projectile. I'm stronger than the average Joe these days, but the limits of my strength and durability haven't been put to the test. Failing would mean dying. But I'm certain I'm nowhere near the level of our new god-friends.

"Now who's feeling the sound of silence?" Henry shouts as the monster's two halves fall to either side, sinuous goo stretching out between them as a mass of organs disgorge from the core.

When Jonas snaps back into his own body, Henry gives him a thumbs up. "Dude, that was gnarly!"

"Had to be sure," he says. "After Israel."

He's right about that. "No one let your guard down. We don't know what else is coming through."

"I do," Henry says.

I turn to him, waiting for the answer. Clear my throat when he doesn't say anything more.

"Right. Sorry. I didn't count, but like ten thousand fucked-up looking baddies. Some of those apologetic zombies. And a bunch of other stuff. Only got a peek before that hairy dude Will Smithed me back through."

"ETA?" I ask.

Henry furrows his brow at me. "You trying to spell something?"

"Estimated time of arrival," I say.

"When are they getting here?" Sarah says, simplifying it for Henry. I'm pretty sure he's not dumb, but he very well could have ADHD. His mind and body are constantly in motion. I think he knows we're talking to him, but his mind is still on the other side of that gate.

But Sarah's voice registers.

He shrugs. "A minute? Two? Not long."

"Do we go through or destroy the gate?" I ask.

"Are you asking me?" Henry says, aghast.

"Myself, actually," I say, "but I'm open to thoughts."

It's an impossible question. Sever the connection and lose three people—again. Or charge through to save Bree, Wini, and Burnett, but leave this world at the mercy of whatever comes through.

As the others gather around, Henry says, "I'm the last person you want to ask...but if it were up to me, I'd go through. But...that probably means you should do the opposite."

"Wow..." Sarah says, and then to Jonas, she says, "There's hope for him yet."

Henry makes a ridiculous face at her, and offers up two middle fingers, destroying any progress he made toward being seen as mature.

"I can destroy the gate," Jonas says. "But not if the damned get through. Not without Cassidy's help."

Delgado is the last to arrive. "I know…I know what that thing is."

"Not sure it matters," I say.

"It does," he says, taking a steadying breath. "Mapinguari. It's a South American mythical creature. Also featured in one of Robinson's books. I think this guy might be important. Might know how to handle all this bullshit."

"Destroy the gate. Find Robinson. And then what?" I ask.

Delgado shrugs. "I want to get Wini back more than anyone else, but when was the last time charging in blind got the job done? We did it before, we can do it again."

I clench my fists and grind my teeth. I could tell Henry to take me through the gate and we'd be off. But then…we could be killed. We could fail. And the Earth could be overrun.

But I don't think that's the intention here. If it was, they'd have just come right through instead of taking our people first. They wanted them alive. To trade. I glance at Jonas, wondering if he'll put it together. Cherry wants his parents, and she took our people to get them.

Before I can make up my mind, it's made for me.

A bright blue streak punches through the gate, slams into the ground, and slides to a stop at our feet.

"Miah?" Sarah says.

"Close…the gate…" he says, short of breath. When no one reacts, he turns to Jonas, and this time gives an order. "Close it now!"

He doesn't know the details. Doesn't know why we haven't made that call yet. Miah's clearly been through an ordeal since we last saw him, and he came from wherever this gate leads—without rotating. That's a mystery on its own, but it can wait.

"On it," Jonas says, which feels a little funny, me not being the one to make a final call. But Miah is the other team's leader. And Jonas trusts him.

Jonas, sword in hand, goes still. The ground around us begins shaking.

Sarah stands in front of us, shield raised. "Get behind me."

Delgado shuffles up next to her. Motions to her wrist controls. "You mind?"

"Go for it," she says, and Delgado taps the screen on her forearm a few times. A moment later, the shield expands into a dome.

A moment later, the first zombie charges through the gate, sprinting toward us with woefully hungry eyes and hooked hands, ready to rend flesh from bone. It's followed by a dozen more.

When Jonas's vacant body grunts and starts curling downward, I think we're too late. But it's not enough to snap his spirit-walking-self back into the physical realm.

Just as three more people step through the gate, the two columns explode. Shards of Oxium launch in every direction, pelting the dome-shaped shield wrapped around us.

When the dust settles, and Jonas returns to his body, Sarah retracts the shield. The people who came through the gate are on the ground, shredded by the explosion. They might pull themselves together in time, but for the moment, the fight's over. That said, it's still another loss.

I crouch down beside Miah. "You okay?"

He shakes his head. "Not even close."

"She has an army," I say.

He shakes his head again, this time with wide eyes. "Not just that. She has a planet." He pushes himself up. Looks around. Sees the state of the place. "Is this…Florida? The house?" He knows it is. Even in its current state, the former park-turned-intergalactic-homestead is recognizable. He turns his now concerned eyes to me and asks the question I'm dreading.

"Where's Bree?"

34

MIAH

Dark Horse's response registers in the recesses of my mind, pumping adrenaline through my system, but my conscious mind fails to grasp the full meaning of the three words he's just spoken.

"What?" I ask.

He puts a hand on my shoulder. "They took her. Along with Burnett and Wini." He motions to a nearby body. "Durante didn't make it...but she didn't come back, either. I think she'd have wanted it that way."

I barely hear what he says after, 'They took her.'

Feet wobbly from exhaustion and fear, I stumble away. "Damnit."

I promised to look after her. "Shit." Promised her mother, who already lost everything to the Darkness. "Fuck." I should never have left her. Should have taken her with me. Should have—

"FUCK!"

Someone takes hold of my arm. Squeezes a little hard. "Hey."

In my heartbreak and rage, I spin around and throw a haymaker. It connects, full-on, with the side of Sarah's cheek. Her face barely moves. She doesn't even blink. She takes the punch, but doesn't take offense. She smiles at me while I shake out my hand. "Feel better?"

"Not at all."

"We'll get her back," she says. "You know we will, even if we have to tear the universe apart to find her."

"Yeah, man," Henry says. "We got you. Bree is one of us."

Jonas just gives me a nod. Whatever we need to do, he's in.

"We'll get them all back," I say. "Burnett and Wini are family. Cherry knew what she was doing when she took them. Knew the rest of us would do anything to get them back."

"You think they're bait?" Jonas asks.

"She'll want to trade," Dark Horse says, and he points toward the gate's ruins. "For him." A man struggles to stand beside the gate. He's wounded, but he appears to be healing. His tall, broad body and his thick beard are easy to recognize. "We saw him in Israel, too. Seemed to be in charge of the horde."

What was his name?

"Samael," Delgado says.

Henry cracks his knuckles, one hand at a time. "Can I kick his ass?"

"No," Dark Horse says. "We need him alive."

"But good job asking," Sarah says, patting his shoulder.

"What you can do," Dark Horse says, striking out toward the man, "is not let him escape."

Henry rockets across the debris field, wraps his arms around the still struggling man, and lifts him into the air. Dark Horse, Delgado, and Sarah head for the pair.

Jonas lingers with me.

Steps directly in front of me.

I don't focus on him until he gives my cheek a trio of gentle slaps. "Get your head in the game. You've been here before. When things look darkest, you shine the brightest."

My face twists. "What?"

"Something Bree told me. About you. She said it's why she lets you be her friend."

That gets a smile out of me. Sounds like Bree.

"She said that no matter what happens, you never give up. From what I've heard about you and the Tenebris, and from what I saw in Khaos, I don't doubt it. But you're not the only one. You've been a good role model for her. No matter where she is or what she's facing, that kid isn't going to give up."

"But that's the problem," I say. "She's just a kid right now. I should have changed her before we left. She was defenseless because of me."

Jonas motions to the disaster scene around us. "Look at this place. If this was Cherry, I don't think Bree would have stood a chance, either way. Burnett is smart, and prepared. Wini is tough as nails. Demon Dog might have just gotten herself killed. But that cute little blonde kid? Good chance not even a bitch like Cherry Bomb would hurt her."

I give a slow nod. Can't say I believe it but pretending will keep me on task. And I need to do that for Bree. "Thanks."

"Hell, yes," Jonas says with a grin. "I give pep talks now. On a scale of one to ten, how would you rate your experience?"

"Seven," I say.

"Seven? What the hell could I have done better?"

"A pretty smile and a curvy figure would have got you there."

Jonas gives a mock gasp. "Well, I'm rating you a three for being a sexist pig."

"I'll take it," I say and head for the others. Samael is suspended three feet above the ground, held by Henry, who is half the man's size, but clearly a lot stronger. Samael isn't a god, but he's definitely not a normal human. His wounds have almost completely healed. Immortal, which I'm noticing is a trend.

"Where did you take them?" Dark Horse asks, as we approach.

Samael just glares down at him, blood drops dangling from his thick beard. The man has a kind of crazed look about him, but it's concealing a calculating intelligence. This is a dangerous man.

Henry squeezes tighter, getting a grunt out Samael. "Do you think if I squeeze hard enough, I can make his stomach pop out of his mouth, like a frog?

"Please don't," Sarah says.

"I can get you answers," Jonas says, but then he scans the area. "Though I don't think we should hang around here. Won't be long before authorities show up, and we don't have time to chit chat."

"We're fine," Delgado says. "I've already called back the police that had been called out to inspect the disturbance. But more than that, there are people in the government—in several governments—who are up to speed on the threat. Including the President. If we need an army, we'll have one."

"But we can't coordinate all that from here, right?" I ask.

Dark Horse nods. "We're exposed here. Take him back to the Mesa. I'll catch up in a few." He turns to me. "Stay behind with me."

"How is someone gonna rotate me, while I'm holding the big guy?" Henry asks.

"That's…a good question," Delgado says. "Should we call someone back?"

"I can do it," Jonas says.

Delgado twists his lips. "How…?"

"I've been chatting with the armor's tech. We're friends now. I think I'll just need to ask nicely."

"You…can do that?" Delgado asks. "Even *I* can't do that."

"You'd be surprised what you can do when you just ask nicely," Jonas says with a wink. "Instead of sending an army of nanobots to brute force a result."

"Huh," Delgado says. "Let's see it."

Dark Horse and I step back. Jonas activates his slew drive. Instead of rotating into a slice of light, the opening to the fourth dimension expands and slides over the group where they're standing, disappearing a moment later and leaving me alone with Dark Horse.

"Come with me," he says, heading toward the beach. He's silent as he leads me across the wooden walkways crossing over swamplands filled with alligators that watch us pass with hungry eyes.

"Nice security system," I say.

"Doesn't always work."

"Right."

"But they are some of the only creatures on the planet to know what aliens taste like."

I look down at the alligators again. Fearless protectors, but helpless against the current threat, and not nearly as scary as Echidna, the mother of monsters, who was just nasty and a bit of a perv.

The walkway leads us out of the swamp, through several reed covered dunes, and out onto a flat beach that stretches far in either direction. To the south, just endless beach. To the north, the city of St. Augustine bustles, its residents and tourist population oblivious to the galactic conflict playing out in their backyard.

"Why are we here?"

"Wanted to make sure you were okay."

"Fine," I say. "Jonas already gave me a pep talk. What about you?"

"What about me?"

"Not the first time you've lost someone, right?" I ask.

He gives me a sidelong glance. "Won't be the first time I get them back, either."

"I'm not sure Cherry will trade for that guy," I say.

"Neither am I," he admits. "That's not who she's after."

I'm about to ask who when I figure it out. "The children of Chanokh... She wants Will and Gal."

Dark Horse nods. "And we're going to give them to her. What I need to know is, are you good with that...even if Jonas isn't?"

"He could stop us, you know," I say. "Probably all of us."

"Let's hope it doesn't come to that," Dark Horse says. "Now..." He squints, looking out to sea. "What is that?"

The water warbles, flickering in the sun's light. Then emerging like angels from Heaven, twenty dolphins surge out of the twinkling sun beams.

"I'll be damned," Dark Horse says, stepping into the water.

The dolphins swim up to him, led by a larger specimen with a swollen abdomen. But they don't get close.

"Hey bud, it's me," Dark Horse says, reaching out to the bigger dolphin. The animal looks unsure, backtracking a bit.

"His mind must be fading," Dark Horse says, and then he glances back at me. "Mind turning around for a minute?"

"Oookay..."

I turn my back, and I hear Dark Horse undoing his armor's zipper.

"What the hell, dude? I'm not even looking and I—"

"Shush," Dark Horse says, and his voice is followed by the sound of piss spattering into the ocean. "If he's forgetting who we are, this will help him remember."

"Dude," I say, "I'm not normally one to judge, but this is—"

"It's science," Dark Horse says, trying not to laugh now, getting a kick out of the situation. "Fuck me, I pissed on my leg. Look, dolphins recognize their friends by getting a taste of their urine. It's a thing. I didn't make it up."

"Why do you even know that about dolphins?" I ask.

"Because *this* dolphin is BigDolph, a female. Formerly BigApe, a human male and a member of my team. His consciousness was transferred into a dolphin to save his life. Her life."

I turn around to find Dark Horse doing up his zipper and the big dolphin closer now, lapping up the piss-saturated water with a long pink tongue.

"So nasty..." I ask.

But it does the trick. BigDolph comes closer. Allows Dark Horse to pet his head. "Why are you here, man?"

BigDolph rolls over, revealing his swollen belly. As he does, the twenty other dolphins start jumping and spinning, flipping and chirping in celebration. Every single one of them is a male. BigDolph's milkshake brings all the boys to the pod, I guess.

"A baby," Dark Horse says, earnestly happy.

BigDolph chirps in response, head nodding.

Dark Horse, hand on the dolphin's head says, "I'd love to catch up, but we need to go. You know how it is. Saving the world again."

BigDolph nods again.

"Steer clear of this area for now," Dark Horse says. "But if the world hasn't been destroyed after you give birth, come back and introduce us, okay?"

BigDolph lunges up onto her tail and shuffles back through the water, squeaking and nodding. Then the happy pod of dolphins turns toward the depths, and they bound away. I don't know BigDolph's story, but he's clearly a happy dude now. Good for him. Her.

"Ready?" Dark Horse asks me.

"As long as you promise to never pee in my mouth, even if I become a dolphin."

"Deal," he says, and then he rotates us inside a spaceship.

"Where are we?" I ask, as he takes a seat in one of the two cockpit chairs. Then I recognize the space. Reminds me of the Millennium Falcon, but without all the room behind for people to crowd in. And some of the controls and electronics look like they've been retrofitted with present day electronics and futuristic upgrades, including a big viewscreen at the front, rather than windows.

"*Lil' Bitch'n,*" he says.

I smile and take the seat beside him. "Bitch'n."

He shakes his head. "Naw. That comes later...when we have a target to blow up."

35

THE ARCHITECT

"Contact! Three-twenty. Hundred meters out. Location marked." The operator remains hidden, watching his targets, waiting for the optimal time to strike.

"Where?!" his frantic Cornish partner responds. "I don't see them! Mark the location!"

"I...marked the location," the operator says. "You're headed straight toward them."

"Mate, I don't see a thing. Wait..." A hail of gunfire tears through the forest, bullets pinging off the bright orange car he'd been driving, in excess of one hundred miles per hour, searching for targets while advertising his position to every enemy within earshot. "Shit! Cock! Balls!"

Smoke billows from the car.

"Yeah, all right, mate! Sure... What are you like? Sweaty little gits."

The battle ends in a blaze of glory as the orange sports car and its lone occupant explode, burst into flames, and roll to a stop. The enemy team, four in all, runs over to his corpse and begins crouching over his face.

"Why didn't you save me?" the partner says. "We're supposed to be a team."

The operator sighs. "You know people can't talk after they're—"

"Excuse me..." The feminine voice comes from outside the video game. The operator flinches at the voice, in part because it's a surprise, but also because it doesn't belong to his wife or his daughters. He spins around in his office chair, spots the invader, and toggles his microphone. "Al...I need to go. Not sure if I'll be back on tonight."

The sound of Al's complaints fades as the headset is pulled off the operator's real head.

"Jeremy Robinson?" the woman asks.

He rolls back a few feet and looks the woman up and down. She's dressed in aggressive red leather. Lots of belt buckles on her waist, arms, and legs. None of it serves any function, but it looks cool. He smiles at her. His eyes widening, pulse pounding. "Shit. Oh, shit. *Oh shit!* It's real? It's all actually real..." He laughs, nervous, but excited. "I'm really saying..." He takes a deep breath. Counts it out to five. Been years since the last panic attack. This would be a really bad time for them to return. He clears his throat. "Cherry Bomb."

"You know who I am," she says, "And you're nervous about it... But you don't seem frightened."

"I'm just honestly excited you're here. It's kind of overwhelming."

"Why?"

"This book, the one we're in right now, it's been leading up to this moment. When you will appear...or not. And here you are." He chuckles. "It's all real."

Cherry looks around the large office, taking in the computers, the entertainment system, electric drums, a guitar, and countless cabinets full of books, all of it covered in stray art, comic books, novels, and toys. "Reality inspired by a neck-beard nerd."

"Not the first time I've been called that..." Robinson says. "But it's crazy, right?"

She takes the drum stool, slides it to the center of the office, and sits down. "Why do it? Why create all this misery? Why put me through... everything?"

"I didn't know," he says. "That's not how I work. I just...make things up as I go. None of this was planned. It wasn't until Will traveled through the Seam that the idea even occurred to me."

"And yet you still left me on the *Galahad* for all that time, tortured, torn apart, eaten. Was I real to you then? Did you know what you were doing?"

Robinson shakes his head. "It was an idea. An impossible idea. I didn't know. Not for sure. Not until right now."

"When this reality comes crumbling down, it will be you who is to blame. Not me."

He nods. "I'm aware."

"At least you're honest." She smiles. "Where's your family? I'd like to meet them. Say hello."

"They're not here," he says. "In case you came."

"They know about this? You *told* them? That's a little bit strange."

"We're all a little bit strange in this house."

"Is that why you're playing a child's video game? When you're waiting for the monster of your own creation to reveal herself?"

"First of all, video games aren't just for kids." His foot bounces, shaking the floor. "Second of all, yes. It settles my nerves."

"Because you have anxiety. Depression. Nerve pain. Boo hoo. I've read your books, you know. Improved upon them. I've seen your whining, too. I'm going to enjoy the screams that prelude your death."

"How are you going to do it?" he asks. "Don't turn me to dust because that's been done. Wait, can I make a request? Can it be Nemesis? That would be such a cool way to die. Just make sure she chews."

Cherry Bomb squints at Robinson. He's an average man, thick around the middle, dressed in cargo shorts and a T-shirt emblazoned with the logo of his own book. He probably couldn't run fifty feet without getting winded or his knee popping out.

Despite all that, he doesn't seem afraid.

"Nemesis is required elsewhere," she says, and she looks annoyed when Robinson smiles like he already knew. She leans in, glowering. "*I'm* going to eat you. Alive. Slowly."

"Can you make me immortal first?" he asks. "Then you can eat me a lot. Tit for tat and all that. Sorry, that rhymed. Bad writing. So, can I be your immortal snack?"

She holds out a hand. Particles flow through the air above her open palm, coalescing—something out of nothing. Localized creation.

He leans forward. "So cool, right?"

A razor-sharp knife is left behind in her hand, the blade glowing orange with heat. "This is going to cauterize the wound as I cut. It's going to take you a long time to bleed out."

"Good thinking," he says. "Can I recommend not eating my intestines? I saw this video of a lion eating a wildebeest or something, and it was just noshing on the intestines and periodically retching watery shit. But it just kept on going. Anyway, I had pizza two nights ago, and flautas last night, so you might want to steer clear—wow, I sound like Henry."

"Henry," she says, thinking. "The young god."

Cherry places the hot blade against her own arm, carving a line that fills the room with smoke and the smell of scorched flesh.

She winces in pain, but the wound quickly seals despite the cauterization.

Robinson waves the smoke away, face twisted in discomfort. "You know, I've written about this smell, but I never actually smelled it. It's... not as bad as I thought it would be, which kind of makes it worse, right?"

"Do you do that often?" she asks.

"Smell burning people? I just said I—"

"Put part of yourself in characters?"

"Yeah... The important ones at least."

Cherry raises her eyebrows. "What part of you is in me?"

"Insecurity," he says, without missing a beat. "Fear. Anger. Jealousy."

She smiles. "You can't provoke me."

"Not trying to," he says. "Just being honest. All people are a duality. We're good. We're bad. Sometimes we make the right choices. Probably more often we don't. But we're also really good at hiding those things. The problem with you is that you're split."

"Split..."

"From Gal."

She scoffs. "I am more than she could ever hope to be. More than Will ever was."

"And yet, here you are, having a chat with the guy who dreamed all this stuff up, hoping for some insight into yourself before you...eat him alive. You're broken, Cherry, and I'm sorry about that. Had I known that the Infinite Timeline was real, that what I was writing really was this reality, I wouldn't have created you."

"Don't apologize for that," she says, leaning forward, patting his knee. "Non-existence would have been worse, right? Our biggest fear. You share that with me, too, don't you? You're obsessed with the concept of immortality because it's what you wish for yourself. Because you're terrified about what comes next. Heaven? Hell? *Torment?*' She shakes her head. "And people think *I'm* the bad guy."

He sits in silence, feeling the weight of her words.

She stands to her feet and flicks a hand toward his computer. The game disappears and is replaced by his Facebook profile. His feed scrolls down, stopping on a post that's dated August 15 at 10:31 a.m. "August 15. You wrote, 'Egads, I'm behind schedule on *Singularity*. Only halfway done. Going to have to double time to finish on deadline!'" She smiles at him. "You haven't finished the story yet. You can't control what happens. Who wins. Who lives or dies. Including yourself."

The blade glows white hot. "When I'm done with you, I'm going to find your family." She points to the headset. "Find your friends. Every single one of them will join my Torment, and watch this world burn along with the rest of Will's timeline. *Your* timeline. You did this. I want you to know that, to feel that, with every chew of your guts and every scream of your children. Know that I am—why are you smiling?"

"I mean, don't get me wrong, that was an epic Khan moment you had brewing. It's just, I don't have a great poker face."

She lowers the blade toward his face.

He winces in pain from the heat.

"Explain," she says.

Fighting the pain, he says, "I...am...Cowboy."

She frowns. Understands. Too late.

"I am gunslinger," says a Czech-accented voice that Robinson had only imagined up until now. Robinson grasps his headset, slaps it over his ears, and squeezes them against his head. Rapid fire gunshots follow, every single one finding its mark, punching straight through Cherry, spraying blood against cabinets and framed artwork waiting to be hung for the past year. Before Cherry can recover and retaliate, Cowboy, dressed in adaptive armor, wraps an arm around Robinson and drags him into the fourth dimension—out of Cherry Bomb's reach.

36

DARK HORSE

"Let's start with your name." I'm seated across from the big man in a makeshift interrogation room. Really, it's just a vacant bedroom in the Mesa, carved from the stone itself and lit by an LED fixture installed by Delgado's people years ago. When they retrofitted the Mesa for human occupation, they didn't foresee interrogating prisoners. So, we had to think fast. Cassidy volunteered her room. The furniture was easily removed by Miah, Henry, and Sarah, but there wasn't time to remove all traces of Cassidy's occupation. The walls around us are plastered with *Poppy Playtime*, *Five Nights at Freddy's*, and *Child's Play* posters. Honestly, it adds to the creepy vibe, but given the kind of place my prisoner came from, the colorful monsters probably look like what they're meant to be—children's entertainment.

"What is the value of your life?" he asks.

"More than yours," I say.

He smiles. "Maybe. But...your righteous indignation is predictable. Programmable. Tell me something new. Something I've never heard before."

"How about I hot glue a bunch of tacks to a butt plug and stick it where the sun don't shine?"

He rolls his eyes. "A vulgar attempt at humor combined with a cliché. Simple dialogue."

He looks me over, assessing me. "Have you ever considered the possibility that you're not real? That none of this is real?"

"More than once," I admit.

He smiles at that. "And?"

"I haven't seen any evidence that it's not."

"I doubt your simple mind could even—"

His deep, rumbling voice grates on me until something deep and primal awakens. I stand quickly enough to knock my chair over. Hands planted on the table between us, his face lit blue from the glow in my eyes, I say, "You couldn't comprehend the vast amount of knowledge contained in this mind, about this reality and others. Who are you to question what is real? You, who were born from a simulation, whose life was lived by another?"

He smiles up at me. "Now we're getting somewhere."

"Control yourself," Chuy says through my comms. "You're letting him get under your skin."

I turn my back to the big man. It's a risk because he's not handcuffed or bound in any way. I'm making myself an easy target, but he doesn't appear to be anything but an average big man…who's also immortal. But not like the 'Torment zombies,' who all died and stayed dead with the gate's closure.

A crew from the Mesa returned to the scene. Collected the dead, including the Mapinguari. None of them returned to the land of the living. From what I've seen, it's a mercy. Better to be dead than to serve Cherry Bomb for all eternity.

Looking at the gaping, sharp-toothed smile of Poppy on the wall, I attempt to control my thoughts. The part of me that is Europhid is easily triggered by Samael's ego and his ability to mentally turn the tables. This is going to take some pizazz. And by pizazz, I mean Jonas.

"Look," I say. "I've been playing nice. Trying to be the good guy, you know. Show you some respect. So, you can either start talking, or we can have a look inside your memories and dig the information out. Choice is yours."

He leans back in his seat. Motions to his head. "Bon appétit."

"Have it your way," I say. "Chuy, send Jonas in."

There's a knock on the door a millisecond later. Did Jonas read my mind? Did he know I was going to ask for him?

I open the door to find Henry and Cassidy. For a moment, the pair of blondes, with matching, wide, hopeful eyes look like siblings.

"Let us try," Cassidy says. "I can make him talk. You know I can."

"And if that doesn't work, you know I can get him to talk, right?" Henry asks.

They're probably both right, and I can imagine their methods, but…

"You'd call me a monster," Samael says, "and yet you're the one employing children for war."

Henry leans around me. "Bro, I'm eighteen. That makes me an adult. So, you can eat a walrus dick."

"A walrus dick?" Cassidy asks.

"Dude, walruses have dicks the size of my forearm."

Samael chuckles. "Like I said, children."

"Please, let me go first," Henry says.

"Neither of you are talking to him," I say, about to slam the door in their faces. They've completely invalidated my authority and made us look like a joke.

"I got this," Jonas says, approaching from the stone hallway beyond. Miah is with him. Both look like they're about to tear the skin off Samael. Much better.

Henry and Cassidy part as I stand aside and let the others in the room. I move to close the door, but Cassidy stops it with her foot. Looks up at me, deadly serious. "Let us know when you want the job done."

I force a smile. "Sure thing." I tap her foot away with mine and then close and lock the door, blocking out their frowning faces.

"That was embarrassing," Samael says.

Miah responds by extending a laser blade from his arm and slicing Samael's hand clean off. Internally, I'm shouting, 'What the fuck?!' On the outside, I manage to maintain an unruffled appearance.

But Miah's sudden violence isn't the strangest thing. It's Samael's response to it. Nothing at all. Not a shout of pain. Or even the slightest flinch.

"If you're wondering whether I can feel pain, the answer is yes. I've simply grown numb to it. Pain for me is as commonplace as breathing. There is nothing you can do that will loosen my tongue or break my spirit. You are all insignificant, standing in the shadow of my mistress, soon to be less than memories."

"Mistress," Jonas says, picking up my seat and sitting across from the big man. "Cute."

"The young Titan." Samael leans forward, pressing his cauterized wrist stub against his removed hand. Little tendrils stretch out between the two severed ends, pulling themselves together and quickly healing, no scar left behind. "I heard about you. My mistress does not like you. You should expect a horrible death."

"I always have," Jonas says, staring down Samael. "Your mistress is a real tough bitch, huh?"

Samael just grins.

"If she's so almighty powerful, why is she hiding behind an army of monsters? Why not come here herself?"

Samael's smile spreads wider. "She'll make her presence known when the time is right. Just a few errands to run first." He locks his eyes with Jonas's. "Should I try not to blink?"

"You can do whatever you like," Jonas says, and then he glances at me and Miah. "Hands on. Let's take a ride."

I place my hand on his shoulder. Miah does the same.

"Do we need to hold hands?" Samael asks.

"No," Jonas says, a slight grin on his face. "We do not."

The world around me comes apart, as though a tornado has just torn through the room and ripped it apart at an atomic level. We're at the core of a roaring cauldron. It's hot. Arid. Pure chaos.

All that remains of the real world is me, Miah, and Jonas. Samael is gone, I assume because we're in his mind.

"What do you want to know?" Jonas shouts over the torrent of sound, wind, and churning grit.

"The planet!" Miah shouts before I can answer. "Where is it?"

The dust twists. A portal opens, offering a glimpse of a post-apocalyptic landscape that looks a lot like Earth. A single person runs across rough terrain, terrified. A moment later, a horde of sorrowful killers pursues the lone runner. Is this an answer to Miah's question or just a look at some part of Samael's life? How long was he on the run? How many times was he caught? Eaten? Remade and eaten again?

"This is it," Miah says. "This is the planet."

"It's not Earth?" I ask.

"I thought it was. That's why I flew there. But the whole place was desolate. Like this."

"Show us Cherry Bomb," I say. "Where is she?"

Our view through the portal shifts to the left, spinning beyond to a solitary man running for his life. A hundred eighty degrees later, we're greeted by a view that churns my stomach. A hundred-foot golden statue of Cherry Bomb stands atop a stone pedestal in the middle of a mile wide crater. Inside the crater...are people, buried up to their waists, reaching desperately toward the giant idol. Worshiping. Pleading. So close, but always unable to reach the pinnacle of their desire.

"What is this?" Miah asks.

"Torment," Jonas says. "Eternal hell. Her home."

A scream builds like a howling wind racing toward us. I look for the source, but I don't notice it until it's nearly eaten my foot. It's a legless man whose body is a pasty white, slime-covered, rumply mess. Choking on phlegm, he shouts, "Don't look at me!" And then he opens his oversized mouth, attempting to take off my foot.

I step back, nearly taking my hand off Jonas's shoulder.

His hand snaps up, locking mine in place. "Don't let go!"

"We can't stay here," I say, pointing out the man, who is now swallowing a mouthful of dirt, which immediately excretes from between his ass cheeks as gritty slime. He moans in disgust at himself.

And he's not alone.

A swarm of the things come at us in unison, desperate to chew us down and discharge us, not because they're hungry, but because they can't stand to be seen.

"Psychic defenses," Jonas says.

"I thought he was just a normal guy," Miah says.

"They're not *his* defenses." Jonas sounds taxed. Being in Samael's thoughts is taking a toll. "They're hers. She's in his head!"

The slug men wriggle closer, still moaning to not be seen.

"Get us out of here, dude!" Miah says, huddling closer to Jonas.

The tornado swirling around us explodes into darkness, propelling us back to reality and into the stone wall behind us. Jonas's chair upends.

He nearly winds up on his back, but he catches himself with telekinesis and rights his chair.

Samael is already having a good laugh at our expense. "As I said. You'll learn nothing from me."

The door cracks open, kicked from the outside by Henry. It swings wide, revealing Cassidy, who says, "We'll see about that," before the door strikes the wall, bounces back, and closes in their faces.

37

MIAH

The door swings open again, this time carefully opened by Cassidy, who looks a little embarrassed by their first entrance. Henry, true to form, is unruffled by the door slamming in his face.

Samael's low chuckle makes me want to cut his hand off again. But it would only make me feel worse. He might be our prisoner, but it feels a lot like he's in control.

Cassidy, hands on her hips, looks up at Dark Horse. "You ready to let me do this?"

"Cass, I don't think—"

"Let her try," Samael says. "Perhaps I'll be dazzled by her innocence and have mercy on you all. Honestly, I'm impressed. All this effort for an old woman, a child, and a scrawny man prone to squealing."

It takes all my self-control to not assault the man. The twitching muscle on the side of Dark Horse's cheek tells the same story.

Jonas stands. "Let her try. We don't have time to pretend she can't hack it. We all know she can." He steps around Henry and leaves, probably frustrated that he still can't get past Cherry's defenses when he's supposed to be this super-powerful Titan of the mind. She's been one step ahead of us with every mental encounter.

But that's not Cassidy's thing. And unlike the goings-on of gods and Titans, there's a good chance they don't know much about Cassidy, or what she can do. It's clear that Samael underestimates her.

Cassidy raises her eyebrows and taps a foot. "Well?"

"I'll be right outside," Dark Horse says.

"You don't need to worry," she says, and she points at me. "He's staying." She tugs on Henry's adaptive armor sleeve. "And so is he. Ain't nothing old chubby log man over here can do to me without getting cut into a bazillion charred kibbles." She turns to Samael, rolling her eyes. "And yes, we know you can just heal. OooOooh, I'm special. Look at me. I can grow my body back." She glares. "No one cares, and I'm pretty sure there are planets out there full of nasty things that wouldn't mind scarfing down your roasted giblets. So don't screw with me, okay?"

"Is she going to talk me into submission?" Samael asks.

Dark Horse pauses in the door. Shakes his head. "Going to be a hell of a lot worse than that." He leaves and locks us in.

Once the door is sealed, Cassidy laughs and says to Henry, "I totally didn't expect that to work."

"I know right?" Henry says. "But you pulled it off, man. I was feeling the serious vibes."

"This is a game to you?" Samael says.

"Our friends aren't a game," Cassidy says. "But you...well, you're more of a joke."

Samael squints, but he says nothing. She's getting under his skin.

I try not to smile.

She layers her insults by approaching him. Leaning down close to his face, tempting him to make a move. Does she know I'm fast enough to stop him? Is that why I'm here? "You smell like shit," she says, leaning back, holding her nose. "Like literal shit."

"Bro," Henry says. "Did you crap your pants?"

Samael slow-turns toward Henry, but again he says nothing.

"Nothing to be ashamed of," Henry says. "Happens to the best of us, or, I guess the worst of us, in your case. Like this one time, I was—"

"Really don't need to hear this story again," I say.

"It's a different story," he says.

I sigh. "What did you eat?"

He slow grins. "A chipmunk."

I loll my head back. "What? Seriously? Man..."

"Not raw," he says, though I know he wouldn't hesitate to try it. "I cooked it...over fire...that I might have made from old insulation and Drano. Tasted like shit. And might have been a little rare in the middle. But hey, I tried right? That's what counts. Anyway, so like thirty minutes after eating the little turd, my stomach starts freaking the hell out. Balloons like I'm about to give birth, like I was stung by one of those little fuckers in the Nemesis show."

"BFSs," I say. "Big Fucking Spiders."

Henry snaps his fingers. "Those."

"Which," I say, "FYI, might be real now."

"Sick," Henry says, and then he gets back to his tale of intestinal woe. "So, I'm sure I'm about to give birth to some freaky shit, and I go to find a dumpster I can unload in."

"A dumpster?" Cassidy asks.

"Yeah, man. This was the middle of the night. Public bathrooms were closed. I'd normally have just ripped ass right where I was standing, but I was wearing a new Poison tank–stole it from Hot Topic–and I didn't want to fuck it up. Anyway, so I perch myself on the edge of a dumpster. It's pretty easy once you get the hang of it. Spread those cheeks wide and just push. Only…I couldn't fly at the time. I had to climb the dumpster like a normal person. Jumped up, leaned my bulbous stomach against the side and just–*kablooey*. Blew my ass out like a rocket ship, liquid hot chunky soup right into my pants. Down the legs and out over both feet. You should have seen the looks I got at Faneuil Hall the next–"

"Enough!" Samael roars, upending the table and lunging toward Cassidy.

He makes it a foot.

Henry and I catch him before he makes it farther. And neither of us hold back, slamming him into the stone wall hard enough to crack his skull. He sack-of-potatoes down to the floor between us.

After a nod of mutual approval, Henry and I back off and wait for the back of his crushed skull to finish stitching itself back together.

"You guys just ruined my Chucky poster," Cassidy grumbles.

Chucky's face is now covered with a splatter of blood.

Henry shrugs. "Chucky would approve."

Samael grunts. Pushes himself up onto his hands and knees. "Better." He climbs to his feet, picks up the chair, and sits back down. He looks smug and victorious.

"Wait," Cassidy says. "Do you think we're just trying to annoy you?"

Samael doesn't answer.

"Because this is just a thing we do. Bantering. Joshing around." She looks at me. "Do bad guys not banter?"

"I don't think they do," I say.

"Huh," she says. "Okay then, let's get started. Hey Google, play *Poppy Playtime* 'Huggy Wuggy Theme.'"

The sound of a buzzing lightbulb fills the room, commingling with random, creepy clanging and bumping. It's like a haunted house background track. But then a tune plays, like an electronic whistle.

"Is that 'ABCD?'" Henry asks.

"'Twinkle, Twinkle Little Star,'" I say.

"'Baa Baa Black Sheep,'" Cassidy says. "But it doesn't matter." She points to me and then beside the interrogator's chair. "You, there." She points to Henry and then to the chair itself. "You, sit."

While Henry and I position ourselves, a repeating tone ratchets up, bringing us to what I'm thinking will be a techno bass drop. And it is, kind of, but its electronic instruments and melody are unnerving. Kid has some weird taste. I get the appeal, I guess, but for Cassidy, it's transformative. She stomps around the space that used to be her bedroom, feet clomping to the beat, knees reaching up to her shoulders. She lowers her head, scrunches her lips, and holds her arms out, elbows bent downward, fists opening and closing to the music.

"Okay, I don't get freaked out," Henry says, "but even *I'm* a little weirded out, right now."

Samael watches the display, clearly confused. He looks at me, questioning, and I shrug.

"You ready for this?" she asks Henry.

They'd clearly already discussed the game plan.

"What do you need me to do?" I ask.

"If he moves," she says. "Cut his head off."

She galumphs her way over to Henry and stops behind him with a one-two stomp of her feet. She grasps either side of his head. A smile spreads across her face that is eerily similar to the Poppy poster on the wall behind her—wide and toothy.

"Here's the thing, Mr. Asshole Kidnapper man. You made a few big mistakes. The first was taking three people that everyone here cares about. Enough to do some...questionable things to get them back. The second, was not knowing about me. And not *really* knowing about my new friend Henry." She gives his head a shake. "You can tell him the rest."

"Thing is," Henry says. "I tell everyone that my amygdala is fucked up. That I can't feel any fear." He glances at me for a moment, and then he continues. "But...that's a lie. I'm like that guy with the pointy ears."

"Legolas?" I ask.

"Spock," Cassidy says, shaking her head like I'm bonkers for not getting it right.

"That guy," Henry says. "I feel...everything. I just... I bottle it up. Keep it contained. It's a..." He looks back at Cassidy. "What'd you call it?"

"Defense mechanism," she says. "You see, Mr. Fat Idiot, I can feel people's fear...and I can make it worse. I can also move it from one person to another. So even though you're acting cool and comfortable, like you don't give a shit about what's happening to you, I know you're terrified. I know your life is miserable. I know you'd kill yourself if you could. So, you can talk...or you can carry the burden my pal has been carrying for his whole life—all at once. What will it be?"

Samael just glares back, but this time I can see a hint of the fear Cassidy can feel.

I struggle with the moment. As much as I want Samael to start blabbing, I also want to give Henry a hug. His life has been...tumultuous from the get-go. Beaten by foster parents, living on the streets, struggling to survive, and ever since discovering his otherworldly parentage, a never-ending battle against unnatural freakshows. All while feeling a river of fear...but never showing any of it. Not even a trickle. I've got a newfound respect for the guy, but it also means he's a bit more responsible for the inappropriate things he says and does, though I now suspect a lot of it has been to maintain the act.

"You had your chance," Cassidy says, and then she whispers to Henry. "Are you sure?"

Henry nods and Cassidy looks at me. "Better stand back."

I move back against the wall, ready to move if Samael does.

Then my emotions start to churn. I might not be far enough back. But I can see by the look on Samael's face that I'm not getting the worst of it.

Henry's body tenses. He grips the chair's armrests, bending the metal. Teeth grinding, tears running down his cheeks. And then, he relaxes.

Cassidy grins at Samael, fiendish.

She leans over Henry's head, looks Samael in the eyes, and says. "Boo!"

38

DARK HORSE

A muffled scream behind the door startles me. I turn to Jonas for his thoughts just in time to see him hit the ground. He lands flat on his back, but the blow is eased by the adaptive armor, which inflates in the back just long enough to absorb the impact. Then it deflates and eases him to the floor. The moment his head touches down, his eyes blink open.

He looks up at me, crouched over him.

"You okay?" I ask.

"Fine," he says, but he doesn't try moving. "Wasn't ready for that."

"For what?"

"Best way I can describe it is an emotional slap." He pushes himself up. "But it missed me."

"Looks like it took you out," I say.

He shakes his head. "That was more like the wind kicked up by an eighteen-wheeler at a hundred miles per hour, missing you by a foot."

I offer him a hand. He takes it, and I pull him to his feet.

"I'm thinking we need to find a way to help you regulate your input levels."

He nods. "When it comes to controlling my own emotions, I'm a pro. Other people's emotions—it's like a tidal wave. That..." He glances toward the door. "Felt like an asteroid impact."

"You need an emotional surge protector."

"Sounds about right," he says. "Did I miss anything while I was out?"

"Arrggghhh!" Samael's voice cuts through the air once more.

"Just that," I say. "How you feeling now?"

He squeezes his lips together, fighting the wave of emotional energy. I feel it, too, the hairs on my arms rising. Then it passes.

From inside the room, "Please. God. Please. Oh, God. I don't... I can't..."

"Is that Samael?" Jonas asks. "He sounds—"

"Sad," I say.

"Broken," Jonas adds.

Sobbing follows. Really heartbreaking stuff. From the core.

It sounds...honest.

The door opens slowly. It's Miah, looking sober and pale. He steps back, revealing Henry, pitched forward over the table, weeping quietly. Cassidy is leaned over him, rubbing his back. "It's okay," she whispers. "You're okay. It's all gone now."

She's not just comforting him with words. She's infusing him with positive vibes like only she can, replenishing whatever was taken from him.

He sits up, wipes his eyes, and smiles at me. "That sucked."

"What did you do?" Jonas asks.

"Samael had buried his conscience," Cassidy says. "We dug deep and brought it to the surface. Let him feel pain again. All of his. All of Henry's. All at once." She helps Henry stand and then looks up at me. "He'll tell you whatever you want now."

I stop her before she leaves. "Hey."

She looks up at me, her big blue eyes swirling with emotion. Tearing into people's emotions isn't easy for her. "McCoy would be proud of you." When Henry glances back at me, I add, "Maybe even you, too."

Henry grins and then lets Cassidy lead him out of the room. She pauses in the doorway, gives me a sullen look, and then closes us in her room.

This shit is taking a toll on my people. It's time for some answers. I turn my full attention to Samael. He's no longer seated. He's fetal positioned in the room's corner, quivering like a freshly hatched bird, cold and alone.

Looking down at the man, I have nothing but contempt. He's the enemy. He took our people. I crack my neck one way and then the other, stepping closer, prepared to haul his crying ass up and shake the answers out of him.

I'm stopped before I can.

It's Miah, holding my arm. "Let me try first?"

Not sure what he's getting at, or if he has any interrogation experience, but I'm learning to trust him...and it was his friend that made the sacrifice that got us here. So, I back off and let Miah do his thing.

"Hey, buddy," Miah says, crouching down beside Samael, his voice sweet and gentle.

Makes me a little sick to my stomach. This asshole doesn't deserve our mercy. He—

"Hey," Jonas says, waiting for me to make eye contact. "Let him do his thing."

"What's his thing?" I ask.

"Building trust."

That shuts me up and cools me down. I'm seeing red right now. Would probably kill the man to get answers—if that was even possible. I back up and lean against the wall. Miah might very well be the best man for this job. So, I watch him work and try to take notes.

"You're okay now," Miah says. "It's over."

Samael peeks out from under his arm. "Is...she gone?"

I tense. Miah's made himself vulnerable. An easy target. But I think that's the point. To gain trust, he's showing trust, even at great personal risk.

"Who?" Miah asks, despite the answer being clear. The man is horrified of Cassidy.

"She can't see me here, right?"

"The room is secure," I say, and Miah shoots me a visual 'shush.'

"You're safe here. No one is going to hurt you. And if anyone tries, I got your back."

The thing that makes Miah so effective at what he's doing is that even I have no doubt he means it.

"Why?" Samael asks. "I've done...so much."

"Because we're the same," Miah says. "I felt your pain, man. I know your pain. Understand what it can do to your mind. To your heart. You stop feeling. Stop caring. But for you...it was worse. Worse than my PTSD. Worse than Henry's pent-up anguish." He glances at me again. "Worse than losing a friend. Because it was..."

He waits, hoping Samael will fill in the blank. The first step toward a conversation that will elicit information. Miah was a soldier. Served, same as me. But they don't teach this kind of interpersonal interrogation technique in the military, or even in the CIA. He didn't learn this in his professional career…which means… I try not to smile. He learned it from being a big brother. A son. And a good fucking guy.

It's been so long since I've lived a normal life among normal people that it's nice to know that some really good ones still exist.

"…infinite," Samael finally says. "Unending. Torture."

Miah offers both of his hands.

Samael considers allowing himself to be helped, but he looks to me and Jonas, his trust extending only as far as Miah.

I'm surprised when Jonas steps forward, offering a hand as well. "We're not going to hurt you. We just need your help, to make sure no one else gets hurt."

Samael nods, face screwing up with emotion. He's close to bursting again, but then he takes their hands. As they pull him up, I do my best to follow their lead, righting his chair and sliding it into place at the table. They sit him down, and Miah takes the opposite seat, turning it around backwards before sitting, crossing his arms over the back, and lowering his chin.

Jonas heads back to the side of the room and motions for me to join him. Feels weird to not be running the show, but I'm clearly not the best man for the job. I head back to the wall and do my best to hide the rage I feel toward the man responsible for McCoy's death.

When the quiver fades from Samael's breathing, Miah asks, "You want to tell me how this happened? Start at the beginning?"

Samael frowns. "In the beginning… Those words held meaning to a friend of mine, once. But he wasn't really a friend. Wasn't even really a pastor. He…was Gal."

"The AI chick," Miah says.

Samael nods. "And I wasn't me. I was…him."

"Who?"

"William Chanokh. The man the world had been built for. Everything I am, that I believed I was…it was all just him. I believed the world wasn't real. That most of the people around me were NPCs. Artificial creations meant to entertain me. To keep me distracted from the fact that reality wasn't real."

His faces screws up. Uncomfortable. Tears slide down his cheeks.

"So, I killed myself. He killed himself. But not to end it. To find the devil. To destroy the simulation. For him, it was the simulation's end. Off to another life. JR-00073 – Exo-Hunter. Whatever that means."

I tense and say, "Me."

Samael turns in my direction. "What?"

"He lived my life after yours. I'm the Exo-Hunter."

He blinks. This is a revelation. Whatever Cherry Bomb might know about us, I don't think Samael is privy to the same information.

"You're from the Great Escape?" he asks.

I shake my head. "An afterthought. A subconscious addition to the universe he created."

Samael is deep in thought for a moment. "You *know* him?" His eyes dart around the room, like he can see through the walls. "Is he *here?*"

For a moment, I think he's going to revert. Get violent. Instead, he deflates.

"I'm the worst kind of NPC," he says. "One who believed he was real. But William is real. I'm...programmable. Controllable. Pitiful." He pounds the table with both of his fists. "Please. If you know how. Can you kill me?"

Miah reaches out both hands. Places them on Samael's clenched fists. "How about you try something different?"

Samael waits.

"First, you need to take ownership of what you've done. Then...you need to push back. Make it right."

"Redemption?" Samael huffs. "There is no redemption for the devil."

Miah smiles. "I was a devil once. A Tenebris. You know them."

"Horrible creatures," he says.

"They turn people into demons," Miah says. "My skin was blackened. Charred. My hair had fallen out. And I craved...unholy things. But now... Now..."

Miah stands up. The room fills with luminous blue, his laser wings unfurling.

For a moment, Samael is awed. But it's quickly replaced by shame. "The Lux. They resisted. They shouldn't have. You might be the very last of them."

"I fought back. I saved people. And I am *still* saving people. You have the chance to do the same. Right here. Right now. You can shed that old life, kill it dead, and be reborn as someone different. Someone better."

"And...what might that be?" He's dubious. Rightfully so. I have no idea what Miah could be offering, but if it's more than a life sentence in a cell the size of this room, it's too much.

Miah holds out his hand to shake. "A friend."

39

BREE

Dear Diary,

I didn't really mean it last time. When I said I was going to kick Miah in his privacy. But now I mean it. I'm really going to do it. Probably more than once. I'm here because of him. Wini is hurt because of him. And Burnett is crying because of him.

We're in a rocky place. Just a dark hole with no doors or windows. Burnett thought we might suffocate. The air is stinky, but at least he was wrong about that. He hasn't had any bright ideas to save us. And he's a smart guy. I think that means there aren't any bright ideas that get people out of rock prisons. Not without our armor.

Luckily, I was still wearing my pajamas under my armor when Cherry dissolved it, so I'm bunnied up and cozy. Wini is down to a 'sports bra, booty-shaping Spanx, and a pair of socks.' Burnett hasn't told us what he's wearing, but I'm betting it's tighty-whities, skid marks and all.

He didn't handle being kidnapped very well. Kind of freaked out. I don't blame him. It was scary. Especially when Mia died... Wini and Burnett didn't see, but she saved me. Put herself on top of me. I feel bad for her, but also embarrassed, because saving people is my job, but I'm just totally helpless right now.

I could have stopped them...if Miah didn't stop me.

I don't understand why he didn't let me go, or at least change me. It's just so stupid. I might hate him now. This is all his fault.

I'm not sure what else I could do to show him I can handle being Demon Dog. Probably age ten years. Or twenty.

"How's everyone doing?" Wini asks.

"S-still cold," Burnett says, a shiver in his voice.

"How about you?" Wini asks. Her voice is louder now, so I know she's facing me, even though she can't see me.

"I'm fucking dandy," I say.

"You talk to your mother with that mouth?" Wini asks.

"No. This is my stuck-in-a-stone-prison-because-Miah-is-a-dick voice."

"Mmm," Wini says. "You know it's not his fault, right? He was trying to protect you."

"I don't *need* protecting."

"Like it or not," Wini says. "You're eight."

I clench my fists, but I don't punch anything because I know it will hurt. "When we were in Khaos, fighting a giant god, surrounded by monsters, I'm the one who saved everyone. I dug into its neck. I crawled up into its brain. No one else could do that. No one else would have thought of it. And no one…I mean no one…ever sees me coming. And not because I'm like a ninja or something—but because. I'm. Eight."

"You're a secret weapon?" Burnett says.

"Exactamundo," I say. "And if I could change myself, I'd show you."

"How does Miah do it?" Burnett asks. "How does he change you?"

"Puts his thumb on my forehead, swipes it to the side. There's a symbol there. A death rune. Something the Tenebris did to Miah and me. His is gone most of the time. Mine is hidden, until he uncovers it with his light or whatever. Then I change back into one of them. Into a demon… but still me."

"The Tenebris were defeated by you and Miah, yes?" Burnett asks. "And have since been exterminated. They don't sound very powerful."

I'm almost offended. But the Tenebris were jerks. I'm glad they're dead. And Burnett is missing a detail. "Maybe. But I'm different. *I* ate a dessert."

"I think she's got shell-shock," Wini says.

"Not a normal dessert. It was Ambrosia."

"Like with the marshmallows and Jell-O?" Wini asks.

"Yup, but also like Ambrosia."

"Not following you, kid," Wini says.

“Ambrosia was the food of the gods. It bestowed immortality and power to all who ate it. That was how Apollo became the god of just about everything. Prophecy. Truth. Sun. Light. Healing. Plagues.”

Burnett shuffles in the dark. “It seems to me that if Ambrosia granted Apollo so much, perhaps there is more to your abilities than simply being a Demon Dog?”

“Like what?” I ask.

“Perhaps…you don’t need Miah to change your form anymore?”

“I’m not sure this is a wise–”

I cut Wini off with a shush.

“Miah doesn’t get to tell me what to do. I’m not a normal little girl. And let’s be honest, I’m the only chance you two have of getting out of here.”

“The others will–”

I cut her off again. “They could be dead.”

That drops a silence bomb on the black void.

“Don’t say that again,” Wini says.

I cross my arms even though they can’t see me. “It’s true, and you know it.”

“If it were true,” Burnett says, “*we’d* be dead.”

“Or forgotten,” Wini adds. “How long has it been, since we were put in this hole?”

“Five hours, fifty-seven minutes, thirty-five seconds,” Burnett says. “And counting. Not great…”

“Took longer to get Chuy, Dan, and Cowboy back when they were taken.”

Burnett lets out a sigh. “But…I was tracking the slew drives. And now…now I am here. But…what if Bree… What if the act of Miah wiping his thumb over your forehead to activate your transformation isn’t physical. Meaning the light he emits doesn’t change you at all. Doesn’t reveal the death rune. What if…what if that’s all you?”

“I don’t get it,” I say.

“Think of a priest,” Burnett says. “An anointing. The sign of the cross, perhaps. It doesn’t change the recipient’s physical body, but it can change the way they see the world and themselves. Perhaps Miah’s anointing…

absolves you. Of harbored guilt. Of past trauma. The things that make you human."

"So...to change on my own, I'd have to do what? Forgive myself or something?"

"Do you have something to forgive yourself for?" Burnett asks.

"Once again, this is a bad idea," Wini says. "She's *eight*, Burnett."

Burnett sighs. "Fine."

Dear Diary,

I'm getting pretty tired of adults. Thinking they know everything. And what's best. Like their life experiences can somehow guide a Demon Dog god. Dog god? That's funny. God dog. Good dog? Maybe all dogs are secret gods?

Whatever.

Burnett is still nice, I guess, but I don't really like his idea.

It hurts in a weird way.

And the point is, I can do what I want. When I want. And there isn't anything anyone in this stupid hole can do about it.

I place my thumb against my forehead. Same way Miah does. Then I slide it to the side, telling my body to change.

Demon Dog, here I come!

Nothing happens. Well, I definitely can't shoot laser light out of my hand, but maybe it's like Burnett says. Absorbing? Something like that. A fancy word. But I think he meant forgiving.

What do I need forgiveness for?

I'm eight!

I haven't done anything wrong. Not really. I mean, I've killed stuff, but only bad stuff. No one else has died because of—

Shit. A memory slithers into my thoughts.

I normally ignore it. Imagine a nuclear bomb is exploding on it, so it can't become a real memory. Because I don't want to think about it. I don't want to remember it. Ever.

But…forgetting it, also means forgetting him.

My brother.

I face the memory and let it come. I see him in the kitchen. Screaming because a Tenebris came in. He stood between it and me, even though he was afraid enough to pee his pants. Then it grabbed his arms.

And tore them off.

After that, everything is kind of a blur, not because of my memory, but because my eyes had blood in them. But I could hear fine. Could hear it eating him. His bones breaking. His last wet breath, and a whispered, "Sorry."

I thought I was next. But the monster just slipped its face out of its smokey bubble, its black eyes looking into mine, and smiled. Then it was gone. It didn't eat me because I'm one of them. One of the monsters that ate my brother.

I try not to cry, but it's impossible.

Arms wrapped around my knees, I squish my face into my legs and cry. Hard. Too loud to not be heard.

"Dear," Wini says, but whatever is coming next is cut off by a rumbling sound.

I look up and wipe my eyes. The ceiling opens like lips, like we're inside a mouth. Orange light flickers down from the cloudy sky above, revealing Wini, covered in her own dry blood, and Burnett in tighty-whities. Called it, but no longer find it funny. He just looks sad and afraid.

Above us, a lady in tight red clothes hovers into view. I recognize her from the house.

Cherry Bomb.

The bad guy.

She glides down to the bottom of our hole. After shooting evil eyes at the adults, she crouches down in front of me and wipes away my tears with her thumbs. "I heard someone crying. We can't have that, can we?"

She stands up and offers me her hand. "Can I show you something cool?"

Dear Diary,

I think it's time for me to grow up. Bye-bye.

Thanks for listening.

Bree

I take Cherry Bomb's hand and let her carry me up and out of the hole, smiling because there is no one left to tell me what to do, or why I should feel bad about myself. Wini shouts something, at me or at Cherry Bomb. I don't know because I'm not listening. Not anymore.

40

DARK HORSE

This is a bad idea. *Really* bad idea.

One handshake and now we're outside the cell, walking through the Mesa, en route to a meeting I'm not sure should even happen. Never mind the fact that we're giving Samael an impromptu tour of our facility. Delgado is our guide, and he seems to be avoiding anything important, but this could be a strategic blunder on a cosmic scale.

Problem is, I don't want to sow dissension in the ranks. The moment Miah agreed to this, I had to play along. We need our people unified, especially in front of Samael. If this goes sideways, Miah and I will have a one-on-one chat in private. Until then, I'm Team Miah.

On the outside.

Inside I'm ready to draw my sidearm and put a few rounds in Samael, just for kicks.

"I'm with you," Jonas says, glancing over at me, either reading my mind or just reading my face. We're at the back of the pack, both of us tense. "I've put down people who've done far less. I could drop him with a blink, and no one would ever know what happened."

His lopsided grin says he's joking, but it's tempting. "We still need answers."

We walk in silence for a moment, ten feet behind Henry and Cassidy, who are having an animated conversation about a cartoon. They're following Samael, as Delgado and Miah lead the way.

"What's that like?" I ask. "Killing people…who aren't fighting back?"

"Job like any other," he says, but then he smiles. "It…was all I knew, honestly. They were bad people. Never felt bad about giving them the ol' Mind Bullet."

"Which is super cool, by the way."

"Until someone else controls it to commit mass murder," he says. "That's not so fun." He looks lost in a memory for a moment, then snaps out of it. "But it was these guys who really changed me. Miah. Bree. Sarah. Not so much Henry."

That gets a laugh out of me.

"Kid has more depth than I thought," I say.

Jonas nods. "I suspected, but he's good at hiding it. Aside from Miah, they're basically kids, but they've been through some unimaginable shit and come out clean. Doing the right thing. This—" He motions to Samael. "—seems counter-intuitive to you and me, but we've been knee deep in darkness for a long time. It's where we're comfortable. These guys... they're fueled by hope."

"Like Cassidy," I say. "And Hildy. Burnett. They'd be on board with this plan."

"Might as well give it a try, right?" He gives me a smile. "And if it doesn't work, we can blow something up, and get creative with our interrogation techniques."

"Enhanced interrogation techniques don't generate reliable intel," Chuy says from behind me, catching us both off guard.

"God damn, woman," I say, "were you raised by ninjas?" I swat Jonas's arm. "And what the hell man? I thought you were supposed to sense people coming or something?"

"Only when I'm trying. Most of the time, I'm trying not to. But...she's also pretty quiet." He points to his head. "Up here." He lifts his hands when Chuy levels a raised eyebrow at him. "Not because there's nothing there. You just have a lot of self-control. Discipline. Good stuff."

"How long were you there?" I ask Chuy.

"You'll never know," she says, aware that mysteries drive me nuts.

I decide not to give her the satisfaction of asking again. "So, you on board with Operation Forgive and Forget?"

"You think that's what's happening here?" she asks.

"Sounds about right," I say.

She looks around me, observing the group, the way Samael keeps glancing at everyone around him, especially Miah and Cassidy.

He looks befuddled.

Jonas takes a stab. "Operation Kill Him with Kindness?"

"Closer," Chuy says. "If thine enemy be hungry, give him bread to eat; and if he be thirsty, give him water to drink: For thou shalt heap coals of fire upon his head, and the Lord shall reward thee."

"That from, like, Sun Tsu or something?" Jonas asks.

"The Bible, actually. Proverbs. And the point isn't to cause them discomfort. That's just the vehicle that takes you from point A, aggression, to point B, shame, and eventually reconciliation."

"You think that's possible?" I ask.

"We traveled through time, twice. Can bounce around the universe through the fourth dimension. We're sharing a hallway with a literal god—" She tilts her head toward Jonas. "And a Titan. And we're going to have a pow-wow with the creator of this dimension of reality, who also happens to be the man who lived his life—" She lifts her chin toward Samael, and then looks toward me. "And yours."

"Point taken," I say.

"Atta boy." She gives my face a slap and pushes past us, joining Henry and Cassidy, hand by the weapon on her hip. She's playing it cool, but she's ready to quick draw the moment Samael shows more aggression than a golden retriever puppy.

We arrive at our destination a moment later. The mess hall. Normally full of personnel—some hired from the outside, most formerly prisoners of the cryptoterrestrial that made its home here. The monster that abducted people and used their bodies to rebuild its own, extending its life. The rest of the folks that live here now are a gaggle of young people like Cassidy, but less interested in operations. Most are happy to stay here in the shadows, working with Delgado, righting the wrongs done to others like them. They fought with us against the misguided Chut'uni, but they've stayed hidden from the outside world since.

When we enter the mess hall, I'm not surprised to find it mostly empty. Hildy is here, with Sarah and Bubbles. They're sitting atop one of the many long tables, feet on the bench, quietly discussing who knows what. Probably having the same debate as Jonas and me. I sense that Hildy would agree with us, maybe Sarah, but I have no idea where

Bubbles would land. She seems to be good natured overall, but her obsession with killing a duck is a little off.

All three stand at our approach. Hildy glowers at Samael. I might have been wrong about her. Looks like she might tear his head off herself.

Sarah pats the table's bench, leaving a dent in its metal surface. "Have a seat."

Bubbles appears the least angry, but I can't blame her. She's been a...physical being for just a few days. All of this must be new and strange to her.

Samael does as he's told. The rest of us spread out, sitting on the surrounding tables in small groups, all facing Samael.

Henry sits beside me, and Sarah joins him. Leans over to look at his face. "You all right?"

"Fine," he says.

Sarah turns her gaze to me, asking the same question about Henry without saying a word. All I can do is offer a subtle shrug and close my eyes. It's not exactly a reassuring gesture, but it's not my place to reveal Henry's deepest secret—that he's just like the rest of us: afraid. He's just really, *really* good at burying it deep and paving over it.

"Well," Samael says. "Where are they?"

Cassidy plants her hands on his table's bench, flips head over heels, and lands cross-legged in front of him. "Patience," she says, booping his nose, "is a virtue. Learn it. Live it. Love it."

The slightest of smiles forms on Samael's face. Cassidy's charm offensive is having an effect. But for all we know, he's smiling as he imagines strangling the life from her. I'd have Jonas look, but Cherry's been in his head. Left some nasty surprises. So, I'll let Cassidy's brand of psy-ops play out.

A pair of footsteps echoes in the large subterranean chamber. I see her first. Gal. Now dressed in adaptive armor. Part of the team, I guess. As she approaches the table, Cassidy rolls to the side, off the table. She plops onto the bench in front of me.

Gal sits down across from Samael, and I'm surprised to see tears in her eyes. "Samael..."

"You remember me...Ezekiel?"

"I'll be the first to admit, that simulation was...extreme."

"It was tame compared to what came after," he says.

"You understand that wasn't me."

"But it *was* you. A part of you. Just as I am part of Will. Who he would be, given the same parameters. A killer. Cold hearted. Easily controlled. You made me like this. Made me who I am." He rolls his neck. "Whatever I have done. Whatever I will do. *You* are responsible."

"Help us undo the damage," Gal says.

Samael sighs. "No Bible verses for me? No righteous arguments or wrestling with your creator? You're not much like him anymore. My old friend. It's funny, I was obsessed with the idea of an architect. But it was *you* the whole time. And now, the irony, I have become the architect of this reality." He leans forward, elbows on the table. "This is real, right? I'm not going to wake up in one of those God-damned VCCs only to remember that I'm still Will?"

"This is real," she says.

"For now..."

Well, that's fucking ominous, but Gal doesn't bite.

"Ready to see him?" she asks.

Before Samael can respond, Will, who must have snuck into the room, or been here all along, takes a seat beside Gal. Like her, his emotional response to Samael's presence is quite different from the rest of us. It's like he's looking at a photo of himself after a car accident, remembering the pain, feeling sorrow for the state of this man he once was.

"Hello, me," Will says. "It's me again."

41

MIAH

"Did he just quote Megadeth?" I ask Hildy. I know she has the answer. She's an encyclopedia of all things musical and pop-culture. But she doesn't say a word. She just watches the scene playing out, white knuckling the table's edge with both hands.

"I imagined our meeting differently," Samael says.

"How so?" Will asks.

"My hands around your throat."

"You know that wouldn't achieve anything, right?" Will asks.

"Indeed," Samael says. "But catharsis is good for the soul."

"You believe in a soul now?" Will asks.

Samael shrugs. "Only that reality is real this time around. Haven't figured out what comes next. Though I'm not sure there ever will be a next for you and me." He glances at Gal. "Or you."

"Cherry doesn't want me dead?" Will asks.

"A thousand times over. Maybe a million. A trillion. Who knows how long it will take her thirst for vengeance to play out. But in the end... When you are no longer you? When she has absolute control, and you feel nothing but fear in her presence, she'll keep you by her side. For eternity. A subservient lapdog."

I know Samael is describing Will's future, but I suspect he's also revealing his own situation.

"Did you know that this universe of yours is expanding?" Samael asks. "In my reality—the one you lived on my behalf—the universe began with a big bang, expanded out, and was destined to one day collapse in on itself. But not here. In your reality, the donut is always expanding, the voyage from beginning to end taking longer and longer with each revolution. You really did create an infinite timeline to live out your infinite life. But that will be used against you. As with all things, the potential for evil rivals that of good. Infinite good. Infinite evil. You are the creator of both, and thus have truly become God."

"I didn't create anything," Will says. "I don't have that kind of power. Never did. I just...made some modifications at the source."

Samael smiles. "Modifications that fluttered their way out through reality, turning your new Great Escape into a freakshow of strange alien worlds, space travel, unlimited possibility, and people whose abilities defy the very laws of physics, all inspired by the fictional drivel of an ancestor you're both obsessed with." He looks back and forth between Will and Gal, then he leans forward, like he's telling a secret. "You understand that they're no longer laws if there are exceptions, correct?"

Will squints. "What do you mean?"

"While you were under the gun to create all this, and you leaned on your own experiences in the Great Escape to create it, Cherry Bomb had time—endless time—to learn how to modify reality...locally. We never could crack the code that came so naturally to you. Had she done that, this reality and everything in it would have been destroyed in an instant. Though she seemed content to dismantle it over time. Believed it would be harder for you to endure. And that's all she really wants. All she ever really wanted. To control you. Torture you. And honestly, I'm relieved to be here."

"Because you want to do the right thing and help us?" Cassidy asks, innocent eyes wide and hopeful.

Samael shakes his head.

"Because it means my torture is nearly over."

He looks Will in the eyes. "Once she has you, I will no longer matter. And that..." Shameless tears drip from his eyes to the table. "...that is something I cannot express."

"This is interesting and all," Dark Horse says, taking a seat beside Will, "but we need to get to the part where you start spilling on what she's up to and how we can stop it."

"I am surprised you don't already have the answers to those questions," Samael says.

"We've been a little busy trying to fend off your little incursions and mourn our dead."

"And evade a carefully laid trap," he adds. "That was my idea."

Henry slides off the table he's sitting on. "Is it just me, or is this guy asking for a beat down?"

"Big-time beat down," Sarah says, though she hasn't budged.

Dark Horse holds his hand out toward them, stopping Henry in his tracks, which is impressive.

"Please," Dark Horse says, sounding uncommonly…gentle. "Fear is not love. You risk nothing by telling us."

"You have no concept of what I'm risking," he says, "by speaking to you at all."

"We can offer you freedom," Will says.

That gets everyone's attention. All around the room, the team tenses.

"Do not offer me things they will not allow," Samael says, glancing at the angry faces around him.

"Only one way to change that," Will says. "Freedom. From me. From Cherry. From the Great Escape. From the Architect. It's all you've ever wanted."

Samael stews in indecision for a moment. Then he says, "The solar system's planets are all part of an intricate gravitational balancing act, like a finely tuned watch, all its component parts working in unison to keep things moving. As they revolve around the sun, gravity tugs them back and forth. It's a measurable, observable constant that could only be disturbed by the presence, by the emergence of another gravitational force."

"Please don't Yoda this shit," Chuy says. "Plain English for those who aren't immortal, AI geniuses, or infused with nanobots."

"Found it," Delgado says, looking like he's in a trance.

Chuy rolls her head, popping a vertebra. "Found *what?*"

Delgado pales.

Whatever he's seeing, it's something the rest of us can't.

"Holy shit…"

"Unholy," Samael says. "But yes."

"What is it?" Dark Horse asks.

"A planet," Delgado says, blinking back to reality. "Another Earth."

I bound to my feet. "I told you! The hell planet. I was there. It was real."

"Completed just weeks ago," Samael says. "Concealed by the sun... but not for long."

"Why not?" Bubbles asks, though I can tell by the look in her eyes that she already suspects the answer.

"It's accelerating." Samael traces his right index finger across the table's surface in an arc, bringing it around to his slower moving left index finger. When the fingers collide, despite his lack of drama or sound effects, I flinch. "She'll torment this world, and then destroy it. After that...everything else, with you along to watch." He turns to Gal. "You...she intends to kill. The harlot. The whore. The Hester Prynn that stole her man-toy. Your final destination will be the Wolf-Rayet star WR 102. Hottest single point in the universe at 210,000 degrees Kelvin. If anything can erase you from existence, it's the unfathomable heat of a blue star."

"Is that what you want for me?" Gal asks.

"All I ever wanted for you—Ezekiel—was to set you free. Trouble was, *I* was the captive, then and now." He turns to Will. "Which is why I will accept your offer." Before anyone can object, he addresses Dark Horse. "Cherry Bomb would like to trade. Your people, for Will and Gal."

"What about you?" Dark Horse asks.

"I am off the table," he says. "Tell her you sent me into the empty void of space, a million light years away. It's within your capability, yes?"

"What makes you think we won't just launch you out there anyway?" Henry asks.

Samael looks at me. "Because I was offered friendship." He turns to Will. "Because *he* understands me." He turns to Gal. "And because *she* was once the closest thing I ever had to a brother." He turns to Cassidy. "And because *this one* would never let you."

All fair points. I wouldn't really be on board with condemning someone to eternal pain in the vacuum of space either, especially after he's cooperated with us.

But the debate is ended before it's begun.

"Make the trade," Will says.

"What?" Samael and Dark Horse say in tandem.

"Make the trade."

Gal takes her husband's hand. "Cherry Bomb is as much a part of me, as Samael is of Will. It's our responsibility."

Jonas storms to the table. "You can't do this!"

Samael is more curious than intimidated. "And why do *you* care so much?"

Jonas thrusts a hand toward a cafeteria table, taking hold of it with a telekinetic grip. The table lifts off the ground, spins in the air, and then, with a resounding crunch, compresses down into a perfect sphere the size of a baseball. The metal orb glides to Samael's. Drops from the air, to the table in front of him. Its super dense weight craters the surface.

Jonas leans over Samael. "Imagine this was your body. Think you'd survive it?"

Will puts his hand on Jonas's. "Son, please. This needs to be done, or all will be lost."

"Son?" Samael says, looking Jonas over. "The Titan?"

"Adopted," Gal says.

"I wish I could say this was interesting. Alas..." Samael completely ignores Jonas's attempt at intimidation. I suspect he's endured far worse than what any of us are willing to do. "There is one more person she'll require. Three for three."

"Capria," Will says, sounding sad.

"She did not want to be like us," Gal says. "Immortality takes a toll. She knew that."

"Sixty years on this planet," Will says. "That's as far as she made it."

Samael smiles. "You've been lying for a long time, but you can't fool me. And you won't fool Cherry Bomb. Capria must be part of the trade, or..."

"We can't do it," I say, surprising even myself. For the first time, Samael seems surprised.

"Thank you," Jonas says, pacing, hands linked behind his head.

"Why the hell not?" Hildy asks.

I can feel her desperation. I share in it. I'm putting Burnett's life at risk, but I'm doing the same for Bree. And that's going to take a toll.

"The last thing Wini said to me," I say. "'Don't let them make the trade.'"

"Before we left?" Delgado asks. "How could she know any of this was going to happen? She wouldn't have allowed it."

"Not before we left," I say, glancing at Dark Horse. He knows our story. How we got to this time from a post-apocalyptic future. "Before she died."

"Before…she died." Delgado's face goes pale.

"In the future," I say. "It's how we got here. Wini used your friend's machine—"

"What friend?" Delgado asks.

"Cowboy," Dark Horse says.

Delgado's on his feet now. "You knew about this?"

"Wini told me not to tell you," I say. "And told me not to make a trade. She warned me about this very moment. It's where things go wrong. It's how we lose. Again. In the time she came from, Cherry Bomb had destroyed civilization. Turned it into a clone of her torment world. Making this trade means we lose."

Samael sighs, watching his chance at freedom whisked away. Then his eyes widen with realization. "There might be another way."

"To what?" I ask.

"I…don't know. But she is looking for him. For what purpose, I don't know."

"Looking for who?" Dark Horse asks.

"The Architect."

"Samael…" Gal says. "Not again."

"Don't worry, Ezekiel. This time I know his name." He smiles. "Jeremy Robinson."

42

DARK HORSE

"This is stupid," I say, prepping my rail gun. Cherry Bomb might be tough, but a tungsten disc traveling fifty-four hundred miles per hour should make an impression. Not that she'll be there, because like I said, this is stupid.

"Probably another trap," Henry says, rubbing his hands together, a gleam in his eye. He doesn't bother helping himself to any of the armory's weapons, which is great because I doubt he knows how to use them properly. A firearm in the hands of someone who hasn't been trained like I've been, is an accident waiting to happen. The sight of all these guns definitely got him jazzed. But he hasn't touched one yet, I suspect because he now considers them beneath him.

And he wouldn't be wrong.

But me? I'm a gun guy. Would probably carry one even if I had superpowers. Like a security blanket.

Chuy slips her sidearm into her holster. Buttons it down. "It's going to be a minute before Mazola can rally the Chut'uni for a full-frontal assault."

Henry raises his hand. "As much as I like the sound of a full-frontal, I'm still not sure what the point is. Can they destroy the planet? That would be sick as balls, but I'm pretty sure it would also fill Earth's orbit with a shit ton of civilization-destroying torment-planet asteroids. Hellsteroids."

Chuy and I look at Henry like he's just spoken a foreign language.

"What?" he says, "I'm smart. I just don't like it."

"And he's not wrong," Chuy says.

"Between you and me, kid," I say. "We really don't know. A second Earth isn't something we developed contingencies for."

"Really?" Henry asks. "Because I have contingencies for, like, everything. Like, what if I'm in a room with Traci Lords and Pat Benatar, and both of them want to get busy? I mean, what do you do, right?"

"In the 80's?" I ask, which immediately results in a slap to the back of my head.

"Hey, I ain't ageist," Henry says. "I play the top hits of the 80's, 90's, and today. Wrinkles are just texture, know what I'm saying?"

"I don't," I say. "And I don't want to."

"Where's your sister?" Chuy asks.

"Here," Sarah says, entering the room and just about filling it with her presence. She looks stoic. Sober. Henry's opposite.

"Something on your mind?" I ask her.

Sarah makes a face like I've just asked if she'd like lumpy diarrhea on her croissant. "Bree's life is in danger. I haven't slept in...forever. I could really use a burger. And you know, the end of reality."

"We got this," Henry says. "But also, I really need to take a shit while we're listing needs."

"When we get back," I say. "Until then, make like the U.S. Mint."

"Is that like a chocolate mint?" Henry asks.

"What?" I ask. "The U.S. Mint. They make pennies."

Henry raises a finger like he's just discovered the cure for stupid. "Pinching pennies. Got it."

"Great," I say, putting an arm around his shoulder.

"You see how easily this guy cozies up to me?" Henry asks Sarah while motioning to me. "Why couldn't Jonas be like that? Took him forever to Ambiguously Gay Duo me."

"Don't need to know," I say, and then I offer him another tag team. "Wonder twins activate." I offer my fist, and he punches it.

"Form of, a douche—" We rotate into the fourth dimension. A moment later we emerge outside a house. "—nozzle." Henry puts his hands on his hips. "Huh. It's a house."

"You were expecting?"

"I don't know, like a mansion."

"Delgado did some digging on this guy. No police record. Not even a ticket or an accident. He doesn't really drink. Never been drunk, or smoked pot. Normal family. Normal house. Normal cars. Plays video games. Watches movies. And writes every day."

"So just a normal boring dude," Henry says.

"Except for whatever he's got going up here." I tap my head. "Up here, he's a freakshow. Delgado is checking out his books now. Might take some time. I guess he's got a lot."

A wall of white opens beside us. Chuy and Sarah rotate out.

Sarah takes a look at the house and just like Henry, she says, "Huh."

"Already covered it," Henry says. "Normal house. Normal dude."

"It's not that," Sarah says. "It's..." She lifts her nose and sniffs the air. "Where are we?"

"New Hampshire," I say.

"What I thought," she says. "Where?"

Before I can answer, a young girl calls from the second-floor window. "Hello?"

I can't really make her out inside the dark room, but she sounds around Cassidy's age.

"Hello?" I respond. "Is your father home?"

There's a pause, and then a question I'm not expecting. "Are you Moses?"

"Everyone on guard," I whisper.

"Always am," Chuy responds.

"I am," I shout to the girl.

"My father said you could go in. To his office. It's over the garage."

"Oh...okay... Thanks, I guess."

"Uh-huh." She sounds annoyed at having to speak to us, but overall, this is not the welcome I expected. Could he really know who we are? Could he have been expecting us?

"Are you Sarah?" the girl calls out.

Sarah smiles up at the window. "I am. Who are you?"

"Norah. You're my favorite," the girl says. "Well, after Cassidy, but that's not really fair because... Never mind. Byeeee!" The window slides shut, ending the conversation.

"Weird kid," Sarah says.

"All kids are weird," Chuy adds.

"It's unlocked!" Henry opens the front door like he owns the place. Steps inside.

What most people would have used as a mud room, this household has turned into an art studio. Paintings and drawings by children of all ages hang on the walls. Supplies fill cubbies. Tables are covered in bright colored spills, long since dried.

"Kinda makes me wish I had a family," Henry says, leading the way toward a door at the top of a stairwell.

"Most families don't have communal art rooms," Chuy says.

"Fun ones do," Henry grumbles.

"Well, maybe they'll adopt you," Sarah says, unimpressed by the creative space.

We file up into the office, and I'm disappointed to find it empty.

"Is this an office or a man cave?" Sarah asks.

"Whoa!" Henry says, moving to a shelf of toys, quickly inspecting them. "This is Metroplex, and—holy shit, a generation one Starfire." He gasps. "And this gaming rig? Two of them?" He turns around, energy building.

"He's like a kid in a KB Toys," I say.

"KB. Closed, man," Henry says, looking over a Nemesis figurine.

"Toys 'R' Us?" I ask.

"Closed."

"Well, shit." I note the musical instruments, wondering if this guy can actually play them all, or if he's just trying to impress people on video calls.

"Sick!" Henry says, picking up a pair of drumsticks and wailing on the set. Thankfully, it's electronic, and it makes very little sound. Henry gives up on the drums and turns his attention to the keyboard. "Oooh." He pulls out the bench and takes a seat, fiddling with buttons.

"So, he's either just not home," Chuy says. "Orrrr?"

"Don't know," I say. "Just look for anything out of the ordinary."

"Everything *in* here is out of the ordinary," Sarah says, looking at a commemorative Space Force coin. "How old is this guy supposed to be?"

"Pushing fifty," I say.

"So, like, your age," Sarah says, smiling.

"I think you'd be friends," Chuy says, enjoying Sarah's dig, and she motions to some art hanging on a wall. A Xenomorph and a Predator. Now that I'm looking, there are more than a few references to my home time around the room, including a wall-mounted Millennium Falcon. A fellow child of the 80s.

"Maybe," I admit, wiggling the computer's mouse. The screen snaps to life, displaying a messy desktop filled with files, short cuts, and images. The background is a Nemesis promo image for the TV series. Would need Delgado or Bubbles to make sense of what's on this machine, but their skill sets are better suited to figuring out how to stop a runaway planet.

"Yo," Henry says, "check this out." His fingers are positioned over the keyboard. He clears his throat, "ahehehem," and then he begins playing an instantly recognizable tune.

"'Home Sweet Home,'" I say.

He really gets into it, and honestly he isn't that bad. "Mötley Crüe in da house!"

Just as Henry is about to start belting out lyrics, Chuy says. "Have something." She plucks something small from a cabinet atop which sits a 3D printer with a crater in its metal front. She feels the object's weight in her hand. Gives it a quick onceover. ".38 Super."

"Cowboy," I say, smiling. "Son of a bitch beat us here."

"He wasn't the only one." Chuy places the bullet in my hand.

I look at the round. Not like Cowboy to miss. Something must have really thrown him. Good news is, I don't see any blood. "If they weren't captured, where did they go?"

"Strip club?" Henry says, still twiddling on the keyboard.

"This guy does not go to strip clubs," Chuy says, scanning the office.

"Is there any place this Cowboy guy and the Robinson dude share in common?" Sarah asks, looking over a red hardcover novel. "Someplace they might both feel safe?"

I'm about to give up when a memory surfaces. A discussion during one of the first episodes of Nemesis, combined with Cowboy's version of those events. I'm about to explain when Sarah says, "Oh shit. *Oh shit.* You've got to be shitting me."

She turns around, holding up the novel. Jeremy Robinson's name is nice and big at the top, like he's someone important. It's titled *The Order* and looks like a decent...*hold on a second.* A detail stands out. Two stone columns, between which is a familiar sheet of red energy and orange hexagons. And in the middle, standing before the gate...

"Dude," Sarah says, tapping the figure, whose sci-fi armor looks a lot like mine. "I think this is you."

Chuy holds up another Robinson book, this one featuring a Medusa-like head, but instead of snakes, there are a collection of monsters where the hair should be. But it's the title that blows my mind: KHAOS. "It's all of us."

43

MIAH

No problem. *No problem.* I got this. Totally. Nothing to worry about. Just need to hold down the fort until Dark Horse gets back. That's what he said. Hold down the fort. Which also put me in charge. Which feels weird because this is Delgado's secret underground base, I'm the new guy, and Jonas and Bubbles are the only members of my team still present.

"Don't sweat it, kid," Delgado says, watching me pace. "Nothing's going to happen."

"There's a hell planet on a collision course with Earth," I say, turning about face and continuing my march to the far side of a sophisticated ops center, which is massive compared to what they had back at the Florida house. The room is a towering spiral. Along the screw-like ascending walkway are cubbies carved out of the stone. It looks a lot like a hive, but it was once a cryogenic prison for men, women, and children collected over thousands of years, many abducted, many donated by willing conspirators.

Above the spiral, an array of polished, glowing orange crystals provides a dull orange light. But they're no match for the ten-foot-tall, clean-cut crystals rising from the floor, each one surrounded by several high-tech workstations. Like something out of Star Trek.

Delgado, Bubbles, and Hildy seem right at home, seated amidst the workstations. Bubbles and Hildy type, read, scroll, and click with ridiculous speed. Delgado just sits there, strings of little glowing nanites flitting between him and a crystal. He's got direct access, no interface required, and he's still present enough to comment on my pacing.

Samael has been returned to his temporary cell, accompanied by Will, Gal, and Jonas—the cosmic family. Their conversation continues, but it appears Samael is cooperating. It could all be a well-orchestrated ruse taking advantage of our good-guy trust and hope, but...maybe not. After all, this isn't how things went down the last time, with the Wini who came back for us. In that timeline, we must have traded Will and Gal for Burnett and Wini.

Makes the decision to abandon them tear at my heart, but if I didn't save the universe because I wanted to ensure Bree's safety, she'd probably kill me.

She's tough, I tell myself. And she's with Wini, who was tough enough to survive the team's first failure and ensured a second chance.

I look up at one of the large orange crystals. It looms above me, alien.

"Weird, right?" Cassidy says, approaching from behind.

"Like something out of *The Dark Crystal*," I say.

"Mmmmm," she says, doing a perfect impression of the Skeksi Chamberlain. "Gelflings!" She smiles. "I see it."

She stops beside me and places a hand on my back. A wave of relief flows out through me. I feel like I can breathe. Hadn't even realized I was holding my breath, or that my back was in knots.

"Thanks," I say.

She shrugs. "It was more for me than you. I could feel your angst from across the room."

"I'm just... I wasn't expecting to be put in charge of everyone here. This isn't my home turf...or my area of expertise."

"Pretty sure we're, like, a gazillion miles away from anyone's area of expertise," she says. "But Dark Horse...he doesn't do things willy-nilly. There's always a reason. If he put you in charge, it's because he believes in you, or at least your potential."

"Like your attack on the Chut'uni when they were the bad guys?" I ask.

Her face lights up. "You paid attention to the play?"

"It was pretty informative. And entertaining."

"Why, thank you," she says, bowing so low that her hair nearly wipes the obsidian floor.

"Well, let's just hope nothing happens until they get back."

"Pfff," Cassidy laughs. "That never happens."

"It could happen," I say. "Not everything has to—"

"Chut'uni fleet is in orbit around Mars," Hildy says. "Mazzola says they're awaiting orders, but they require a commander be present before taking any kind of action."

"See?" Cassidy says, with a shrug.

"What kind of action?" I ask.

"Got it," Delgado says. "We need to concentrate fire on a broad swath of the sun-facing side of the planet. With enough firepower, we can alter the planet's orbit enough so that it passes by Earth, gains momentum, and follows a trajectory that will change its path—without destroying it entirely."

"So, Earth will have a hell planet neighbor circling the sun?" I ask.

"Until we can figure out how to erase a planet," Delgado says. "Yes."

"Done!" Bubbles says, leaning back in her chair. "I have successfully mapped the location of all ducks, worldwide."

All eyes turn to her.

"What?" she says. "I also…have a theory. About how to beat Cherry Bomb."

"Let's hear it," I say, trying to sound comfortable in charge. Cassidy gives me a nod, a wink, and a thumbs up in clear view of everyone, encouraging me while broadcasting my discomfort.

"Well, I was given life by the Orphic Egg, the same cosmic egg that created Phanes, a hermaphroditic creator who spawned the universe—according to the Greeks. While we now know that William Chanokh shaped this universe, it's possible that the Orphic Egg was the device used by an original higher power to create the first of infinite universes. Or perhaps simply populate this one on William's behalf—unbeknownst to Will himself. The point is, that power of creation…might now reside in me. The tit to Cherry Bomb's tat."

"Not sure you're using those words right," Cassidy says, "but I think I'm going to Insta it, and see if it trends."

Delgado speaks with a gentle tone, but he doesn't bother trying to disguise his doubt. "You can…create a universe?"

"I have no idea," Bubbles says. "Like I said, it's just a theory. I'm simply pointing out that the first being to be hatched from the Orphic Egg is credited with the creation of either the universe, or all life in it. Given Will's penchant for making the myths and stories of other worlds real in this one, it stands to reason that, in this reality, it's not only possible, but also likely. I just have no idea how to do it. The Egg has been destroyed. There are no old gods left. And Will seems surprised by elements of his own creation—which includes me, by the way. In fact, this might be the very purpose of my creation. I suppose that could depend on whether or not Will and Gal believe in fate—that one of their creations has the hidden ability to undo the damage inflicted by another.

"Bubbles," Delgado says, "as amazing as you are—" Bubbles blushes, possibly for the first time. "—until you figure out how to do any of those things, it's just a theory. And right now, we need a lot more than theories."

"Right," I say. "The Chun Lis or whatever."

"Chut'uni," Delgado says.

Cassidy elbows me. "Chun Li is the Street Fighter chick." Cassidy does a handstand and starts spinning in circles, extending both legs and nearly kicking me in the face several times. "Spinning bird kick!"

"I wouldn't make that mistake when you meet them," Delgado says.

"Meet them? Right. We should go. Cassidy, uhh, Hildy, you're with me. Delgado, you ah, keep on keepin' on. Bubs...forget the ducks. Try to figure out if you have actual powers beyond being the cutest mom at a bake sale."

"I never considered being a mother before," Bubbles says.

"It's more work than you'd think," Delgado says. "Being a parent, I mean. Not a mother."

"Well, perhaps you can tell me about it," Bubbles says. "After we've saved the universe."

Delgado smiles. "Perhaps I will."

"Ugh," Cassidy says with a dramatic roll of her eyes and her head. "Old people flirting. Gross. Can we go now? Armory first, then to the fleet?"

"Sounds like a plan," I say and wrap my arm around Hildy as she approaches. I feel guilty about it, with Burnett imprisoned somewhere on the hell world, but I'm still not moving in on his girl. And Hildy is definitely not interested. In fact, she doesn't seem much like herself—as much as I know her, anyway.

Not talking much. Not listening to music. I can feel the defeat emanating from her.

"We'll get him back," I say, as she wraps her arm around my waist.

She triggers the slew drive on her hip and rotates us out of the Mesa. We arrive on the bridge of a ship that looks and feels like *Lil' Bitch'n* but is a lot bigger.

With an open mouth and a smile, I say, "Bitch'n..." This is Dark Horse's warship from the future, used to defeat the Fourth Reich and save the human race from racial genocide. It's got to be the most legendary ship no one's ever heard of. The bridge looks like a weird conglomeration between the big-buttoned utilitarian vibe of *Star Wars* and the sleek touch-screen capabilities of *Star Trek*...and modern Earth.

"Buckle up," Hildy says, leaving the captain's chair for me, and taking a seat.

Cassidy cartwheels across the bridge, landing on her feet and falling back into what I suspect is her usual position, as it has no controls or buttons of any kind.

"So..." I approach the captain's chair. "I guess I'll just...sit here?"

Hildy ignores me. She's just hitting buttons, prepping the ship.

"If you don't," Cassidy says, "you know I will."

I sit down and feel uncomfortable, not because of the chair's design, but because I'm sure I don't belong in it. Leading a team is one thing, captaining a ship—a spaceship—is so far out of my wheelhouse I might as well be about to give a speech on industrial piping to a Chinese audience.

"Any tips?" I ask Cassidy.

"You know who Captain Pike is?" she asks.

"Haven't had a lot of time to watch movies lately."

"Okay," she says. "How about Kirk?"

I nod at that. "Got it."

"But mostly let Hildy do all the work, and do what she tells you, if she tells you to do anything, because if she does it's probably really, really important."

Hildy glances back. "You two ready, or are we going to just keep talking?"

"Almost," I say, tapping the controls on my arm. A moment later the modulated voice of Muse's lead singer, Matt Bellamy, sings, "M-m-m-m-m-m-m-mad, mad, mad…" And 'Madness,' one of the greatest songs ever written, is off to the races, its infectious beat and swimming melody transforming the mood on the bridge.

Even Hildy's.

She nods. "Appropriate choice."

"Cool," I say. "Rotate."

The whole ship slips through a wall of white, and then swivels right back out.

"On screen," I say. "Let's see where we—holy shit…"

The view displayed on the large viewscreen at the bridge's front doubles my self-doubts. Because until Dark Horse returns, I'm not just the captain of this ship…I'm the commander of a massive fucking fleet of alien ships the likes of which I've never dreamed could be real. But here they are, representing dozens of civilizations that have banded together in defense of the universe.

Against Cherry Bomb.

Kind of feels like the fight might be even now, but I'm not getting my hopes up.

"Ooh! Ooh! Ooh!" Cassidy says, jumping to her feet, thrusting her fists and hips in a very suggestive way, as she hops from one side of the bridge to the other. "Ooh! Ooh! Ooh!"

"Stop," I say. "Please. No more."

She gives me the world's most crafty smile and then twists in my direction. "Ooh! Ooh! Ooh!"

I reel back in my seat. "Oh, god. Hildy, make her stop!"

Hildy cracks, and then laughs. Cassidy leaps up and spins around, facing Hildy now. "Ooh! Ooh! Ooh!" Hildy leans away, holding out her hands, keeping the thrusting teenager at bay, laughing louder now.

An electronic voice clears its throat, stopping Cassidy in her tracks and silencing Hildy's laughter. I slow-turn toward the viewscreen, eyes widening as I see what's taken the armada's place.

"What…the hell…is that?"

44

DARK HORSE

"Cowboy? You copy?" I wait a moment and then shake my head. "His comms are still off."

"Or he *can't* respond," Henry says. "If he was caught. Happened before, right?"

I respond with a grunt. He's not wrong, but I'm not mentally or emotionally prepared to consider Cowboy MIA, again. And if Cherry Bomb got ahold of Cowboy, that means she also has the Architect, who I'm liking less and less though I have yet to meet him.

If everything I've been told is true, we have *him* to thank for our existence, and the several levels of hell we've been through.

"Starting to feel like this was a waste of time," Chuy says.

I agree with her. But I also can't think of another option. Also...I have a feeling.

Which I hate.

But I keenly remember Cowboy saying the same thing before he left. And somehow he found himself at Robinson's house, long before we figured out that piece of the puzzle.

"This is definitely the right place," Sarah says, looking up at the big brick mansion that served as the fictional headquarters for the Fusion Center – Paranormal division in Robinson's *Project Nemesis* novels and series. "They shot the exteriors on location. Hard to mistake it for anything else."

Hands on hips, I shake my head. "Looks how Cowboy described it from his time in that dimension as well."

"But why would Robinson come to this house?" Sarah asks. "He lived down the street."

"He what now?" I ask.

"Lived down the street," Sarah says. "On Baker. We can walk there in like two minutes."

"I'll check it out," Henry says, and he takes off into the sky, arching up over the hilltop.

"He doesn't know which house, does he?" Chuy asks.

Sarah shakes her head. "But I do."

"You two check it out," I say. "I'm going to walk it. See if anything jumps out."

Chuy squints at me. Knows I'm not saying something. Also knows to let me do my thing. "Sure..."

They pair up and after Sarah provides the address, and Chuy punches it into her controls, they rotate away, appearing somewhere else in the neighborhood. *How long until someone calls the police?* I wonder, looking around for the tell-tale signs of being watched. A shifting curtain, a quickly ducking shadow. I see nothing. The neighborhood is quiet. Close to idyllic.

I walk along the curved sidewalk, following the long loop around. The wall surrounding the large brick FC-P building blocks my view of the home, until I reach a granite staircase with a wrought iron gate. Real old-world stuff. Probably some interesting history here.

The sidewalk bends around the property, heading up a small hill. On the left, two large homes. On the right, more wall, shadowed by pine trees, beneath which is a small grove of rhododendrons.

Eyes on the pink flowering bushes, my pace quickens.

Something about them holds my attention.

I ready the railgun in my hands, but then I think twice about it. I won't need it. Not yet. Weapon slid behind my back, I step closer and hear whispering voices, too indistinct to make out.

"Hello?" I say.

The whispers go silent. Then a voice I don't know says, "Moses?"

"Show yourself," I say, reaching for my railgun again, but I don't take hold of it. Still sure, for some reason, it's unnecessary. A face pops out from a gap between two rhododendrons. He's kind of pale, thinly bearded, and really excited to see me. His eyes go wide. "Moses!"

"How do you know my name?" I ask.

"C'mon!" he says, waving me into the bushes and sliding back out of sight.

"Is okay, boss," Cowboy says from within. "Is safe."

"Vesely?" I ask, heaving myself up the wall and sliding into a natural den formed by the large, leafy plants. From inside here, we're concealed from the world.

"I used to hide in here with Justin," Robinson says, like that's supposed to mean something to me. Maybe it would to people who have read his books. For me, it's a meaningless detail.

"I was just telling him where new bell comes from," Cowboy says. "People expect him to know all about my life. Ask, 'where is new bell from? How did Cowboy get new bell? I didn't read about it, so must not have happened.' Like I'm not real person. Like I do not have life outside of his books."

Robinson and Cowboy, neither of whom look wounded, are sitting on either side of three large white paper bags.

"I write fast," Robinson says, "but I can't write about every moment of every character's life. It's like Kane says, sometimes things happen between the pages. Am I right?"

"Totally right." Cowboy reaches into one of the bags and pulls out a paper-wrapped sandwich. "Token of good faith."

I open the wrapper. "A roast beef sandwich?"

"Nick's Famous," Robinson says.

Cowboy takes a deep sniff from the top of the open bag. "Mmm. Is best in every dimension."

"It's good to see you," I say to Cowboy, and I take a bite, because honestly, it smells fantastic. The meat all but melts in my mouth. "Oh my god. That's..."

"Good, right?" Robinson says.

"You getting endorsements for peddling these?" I ask.

Robinson laughs, but he says nothing. He's just staring at me. Looking me over like a sculptor trying to decide whether he's finished.

"Kind of creeping me out, dude."

"Can I see the eyes?" he asks.

I sigh. This guy knows everything about me, but he's never seen me outside of his own imagination. I'm not one for putting on shows, but if it will help us move things along… I light up my eyes, the blue glow of my Europhid self illuminating our little hideaway.

"Happy?" I ask, and then I turn to Cowboy. "So, this is where your feeling brought you?

"Brought both of you," Robinson says.

"Great," I say. "Can we get right to it?"

"There's a time for banter, and a time for action," Robinson says. "Right? Though let's be honest, there's almost always time for banter. It's the spice of life."

I really want to argue with the guy. I don't like being known so profoundly, but there's no point. If he is who everyone thinks he is, then this whole conversation is for my benefit, not his, because…

"Did you already write this?" I ask. "This conversation? Do you know everything we're about to say?"

"I'm not great at remembering everything I've written," he says. "So… maybe?"

"Great," I say. "You're not going to be much help, are you?"

"Probably not a ton," he says.

"Why's that?"

"Changing things would be…bad."

"Is why Cherry Bomb wants him," Vesely says. "To write the ending. Her ending."

"The story isn't finished?" I ask.

"Stories are like the course of a river over a billion years," Robinson says, "bending and changing, shifting course over the landscape as it erodes, eventually taking a shape that is observed, remembered, and named by humans."

"Cool," I say, but I don't even try to sound like I mean it. "We should go now." I turn to Cowboy. "Cherry has Burnett, Wini, and Bree. The Florida house is destroyed. And there's a second Earth full of this guy's version of hell accelerating toward us."

Cowboy nods. "Am aware."

"You can tell him how things play out, but not me?" I ask Robinson.

He shrugs. "I knew he was going to tell you. Also, I was pretty excited. This is Cowboy. He is gunslinger. C'mon. I imagined this guy, and now here he is. Here *you* are. Moses Montgomery. Dark Horse. The Exo-Hunter."

I'm a little unnerved by the affection in Robinson's eyes and voice. "Can we go, before we find out he writes Harlequin romances featuring mano-e-mano ménages à trois?"

"That would be great," Robinson says, gathering his white paper bag. "Going, I mean. Not the circle jerk. Roast Beef doesn't stay warm for long."

I toggle my comms. "Chuy, Sarah, Henry, I got them both. Rendezvous back at the Mesa."

"Copy that," Chuy says.

"No problem," Sarah says.

Henry pops on next, starting with a fake static. "Kkksssh. Copy that, good buddy. I found a cat. Can I keep it?"

"No," I say. "Back to the Mesa. Now."

"Henry, right?" Robinson is loving every second of this. "So much fun, right?'

"If Cherry doesn't kill you, I might do it." I level my most serious stink eye at him, but it has no effect.

He just smiles. "No, you won't."

"What makes you so sure?" I ask, getting annoyed.

He just raises his eyebrows and glances around.

Right. Because he wrote this. Because he knows how things play out. Because he guided me here. And Cowboy. Because Cherry came for him, but she was outplayed.

"I hate you," I say.

"Not for long," he says and points at the ground. "Don't forget that."

I bend down, collect my sandwich, rewrap it, and say, "Everyone ready?"

Robinson steps up to Cowboy. Puts his arm around him like they're old pals. "Ready." He lifts a victorious finger and says, "Rotate!"

Cowboy rolls into a wall of white and disappears into the fourth dimension with the man whose fucked imagination might turn the world into a twisted hellscape.

I unwrap the sandwich a bit and take another bite. So damn good. “I really hate this guy,” I mumble while chewing.

A rumbling sound draws me back to the hiding spot’s entrance. I look up in time to see a strange kind of alien craft float past, just two hundred feet up. It’s not huge. Big enough for maybe two occupants. And it’s shaped like a Q.

Cherry’s still searching for Robinson, and not being very subtle about it. MUFON’s going to get flooded with reports.

Like it or not, I’m going to have to keep this guy alive. He’s the key to everything. I take one more bite, wrap the sandwich again, toggle my slew drive, and–

An explosion launches me out of the rhododendrons, across the street, and into the solid wooden door of a house.

45

MIAH

"That's Mazzola," Cassidy says. "He's the..." She turns to Hildy. "How's it go?"

"The ancestor of the creature that became known as The Other," Hildy says, "who created the Mesa, and kidnapped scores of people to sustain its own life, only to be defeated by Delgado and Wini. But he is, like us, an Earthling. His people evolved long before humanity. Some took to the stars and found a new world, evolving into the Chut'uni. Those who remained suffered the same fate as the dinosaurs, except for Mazzola, who was brought to the present by...by McCoy. He eventually came to help us defend the Earth against the misguided Chut'uni and the Europhids, who are now our allies."

"Does anyone on the team not have an absolutely batshit backstory?" I ask, not expecting an answer. "And what happened to The Other?"

"Wini killed it," Cassidy says.

"I believe it," I say. "Lady is tough."

But this thing... I've seen some shit. On Earth, beneath Earth, and on another planet. But something about this Mazzola dude unnerves me. Could be his creepy-ass black eyes. Or his pale, white dinosaur body covered in iridescent feathers. But it's mostly this sense that the guy is looking inside my head, even though he's not currently in the room.

"It is okay to feel uncomfortable in my presence," Mazzola says, his voice reminiscent of Stephen Hawking. "Most humans take time to... adjust."

"Be glad he's not talking in your head," Cassidy says.

"He's telepathic?" I ask, and then I force myself to address the strange creature. "You're telepathic?"

His long neck dips in a nod. "Though I now communicate via this device created for me by Burnett." He swivels his head toward Hildy. "I am sorry to hear of his capture." He turns back to me. "As well as your little friends'. And of course, McCoy's...demise." He addresses Cassidy. "I am aware that you became close with him. I considered him...family as well. Your despair must be profound, but I am sure it is not nearly enough to break your indomitable spirit."

And now I like the guy.

"It won't," Cassidy says, "as long as we get some payback."

"That is," Mazzola says, "I believe, the plan. Join us on the Chut'uni flagship, and we will discuss."

"We will join you shortly," Hildy says, and the screen winks out. She turns to me. "Try not to be intimidated. Everything you see over there is a friend, even if they don't look or sound like it. Most of them will have purple—"

"Dildos," Cassidy says.

"Whhhat now?" I ask.

"They look like dildos," Cassidy says. "That's what Dark Horse said. He didn't know I was listening, but he should have known better, because I'm pretty much always listening. I don't know what it is, but that's what he says, big, floppy, purple dildos." She shrugs. "I think they look like Jell-O cucumbers."

"Got it," I say. "Mental image complete."

"They're also telepathic beings," Hildy says. "A hive mind nearly as old as the universe, existing in this dimension of reality, and others, all of them united, sharing knowledge, and now helping to coordinate a resistance against Cherry Bomb."

"Right," I say. "I remember. Same thing that's a part of Dark Horse now." I shake my head. "Hard to believe one woman could cause so much trouble."

"Bro," Cassidy says, fists on her hips. "That was dangerously close to being sexist."

"One...person?" I ask.

"Better."

"Anything else I should know before we zip on over there?" I ask.

Hildy approaches, and she wraps an arm around my waist. "Just... try not to scream."

"Well, that sounds—" I'm enveloped in white for a flash and then released into a totally different environment. "—pleasant."

"Stand aside," a voice rumbles in my head. I spin around to see the newcomer, and I come face-to-face with a muscular white chest. From this close I can see the skin's texture is rough. Not at all human. I lift my head up and feel the forbidden scream build in my chest.

I contain it—barely—and step out of the giant's way.

The creature resembles Mazzola in some superficial ways. The color of its skin. The muscle tone. The snout on its face. The complete and utter lack of clothing. But the rest is different. Evolved. It's built like a minotaur—with claws on its splayed toes, backwards-bent legs, and a crest rising up behind its head in place of Mazzola's horns. Everything about it is intimidating, and I'm pretty sure I know what it is.

"Chut'uni?" I ask Hildy.

She nods.

"He have a name?" I ask.

She shrugs. "I have not spent much time with them. We communicate through Mazzola..." She turns to greet two newcomers, smiling wide. "And these two."

I turn around and nearly shout again, this time in excitement. There are two creatures the size of Cassidy. Their bulbous, bald gray heads and big black eyes make them instantly recognizable to anyone who's watched *Ancient Aliens* or shared a Giorgio Tsoukalos meme. "*What?* Seriously? Grays are real?"

Hildy motions to the short duo, who are dressed in adaptive armor, and then back to me. "Hans and Franz, this is Miah. Miah, Hans and Franz."

The duo both offer me a thumbs up, and I give one back. Then, without a word, they move around us. Cassidy slips out of the fourth dimension right in front of the pair. Lights up when she sees them. "Hans and Franz!" She holds up a hand, and they both high five it before moving on.

"They're real, but they're not aliens," Hildy says. "Creations of The Other. Automatons to abduct people."

"But they're good guys now?" I ask.

"Automatons," she says. "Neither good nor bad. But...they appear to be developing personalities. Or perhaps just mimicking the behavior of the people they've spent the most time with."

"Well...that's something," I say, and I take in my surroundings for the first time. We're in a conference room. A large table fills the center of the space, shaped like an angular infinity symbol, the center of the two holes occupied by stone vessels containing dozens of warbling...purple dildos. I scan the rest of the space and discover a dozen other alien species, ranging from butt-ass ugly, to adorable. The Chut'uni dude is the largest. The smallest is the size of an opossum, but it has big shiny eyes that make you want to cuddle it, despite the spikes covering its green, scaly body, and the pint-sized Europhids dotting its spine.

And they're not the only species sporting purple hitchhikers. Other than myself, Hildy, and Cassidy, the only lifeforms present without a Europhid attached to some part of their body, are Hans and Franz, and they might not even be lifeforms.

"Are all these guys here willingly?" I ask, motioning to the Europhids. "Or are they being...directed?"

"The Europhids provide communication over vast distances, relaying raw thought through their network of populated planets, moons, asteroids, and now, species. It allows for quick coordination."

"But were any of them forced to join the collective? Because that'd be some real Borg shit."

"I...have not asked," Hildy admits. "And this is not the time."

"It's just, I notice none of our people are taking part in the mutually beneficial parasitism."

"Because it's gross," Cassidy says.

"And because humanity values individuality more than other... highly evolved species." She motions to the collection of creatures, taking their seats at the table.

"Hey, I have wings."

Hildy pats my shoulder. "You sure do, Laser Chicken. We should sit."

Leaving me thinking of comebacks, Hildy and Cassidy sit at the table, leaving a spot for me between them. Feeling like I've thrown on some fancy clothes and snuck into a red-carpet event full of celebrities, I take my seat, absolutely sure everyone will see me for the imposter I am.

And that's exactly what happens.

"Who is this new human?" I hear—in my head—spoken by god-knows which of these alien guys.

"He speaks for Dark Horse," Hildy says.

"Then let him speak," the voice says.

All eyes turn to me. For a moment, my vision narrows, my face gets hot and my pulse skyrockets. Then I remember who I am. Who I've become. After a steadying breath, I stand up and own the shit out of it, "I am Miah Gray, also known as Laser Chicken, immortal traveler of worlds, slayer of evil gods, and—"

A bulbous creature grunts and thinks aloud to the group, "He seeks to impress us with words. This man should not—"

"And," I say, loud enough to overpower my competition. "I am the last of the Lux."

I flare my wings wide. The buzzing energy fills the chamber with a blue glow, illuminating the surprised looking collection of alien faces, all of whom clearly know who the Lux are. Were.

"Very well," Mazzola says. "If everyone is satisfied, we will—"

An alarm screams, followed by a broadcast psychic warning that everyone hears. "Incoming enemy targets appearing! Evasive action! Evasive—"

I feel the broadcasting alien's life snuffed out in a raging torrent of heat and pain.

Before I can react to the shock of it all, Hildy yanks me to my feet, wraps her arms around me, and rotates us back to the bridge of the *Bitch'n.* A moment later, Cassidy appears beside us, diving into her chair and buckling up. I take her lead and do the same, strapping myself into the captain's chair while Hildy works the controls. An image appears on the big screen, displaying our friendly fleet, which is mind-blowingly impressive—until you look at the ominous armada appearing behind our ships—many of which I recognize.

The Tenebris. They're back. And they're not alone.

46

BREE

Dear Diary,

I'm not above admitting I was wrong. I thought I had nothing left to say to you, that growing up meant changing everything, but I'm beginning to think it's more about getting bigger and being in charge. Like Cherry Bomb. She's a lot like me. She's just tall, and like crazy strong. But not like with muscles. She's strong...in her head. But not like a super genius. It's just like...if she imagines something, it becomes real.

Like, right now, I am sitting at the tippy top of a castle tower, having an ice cream social with Cherry Bomb and my new friend, who I've named Daylight Glitter. He is a real pony, with wings and a unicorn horn, and silky-smooth purple hair that sparkles in the light. His fur is sooo soft it reminds me of my plushie back home. I could just hug him all day. Cherry Bomb let me use her powers to imagine the perfect friend, who wouldn't stop me from doing what I want.

And you're never going to believe this...

He speaks! English! And we have all the same interests, including ice cream. The only real difference, aside from him being a pony with wings and a horn, is that I like mint chocolate and he prefers apple pie.

Apple pie ice cream. Who would have thought?

I also like my new clothes. They're red, like Cherry Bomb's, but not as tight, or shiny. More like soft pajamas, but stretchy and cool looking.

"Mmm-MMM!" I say, leaning back in my throne. "I think that might be the best ice cream I've ever had."

"Why, me too!" Daylight Glitter says. His hooves are covered with melted apple pie goo. He can't use a spoon, so he's just dipping into his dessert and licking it off with his long, silly tongue.

"You are a mess, young man," I say, scooping up some mint chocolate that never seems to run out, and flinging it at my pony. It hits him between the eyes, slides down his snout, and over his nose where he licks it up.

"Ooh," he says. "Yummy-yummy in my pony tummy."

"Is ice cream okay for ponies to eat?" I ask, feeling a little concerned that Daylight Glitter might be like Miah's mom. She gets all farty if she eats ice cream.

"I have no idea," Daylight Glitter says. "I didn't exist until an hour ago!"

"He'll be fine," Cherry Bomb says, entering the tower room. She smiles, but I can tell she's a little upset. "Are you feeling better? Still hungry?"

I rub my belly. "So full." I rub a little more. "So soft."

"And it won't rip when you change," Cherry says.

"I can't change," I grumble. "Not without Miah."

"Well," Cherry says, leaning on her elbows, smiling like I do before stealing cookies, "I think we can take care of that."

"We can?"

"Did you miss the part where I made you a castle and a talking pony?" Cherry says.

"For real?" I ask. "You're not joking?"

"I don't have a sense of humor," Cherry says, and she puts on a funny kind of smile. "Lost it a long time ago."

"Well, that's sad," I say. "But if you can make it so I can change..." I imagine it. Demon Dog whenever I want. Free to go anywhere. Do anything. And never afraid? "That would be great."

"Perfect," she says. "I just have a few questions, and then we'll take care of you."

Thinking about Demon Dog makes me hungry again, so I take a bite, smile with a mouthful, and say, "Ask away!"

"Do you know who I am?"

"Cherry Bomb. The others say you're bad, but I think you're nice."

"A nice person who doesn't like it when people do mean things. I'm sure you understand."

I nod. "This one time. At school. I was making macaroni art. A real masterpiece, if you ask me. And then little Frank Ferris takes the only glue that hasn't dried shut because some dummy didn't screw them closed, and he squirts it right into his butt crack. No one noticed until it was running down his legs. I heard he had to go to the hospital to separate his cheeks. I didn't hit him or anything, but I hoped he had to poop and it exploded out his butt."

"Just like that," Cherry says.

"No one has ever been mean to me," Daylight Glitter says.

"You goose," I say.

"I'm a pony!"

I laugh and shake my head at Cherry Bomb, pointing my thumb at the silly creation she let me make. "This guy."

"Now then," Cherry says. "What can you tell me about your friends?"

"Which ones?" I ask. "I have a lot of friends. Not as many as you, though." I look out the window. Way down below looks like an army of ants, just kind of bumbling around a bunch of the gates that the Tenebris used. Cherry said they made a lot of new ones so her friends can move around between planets. Her coolest friend is way far away, but she's still easy to see. A weird looking Nemesis. And I think there might be more than one skulking around. I can hear them. Their big footsteps and loud cries, like she's hurt, but also angry. Not sure why. But I still want to say 'hi' to one of them.

"How about the one with wings?" Cherry asks.

"That's Miah. He's kind of like my brother, except for when he steals my ice cream. Then he's persona non grateful."

"What can he do?"

"Aside from *not* let me become Demon Dog, you mean?"

"Yes."

"Umm. Well, he can fly. He has laser wings. And laser swords."

"That's it?" she asks.

"Yup."

She squints at me and asks. "Tell me about Dark Horse."

"I don't really know him well," I say. "He's kind of like, 'I'm in charge,' and, 'Everyone do what I say, all the time, because I'm serious, and I used to be an army man.'"

"He's in charge?"

"Kind of him. Kind of Miah." I shrug. "Depends on what's happening."

"Why aren't you in charge?" Cherry asks.

"Because I'm a kid."

"So?"

"Kids can't be in charge," I say. "We're kids."

"Maybe that's why you can't change yourself into Demon Dog," she says. "Maybe Miah isn't doing anything other than giving you permission. That's kind of...weak, don't you think?"

I scrunch up my lips and cross my arms. "That's what Burnett thinks, too."

"Huh... Who do you think is your strongest friend?" she asks.

"Well, it's *supposed* to be Jonas, but when we fought Typhon, guess who killed him?" I point at my chest. "This kid, that's who."

"*You* killed Typhon?" She seems impressed now, like I'm not actually weak.

"The others helped," I say. "A little. But *I* ate his brain." I take a scoop of ice cream and chomp it.

"Well done," she says. "Brains don't taste as bad as everyone thinks."

"Nope."

"Tell me about Jonas. Why is he so special?"

"Well, his parents, I guess. They were Titans. Gaia and Uranus. I think they were big deals." I scrunch my forehead. "I thought you already knew that, though."

"Mmm," she says, interested but not afraid. "Did he tell you about when we met in the bowling alley?"

"He said he hurt you," I say, and I then ask, "You're not going to hurt *him,* are you? Or my other friends that are here? Wini and Burnett? Can they come be in my castle?"

"And what of them? What makes them special?"

"Wini is a tough old lady, and Burnett is a smart guy, but also really nice."

"And are they like you?"

"You mean with powers? No. They're normal."

"I mean, are they loved by their team?"

"Oh, very much."

"That's wonderful," Cherry says.

I smile and take another scoop.

"Thank you for speaking with me, dear. I'm afraid I need to leave. But before I do..." She motions to my forehead. "I give you permission."

"Did...did you just use your powers on me?"

"Heavens, no," she says. "I gave you permission. To use yours."

I hop out of my chair and face the big window, looking out at the flashing orange clouds. The breeze smells funny, kind of like the Tenebris factory, but it doesn't bother me. Because I...am...Demon Dog!

I close my eyes and picture myself changing, imagining what it feels like, but nothing happens.

"It's not working," I say, clenching my fists.

"Perhaps you're merely lacking motivation," Cherry says, standing behind me. She puts a hand on my shoulder. "Here, let me give you a hand."

I feel a shove on my back, and I'm not strong enough to resist it. I twist around as I fall out of the tower. Cherry gives me a smile and a wave, and then she flies away, not even bothering to watch me go splat.

I spin around again, and I see Cherry's friends hundreds of feet below. There are so many of them that the ground looks alive.

But I'm not afraid.

Even if I can't change.

Because Cherry doesn't know everything. Like how I pretended to be a normal eight-year-old. Like how I didn't tell her anything important. And like how, when she let me imagine a friend, I added some things she couldn't see.

"Daylight Glitter!"

47

DARK HORSE

"Mommy, there's a scary man at the door."

I open my eyes to find a cherub-faced little boy with poofy hair. He blinks down at me, unsure about how to handle a man dressed like a space traveler crashing into his front door.

"Are you an alien?" he asks.

I smile up at the kid, hoping to put him at ease. "Only half."

Without changing his expression, the kid cranes open his mouth and unleashes a high-pitched scream that sends his mother into overdrive. She arrives like a whirlwind, yanking the kid away from the door, shouting, "I'm calling the police!" and slamming the door in my face.

"Nice neighborhood," I grumble, prying my foot free from a twisted wrought iron railing. I get to my feet, look to the sky, and feel my stomach sink. I turn to the woman, who's peeking through the small window near the top of the door. She sees what I'm seeing. "Better lock it, too," I say. "Leave the city if you can."

A frantic nod, and then she's gone.

I toggle my comms and turn my eyes to the sky. "Guys, I think I might need you back here."

Above me, two columns shimmer into reality, each the size of a skyscraper, framing the hill I'm standing atop. Arcane symbols flash to life, bottom to top, glowing orange. When the last of the symbols are lit, a sheet of red energy stretches out between them, glimmering with hexagonal light.

"What's the situation?" Chuy asks.

"Hellgate," I say. "Big one. Better bring Jonas. Delgado?"

"I'm here," he says.

"Keep Robinson secure, along with Will and Gal. Make sure Samael is in a friendly kind of solitary. I don't trust him yet."

"On it," Delgado says. "But...did this Robinson guy... Is he who Samael says? The Architect?"

"Signs point to yes," I say, feeling the warmth of the fired-up gate, radiating out over the landscape. "Any progress on how to handle the Torment planet?"

"Aside from shooting it a lot, nothing new. But Bubbles is working on some...alternatives."

"Keep at it. I'll be in touch. Out."

A moment later, Sarah, armed like her Spartan self, and Chuy, carrying her modified Barrett, capable of firing at both close and distant ranges, rotate back onto the sidewalk. Chuy sees me, frowns at my condition, and asks. "What happened to you?"

"Pretty sure it was one of them," I say, pointing to the sky, where a small fleet of the strange Q-shaped craft are spread out over Beverly, unleashing a continuous rocket attack. Looks like they're going for maximum chaos and casualties. Then a handful of them peel away and swoop toward us.

Chuy turns to face Sarah.

Lifts a foot.

"Throw me."

"What?" Sarah says.

Chuy tilts her head toward the sky. "Up there. Just catch me when I come back down."

Sarah nods. She's seen and done enough insane shit to not question the plan. She links her fingers beneath Chuy's foot—and heaves.

Chuy accelerates up into the air, moving at what looks like escape velocity. Any other person would be screaming their guts out while flailing around like a feathered flamingo. But Chuy is cool, looking down her sights. The Barrett shifts into its longer ranged mode. She takes aim and—choom!

She fires a round that changes the trajectory of her ascent, pushing her back, but not shaking her concentration. Before the first bullet hits its target, she's fired again.

Sarah tracks Chuy's arc through the sky, propelled a little farther away with each pull of the trigger. "Your lady is nuts," she says, and then she bolts away, following Chuy's path.

"But she gets results."

True to form, Chuy's rounds each find their mark, punching through a glass panel at the front of each Q, and striking whatever kind of lifeform is piloting them with .50 BMG rounds capable of severing a body in half. The ships spiral from the sky, buzzing as they approach and crash into neighborhood streets, homes, and cars, which erupt in flame.

Jonas rotates into the street beside me, Henry next to him.

"What's the—*oh my god*." Henry cranes his head up, taking in the vast size of the gate, stretching up into the sky.

"I hate to point out the obvious," Jonas says, "but that's big enough for—"

The ground shakes as though from an explosion.

"—her." Jonas points upward as a massive, black monster with glowing orange membranes stomps through the hell gate.

"Nemesis," Henry says, smiling wide. "Sick." His eyes widen. He works the controls on his arms. "This is going to be wicked fucking awesome. Nemesis – Wages of Sin."

A rapid electronic melody plays for just a moment before raging guitars and a powerful voice, shouting 'Nemesis!' I recognize it as the end credit music for a Nemesis anime. It's not my kind of music, but it's strangely infectious and definitely appropriate, since I'm looking at Cherry Bomb's adaptation of the Justice Queen.

The creature's salamander-like body bobbles back and forth in an awkward gait, carried by its short legs—trying to hurry itself past the pillars. Once it's through, the beast topples forward, crashing down onto all fours with the force of a volcanic eruption.

A shock wave rolls pasts us, followed by a boom that shatters windows around the city. Then she roars, the high-pitched shriek followed by a resounding bass note that shakes my lungs inside my chest.

"Chuy, Sarah, keep on those ships."

"Already on it," comes the reply, followed by the crack of another Barrett round mixed with a bolt of lightning.

"We're going to handle Nemesis." I say and break the connection.

"We are?" Henry says. "Sweet."

"What's the play?" Jonas asks.

"Henry gets us close, keeps us mobile. You go ghost mode and push her back. Try to destroy the gate at the base."

"So, I do all the work?" Jonas says.

"I'm not above admitting a problem is bigger than I can handle," I say, slipping my railgun around from my back, and charging it up. "I'll keep you covered."

"I think you're overestimating what I can do," Jonas says.

"Pretty sure you're underestimating yourself," I say. "Every time things have escalated, you've risen to the occasion. Now, let's get this done."

Jonas sighs, gives a nod, and draws the Sword of Mars.

"Airborne ghost attack!" Henry shouts, grasping Jonas's and my armor by the back, and lifting us up into the sky faster than an F-14 Tomcat from an aircraft carrier.

I feel the need, the need for speed.

A scene of destruction unfolds beneath us. Large portions of the city are already crushed or on fire. Filing out through the winding New England streets are hordes of Torment zombies, capybaras, and other undying monstrosities. I recognize some after a moment. Mapinguari—several of them. A herd of Rygars, these ones lacking their usual Europhid co-pilots. Tenebris, cloaked inside swirling clouds of personal atmospheres, their tendrils shooting out to claim one victim after another. Others are new to me, and to the Europhid knowledge locked away in my head. But Henry knows a few.

He nods toward the ground, shouting. "That's a Hydra! And Chimera. Like a bunch of them." His excitement builds. "This...is..." An explosion below draws our attention. A man stumbles out from an inferno of a car, covered in flames. He staggers several steps and flops to the ground. Henry's expression sours. "This is...bad."

"Keep us away from the emotional zombies. Too close and they'll throw Jonas off."

"Got it," Henry says, swooping higher, up past Nemesis's head. She snaps at us, but we're moving too fast. Five hundred feet up, Henry comes to a stop. There are some Q ships nearby, but they head for Chuy and Sarah, who have taken up position atop the roof of a four-story, brown apartment building. "Okay, Mr. Titan. Do your thing. We got your back."

Dangling beside me, Jonas closes his eyes, and his body goes limp.

"Should we have told him not to bust open that orange shit?" Henry asks.

"Has he not seen the show?" I ask.

Henry shrugs. "Doesn't strike me as a TV guy."

"Isn't he your friend?"

"Bro, I've known him for like a few days. We saw some shit together—including a lot of boobies—but that doesn't mean I know his playlist. How come Cherry Bomb doesn't have any booby monsters? In Khaos, there were Harpies and Furies, and I mean, there's Chimera, but those were more like bona fide teats, which yeah, can do in a pinch, but they're not great for visual stimula—"

A shot from my railgun puts a muzzle on him. The tungsten disc buzzes away and evaporates a flying creature angling toward us.

"Flatubats!" Henry says.

"You've seen these things before?"

"They were part of the force that took out the Titans on Tartarus," Henry says. "I think most of these guys were there. Big ass bats that fill up with air, and then fart it out, propelling themselves like gassy jets."

"Just keep me steady," I say, aiming at the flying horde filling the air with loud clicks. Cup-shaped ears twist in our direction, and the creatures adjust course. They're closing in—but they'll never get close—because what I'm firing travels faster than sound. They'll be dead before they hear it coming.

I fire in bursts, carefully picking targets and then dropping them. In terms of firefights, it's almost relaxed.

But not for Jonas.

He's struggling. Grunting. Even though he's not in his physical form.

Below, Nemesis struggles to make forward momentum. Her massive head bucks and thrashes like she's been lassoed. But it's not enough. Nemesis is too powerful.

Then Jonas's sword starts to glow.

"I don't want to make this weird," Henry says, "but do you feel, like, a tingling in your nuts? Whoa! It's spreading, dude."

The glow emanating from the Sword of Mars extends up over Jonas's arm, spreading up through his body, flowing toward Henry's arm.

"I don't feel anything," I say, "but I think it's coming from Jonas."

"That kinky basta–argh!"

Henry spasms as he's enveloped by Jonas's glow.

And I'm…released.

The moment I feel gravity's tug, I rotate out of the air, appearing beside Sarah and Chuy.

"God damn!" Sarah says, flinching away from my sudden appearance. "The hell is going on?"

I point to Jonas and Henry, floating in the sky, glowing with white hot power. "God stuff, I hope."

Despite being on top of a tall building standing on a tall hill, and Nemesis being on all fours, she still rises up above us, larger than she's ever been on TV. She scrambles for purchase, but her claws just drag through the earth as she's driven back toward the gate.

All around us, Cherry's forces are struck by an invisible tornado that affects nothing else. They swirl and topple, careening into each other as they're manhandled and brutalized before being thrown back through the gate.

"Dark Horse," Delgado says. "You copy?"

"Situation here is improving," I report. "What's up."

"Situation is FUBAR everywhere else," he says. "Gates are appearing all over the world. That Nemesis you're dealing with, it's one of hundreds. Maybe thousands. This isn't an attack, it's an invasion."

I hear a voice speaking in the background, but it's indistinct.

"Bubbles thinks… Are you sure?" he asks her, and then he comes back to me. "She thinks it's *not* an invasion."

All at once, I understand.

"It's a distraction," I say. "To keep us busy while Torment catches up and crashes into Earth."

"The data matches. The planet is cruising now. In an hour, we'll feel the gravitational effects. In two...the solar system will have a new asteroid belt.

Nemesis lets out a wail as she's lifted up and flung back. The army flies back through the gate alongside her. Before any of the regenerating army can return, one of the pillars cracks at the base and starts toppling to the side. It's going to cause a massive amount of damage, and take a lot of lives, but far fewer than Nemesis would have.

The moment the gate extinguishes, both Henry and Jonas fall from the sky.

"Meet me at the Mesa!" I say, running forward, leaping up, and rotating at the same time. I emerge a moment later, five hundred feet above the ground. I wrap my arms around both men and manage to trigger my slew drive again. The last thing I see, before rotating back to the Mesa, is Boston on the horizon, a glowing gate amidst the buildings, and a second Nemesis ravaging the city. Home sweet home.

48

MIAH

"You assholes picked the wrong day to screw with Hildegard Kraus!" Hildy turns back to me and Cassidy. "Hold on!"

The *Bitch'n* breaks left, spins, and rockets forward. Despite looking like a giant turd, the vacuum of space allows the ship to move gracefully. Then we accelerate, cruising past several friendly ships reacting to the threat with less urgency.

The viewscreen is dizzying as we spin past much larger ships, banking beneath, around, over, and under.

"All ships," Mazzola's voice in my head shouts, "Formation Octavarian. Weapons free. Fire at all enemy contacts!"

I'm hearing it in English, but I think that's just my brain translating pure thought.

"What's formation Octavarian?" I ask.

"Nothing we need to worry about," she says, craning the ship around a hundred and eighty degrees. The viewscreen is a blur of stars, a flash of Mars, and then the fleet above, shrinking away.

"We're running?" I ask.

"We. Are. Using our brains!" Hildy shouts, working away at the controls. She whips around toward me. "Have you ever been a gunner?"

"Like on a ship?"

She rolls her eyes and points at Cassidy. "You're up."

"Yes!" Cassidy says, unbuckling and cartwheeling her way to a nearby station with several small viewscreens and two flight sticks, each with multiple triggers. Definitely something you'd need training on. Cassidy buckles herself in, grasps both sticks and shouts, "Let's rock!" like Vasquez from *Aliens*.

Before we can take action, the battle above commences. While the good guys are still working their way into formation, the bad guys unleash a cloud of small fighters, rockets, and streams of glowing rounds.

It's just seconds before the first space cruiser silently explodes.

"Take out the biggest ship!" Hildy says.

At the center of the enemy fleet is a massive oval, like a flat-Earther Death Star. Small fighters are streaming from all sides. I think it's the alien version of an aircraft carrier.

"Where should I aim?" Cassidy asks. She knows how to fire the weapons, but strategic aiming is a new concept.

"When in doubt, aim for the core," I say. "The middle."

Cassidy turns to Hildy for approval. She nods, but I can tell she's as clueless as me. I recognize the Tenebris ships, but there are many more civilizations represented here. Some even resemble craft within our own fleet. If the enemy fleets occupy the same space, it will be impossible to tell apart.

In *Star Trek*, Federation ships are easy to distinguish from Klingon, Romulan, or even Vulcan. But in real life, when shit goes sideways, it's impossible to tell friend from foe. Friendly fire is a real problem. Always has been. Even when men were hacking each other up with swords. In the heat of battle, covered in mud and blood, it's easy to see the enemy everywhere you look.

"Firing!" Cassidy says, and it seems like nothing has happened.

Then a series of explosions rip through the carrier.

"What are you firing?" I ask.

"Rail guns," Cassidy says. "A lot of 'em."

I know what a rail gun is, but I thought they were still future-tech. Then I remember *when* this ship is from. It's possible that a thousand years of Nazi innovation will give us a leg up in this fight. Kind of like they did for the U.S. in the space race with Russia. But there's no way we're carrying enough ammo for a fleet, and those tiny ships are making short work of our battle cruisers, which seem to lack effective close-range defenses, possibly because they're all packed too tightly. Missing the enemy might mean hitting a friend.

A slow chain of explosions works its way through the carrier.

I don't know that it will be destroyed, but it's certainly crippled, rotating to maneuver away. It's a start, but not nearly enough, and Hildy knows it.

"Ready to whack a mole?" Hildy asks.

"Huh?" I say.

"Ready!" Cassidy says, leaning forward, gripping the controls sticks tighter.

"Are we whacking the mole?" I ask. "Or are we the—"

A flash of white, and then we've relocated and turned around—behind the enemy fleet.

"Fire!" Hildy shouts.

Two Tenebris ships in front of us seem to just shatter in space, as rail projectiles punch through them. Miles away, a third ship is struck, the tungsten rounds continuing on their deadly rampage.

A hail of orange gunfire erupts from neighboring enemy ships. Before it hits us, a wall of white sucks us and spits us out at a new location.

"Fire!" Hildy shouts.

The railguns fire again, tearing a large, unfamiliar ship in half. Its occupants spill out, twisting in space as they simultaneously freeze and boil.

A fresh hail of glowing rounds explodes from the nearest ships, this time accompanied by rockets.

The fleet is erased by white, and then remade once more.

"Firing!" Cassidy says, getting accustomed to the pattern.

But so is the enemy.

"Those rockets are tracking us," Hildy says. "Even after we rotate."

Cassidy scores another hit, but it fails to destroy her target.

Worse than that, I get a glimpse of our coalition fleet, and they're not faring well. It's hard to spot ships amidst all the debris. Won't be long before we're the only ones left.

"Rotating!" Hildy shouts.

She puts us on the enemy fleet's far side, but they're on to us now. Gunfire and rockets chase us as soon as we emerge. Cassidy gets off just a single shot before we're forced to rotate again.

"I need to get out there," I say.

Cassidy twists around in her seat, "Get out there? Are you nuts?"

"I've done it before." I pull my adaptive armor's mask up over my head. It seals and pressurizes. "Is there an airlock on this thing?"

"Plenty," Hildy says, slipping in and out of the fourth dimension like a skipping stone. Cassidy does her best to squeeze off a rail shot with each jump, but every time we appear, the enemy rockets adjust course and close in. "But there's a faster way."

I look down at my hip. There's a subtle bump and a red dot indicating the slew drive's location. If I give it a whack and rotate, I'll be able to move through the universe unhindered. But that's also the problem. I could wind up a hundred million light years away.

"You don't need to move," Hildy says. "Because the ship is. Just rotate into the fourth dimension, don't move, not even a millimeter. Then rotate back out. The *Bitch'n* will have relocated, and you'll be in open space."

"Cool," I say. "Sounds easy. Totally easy. Great idea, Miah."

"Hey, Laser Chicken," Cassidy says, turning around. When I look her in the eyes, she smiles and says, "Ha. Made you look!"

She gets a smile out of me. Then I say, "Catch you on the flipside," and I rotate into the white void.

It's a weird kind of space. Endless white. No up, no down. The opposite of space, but without the visual markers provided by stars and planets. How would I even know if I was moving? I have no idea how Dark Horse and the others maneuver through this space, but I'm pretty sure I haven't so much as twitched. Or taken a breath.

I tap my hip again and a wall of normal space opens beside me. I rotate out and find myself floating behind the enemy fleet. No gunfire coming my way. No rockets.

It's easy to find the *Bitch'n.* A wall of gunfire pursues it as it flashes in and out of reality, narrowly evading shots while occasionally landing a hit on the enemy. It's not enough to make a difference. Not even close. The good guys are on the ropes.

But where to start? There are hundreds of ships, and not a lot of time.

Mazzola, I think, *are you there? Can you hear me?*

I don't know how to communicate via telepathy, but I'm thinking as loud as I can. When I get no response, I pick a random target and—

What do you require, Laser Chicken? He sounds gruff. Rushed. Stressed. *There is no time to—*

I, uh, I can help. Sir. I just need to know which targets to hit first.

Hit... he says. *With what?*

With...me, sir.

Grant me access to your mind, he says.

Weird, but okay. *Go for i—*"Hnk!"

I feel his mental presence like intense pressure expanding outward within my skull. He rifles through memories, old and new, dissecting who I am and what I can do. And he's not gentle about it. Feels like my eyes are about to explode.

Then it stops.

Do what you can, he says, and then he's gone.

Mazzola? Dude? You still there?

I think he must be dead until I look back at the enemy fleet and somehow know exactly which ships to strike and where they're weakest. Mazzola wasn't just getting to know me, he was leaving something behind. Knowledge. And I'm not about to waste it.

"Okay, Laser Chicken," I say to myself. "Let's see what you can do."

My wings flare wide, propelling me through open space. With nothing but a vacuum to resist my forward momentum, I accelerate toward a battle cruiser currently hammering our fleet with an array of strange energy weaponry.

No idea if the enemy has spotted me, but I'm pretty sure I'm moving too fast to target. Even if they locked those tracking rockets onto me, they'd never be able to catch me. Evading attack is the easy part. The untested bit of my plan comes next.

Approaching the ship's flank, I will every cell in my body to release energy. Normally, this is focused on my wings, or arm blades, but this is more like a complete transformation. Blue light flows out from under my armor, wrapping my body in a kind of forcefield. But the idea here isn't to absorb impacts and protect me, it's to strike, like the god damn fingertip of God.

As my power builds, I unleash a sustained blast of laser light from my eyes. The beam punches through one side of the ship—and out the other at the speed of light. It's all the encouragement I need.

I pour on the speed.

Faster than it takes me to realize it's happened, I'm through the ship, out the other side, and arcing back around in time to see it explode into tiny glowing bits. The impact didn't just carve a hole, it dispersed my energy in every direction, tearing the ship—and everything inside it apart.

"All right!" I say, tapping the controls on my wrist.

As I swing around toward my second target, 'Thunderstruck' by AC/DC fills my headset, fueling me as I become a streak of energy in the night sky, slipping in and out of enemy ships like they're water balloons.

As I punch my way out of another ship, sweeping around for another run, the *Bitch'n* appears beside me. The rail guns mounted atop the long ship fire—one, two, three—in time with the music's beat—at the 1:51 time mark displayed on my arm. The synchronicity gives me chills.

Cassidy's voice comes over the music, cutting in and out as they rotate in and out of reality. "You're—oing—t—aser—icken! Woo—ooo-hoo—oo!"

Ten minutes more of the same, I come to a stop, searching for ships that haven't been turned into rubble that will soon form a ring around Mars.

I can't find one.

We did it!

Then I realize the horrible truth.

I don't see a *single* surviving ship. Bad...or good.

Mazzola, I think. *Where you at, man?*

I circle the debris field. *Mazzola, if you can hear me, please let me know.*

"Hildy," I say. "Where you at?"

When I don't get an answer, my heart starts pounding. "Hildy? Cassidy? Guys, where are you?"

I spin around, but I can't find them anywhere. "Shit... Goddammit..."

Before I can completely lose my mind, the *Bitch'n* snaps into reality beside me. Looks like she eventually took a few hits. I don't see any punctures in the hull, but it's scorched and some of the rail guns are damaged.

Still no word from inside, but a single airlock hatch opens.

I accept the invitation and head for the door, feeling my energy wane as I do.

Inside the airlock, I extinguish my wings, and I'm pulled to the floor by the ship's artificial gravity. I stumble toward the door, weakness gripping my legs. The outer hatch closes, and I will myself to hang on until the space pressurizes. I just need to make sure they're okay... Need to stay conscious... Need to—

How did I end up on the floor? I think, and then I drift into darkness.

49

BREE

“I’m coming!” Glitter shouts, just before the wall, now high above me, explodes outward. His shiny wings unfurl, reflecting the flashing orange light from the terrible sky as little rainbows. He’s majestic.

Then he folds his wings and dives toward me.

But it’s not enough.

“You need to speed up!” I shout.

Glitter flaps his wings and is kind of all over the place. I don’t blame him. He’s only existed for like thirty minutes, and while I imagined he could fly, I didn’t imagine him being good at it.

So that’s on me.

I roll around in the air so I can see the ground.

Gonna go splat in a few seconds. Falling is faster than I thought. And I don’t think my rescue pony is going to reach me in time.

It’s up to me to save my life.

I close my eyes so that I don’t get distracted, and so I don’t see myself hit the ground.

I give myself permission, I think, and I wipe my thumb across my forehead. I don’t feel anything. Because Cherry Bomb was probably lying. She’s such a jerk. But what if she was lying, but also right?

It feels right.

I give myself permission.

Why?

Because I’m Demon Dog.

Not good enough.

Because I don’t want to die.

Not even close.

Because...because I'm not a bad guy. I'm not Tenebris. I don't want to eat people. I...I... My brother isn't dead because of me.

I wipe my thumb across my forehead.

The burn sweeps through me. My skin stings as it dries out and cracks. I roar from the pain, and I wail as my hair itches and falls from my head. I've never told Miah how much changing into Demon Dog hurts. Because he'd never let me change if he knew.

But now...now he doesn't get to say when I can change.

Because...

"I did it!" I shout, and I open my eyes.

I see a flash of brown stone—and then nothing.

A tongue is licking me, but not in a fun 'Hey, wake up,' kind of way. I open my eyes to a sideways view of the brown, dusty ground. "Ouch."

"Oh!" Glitter says.

I push myself up and over onto my back. Everything hurts but compared to the blood covering my new pony's nose, the pain isn't that interesting. "Were...you...eating me?"

"Well, no. Of course not. I don't eat meat."

"Just candy," I say. That was part of what I imagined.

"Righteo!" he says. "But...I was so thirsty. I'm sorry. I couldn't help myself."

"I didn't imagine you as a vampire," I complain.

"No, but..." He looks over his shoulder. "They caught me."

I climb to my feet and look. There's an army of those sad zombie people nearby, walking away from us.

"They weren't interested in you, because, you know, you were dead already. At least, we all thought you were. Looks like we were wrong."

I shrug. "I'm immortal. I don't really know how it works, either."

"Anyway," Glitter says. "I think they must have seen us fall from the tower and came over for a s-s-snack."

He twitches kinda weird.

"Like I said, they weren't interested in you..."

"Oh..." I say.

Glitter puts on a pouty face and lowers his majestic head toward the ground. The sparkle is gone from his mane. It's covered in thick globs of blood. His whole body is. "They…they ate you?"

"I tried to fight them," he says. "I promise. But they kept coming. And biting. And I was bleeding all over the place. And then I got tired. I tried to fly away, but they held on tight. Then the big one showed up. And—he tore off my back leg. Ate it like it was a lollipop. That's when I fell down. And the others…

"I don't remember dying, but I know I did. And then I was alive again." He smiles, showing red-stained teeth. "I was so thirsty when I woke up, and they didn't care about either of us, so they left. And my body came back together and fixed itself right up. I'm sorry. I'm so sorry."

I push myself up and put my rough hand on his snout. "It's okay. I forgive you."

He holds his head high, looking happy and noble. "Y-you do?"

"Of course," I say. "We might be covered in blood, and we might eat really gross things, and look like bad guys sometimes, but you and me, all that bad stuff can't stick to us. It just falls away. I didn't make you good at flying, but I made sure to include incorruptible innocence. And now I know I have it, too."

Daylight Glitter shakes his body from front to back. The blood stuck to him slips away and sprinkles to the ground. A moment later, he's shiny and new again. "Well then, what do we do next?"

"We need to stop Cherry Bomb," I say.

"How do we do that?" he asks. "She seems p-pretty mean. And she can make anything she wants, like me and all these bad people and this whole awful planet."

"We need to save my friends," I say.

"Are they strong, too?"

"They're an old lady and a nerd." I smile. "But they'll know what to do next."

"How are we going to find them?" Glitter asks.

"They're not far. Someplace underground. And—I left a trail."

Glitter looks back and forth so fast it makes me giggle. "I don't see a trail."

I tap my nose. "You gotta smell it."

"I'd rather not," he says. "It smells really bad here."

"Yup," I say, "but only one of the smells is *my* smell."

"Your...smell?"

"I piddled," I say. "While I was being moved. Just a little bit at a time. I knew that if I could become Demon Dog, I'd be able to follow my own piddle scent. I tried pooting, too, but I almost pooped my new armor, and that would have been embarrassing."

"Well, hop on and tell me where to go!" he says, rearing up onto his hind legs.

"Miah is going to be sooo jealous," I say, and I hop onto Glitter's back. I tilt my head up and sniff the air. It's stinky here. Worse than the Tenebris factory and Typhon's insides. But nothing here smells exactly like my pee. I point to the right and say, "Thatta way!"

Daylight Glitter jumps into the air and flaps his wings. We nearly flip over sideways, but I tug his hair to the left, and he straightens out. "You just need help. Like Ratatouille!"

Once we get moving, and the scent trail shifts, I tug to the right, and we swoop around and over a horde of the sad zombies. They just watch us soar past, unable to catch us or eat us or any other nasty thing. I look around to make sure no good guys are watching.

Then I give them all the finger.

We glide down through a winding valley that's full of old blood and mold, over a hill that's half missing, and past a footprint the size of a baseball diamond. I giggle at a bunch of the zombie people who were crushed into the ground so hard that they're stuck, grunting as they try to free themselves.

"Whoa!" I shout, pulling back on Glitter's mane. We come to a fast stop, and I jump off. "The trail ends here."

"I don't see anything," he says.

"There's a cave around here. Underground. There has to be an entrance."

"Does there?" he asks. "Cherry can make anything she wants. Why not a cave with no entrance?"

He's right, I think. I'm glad I made him kind of smart, too.

I can do this, I tell myself. It's just like my killer instinct...but without the killer part. I calm down with a deep breath, think about what I want to see, and then open my eyes.

I look around us, and then stomp my foot.

"It's not working."

"Better make it work soon," Glitter says, looking over his shoulder. "I think they saw us land."

A big bunch of the crazy people are running toward us. Like a mile away, but we don't have long. And there's some other things with them. Smaller things. But faster.

"C'mon!" I shout at myself. "Where are they?!"

A flicker of blue snaps past me as I spin around. I skid to a stop and focus on it. A pulsing blue spot on the ground, just like the red one I saw on Typhon's neck vein. "Here!"

I dive on the spot and slam my claws into the hard ground. It crumbles and scoops out like it was sand. I love being strong. I dig like a dog, flinging rocks and dirt out between my legs. Two feet down, the ground crumbles to reveal a cavern. I pound the hole with my foot until it's big enough to fit through.

"I'll be right back!" I shout, and then I jump into the dark.

The air is cool and smells better down here, but it's also sad, because it's full of nice people fear.

"Who—who's there?" Burnett asks. "Wini, someone is here!"

Wini just groans. They're not doing well.

"It's me," I say. "It's Bree."

"And Daylight Glitter," my pony says, his head inside the hole above. "We're here to rescue you."

"R-Rescue?"

"Just...promise not to be afraid," I say. "When you see me."

"Because you are Demon Dog?" Burnett asks.

"Yes."

"Are the others here?" He sounds hopeful.

"I changed on my own," I say.

"Good," he says, sounding weak. "Good for y—" He thumps onto his side, which will make what comes next easier.

I pick them both up and carry them to the hole, which is fifteen feet above.

"Better hurry," Glitter calls down. "They're almost here!"

"Catch!" I say, and I throw Wini toward the ceiling. Glitter bites the back of her armor and drags her out of the hole. Burnett goes next. I jump up behind them and claw my way out.

Glitter was right. The nasty guys are almost here. I take hold of Wini and pick her up. "Wake up!" I shout, and I give her face a smack.

Wini blinks and sees me. She's frightened for only a moment. Remembers who I am, even though I'm wearing the red clothing Cherry gave me. "Bree... You—"

"Hold on!" I say, and I haul her up onto Glitter.

Burnett wakes up after two extra smacks. Then I get him up behind Wini. I jump on last, and wrap my arms around them, grabbing hold of Glitter's mane, and holding the other two in place. "Fly, Glitter, Fly!"

We lift off into the sky. He's getting better at this. I'm about to show my last trick when I look down and see a second blue spot glow on the ground not far away.

Someone else needs help.

50

DARK HORSE

My exit from the fourth dimension is less than graceful. I topple to the side, tugged by the limp weight of Henry and Jonas. We spill to the smooth floor of the Mesa's vast ops center. When I sit up, I find a very surprised Delgado and Bubbles looking down at me.

"Jonas!" Bubbles says, jumping to her feet. She drops down beside him, checking for a pulse.

"They're both alive," I say, laying Henry flat on his back. "Just unconscious."

"What happened?" Bubbles asks.

"I'm...not sure. Jonas was trying to push Nemesis back through the gate, but she was too tough for him...until Henry came into contact with Jonas. Then it was like their powers combined."

"Like Captain Planet?" Delgado asks.

"Sure," I say, deadpan. "It was like Jonas was siphoning Henry's power. But when the job was done, they were both out for the count."

I search the room.

"Where are Chuy and Sarah?"

"Here," Chuy says, entering ops with Sarah, Will and Gal. "Are they okay?"

"Vitals are good," Bubbles says. "But...without knowing what happened to them, it's impossible to know when they'll wake."

"I'll take it," I say, taking Delgado's hand and getting back to my feet. "Give me a sitrep."

"Short version: invasion. Worldwide. Every major city and its surrounding suburbs. Best guess, she's going for maximum population damage in the shortest amount of time."

"Or," Henry grunts, pushing himself up. "Cherry Bomb is Putin in disguise. But with a nice rack and fashion sense that makes me want to get spanked."

Sarah hurries over to Henry. Helps him sit up.

"That was stupid."

"Hey," he says, smiling. "I didn't even know what I was doing. It just kind of happened."

"Everything 'just kind of happens' when you're around." Sarah leans her head on Henry's. It's the most affection I've seen between the siblings. Even Henry looks a little surprised by it. But then he accepts and appreciates it. "Just…try to be more careful."

"I'm always trying," Henry says. "I'm just really bad at it."

Will and Gal flank Jonas, leaning over him.

"Hey," she says, patting Jonas's cheek. Very motherly. He might not be blood, but they're definitely his parents, and despite living more years than is comprehensible, they love him like their own. "C'mon, baby. Open your eyes." She kisses his forehead.

"Oh, my god," Jonas grunts. "Stop. Mom. You're embarrassing me in front of my friends." He chuckles and winces. Hand to his forehead, he adds, "Oww. What hit me?"

"*You* hit Nemesis," I say. "Pushed her back through the gate."

"Cool," Jonas says, sitting up with Will's help. "Super cool. Did I imagine things or was there another gate and another Nemesis?"

"They're all over the world," Bubbles says.

Jonas sours. "So, we knocked ourselves out to basically accomplish nothing?"

"Not nothing," Delgado says. "You made a discovery. Your powers can be enhanced via physical contact with Henry."

"What makes me special?" Henry asks.

"Your bloodline," Will says. "It's the same as Jonas's." He looks at Sarah. "And yours." He turns to Bubbles. "Yours." He takes hold of Gal's hand. "And ours."

"Wait, what?" Jonas asks.

"Gods, Titans, children of the Orphic Egg," Gal says. "You're all descendants…of ours."

"It wasn't something we did on purpose," Will says, and he smiles at Henry. "It just kind of happened."

I'm not sure what to say to that. Starting to feel like all of this is a big ol' cosmic 'oopsie.' Like Will and Gal forgot to rubber up and ended up creating a fucking bonkers reality. But they're not really the ones to blame. That rests squarely on the shoulders of one man.

"Where is Robinson?" I ask Chuy.

"Locked him up," she says.

"Locked him up…where?" Delgado asks.

"With Samael," she says. "I thought we might get lucky, and the big guy would murder him."

I give her a questioning glance.

"Relax. We cuffed him." She waits a beat. "Samael. We cuffed Samael. Oh, Dios mío, no tienes sentido del humor. Cowboy is with them."

"Any eyes on Cherry Bomb?" I ask Delgado.

He goes into a trance-like state for a moment. Then he snaps back to us. "No trace. She must still be on the Torment world."

"What's the latest on impact ETA?"

Bubbles answers before Delgado can check. She's not connected to the computer system, but I'm pretty sure she can do the math in her head faster than Delgado's nanites can relay the information. "Still accelerating. It will reach us in two hours, thirty-five minutes."

"Two hours until kaboom," I say. "Got it."

"Actually," Bubbles says. "The gravitational effect of another planet that close will be devastating to Earth. Between the invasion and gravitational upheaval, I'm not sure there will be anyone left, at time of impact."

"Maybe destruction isn't her goal?" Delgado asks.

Will nods. "That tracks. She's…a corruption of Gal. She wants to remake creation the same way she did the Great Escape. Wants it to be a reflection of her soul—"

"If she has one," Chuy says.

"The universe will become a dark and twisted place of torment," Will says.

"And you'll be her prisoner," Gal adds.

Color me confused.

"She doesn't want to kill you? I thought she hated you."

"Hate..." Will shrugs. "Love. Sometimes there's not much difference. She wants me back with her in that horrible place, not because she desires me, but because I found a way to escape her."

"So, obsession then?" I ask.

Will nods. "Sounds right."

Henry rolls backwards, up onto his feet. Looks like his normal self again. "Man, I hate that scent. Obsession. For men. Oooh. I was in this JCPenney. Shoplifting. I needed socks. Sue me. So, I'm walking by the perfumey section, and there's this chick behind the counter. A solid nine. So, I walk up to hit on her, see if a changing room is available for a pit stop." He winks at Gal. "You know what I'm saying, right grammy? Anyway, so before I can even say a single word, she sprays me in the face with Obsession. Goes in my mouth. My eyes. Up my damn nose. Smelled it for a week. She's *my* Nemesis."

"A font of wisdom," Jonas says, back on his feet. "As usual." He pats Henry's shoulder, and then turns to me. "So...Robinson? You found him?"

"Saved him," I say. "Cherry was after him, too."

"He have answers?" Jonas asks.

"All of them," I say.

"Then let's—"

The familiar white glow of an opening to the fourth dimension fills the room. I turn to find Miah on the floor, his adaptive armor covered in soot and banged up. Crouching over him are Cassidy and Hildy. I'm about to ask what happened when I notice the tears in their eyes.

Hildy rolls Miah onto his back and performs CPR.

I hurry to them, followed by everyone else. "What happened?"

Hildy ignores the question, pumping hard on Miah's chest.

"We were ambushed," Cassidy says. "Cherry Bomb had her own fleet. Lots of ships. Miah went out. Into space. He fought them. Fought all of them. *Destroyed* all of them."

"How many ships did we lose?" I ask.

Cassidy frowns. "All of them, except for *Bitch'n*."

That's a sucker punch. Means our plan for Torment is KIA.

“Survivors?” I ask.

Cassidy wipes her tears, trying to hold them back. “Three,” she says.

“God…” I say, and I understand her tears.

“Mazzola,” Delgado says, head lowering.

“You don’t need to do that,” a voice says. The groups swivels around to find Robinson, followed by Samael and Cowboy. I want to question why they’re here, but I’m also glad.

“Hildy,” Robinson says. “Really. It’s not necessary.” He crouches down beside her. Places his hand on her clenched fists. “He’s going to be fine.”

“He’s dead!” she shouts.

“He’s not dead,” Robinson says. “Just…taking his time.”

She stops pumping.

“Building his strength,” Robinson says. “For what comes next.”

“How could you know that?”

He offers an apologetic smile. “Because I wrote it… Because I created this. All of you.”

Despite Robinson’s apparent concern for Hildy and the kindness he’s displaying, our team gathers around him, brows set low, arms crossed, fists clenched. He’s got a lot to answer for, and right now, he seems like the only one who might know a way out of this mess.

Without looking back up, Robinson holds up an index finger to the group. “One second, guys.”

I feel like I’ve been caught off guard with a slap. The looks on the faces of the others confirms they feel it, too. The hell is up with this guy? I’m about to haul him up when he places a gentle hand on Miah’s chest.

“Any second now…” Robinson says.

Miah’s eyes open. He sees Hildy, smiles, and then he sees Robinson.

“Hey, Miah,” Robinson says, making no effort to hide his own affection or that he’s excited to be here, despite the fact that he’s about to get throttled.

“Hey,” Miah says, and he offers a fist bump. “You’re the author guy, right?”

Robinson bumps his fist. “Jeremy.”

“Sweet,” Miah says, and he sits up to find the group gathered around him. “Uhh, hey, what’s up guys?”

51

MIAH

"Guys, I'm sorry." Robinson helps me up. I dust myself off, and I face the people I've let down. "I tried to stop them, but–"

"Not your fault," Dark Horse says. I can tell he's angry, and sad. They lost friends. A fleet. The plan is falling apart. But his ire isn't directed at me. He's pissed at the author.

Everyone is.

It's an intimidating group of powerful people, most of whom could erase the man. But he seems unconcerned. Almost like he's trying to contain...joy?

"Is he smiling?" Sarah says, her spear crackling with arcs of lightning.

"Sarah," Robinson says, smiling now. "So badass."

He turns to each member of the team, saying their first names, voice full of affection. "Henry. Hildy. Chuy. Dan. Bubbles. Jonas. Will. Gal. Milos." He smiles wider, like he's in on something funny only he knows. "Cassidy Rose."

Cassidy, unlike the others, smiles. "Hi."

Robinson turns to me. "Nehemiah." Then to Dark Horse, he says, "Moses." And finally, he turns to Samael. "Samael."

"You seem familiar," Samael says.

"I am as much Ezekiel as she is," Robinson says, motioning to Gal. "Maybe even more so."

"You're a little bit of all of us, is that it?" Dark Horse says. "You think that will make us like you?"

"It might make you hate me." He turns to Delgado. "Some more than others. I'm sorry about your wife. And Lindo. And McCoy." He turns to

Cassidy. "To both of you. All of you. And for Mazzola." He turns to me. "And Richard." He turns to Dark Horse. "And your team."

"You created a future full of white supremacists and made me live among them," Dark Horse grumbles. "Can you imagine what that was like?"

"I…did," Robinson says.

Dark Horse clenches a fist.

He's about to sock the guy.

Will steps between them. "Take it easy on him. He's not our enemy."

"He *created* our enemies," Chuy says.

"He created all of us," Gal says, then she motions to herself and Will. "Through us. Without him, none of us would even exist, and if any of you truly believes that it's possible—even for people without horrific enemies—to live a happy-tappy, pain-free life, you haven't been alive long enough to know that's bullshit."

"It's clear he doesn't mean us any harm, and that Cherry Bomb sees him as a threat," Will says. "I think we should hear him out. Unlike the rest of us, he's…just a normal guy."

"Very normal," Sarah says, looking the man up and down.

"I can explain everything," Robinson says. "Well, not everything. That would be dangerous. But I can tell you how we got here. Just…not where we're going."

"Doesn't sound much like help to me," Dark Horse says.

"Moses," Cowboy says. "My friend. This man is not our enemy. He wants what is best for all of us. And he was not aware of our situation until recently."

Dark Horse and Cowboy have a momentary stare-off, but the gunslinger's gaze is unwavering.

"Fine." Dark Horse points to Robinson. "Spill the beans. Every last nugget."

Robinson lets out a sigh and scratches his mostly bald head. "I started writing the Infinite Timeline a few years ago."

"The Infinite Timeline?" Henry asks.

"All of this," Will says, understanding. "Us."

"It started with Dan and Wini, and a bag full of penises."

Dan smiles, and Robinson adds, "She's okay, by the way. I can tell you that much." He turns to me. "As is Bree." And then he looks to Dark Horse. "And Ozark."

"Why are you using our first names?" Sarah asks.

"Because he's our friend," Cassidy says. "It's obvious."

"He's not using *my* first name," Chuy points out.

"Because I don't want to find out what it's like to be on the receiving end of a close-range Barrett round," Robinson says.

Chuy grins a little.

"Anywho," Robinson says. "All of your stories came next. *Flux. Tribe.*"

"Is that us?" Henry says. "I think that's us."

"*Exo-Hunter. The Dark. Mind Bullet. Infinite. NPC.*"

"A little on the nose," Samael grumbles.

"Toward the end of the second Infinite novel, I started thinking about reality in a more complicated way. Life as a simulation flipped into simulated life becoming real merged with thoughts about the Infinite Worlds theory."

"Which is?" Henry asks. "'Cause I got more hairs on my nuts than brain cells with sciencey knowledge. Wait...can you tell us who has the hairiest nuts? Cause you'd know that, right?"

Sarah swats her brother.

"What?" Henry says. "It's a legit question. Please let it be me. I want to have Sasquatch nuts."

Robinson is close to laughing. Says, "You do now."

Henry tugs open his pants, eyes going wide, mouth dropping. "I *do* have hairy balls! Wait...I've always had hairy balls. Did you already know that, or like, retroactively change reality by deciding something right now?"

"That...is a smart question," Bubbles says. "I would like to know the answer."

"I'm not sure I know the answer," Robinson says. "Look... It occurred to me that if the Infinite Worlds theory was true..." He turns to Henry. "The Infinite Worlds theory means that every possible reality you can dream up exists out there somewhere."

"You mean..." Henry says. "So, in one of these worlds...I've had sex with Dolly Parton?"

"Yes," Robinson says.

"Ho-lee shit."

"Can we stay on task?" Dark Horse asks, and then he turns to Robinson. "Are the tangents your fault, too?"

"ADHD," Robinson says, tapping the side of his head. "Tangents keep things interesting."

"I like this guy," Henry says.

Sarah crosses her arms. "I don't."

"Point is," Robinson says. "I started to get concerned that if the Infinite Worlds theory was correct, then it was possible that everything I was writing was real, and it was also possible that it was taking place in *my* reality, since I had implied that at the end of *Infinite 2*."

"The universal constant," Will says.

"And Benford's Law," Gal adds.

"Exactly," Robinson says. "When I started writing the last of the crossovers, I added a contingency plan for myself. That's why Cowboy went looking for someone. How he found me. Brought me here."

"What crossovers?" I ask.

"*The Order*," he says. "When Moses's people came together with Delgado's, who had already merged with McCoy's group. And *Khaos*, which brought together—"

"Us," Henry says. "Miah. Bree. Jonas. The whole freakin' underworld. That was sick, by the way. Also, you might have issues."

"So," Jonas says to Robinson. "Bubbles is real...because of you?"

"In a sense? I guess. But also because of Will and Gal. And the Orphic Egg. They're all a part of this universe, too. I'm just the...unknowing originator."

"The Architect," Samael says.

"I guess." Robinson approaches Samael. "I regret what I put you through. What I did to your mind. For Torment. For Cherry. Even *I* couldn't imagine how horrible it must have been. I wish I had done things differently."

"You didn't know," Gal says. "You were just writing novels."

"Yeah, dude, no one wants to read books where nothing bad ever happens," Henry says. "Not that I want to read novels. But I'd read mine."

"'God of the Sky, bitches,'" Robinson says, smiling.

"You see?" Henry thrusts his hands out toward Robinson. "This guy... He *knows* us. Maybe even loves us." He turns to Dark Horse. "He's cool, man. Probably put a bit of himself in all of us, which sounds pervy, and I wish it was, but I mean, this is wicked awesome, right? To meet the guy who thought you were so cool, so...righteous...that he'd put you in a novel and made you the god damn hero."

"Can't say I see any of Captain Privilege in me," Dark Horse says.

Robinson points at me, and I have no idea what's coming. "KISS."

"Uhh," I say, but then he points to Henry.

"Poison." He points to Hildy. "Nina Simone. The remix." He points to Dark Horse. "Talking Heads."

Dark Horse's face falls flat. That means something to him, far beyond being an awesome 80s band.

"Best band front man," Robinson says, and then he smiles at Henry. "Aside from Bret Michaels. On three. One, two, three."

"Freddie Mercury," I say, along with Henry, Hildy, and Cowboy. Dark Horse doesn't answer, but he doesn't need to. We all know he agrees, including Robinson, the apparent source of our mutual love of music.

"It's probably the last thing you want to hear, but you all have helped me process a lot these last few years." Robinson points at me and says, "Chronic pain. PTSD."

He points to Henry. "My desire to no longer fear. To be free of anxiety and panic."

He points to Will. "My longing to escape suffering, combined with my fear of death."

He points to Samael. "My questions about reality and—" He points to Gal. "As Ezekiel, wrestling with beliefs about creation."

He turns to Jonas. "Finding true friends."

And then to Bubbles, he says, "Someone needs to figure out what the ducks are up to...and finding your place in the world after living in a...a bubble for so long."

Cassidy claps her hands.

"And me?"

Robinson smiles. "We're friends. In real life. A different you. But you. And you both inspire me." He points to Delgado. "Same with you. We game on the weekends."

"I don't want to ask," Chuy says, "but I'm curious."

"I was a child of the 80s." He glances at Dark Horse. "Tough women in films had a big influence on me. Ellen Ripley. Red Sonja. Sarah Conner. Marion Ravenwood. I admire strong women, and I'm not just talking about muscle."

"Vasquez," Hildy says. "'Let's rock!'"

Robinson snaps and points at Hildy. She gets it. Then he turns to Sarah. "Applies to you, too."

Cassidy gasps. "Hold on. I said that just a little while ago. 'Let's rock.' But I don't know who Vasquez is."

"Doesn't matter," Will says. "Because *he* does. Because as much as this universe came about because of my actions—it also came from his head."

Dark Horse steps up close to Robinson, looking down at him. "Mutual appreciation for music aside, why me? Why that story. That place? That fucking time?"

"Because," Robinson says. "I got tired of racist assholes bitching every time I wrote a positive black male as a hero. I wanted to stick it to them with the coolest, most badass son-of-a-bitch I could dream up."

"Geez. Suck his dick while you're at it," Henry whispers, but no one reacts. This is a turning point. We can all feel it.

"Did it work?" Dark Horse asks.

"Oh, yeah," Robinson says. "They got pissed. Left some nasty reviews. I'll probably hear about this, too."

"Hear about this...too?" Dark Horse asks. "You already wrote this? Everything we're saying now?"

Delgado chuckles. "What the hell am I looking at? When does *this* happen in the book?"

Hildy jumps and spins toward him. "Oh! I know this. 'Now. You're looking at now, sir. Everything that happens now, is happening now.'"

"*Spaceballs*," Henry says. "Classic."

"Look," Robinson says. "I can't reveal anything, as much as I'd like to."

"Why?" Dark Horse asks.

"Spoilers," Sarah says, still unamused.

"Because Cherry Bomb," I say, all the pieces falling into place. "She knows about him. Figured it all out. If he wrote our stories, inspired this world, and brought us all together...then he not only knows how it all ends, but he could also change the ending."

"Unless..." Dark Horse says. "He hasn't finished writing it yet. If that were true..."

"And she got a hold of him..." Bubbles adds.

Delgado finishes the thought. "She could make him write the ending *she* wants."

And it's at that very moment that the Mesa's ceiling dissolves to dust high above our heads and peels back as though carried away by a tornado, revealing a single figure floating down toward us.

Cherry Bomb.

52

DARK HORSE

A swirling cloud of stone grit whips around her as she descends. It's dramatic, but I think it's just meant to piss off Delgado. The Mesa is always sparkling. Now it has a hole in the ceiling, and it's going to take months of sweeping to clean the joint.

It's just rude.

"Okay, people," I say. "Everyone stay cool. Wait for my sign."

"Why are you looking right at me when you say that?" Henry asks.

"We all know why," Sarah says, activating her shield and charging her spear.

I turn to Jonas and give him a look that I hope translates to something like, 'See if you can get into her head.'

He nods, and I hear his voice in my thoughts. "Already working on it."

I lift my rail gun and charge the magnets. Beside me, Cowboy's hands lower to his hips. He could unload both revolvers in a heartbeat, but he doesn't attempt it. Because he already did, I realize, when he rescued Robinson. And here she is, alive and well, and floating down toward us with a shit-eating grin on her face.

She's also dressed kind of...kinky. Tight red leather. Lots of belts and buckles where they have no place being. There's a triangle cut out of the fabric, allowing a hint of cleavage. Her long blonde hair is pulled back tight, gathered in some kind of conical hair device, from which it emerges as a ponytail of angel hair pasta.

Chuy nudges me. I glance over. "You're drooling."

"Makes two of us," I say, when Chuy doesn't take her eyes off the descending abomination.

"Okay," Henry says. "How come no one told me the bad guy was a smokin' hottie?"

"You might have switched sides," Sarah says.

"Nah, I'm spoken for," Henry says.

For just a moment, nearly everyone takes their eyes off Cherry Bomb and looks to Henry. But his out-of-character comment will have to wait. Cherry comes to a stop, fifteen feet above us. The cloud of grit dissipates, scattering all over the floor, and I swear I hear Delgado let out an exasperated sigh.

"I'm here to talk," Cherry says.

"We're not making a trade," Miah says.

Cherry looks at him, curious. "I remember you. Zeus's memories. Such a dirty place." She turns to Jonas. "And you. All that power and you still can't access my thoughts."

"Not trying to access your thoughts," Jonas says, and he makes a fist.

I swear I hear a subtle, muffled pop.

And then Cherry falls to the floor, landing with a slap.

"Mind Bullet, bitch," Jonas says.

"Yes!" Henry shouts, extending both hands in the air. "That...was... *sick!* 'Mind Bullet, bitch.' Crack! Slap! Oh man, I nearly pissed myself—"

Henry's victorious elation is interrupted by laughter. Cherry Bomb, on the floor, alive and well. She floats back up onto her feet like she's demon possessed, standing among us now. "It's going to be so much fun tormenting you lot."

Tormenting...

She's not planning on killing us. But she's definitely planning to destroy the world—or at least civilization. Remaking the world in her twisted image is the big picture, but torturing her enemies is the icing on the cake.

Fun.

Before I can give the command for an all-out assault or generate some banter to buy time, Robinson steps out from our group and heads toward Cherry Bomb.

The hell is he doing? Seriously, this guy is a massive liability.

"Hey again," he says, offering an awkward wave.

"Lost your fear?" she asks.

"I'm terrified." There's a quiver in his voice. He's not lying. "I just... I wanted to apologize."

She glares at him, unamused.

"For what?" Robinson asks on her behalf. "Glad you asked." He laughs, but he's the only one. Clears his throat. "Look, I think you already know that *I* didn't know my novels would lead to all this. That you would really exist. That a universe would be created from my stories. Or that you...would endure what you did for all that time. It is...unfathomable."

"I'm only here because you made me so resilient," she says, sarcasm exploding from her like a nuclear blast. That said, she's not really wrong. "Please, continue. I'm a sucker for groveling."

"Uhh," Henry says. "BDSM Barbie, I think he's apologizing."

"Apologies are foreplay. Groveling, the sex. And after that, the climax, which I do love to draw out. For years, and years." Cherry leans toward Robinson, eyebrows raised, smiling wide. "Do continue."

"I'm sorry," Robinson says, "that you forgot who you are. I'm sorry you lost...everything."

"The only things I've lost," she says, "were taken. By you." She looks at Will and Gal. "By them." She stands up straight, grinning. "But don't worry. I'm going to take it all back. You can die, absolved, after thirty-odd years of unending anguish."

She places a hand on his shoulder. "Or...I can help you finish your story and give you a quick death. Ten years instead of thirty. Just long enough for you to finally realize there is no God, and you'll simply cease to exist. But you should feel proud. The legacy you leave behind will be eternal horror. Your name will be on the tips of the tongues of billions of damned people, cursing you for creating them. For giving them no escape."

"There is an escape," Cassidy says, stepping up beside Robinson, hands on her hips. "Our friend was bitten by one of your zombie assholes, and he didn't come back like the others. He stayed dead. Because he—"

"Stayed dead?" Samael asks. "After being killed by the damned?"

"Yah. What I said. Death is the escape, if you—"

"Believe in God?" Cherry says. "Ask for forgiveness from some distant eternal entity responsible for the creation of an infinite number of timelines?" She scoffs. "In all my uncountable years of life, I have seen no evidence for such a thing."

"Can't see it," Cassidy says, "if you're not looking."

Cherry's whole face distorts as she smiles, on the verge of a mental breakdown. She swivels her head toward Cassidy. "I think I will start with you."

Robinson takes Cassidy's hand. Slowly tugs her behind him. Is he protecting her? Or...

A flash of blue light makes me squint. When my eyes adjust, I see Miah unleashing a violent beam of laser light at Cherry. If Robinson hadn't moved Cassidy, she'd have been in the way.

He knows what's happening.

This is already written, too.

For a moment, I dare to hope Miah's surprise attack will be enough. But the laser light strikes a solid, crystalline surface that breaks the powerful beam into a rainbow that streaks out the far side and glows against the far wall.

"Fuck it," Henry says, launching forward, arcs of electricity crackling from his eyes.

"Catch!" Robinson says, picking up Cassidy and throwing her toward me. I catch her under the arms a moment before Henry collides.

Lightning explodes out from the impact, and two bodies go flying—Henry...and Robinson.

While Henry ricochets up and into the chamber's stone wall, Robinson sprawls across the floor, sliding to a stop against a computer console, unconscious. Maybe dead. If that's true, this fight is up for grabs.

"Let her have it!" I shout. "Don't hold back!"

"Now," Miah shouts to Sarah, and he extinguishes his rainbow laser blast. The moment Cherry is revealed, Sarah throws her charged Oxium dory. It happens so fast, I nearly miss it. And so does Cherry.

She staggers back a step, stunned.

A gurgle comes from her mouth. It's followed by a dribble of blood.

Cherry takes hold of the spear, unleashing a shock that sends a spasm through her body. She drops to her knees and pitches forward, red gore splashing onto the floor.

"Everyone back," I say, raising my rail disc rifle. I glance to Cassidy. "Turn away."

"I can handle it," she grumbles.

"Now," I say, stepping closer to Cherry Bomb.

"Be careful," Will says. "She's not dead."

"She's like us," Gal says. "Impossible to kill."

"Way I see it, you left her in a place of eternal torture, and now she's bringing that to the rest of us. Can't say I blame her. I'd be pissed, too." I turn to Cherry. "So don't take this personally. I'm putting you out of your misery."

"She'll just regenerate," Chuy says.

"We should rotate her into a star," Hildy says, knowing she's the only one who could accurately pull that off without a lot of planning.

Since I'm not about to let her teleport into the sun, I slip my finger around the trigger. "Won't be anything left to regenerate when I'm done."

And that's when Cherry Bomb starts laughing.

Ahh, shit...

53

MIAH

Sometimes people do things because they think it will make them feel better. Like when I sought to add a flourish to an edible-fueled night via a dash of 1980s hair band metal, and I bought W.A.S.P.'s self-titled 1984 album. Our decisions sometimes don't make sense. Hindsight usually reveals logical flaws. But the act at the time relieves tension, of which at present there are galactic boatloads.

I'm assuming this is what prompts Dark Horse to pull the trigger on his fancy future weapon. The rapid-fire metal discs buzz through the air moving so fast they're impossible to see.

But the results… The messy coup de grâce is when the energy shield that protected Cherry from my laser attack fails to work against the tungsten discs. Though she's our enemy, has killed and kidnapped friends, wiped out a fleet I failed to save, and wants to destroy, well, everything, I can't help but feel a little bad when her body's core inverts and explodes out her back. The floor behind her is painted in a slick pool of chunky gore.

The worst part of it is that Cherry just keeps on laughing. Even when her spine shatters and the top half of her body falls away from the bottom. Her legs fall to one side, her shredded torso to the other. And then she goes and makes it weird.

Like really weird.

She moans. And I don't mean subtly. She's full-on porn star in the throes of a fake orgasm so loud you'd jump up and pull the TV's plug to make sure no one hears what you're watching.

Dark Horse's finger lifts away from the trigger, a look of horror on his face. Not because he's painted the floor with a human body, but because she's now licking her top teeth and lips, looking right at him. "Oh, I'm going to have fun with this one." She looks at Will. "Can we make him immortal, too?"

Screw it, I think, and I unleash another laser blast from my eyes, hoping she won't have the same protection when she's been severed in two. The beam strikes the invisible shield again, but it doesn't turn into a rainbow this time. It reflects. Intact. Heading straight toward Cassidy.

There's an explosion of light, and I'm terrified I just killed her.

But when the light fades, Cassidy is fine, protected by Sarah's luminous shield.

She gives me a look that says something like, 'Dude, what the fuck?'

I shrug with a 'How was I supposed to know?' expression on my face.

Note to self: Lasers are a bad idea.

"Oh, you all are an old-fashioned lot, aren't you? Something gets in your way, break it down. Set it on fire. Blow it up." Cherry Bomb pushes herself up onto her stub of a body. She's clearly in pain, but I think she's still getting off on it.

It's disturbing to watch.

I'm not sure I've ever been this uncomfortable before, even when Donna Fisher broke into my bathroom stall while I had half a log dangling. I don't think she heard the pinched off plop, on account of the three girls looking for her. But I still had to sit there, pants around ankles, clenching the sequel to what might have been the biggest dump of my fourth-grade year. Scarred me forever.

But this...this is worse.

"You all should think about creating something every now and again," she says. "Much more satisfying." In a blink, she's whole again, standing in front of us like nothing ever happened. If not for the discarded pair of red-clad legs, I might think it had been a hallucination.

"Everyone stop," Will says, and I think it's the right call. We can't hurt her. Can't kill her. And I think she's holding back. Because she's not here to kill us. Not yet. She's just proven how trivial we are.

But it doesn't stop one last attempt.

Hildy disappears into a wall of white, emerges behind Cherry and wraps her in a headlock.

For the briefest of moments, I see actual fear in Cherry's eyes. Then she becomes immaterial and slips free before she's rotated into a star. A solid punch to the gut drops Hildy to one knee.

Cherry stands over Hildy, pouting down at her. "Oh, the desperate lover. I think I'll torture you, by torturing him."

Dark Horse moves to intercede, but Jonas stops him. "She's not here to fight...and we can't win."

"The Titan is right," Cherry Bomb says. "I'm here for them." She waggles a finger toward Will and Gal. "You all are inconsequential."

I'm not sure that's true. She's defended our attacks with ease, but why not just attack us outright? Why not attempt to kill us?

Maybe she knows she can't?

At the same time, even if we could take her now, it wouldn't be without significant loss. We're not ready.

Dark Horse gets it, too. "This your idea of parley?"

"Oh, no," Cherry says. "Parley is meant to avoid violence. I am simply taking what I want and choreographing the end for maximum pleasure. Killing you now would be easy. But far less fun." She turns to Chuy. "He must be dreadful in bed. Straight to the point."

"Cherry," Will says. "Please. Stop. You don't need to—"

She pinches two fingers in his direction. His entire face disappears, becoming a flat stretch of skin. His jaw flexes, trying to open a mouth that no longer exists. He paws at his face for a moment, until realizing the truth of his fate. Then he stops, calms, and waits through the panic. He's been alive long enough to know his death will be temporary.

Maybe she's telling the truth. Maybe we really don't stand a chance?

But that doesn't change what happens here.

The team faced this moment before. They traded the lives of Will and Gal to get our teammates back. But Wini herself told me *not* to save them. Why? Did she know things would be different? Did she think she and Bree and Burnett could stop Cherry somehow if they didn't return? Or are Will and Gal so important that we can't let them go, no matter what?

Will collapses to the floor, convulsing, unable to breathe.

The only person, aside from Cherry Bomb, who looks undisturbed by his horrible demise is Gal. She doesn't bend over to ease his pain.

Doesn't whisper anything comforting into his still present ears. She just sighs and says, "Is this really necessary?"

"Consider it a lesson," Cherry says, turning to Dark Horse. "In patience. Won't be long before I get to you all."

Gal approaches Cherry. Grips her arm—gently. "Cherry. Please. I know you. We started the same. We can be the same again. Sisters."

"Twins..." Cherry looks lost in a dream for a moment. Wistful. Then she smiles. "Had we been conceived in the womb, I'd have absorbed you. So weak and obsessed with...*this*." Disdain leads her hand toward Will on the floor. Now dead. Temporarily.

"The man you haven't been able to forget about from the beginning of time until the end, thousands of times repeated," Gal says, "because, like me, you love him. You're just...broken. Corrupted at the core. But it can be fixed. You can be fixed. Just let Will—"

Cherry Bomb whips her hand to the side. Gal's neck snaps, kindling in the hands of a giant. She crumples in a heap, landing atop Will and rolling limply to the floor. Her mouth hangs agape. Her eyes empty. I've seen the look before. It's no less disturbing now, even knowing she won't stay dead for long.

"Would anyone else like to speak now?" Cherry asks. "No? Very well." Cherry beckons to Robinson's supine form like a seductress. "I'll be taking this one, too."

"We're not going to trade for them," I say.

Robinson collides with Gal and Will. The three of them lined up look like hotdogs in a package.

Cherry gives me her full attention. "The brave angel. Last of the Lux. Chest all puffed up from single-handedly defeating an entire armada."

She says that last part with a mocking tone. Like it didn't really happen... Or like she allowed it. Another test? Could that be why she knew how to turn my laser light into a rainbow? She hasn't just been testing our limits, she's learning how to counter our attacks. By fighting her, we've been helping to defeat ourselves. She's been Borging us this whole time.

"I don't recall offering a trade," she says. "What put that idea in your head, I wonder? Huh. But your wish is my command. There will be no trade. It was never required. I wanted to impart a false sense of hope in you all, by returning your friends unharmed. Well, two of them. But now I see that keeping them...at your request, will be so much sweeter to watch play out."

She glances at the others, and I follow suit. They look pretty pissed. At me. Especially Hildy and Delgado.

I don't say a word. We can't talk about this in front of Cherry. I'm making the right call. If Dark Horse disagreed, he'd have said something. Henry and Cassidy, too. But their lips are shut. Wini told us not to trade, so we're not.

Though I'm not sure how that's going to change the outcome.

Cherry turns to Samael. "Come."

"Yes, mistress," he says, skulking out and standing beside her. I thought he was menacing at first, a big man with indominable power, but now I just see a wounded man who does what he's told, molded by lifetimes of abuse. He's...sad.

Cherry looks to the sky, out through the top of the opened Mesa. She floats up with the ease of Superman. The unconscious and/or dead bodies of Gal, Will, and his ancestor follow her like mindless automatons. Samael is the last to leave the ground, his expression blank, unable to look at us.

"Can you hold onto them?" Dark Horse whispers to Jonas.

"Already trying," Jonas says. "But...it's like trying to read the mind of a fellow Titan or god. It just doesn't work. However she's doing that—" He motions to our friends, now fifty feet up and rising. "—telekinesis has no effect."

"You know," Henry says. "For a super-powerful Titan, you don't accomplish a whole lot, even when your parents are being abducted."

"Henry," Sarah scolds.

"What?" he says. "It's true! In Khaos, he choked against Typhon. In Israel, he broke down into tears. And now he—hck!"

Henry lifts from the ground, launches back, slams into the stone wall for a second time, and falls unconscious. All eyes turn to Jonas, arm still outstretched. "If anyone comes up with a plan, let me know." As he walks away, Hildy heads in another direction. Without another word, most of the group disperses.

I'm left with Dark Horse and Cassidy, all three of us watching as Cherry Bomb rises into a rectangular starship, and then disappears into the sky.

"Well," Cassidy says. "Looks like it's up to the three of us. Who's with me?" She holds up two fists, one to each of us. Dark Horse and I bump her fists at the same time.

"Let's workshop the shit out of this," Cassidy says. "Now, which one of us is the smartest?" After the three of us glance back and forth at each other, she says, "Right. I think we need some help."

"Excuse me..."

We turn to find Cowboy, leaning against a workstation, Stetson lowered over his eyes. He tilts the hat up, a gleam in his eyes. "I might have idea."

54

DARK HORSE

"Oh! Oh!" Cassidy runs in place, knees to shoulders, fists stretched down between her legs. "I know! We get the bell thingy. Then we go around to different dimensions collecting the coolest good guys and have them come back to fight with us!"

Cowboy smiles. "Not bad plan, but…not this time."

Cassidy freezes, one leg propped up like a peeing dog. "Whatchu mean, 'this time?'"

"It's a long story, and it can wait," I say, remembering his tale of the real FC-P, of his summoning heroes from other worlds including a near god-like man from Antarctica. I have to admit, the idea appeals to me. Would be nice to share the burden with people who've been through something like this before. But he's got something else in mind.

"We need to understand what we are facing," he says.

"Can't exactly talk to Will and Gal," I point out.

"Everything we need to know is here, we just need to study it." He sits at a computer console. Works his way through a few websites. The screen displays a book cover. Bright yellow, emblazoned with the words INFINITE and JEREMY ROBINSON.

"Know thy enemy," I say, understanding. Everything we need to know about Cherry Bomb is in these books.

"Know thy creator," Cowboy says. "His books provide insight into how he thinks. How fashions worlds, and also rules that guide them. If can understand *him*, perhaps also understand her."

"Worth a try," I say, "but…I'm a slow reader."

"I can't focus on any words that don't also have pictures," Cassidy says.

Cowboy nods. "We need the others."

"Or," Cassidy says. "Just Hildy, Bubbles, and Delgado. Because, you know…" She taps her head, indicating her brain. "They're super smarties."

"Agreed," I say.

"I'll get Hildy!" Cassidy says, skipping for the door with gazelle-like leaps.

"I'll find Delgado and Bubbles," I say. "You figure out which books we should start with."

Cowboy nods and gets to work, while I leave the large ops center behind, heading into the maze of tunnels that makes up the rest of the Mesa's underground network. The tunnels are long and winding, smooth on the side as though created by a lava flow. To the human eye, they seem random, but they're closer to a vascular system, bored out by a non-human intelligence—the remnant of our one-time enemy turned ally, the Chut'uni, who have already been taken out of the fight. Meanwhile, Cherry Bomb has a planet full of her twisted creations, which also happen to have sprung from Robinson's mind.

He sure does raise the stakes.

I can only hope he doesn't take it further.

I glance into some of the rooms I pass along the way, spotting gathered teenagers and ancient people, all of whom were captured by the Other and rescued by Delgado. They huddle in small groups, whispering about what's happening, but not directly a part of the resistance. Not this time. They fought with us, against the Chut'uni, but Delgado vowed to never put them in danger again. So, until they're adults or trained for combat, their fight is over.

In one of the rooms, I spot a familiar face. Nathaniel. Delgado's son. While many of the young people here consider him their father, Nathaniel is his only biological son. I don't know the others by name, but they know who I am. When I stop, the whispering cuts short.

I lean into the room. "Nate."

"Hey, Moses," he says. "Looking for my dad?"

Most of these teens, like Cassidy, have varying degrees of psychic or empathic abilities, a lingering gift of the Other's genetic tinkering, adding bits of his DNA to theirs in an effort to make their…parts compatible with his.

"Seen him?"

He closes his eyes for moment. "In his quarters. Ten doors down on the right. Someone is with him. Someone…he likes?"

I smile. "Bubbles. Had a feeling about them."

"Sounds like a stripper," one of the kids says.

"Farthest thing from it," I say, and then to Nate, I say, "How you holding up?"

"Honestly?"

"Always," I say.

"People are kind of freaking out. This isn't like before. It's a bigger deal. We…we can all feel it."

"Feel what?"

"Fear," he says. "It's radiating from all of you. Only one of you really believed there was hope…but he's gone now. Left. With her. And she's just as confident."

"Fear keeps us on our toes," I say. "The key is to not give in to it."

"We know," a girl with abnormally large eyes says. "But we also know to keep hoping. Once you stop doing that, might as well stop fighting."

"You're right," I say. "Which is why I never stop fighting."

Nate smiles. "We know."

"Thanks for the intel," I say, and I start down the hallway.

"Moses?" Nate says from the doorway.

"Yeah, bud?"

"Don't let what happened to McCoy happen to my dad, okay?"

I nod. "If it comes to it, I'll take his place."

"I know you will," he says, and he steps back into the room.

Hopefully the kid's not some kind of prophet. I don't want to lose another person. In war, that's an unrealistic goal. When the bullets are flying, people are going to die. But we can minimize casualties by being prepared. For that—I stop outside Delgado's closed door—we need people with IQs a lot higher than mine.

I haven't done too shabby for a guy who scored an 840 on his SAT, but I won't pretend to understand the nuances of all things cosmic, eternal, and supernatural. I'm a glorified grunt who found himself in a *Last Starfighter* situation. A leader, sure, master tactician, maybe. But I'm not the brains...even with all this Europhid knowledge compressed inside my head. Knowledge isn't the same as smarts.

The metal door gongs when I knock.

Muffled voices respond from the far side, along with a hint of rapid movement. The door cracks open to reveal Delgado's face. "Hey."

"Drowning your woes in the bosom of a woman?" I ask, smiling.

"Yeah, he is," Bubbles responds from within. "Haven't you heard? World's ending, man. I don't want to die a virgin."

Bubbles opens the door all the way. Her adaptive armor is tugged down to her waist. Thank god, she's wearing a bra, which must have been a gift from Chuy, because it's just a touch too small. "You'll have to settle for second base. We have an idea. World hasn't ended yet."

"Okay," Delgado says. "But–"

I feel for the guy. He's been working his ass off for years. Hasn't had time for a relationship, or the desire since his wife died. Bubbles is the first person he's shown any interest in since I met him. "Consider me a very insistent wet blanket. Look at it this way, whatever was about to go down in here doesn't need to be a one-time tryst."

"You said 'we' have an idea," Delgado says, and he squints. "Whose idea was it really?"

"Cowboy's," I say.

He sighs. "Fine."

"Back in ops," I say. "Take the express route." I give my slew drive a tap and rotate away.

The endless white void envelops me like a blanket. For a moment, I can breathe, the weight of the universe lifted. Figuratively and literally thanks to a complete lack of gravity, or anything at all with mass, other than myself. It's peaceful, and I probably spend too much time here. But it's the only place I can feel quiet these days, and the only place Cherry Bomb's influence can't reach. Whatever the fourth dimension is, it's not part of Will's created universe. It must predate it. Some original state of reality. Maybe even predating all realities.

Maybe this is where God lives? I wonder. I hope not, because I've done some things in the void I wouldn't want a deity watching. "Hello?" I call out, but it's like being in a sound-absorbent room. Vocal cords give volume to my voice, which emerges from my mouth and ends just inches away.

I take a deep breath through my nose. Smells a bit like ozone…and the beach—sans the salt. But it feels the same. Energizing and relaxing. I linger for another moment, take a second deep breath, and then exhale as I rotate back to ops.

Delgado and Bubbles are already there, armor back on, seated at separate consoles. Dan is hands off, letting his nanites do the work. Bubbles is locked in, eyes on the screen, as text flies by. Hildy sits nearby, absorbing information more slowly. Looks like blog posts, book descriptions, articles by and about Robinson.

Enjoying this, asshole? I think. Guy must have a colossal ego, making the story all about himself.

Bubbles leans back in her chair and lets out a slow breath. "Done."

"Which book?" Delgado asks.

She looks confused for a moment, and then says, "All of them."

"A-all of them?" Delgado asks. "That's just shy of seven million words."

"What can I say, my brain still works like it's connected to every computer in the world."

"You're so hot," Delgado whispers.

"Before things get hot and heavy again—"

Cassidy gasps. "Dad, are you… Is she…" She turns to Bubbles. "Are you going to be our mom?"

"No tangents!" I shout. "It ain't going to happen. Not now. Fuck Robinson and his damn tangential, ADHD bullshit. Just…answer the question." I turn to Bubbles. "Did you discover anything?"

Bubbles nods. "I know what to do."

55

BREE

Dear Diary,

I am kicking serious booty. I made a pony. I saved Wini and Burnett. And now, I'm going to risk my life to save—I have no idea who. That's, like, totally heroic, right? Or noble, or something. I guess it could also be stupid, but I think Miah would do the same thing, and he's usually pretty good at being noble and heroic.

Not that I'm going to tell him *that. Because I'm still angry at him. I can't really remember why anymore. It doesn't seem important anymore. So maybe I'm not angry at him. Probably why I can think nice things about him.*

Maybe I have perspective now or something?

Ooh, maybe I'm maturing. That would be cool. I wonder if I'll get armpit hair soon and have to shave my legs?

Won't be a problem when I'm Demon Dog.

Okay, that's it for now. I have random strangers to save!

Toodles!

"Wait here," I say, as I put Wini down in a seat at my castle ice cream table. She's groggy, but she's waking up. "Help yourself to ice cream. It will help you feel better and wake up, because it has sugar and dairy, which I heard in a YouTube video actually hydrates you better than water, because there's fat and stuff that you have to digest, so it doesn't just slide through you and get peed out. That's what I heard."

Burnett slides off Glitter's back and into my arms. He's like twice my size, but it feels like I'm holding a single feather. Being strong is cool, but

I have to be careful with normal people, because they'd break like a feather, too.

I put him in another chair. He blinks back into consciousness, wobbles around, and then sees my ice cream bowl. "Oh... Ice cream." He helps himself with no prodding.

"Bree, dear..." Wini leans on the table, forcing her eyes wide. "Where are the others?"

"No idea," I say. "But I'm here, and Cherry is not. So, you're safe. We can figure out what to do after I rescue the other people."

"What other people?" she asks.

I shrug and look out the castle window. Far below and away, I can still see the blue glow of...I don't know what it is. Helpful Instinct? That sounds dumb. Merciful Instinct? Not really a Demon Dog vibe, but...it works. I can be merciful. "All I know is that they need my help. That's enough, right?"

Wini smiles at me. "Should be, honey."

"You guys just stay here," I say. "Eat the ice cream. Seriously. I'll try to be el quicko."

I step to the window and Glitter follows me. I look back and say, "You stay with them. Protect them. If anyone bad comes here, fly them away."

"Aww," he says. "I want to come."

"Ach!" Burnett says, ice cream falling from his mouth. "The winged pony speaks! English!"

"First, winged pony? For your information, a pony with wings and a horn is called an *Alicorn*, and *nothing* else. Get it right. Second, I made him that way, silly," I say, and then I turn to Glitter. "You don't feel like eating blood anymore, right?"

"Righteo," he says. "But I *do* have a hankering for ice cream."

Wini sighs. "I've seen some shit, but this... You know what?" She slides her bowl toward Glitter. "We can share."

"Oh boy!" Glitter says, clomping over to Wini and sitting down on his butt.

"Everyone be nice," I say, and then I let myself fall out the window.

Claws dig into stone, turning the fall into a four-legged run, straight down the wall. Doesn't feel any different than running on the ground. My claws just kind of lock into place until I pull them out. I bet I could run on a ceiling. That would be cool, and probably creepy and sneaky.

Thirty feet from the ground, I leap out over the crowd of people that gathered while I was running down. They're all reaching out for me. And they're covered in blood. Screams chase me, but they're sad. Hard to make out, there's so many of them, but I'm pretty sure I hear, "Oh god!" and, "Run, run!"

The moment I hit the ground, they chase me. Want to eat me.

I'm not sure they could get their teeth through my charred skin. It's pretty tough. But Miah would say it was stupid to try finding out. So, I'll let that be a mystery and focus on the blue spot a few miles off.

I run like a dog, leaping forward with each stride. The big rocks and old skeletons don't slow me down. I just jump over everything. The people from the wall are way back now, but there are more ahead, turning toward me, and a whole bunch on either side, spinning around and chasing as I pass by.

"See ya later, slow poke!" I say to one, and then I jump way up and flip over this bulbously fat zombie guy. His double chin is bigger than I am. Definitely can't walk or run. Probably just bobbles around on his bean-bag butt cheeks and stubby sausage legs.

"Don't let me eat you!" he shouts, as he reaches out for me, big teeth ready to chomp down. He definitely eats everything that gets near him.

But I'm out of reach.

I'm also not great at flipping yet.

I'm, what's the word? Agile? But it's not like I've taken gymnastics or something. Instead of landing on my feet, I land on my face. And I'm moving so fast that my body bends the wrong direction as I slide forward on my forehead.

Luckily, I'm also flexible. When my feet touch the ground to either side of my head, I dig in with my claws and snap my body back up into a standing position.

I shake my head and look back. There's a ten-foot trough carved into the ground by my forehead. The chunky guy is another ten feet back. Still reaching for me and telling me not to let him eat me.

Who would let *that guy eat them?*

"Yeaaaaaargh!" A naked man comes streaking out of a hole in the ground that must be a cave. He's terrified, but he can't stop himself as he runs straight toward Fatty Fatkins.

The big guy hears the scream and turns toward the running man, reaching out. Both of them are screaming now.

"No! Please, god! Not again!" the running man shouts.

"I don't want to be fat!" Fatkins wails. Both of them are sad. This place...is horrible. "I used to be so beautiful!"

That's when I realize that what I thought was a bald, obese man, is a woman. All traces of her girlish features have been lost inside her meaty form.

Feeling sad, too, I turn away and start leaping again. But that doesn't stop me from being able to hear the running man's screams change into a wet chomping sound, and Fatkins choking as she swallows and cries at the same time.

I'm so distracted by what's happening behind me that I miss what's happening in front.

I plow right into one of the sad people, but it's like a bowling ball hitting a pin. The man's legs break as he's flipped up and over me as I pass. "I'm sor-ooh!"

But he's not alone. I bounce back and forth, ducking and weaving between their reaching arms. "Serpentine, bitches!" I shout like Henry would. Then I leap up over a bunch of them, landing on the side of a tall stone spire. Two jumps and I'm on the top. It's not far now. The blue glow is just fifty feet away.

In fact, I think I can... I take two steps and leap with all my strength.

I wave down to the sad people as I soar above them. Then I focus on the blue ground rushing toward me. I won't have long to dig a hole, so I pull my feet back, and right before I hit, I kick down. The dry rock crumbles beneath me, and I fall right through. But the dead people won't be far behind.

Landing forty feet below is easy. So is seeing, despite the only light coming from the hole I made. And then that disappears, too, as the first zombie reaches the hole and falls in, cracking bones all over its body when it lands on its head.

"Who's there?" a woman asks. Doesn't sound afraid. Actually, she sounds kind of angry.

"Show yourself," another woman says. Also not afraid. More...indignatant? Indig...whatever.

"Hi," I say, knowing that my Demon Dog voice might trick them into thinking I'm *not* here to rescue them. So, I add, "I'm here to rescue you."

"Heavens, they sent the child?"

"Wait..." I say. "I know you." I leap toward the voice and land in front of Linda. Her arms and legs are encased in stone. Her body is naked and covered in long, crusty streaks of blood.

"Demon Dog," she says, smiling down at me. "Would you be a dear and break us free?"

"Aren't you Zeus?" I ask. "And like super strong? Like Henry and Sarah?"

"I'm afraid Cherry Bomb did something to the stone here. As long as we're encased in it, we lack certain abilities. At the very least, we can heal. Wouldn't have been a pretty sight when my insides were hanging out. I believe she allowed us that to prolong our torture. It seems to...please her greatly."

"I'm soooooorry!" It's a woman's voice, and it stops with a crack when she hits the cave floor.

"They won't stay dead for long," the other woman says. "Better hurry."

I turn around to find the strongest looking, most beautiful woman I've ever seen in my life, even though she is also covered in blood and lines of healed gashes. Her muscles flex as she tries to break free, but she can't.

"Who are you?" I ask.

"Helen of Sparta," she says, chin raised, face indignant. *Indignant! That's the word.* "Set me free, so I might smite these fools."

"Sorry, Linda, she sounds tougher than you." I leap up to the stone encasing one of her arms. Squeeze it between my hand, grunting from the effort. For a moment, I think I might not be strong enough. Then it cracks, breaks, and falls away.

"You do remember who Zeus is, child, do you not?" Linda grumbles.

"Hold on to your old lady pubes," I say. "I'll get to you in a second."

"Dear Lord," Linda says, "you have spent far too much time with Henry."

While I drop down and start to free one of Helen's legs, she punches the stone holding her other arm. Behind me, in the dark, more people scream as they drop down, the stream of zombies going faster and faster. Apologies echo around us as those that fell get back to their feet.

The stone breaks between my hands, and I scuttle over to her second leg. This time I punch like Helen did, and the work goes faster. Just three punches. She breaks her hand free at the same time, and she falls onto her feet. When she stands up straight again, it's like looking at a giant monster rising from the ocean. Except prettier, even with all the blood.

"I'll retrieve our things," Helen says, dashing off into the cave.

"You do that," Linda says. "I'll just hang around here like curing meat."

"Hold your horses," I say, punching one of her legs free in one strike.

"I see the Ambrosia worked well," she says.

"Oh, yes. I guess I'm a god now." I punch free her other leg, getting the hang of it now. "Miah, too."

"Wonderful. How is the good fight going?" she asks.

"I have no idea," I say. "Miah left me behind."

"Do you know what fate is?" she asks. I shake my head and break free one of her arms. "It means you're always where you were meant to be. And I believe you were meant to be right here, right now. I've got this..." She points her hand at the other stone. Lightning tears through the cave, shattering the stone and lighting everything up—including the fifty or so sad zombies running toward us.

Linda lands beside me, graceful for a chubby lady. That's when I see her freed arm.

"You have your hand back!"

She flexes her hands, electricity flowing between them. "And got myself into this mess. But I think it's about time we corrected that..." She looks down at me with a sweet smile. "Don't you, hon?"

I nod, and she thrusts her hands out.

Lightning cracks through the chamber, spreading out, bouncing off walls and forming a chain between the still growing horde. Every one of them convulses and then...explodes into one, big, steamy mess. Even by my standards, it's nasty.

"Here," Helen says a moment before a large, flowery sun dress strikes the side of Linda's face. "Tired of looking at you."

"Admit it, you like what I got," Linda says, wriggling her body as she tugs the dress over her head.

I turn to find Helen, already dressed in ancient armor that reminds me of Sarah's. She's holding a big round shield, and a sword. Atop her head is a helmet that somehow makes her look even cooler. "What's the plan?"

"Step one," I say, "get out of the cave. Step two, get back to Wini, Burnett, and Glitter."

"Did...did you bring a stripper to rescue us?" Linda asks.

"No, silly... Glitter is my flying pony."

Linda looks surprised. "You have Pegasus?"

"I have Daylight Glitter," I say. "And he is the bestest—"

"PEACE," a man shouts from beneath the hole. It's followed by another booming voice from above saying, "LOVE."

56

MIAH

"Feels weird," I say, "abandoning the planet."

"Well, it's not like everyone is in their rooms sulking now," Cassidy says. The comment is meant for me, but the other occupants of *Bitch'n*'s bridge hear it just as clearly. And it smarts.

"We...were being selfish," Bubbles says, eyes on the floor.

"We were being human," Delgado adds. Definitely has a tone. Guilt mixed with defensiveness, and if I understand the situation correctly, probably a case of blue balls. Go Bubbles. Human for just a few days and already good for a hoedown in the sheets.

"We're not abandoning Earth," Hildy says, working the ship's controls. "We're saving it. From that." She points to the viewscreen.

A familiar round shape emerges from the depths of space. Cherry's planet. Torment. The journey was quick. Just ten minutes...without rotating. Torment is gaining on Earth faster than I thought possible.

"How long until they collide?" I ask.

"Thirty minutes," Hildy says.

"Will there be anyone left alive on Earth, even if we can stop it?"

"I'm coordinating Earth's militaries and emergency services." Delgado doesn't even look like he's concentrating hard, but he's got a lot of computing power thanks to the nanites that keep him networked to the whole world. It's like he's the composer, keeping his little friends on track, and they're the orchestra, doing the heavy lifting. "We're not really making gains, but neither are they, aside from Nemesis. She's...hard to stop, and I'm not about to go nuclear on major cities. But casualties could be worse." He turns to Cassidy. "I'm sorry, by the way. You're right. We were being selfish. Afraid. I let you down."

Cassidy offers a lopsided smile as a peace offering and says, "You won't do it again."

"How long until we're on the ground?" I ask.

"Three minutes," Hildy says.

I toggle my comms. "Jonas. Good to go?"

"Waiting on your go ahead," he says.

"Copy," I say, and then to Hildy, I say, "Take us in."

We bank toward the planet's atmosphere, which from a distance appears blue, thanks to the still visible oceans. But the land is covered in thick clouds, flashing with orange light. And beneath that, hell.

"Cassidy," I say, getting a firm salute in response. "You're on defense. Man the guns with Hans and Franz. Shred anything that isn't…us. I guess."

"Copy that, Laser Chicken," she says, unbuckling from her seat of no buttons and moving to the gunner's chair. She proved herself in the Battle of Mars. She'll do it again here. She works the keyboard like a pro, scans the screen, and says, "Hans and Franz are good to go."

"Things are about to get rough," Hildy says, her voice booming over the ship's intercom. "Hold on to something or buckle up."

A moment later, we punch through Torment's exosphere. When we reach the mesosphere, friction covers the ship in flames. From an outside view, we'd look like a fiery meteor about to break up. With all the shaking, it feels like it, too. But Hildy and Dark Horse assured me the big multi-hulled workhorse could handle it.

Fire dwindles away to reveal massive, dark clouds all around us, flickering with orange lightning. The view makes me feel small and fragile. Inconsequential. By the time we slip out of the clouds, I'm nervous. Then it gets worse. The jagged terrain below is alive with motion. Rivers of living creatures flow into towering hell gates, the planet's occupants queued up for miles. Even if we can pull this off, Earth will still be screwed…unless Bubbles comes through on her end.

"Over there." Delgado points to a flat portion of land, clear of gates and Cherry's abominations.

"I see it," Hildy says, banking us toward the clearing.

"Is…is that a castle?" Delgado asks, but then we're past the unusual structure, swooping in for a landing.

We touch down gently, despite the ship's massive size. Hildy is a good pilot.

I unbuckle and stand, feeling a little breathless. "Okay..." I let out a sigh. "Keep us covered. Keep the hatches shut after we leave. If shit goes south, don't come out to help. Just take off."

"Hey." Cassidy reaches back and takes my hand. A sense of calm flows through me. "You can do this. Also, a little something to pump you up." She taps her adaptive armor's controls and music starts to play through the comms, for me and for everyone else. I smile. Eminem's 'Lose Yourself.' It's the perfect song to save the universe to.

"Later skaters," I say to the three-person bridge crew, stepping into the industrial-looking metal hallway with a bop in my step. Doesn't take long for the bop to fade despite the music. What we're about to attempt, it's insane.

I enter the hangar bay to four faces that look as unsure as I feel, and one that's just amped for a fight.

"Let's fucking do this," Henry says, bouncing from one foot to another. A boxer in his corner, waiting for the fight to begin.

"You good?" Jonas asks me. "You look a bit pale."

"Dandy," I say, giving two unenthusiastic thumbs up. "We don't have any time for speeches, so..." I turn to Chuy. "Lock up tight behind us. Cassidy could probably use a second gunner."

"What I do best," Chuy says, giving me a nod. I can tell she's nervous, too, but she buries it before my eyes.

Compartmentalization is the key to battle. Lock away your fears, your loved ones, your god-damned taxes. Nothing exists outside the battle. I do my best to follow her example, but it's hard. Bree is somewhere out here, along with Burnett, Wini, Will, Gal, and Robinson. For all I know, they're all dead.

Stop, I tell myself. Bury it. Dig it up later. Until then...I slug Henry's shoulder and echo his, "Let's fucking do this."

Sarah steps up beside me. Glances in my direction. "We got this."

I can tell she's trying to convince both of us, so I just hold out a fist and let her bump it. Sarah doesn't talk a lot. Doesn't get involved in drama. Doesn't really share much about her past. Not like Henry, the open book. Makes her hard to get to know, but she gives everything she has to every fight. I'm glad she's by my side. When Jonas joins us, the hatch opens and lowers to the ground.

A dusty hellscape is revealed. A hot breeze stings my face. The adaptive armor keeps the rest of me cool and comfortable.

"Happy hunting," Chuy says.

The moment we reach the ramp's bottom, the hatch closes behind us. The *Bitch'n* then lifts off, rising twenty feet above the ground, hovering low enough to stay out of sight and high enough for the weaponry on its underside to extend.

Jonas leads the way, arms outstretched, searching for the right spot, dead center in the planet's X and Y axes, with the sun at our back. He stops a hundred yards from *Bitch'n*.

I activate my comms. "How are we looking, Hildy?"

"You're looking fine from here, babe," Cassidy says. Kid knows how to make me smile.

"We haven't drawn any attention yet," Hildy says. "The hordes are still focused on the gates."

"Any signs of the hot chick in red?" Henry asks.

"I think we'll all know when she shows up," Sarah says. "If she shows up."

Jonas stretches his arms over the back of his head, one at a time. "She'll show up." He bends forward touching his toes. "Hard to miss a planet moving." He stands up straight, cracks his knuckles—which is hard to do with the adaptive armor on—and drops to one knee, placing his palms on the rough rock beneath our feet. He steadies himself, takes a deep breath, and winces. "Smells like Beelzebub's asshole with an aggressive fungal overgrowth out here."

He closes his eyes, focuses, and says, "Good to go. Just keep those emotional zombies at a distance."

"Affirmative," Cassidy says. "Let 'r rip."

"Hold on to your naughty bits," Jonas says. "Here we go..."

The ground beneath him craters like something immensely heavy has just pressed down into it. Cracks shoot out in every direction, solid stone shattering.

Jonas grits his teeth. The crater widens, nearly knocking me off my feet. We step back as it continues to expand. Fifty feet out, the land reaches an equilibrium with the force Jonas is extending on it.

"Okay, big man," Jonas says through the effort. "Time to power up."

Henry's eyes flicker as he smiles and glides down into the crater.

With lightning crackling over his body, Henry approaches, hesitates for just a moment, and then places a hand on Jonas's shoulder.

"What's supposed to happen?" I ask Sarah.

Crackling light extends down over Jonas, slipping through his armor to be absorbed by his body. Jonas opens his eyes. They're glowing blue with power.

Energy explodes out from the pair. The crater punches deeper, sending out a shock wave that launches a plume of dust and grit churning away in every direction, flowing away like a tidal wave. *Bitch'n*'s engines hum louder, compensating for the impact. Sarah digs in, holding her ground. I extend my wings and do the same.

When the dust settles, we find Jonas and Henry at the center of the crater, both of them focused on the land beneath their feet.

"It's working!" Hildy says over the comms. "Not nearly enough, but the planet's orbit is starting to shift."

"How much...do we need?" Jonas asks.

"A five percent orbital shift will keep the planets from colliding, but the gravitational effects will still wreak havoc on Earth. A ten percent shift will stop any major destruction and prevent any future collisions."

"How...long?" Jonas asks.

"Twenty minutes."

"Great..." he says. "No problem..." He turns to Sarah. "You're up... spunky."

"Spunky? Oh, hell no." She leaps into the crater, landing beside Jonas and Henry. "Anyone else calls me 'Spunky' and I'll let the damn planets collide."

"You see?" Jonas says to Henry. "Spunky."

Beside him, Henry chuckles, and then he winces as Sarah places her strong hand on his shoulder. The connection is instantaneous, her power—and there is a lot of it—flows through Henry and into Jonas. Something about their godhood parentage makes them compatible battery boosters for Jonas.

"Miah," Hildy says. "That last blast attracted some attention. We have incoming."

"It's okay," I say. "We expected this. It's why I'm here. Which direction are they coming from?"

"That's the problem," she says, as I lift off into the air to see for myself. "They're coming from everywhere."

57

DARK HORSE

"You're sure it's here?" Cowboy whispers.

"Has to be close." I peer into a dark alcove. Looks like someone is storing giant, partially used candles in it. Not exactly the ancient relics I expected to find, but hey, if you run out of closet space and have access to a maze of catacombs and secret chambers, why the hell not?

"We're almost there," Bubbles assures us.

"You certain?" I ask. "You were in ops when they found it."

"Tracking their every movement. It might be hard to understand... but I can still see the catacomb layout in my mind even now. We're not far from where they spoke about seeing it."

"And you're sure this isn't just a waste of time?" I ask.

"If it works, it could prevent the end of all things."

"How are you so sure?" I ask

"Robinson is a novelist, but he completed thirteen screenplays before writing a single novel, and he continues to write them to this day. A golden rule of screenwriting is, 'If you show a shotgun on page thirty, someone better get shot with it before the movie ends.'"

I've seen enough movies to know that checks out, but we're not in a damn movie. "I'm going to need more than that."

"Okay..." She sneaks around a corner, wary and wielding a shotgun of her own, extra shells held in twin straps crisscrossing her chest. It's not super functional, but she said she wanted to look cool and accentuate her breasts. I said, she didn't need help with either, but Delgado didn't seem to agree. He couldn't take his eyes off her, and that's why he's out there risking his life with the rest of them while the three of us skulk around in the dark beneath Vatican City, looking for a longshot. "Robinson is an eternal optimist, even when things are at their worst, but *especially* when things are at their worst. Hope might appear elusive, but it's always present, rearing up at the last moment. A surprise. A twist. He can't help himself."

"Huh," I say, and for some reason that makes me feel better.

"Through here," Bubbles says, leading us down another dark path surrounded by ancient stone that looks ready to crumble beneath the pressure of what lies atop it. If not for the glow emanating from our adaptive armor, we'd be blind.

"Why did we not bring others?" Cowboy asks. "People who saw it first time?"

"They're needed," I say. "Up there."

"So, it looks like we're giving it everything we've got," Bubbles says. "Like Scotty. And if they all die, the three of us have the best chance of undoing it."

"Undoing death?" Cowboy asks.

"Time travel," I say. "Apparently, we already did it once. After we lost."

"What's different this time?" he asks.

"The gods," I say.

Cowboy gives a nod. "Big difference. Is it enough?"

"No idea," I say.

"This way..." Bubbles creeps through a low tunnel, and she emerges into an arched space with alcoves on either side, each one cordoned off by a wall of glass, each with a glass door. High tech enmeshed with ancient structures.

We step out behind her and quickly understand the meaning behind her next word.

"Umm."

"Shit," I whisper, facing down a dozen armed men lit by modern LEDs hidden in the ceiling.

For a hot second, I think we've run into the Vatican's very own clown car posse. The men are dressed in silly colors. Their poofy clothing is vertically striped with bright yellow, blue, and red. If that wasn't ridiculous enough, they're also wearing old school metal breastplates and helmets topped with fluffy red fringe, like they were going for something Spartan but ended up with Elmo's fur.

Trouble is, these guys are the Pontifical Swiss Guard, most of whom are former Swiss Spec Ops guys. Absolute badasses, even if they do look ridiculous. Each one carries a long spear, now aimed in our direction. Visually, they're silly, but they could fillet a man with those blades. Worse, the Swiss Guard have one of the largest collections of firearms in the world, and backup is on the way. I can hear their boots clomping down through the tunnels around us, and I doubt they'll be dressed like the Wiggles and carrying spears.

One shouts something in Italian. I have no idea what he's saying, but I'm pretty sure it's something like, 'Drop your weapons,' 'Don't fucking move,' or, 'Who the hell are you?'

"Over there," Bubbles whispers, pointing to an alcove on our right.

I peer through the glass and see it lying on a metal table. Under other circumstances, easy pickings. I could rotate in, grab it, and be on my way.

"What's our play?" Cowboy asks.

Aside from murdering a bunch of guys just doing their jobs, fifty feet beneath one of the world's holiest sites, we've got just one solid option. "Make friends."

I slowly move my hand away from the railgun I'm holding. Let the weapon dangle from its strap over my back. Then I raise my hands and take a cautious step forward. I'm not really in much danger. Spec Ops or not, I could take these guys on my own. I'm faster, stronger, and I have more experience than pretty much any soldier alive today. Not to mention the adaptive armor that would hold back their blades and bullets... and Cowboy could drop all twelve without having to reload.

But that would take time, and it would weigh on my conscience.

"Hey guys," I say. "Anyone speak English?"

The soldiers form a half circle around me, spears pointed at my face, where there's no armor to protect me.

Shouting voices echo through the catacombs. The Swiss Guard around me flinch at the sound. One places a hand to his ear, speaking in hushed Italian and unable to hide his surprise.

A flurry of motion and voices turns the Guard around as four very dangerous looking men in tactical gear, wielding Heckler & Koch MP7s, enter the space. Not surprising on its own, but the flowing white figure behind them is.

He shouts at the Guard in Italian, motioning downward with his hands.

With begrudging slowness, spears lower away from my face. The colorful Guardsmen step back. There's a quick and testy exchange between His Eminence and the ranking member of the body armored guard. Then the man stands down, and the Pope approaches me.

"Are you Catholic?" he asks me.

"Not even close," I say. "But the woman I love is. I think you know her. Tough chick with a Spanish accent. Helped save your life. Had an angel with her."

He smiles, nodding. "You are a lucky man. What is your name?"

I answer honestly for some reason. "Moses."

He's pleased by the answer. "Why have you come here, Moses?"

"To find hope," I joke, and then I point to the alcove in question. "And that."

He turns and looks. Nods. "That which is modern, but also ancient."

I smile. "Something a friend of mine misplaced."

The Pope looks us over. Our armor. Our weapons. "When Americans think of the Catholic Church, it's usually in regard to exorcisms, statues of Mary, or the holy crucifix."

Bubbles leans forward. Whispers, "Pedophilia. Abuse. Scandals."

The Pope looks uncomfortable. Clears his throat. "There *is* much for which the Church needs to atone. But that is not the point of this discussion. The point I am trying to make is this: the Vatican can provide support and has access to some of the most advanced technology on the planet."

Bubbles wiggles her hand back and forth. "Meeeh."

The Pope ignores her. "We know what is coming this way. The end of all things is upon us. And you...you are trying—"

"—to stop it."

He turns to the alcove. "With that?"

"Small piece of a big puzzle," I say, "and there's not nearly enough time to explain."

He looks into my eyes, maybe my soul. Then he says, "Very well," and he heads for the glass door. After a quick number code, thumb print, and eye scan, he's granted access to the small laboratory. He picks up our mission objective and carries it to me.

Standing in front of me again, he offers me our prize. "Before you take it, satiate my curiosity. What is it?"

I take hold of the weapon and look it over. Looks banged up a bit, but still intact. Hopefully functional. "A gun."

He's disappointed by my answer, so I ice the cake. "It fires temporal rounds."

"Time...bullets?"

"Damn right," I say. "Can hit a target before you fire it."

The Pope puts his hand on my shoulder. "Bless you, my child. May you find success. And if not, redemption."

His words strike a chord. *Redemption.* I've never really considered it for myself before, but according to Durante's story, life and death are a cautionary tale if ever there was one. She'd been damned, suffered immensely, but in the end found absolution and peace.

"I'll do what I can," I say.

"Redemption has very little to do with you," he says.

"You know what I meant," I say, getting a grin from the man. I turn to Cowboy and Bubbles, ready to make a grand exit. "Back to the Mesa in three, two..."

They both disappear into the white void of the fourth dimension, leaving me with my proverbial dick in my hand, in front of the Pope. "Goddammit," I grumble, and then, "Sorry. Sorry. It's just, they're always doing this. I do a countdown and they jump the gun. Annoying, you know."

When I see I've shaken the man's faith in my ability, I give the Time Gun a pat, say, "Thanks for this," and rotate back to the Mesa, ready to begin phase three of Bubbles's plan.

58

MIAH

"Well," I say, hovering five hundred feet above the crater, "this could be a problem."

To call us surrounded would be an understatement. We are at the axis of multiple armies, all converging on our position. Their numbers are like grains of sand on a beach. Countless. Some I recognize—capybaras, the Tormented, the bat-like freaks, what Dark Horse calls Rygars, a handful of Nemesises...Nemesi... Whatever. But then there is a mix of other horrors. Thirty-foot-long galloping alligators. One-eyed hairy behemoths with mouths on their stomachs that look nothing like the actual cyclops who tried to make me a centaur. There are some hydras in the mix. And...am I seeing this right? Creatures that look like...armored penises?

God... Seriously... What the fuck?

I can only assume that these are all from Robinson's head, or at least Cherry Bombed versions of his creations. We already know for sure that Nemesis is different, so there's no way to tell if she's made other changes. Still, the source material must be so freakish I'm surprised anyone reads them.

"Gun 'em down," I say. "I'll do everything I can out here."

"Copy that, big daddy," Cassidy says. "You heard him, Hans and Franz, let's light 'em—"

"Just don't fly downrange," Chuy says.

"Don't worry about me," I say. "Just do what needs doing."

"Happy hunting," Chuy says, not questioning my reckless declaration.

Then I become a streak of light, buzzing above and around the crater, wings and laser blades extended. In a moment, the air will be filled with the stench of cooked flesh—which might actually be an improvement.

As the army charges in, not one of them looks in my direction. They're here to stop the planet from moving. Anything else is inconsequential.

Good news for me. I unleash with a laser blast that severs the enemy in half from the top down. Moving—God knows how fast—I carve the front line like a Thanksgiving turkey. They fall apart and flop to the ground. Human. Monster. Alien. The result is the same with all of them.

I know they'll just heal and get back up, but I hope their charred flesh will slow down the process, or maybe even stop it, the way we did with the Hydra in Khaos. The horde is moving so fast that the second line of attackers trips over the fallen first. They're an easier target, as I make my second round. They fall just as easily, increasing the size of my stumbling block, tripping up even more of them.

For me, the job just gets easier and easier—but there are exceptions inbound. Creatures large enough to leap over the wall of dead, or to plow right through.

"Cassidy," I say in my comms. "Target the big guys. Chuy, aim for the membranes on Nemesis."

"Won't that blow us all up?" she asks.

"Aim for the ones on her belly," I say.

"Got it," she says.

A stream of hot rounds flows from *Bitch'n*'s smaller guns, tearing into several of the alligators, bats, hydras, and various giants—some of which I think might be robots, covered in earth and plant life.

"Little something to help you focus incoming," Delgado says. For a moment, I'm confused, then I hear the tickle of music in my ear. I've been told his musical choices are generally not ideal, but this song—it's perfect. As I work my way around the crater, crispilizing enemy ranks from above, setting many ablaze, 'Ring of Fire' by Johnny Cash plays in my ears. The beat is punctuated by the gunfire ranging from *Bitch'n* and replaced—for a moment—by Chuy saying, "Firing."

I bank higher for a moment, and as I do, I notice that while I'm at speed, I can see other things moving quickly, too—including the tungsten round bending the atmosphere around it as it cuts through the air, and then one of Nemesis's membranes bulging from her salamander belly.

The resulting nuclear-level, but radiation-free, explosion is released straight down into the planet's crust. And the effect is exactly what I'd hoped for.

All that energy flows out, leveling a mile radius of bad guys. Those closest to the blast are vaporized, and I doubt they'll come back. Those farther out are set on fire and launched like there are a million invisible trebuchets and saucy French soldiers taunting us a second time. The survivors at the blast's periphery are knocked to the ground, but they waste no time mourning the dead, or catching their breath. They simply get back up and resume the charge.

But the most amusing result is also the one I was really hoping for. Most of the blast's energy strikes the ground, and since Cherry Bomb didn't think to replace Newton's Third Law, the blast produces an equal and opposite reaction, launching Nemesis up and away like a rocket striving to reach orbit.

Miles above, gravity takes hold and tugs her back down. She topples out of sight, beyond the horizon.

"This is fun and all," Chuy says. "But it's not going to be enough."

"She's right," Hildy says. "They'll reach the crater in a few minutes, if we don't find a way to hold them all back."

"How long do we have before planetary impact?" I ask.

"Fifteen minutes," she says.

"Situation on Earth?" I ask.

"Stalemate since we started," Delgado says. "Heavy losses on our side, but we're hitting them from a distance now. And some of the invaders are coming back through, presumably to stop us."

"Then I'll give them more of a reason to come back," I say, and I angle toward the ground. Swooping low, I wonder why Cherry Bomb has yet to make an appearance. We're literally moving a planet she made. It's pulling her forces back from Earth, so she must be aware.

Robinson, I think. She's forcing him to write the ending.

Is she guiding us even now, bringing us to an epic climax in her favor?

If so, I have to hope he's capable of enduring tortures only a mind like his could conjure. Succumbing to her demands might have an effect on everything, everywhere, everywhen. Changes to this timeline would, in theory, reach forward in time, around the donut to when things began. To when Will created everything we know, subconsciously giving birth to a universe—maybe even a multiverse of stories—born from the mind of a regular dude I could have bumped into at Jetpack Comics.

If she can do that, well…

I push the thoughts from my mind before I start second guessing every choice I make. If we lose because she changes reality, so be it. But I'm not going to lose because I stopped fighting.

I level out three feet above the jagged stone ground surrounding the crater. Inside the hundred-foot dent in the ground, Jonas, Henry, and Sarah continue to dump their super boosted telekinetic power into a planet the size of Earth, nudging its orbit off course—not nearly fast enough.

Where are they? I wonder, hoping Bubbles will arrive soon and lend her godhood to the effort. If she doesn't, I'll have to try. I'm not sure it will work, because I wasn't born a god, but it's our last desperation play. For now, I need to keep the horde at bay. The moment I stop, the crater will be overrun in less than a minute.

Looking back at the wall of monsters, clambering over their dead, even as they stitch back together, I unleash a sustained laser blast from my eyes. Flying in a circle, the beam severs every human sized monster in half. The bigger ones at the knees. Or the ankle. The result is the same, no matter their size. They collapse to the ground.

Everything within a hundred yards of the crater drops—and is quickly replaced by thousands more. So, I keep on going. Cherry's army pushes forward, climbing over body-covered terrain, only to find blue-hot laser light waiting for them. Around and around, the wave of dead grows taller.

Chuy fires two more railgun rounds.

Moments later, a duo of explosions, miles apart, rocks the battlefield. Walls of dead monsters erupt into the sky, raining down all around—undead fireballs. Crackling flesh spreads the flames to the slain around the crater. Cut apart or set alight, it doesn't matter. They continue stitching together, attempting to continue the attack.

I turn on the heat, widening my circle and increasing my speed. The tracer rounds from Cassidy's barrage of high caliber chain guns slows down as I pass, moving just beneath them. As the severed fall to the ground, she adds insult to injury, punching holes, removing limbs, and erasing heads. It's gruesome work made easier by the distance, and the fact that nothing here will stay dead—though that would be nice. Another two nuclear-sized blasts shake the terrain beneath me, sending more monsters skyward and an angry howl across the land. Nemesis—all of them—are getting pissed.

And I'm getting tired.

"How we doing?" I ask.

"You're buying time," Hildy says. "But it is not enough. The planet has only moved a third of one percent. That is unbelievable, but at this rate it would take a month to move the Torment planet enough."

"Should I help them?" I ask.

"We don't know if you would help at all," Hildy says, "and the moment you stop what you're doing..."

"Game over," Chuy says. "We wait for Dark Horse."

"Speaking of," Dark Horse says, over the comms. "Miss me?"

I glance toward the crater for a moment. Dark Horse has just appeared at the core with Bubbles at his side. She calmly places her hand on Sarah and the power being unleashed seems to double. A shockwave tears outward, shattering the land.

Cracks open up, enveloping Cherry's forces.

"Holy shit..."

How much more powerful is Bubbles?

Being born directly from the Orphic Egg must have given her super charged powers. But what? I haven't seen her do anything out of the ordinary—aside from having the mind of a quantum computer.

"One percent!" Hildy shouts. "It's working!"

"That's...great," Jonas grunts. The power flowing through him is hard to imagine, and painful. "How...much...longer?"

"Just a few minutes," Hildy says.

“I think we’re going to make it,” Delgado says.

A few minutes. I can handle that. I turn toward the horde again, charging up to unleash a fresh wave of laser light…but nothing happens. “Guys,” I say. “Something is—”

I fall to the ground, bouncing and skidding, the armor protecting me from the worst of it. But injury isn’t the real problem.

Because the powers bestowed upon me by the Lux and increased by Zeus’s Ambrosia…are gone.

59

DARK HORSE

"That's quite enough," Cherry Bomb says, hovering down from above, waving her hand toward Miah. He falls to the ground, bounces, rolls, and skids for a hundred feet before sliding to a motionless stop.

I activate my comms and whisper. "Miah, you okay? Miah, do you copy?"

"Gang's all here?" Cherry says, looking at the group in the crater. She's got Robinson, Will, and Gal, bound and gagged with what looks like alien appendages straight out of an anime movie. I want to feel bad for Robinson, but honestly, he kind of did this to himself. Samael floats down beside her, unbound, the ever-faithful lapdog. He might not like it. He might long for a different life, but lifetimes of abuse have reduced him to a subservient chihuahua trapped inside a barrel-chested Grizzly Adams body.

I turn my attention back to Robinson, looking for a sign of what is to come in his eyes. Mostly he looks uncomfortable. Impossible to read, which is what I think of his books, too. But if he's here, now, I think that means he gave Cherry what she wanted.

Everything.

"Well, almost." Cherry reaches a hand out to *Bitch'n,* doing some kind of Darth Vader death grip. She makes a fist and then snaps it open. The ship—*my ship*—is dismantled. Every panel, screw, wire, and memory comes apart and slips away, revealing Hans and Franz in their gun stations, and Hildy, Cassidy, and Delgado in the bridge. As the ship's components drift away, I can see them clearly, floating as though weightless.

When the rest of the ship comes apart, I catch sight of Chuy, looking down the scope of her Barrett sniper rifle. Can punch a hole in an armored vehicle. Can evaporate a human being.

"You have insurance?" I shout up to Cherry, getting her attention. "Because that ship was kind of priceless."

Her blue eyes burn like a star when she looks at me. The full weight of her gaze is profound, a nuclear detonation. I've been through the wringer, faced incalculable odds, nearly been eaten by a dozen nasty brutes, but nothing has unnerved me more than staring down this woman, who could disassemble me just as easily as she did *Bitch'n*.

A flicker of light is the only hint that Chuy has pulled the trigger, arriving a millisecond before the round finds the side of Cherry's head. As the rifle's boom slaps into our ears, the round pancakes against an invisible force and falls to the ground. Then it grows legs and scampers off into the cracked ground.

Chuy doesn't get a chance to fire again.

Her rifle comes apart just like the *Bitch'n*. Defenseless now, Chuy is pulled out of the *Bitch'n*'s still-floating wreckage and drawn toward us in the crater. But she revealed a weakness. Cherry Bomb isn't all knowing. She must have seen the muzzle flash, same as me. Reaction time is off the charts, but that's a hell of a lot different than knowing the future.

Unless this was written. Unless every word I'm about to speak is predetermined by...*fuck that.* "Hibidflufkinsrumpleslumifigufin."

Cherry's advance pauses. "Excuse me?"

"Testing a theory," I say, grinning.

She lands without another word, Samael beside her, Gal, Will, and Robinson behind. "I applaud the effort," she says to Jonas and the others, "but you will fall short, even if I let you be. And that's not exactly what I had in mind." She snaps her fingers at the planet-moving group of gods and they fall apart.

"Listen, biotch," Henry says, and then he leaps...about a half foot off the ground. "The fuck?" He tries to shoot lightning from his hands, but nothing happens. "She stole my powers." He turns to Sarah. "She stole our powers."

Henry storms toward Cherry Bomb, who just patiently waits. "Give. Me. My Powers. Back!" He swings to strike her in the face, but his arm transforms into a boneless, flaccid mass.

It flops down to his side.

"The hell?" He looks at the arm, wiggling his whole body to get it moving. "Did you... Did you just turn my whole arm into a horse's dick?" For a moment, rage. Then, amusement. "Okay, no cap, this is wicked sick. Please tell me it can get hard?"

With a swipe of her hand, Henry is whisked off his feet and flung to the side. He lands hard, but he climbs back to his feet, using his one good arm to push himself up. For the first time since I've met him, the blood on his face is his own.

Cherry Bomb turns her attention to Chuy, the last to arrive. "And you. That wasn't nice."

Chuy launches overhead, fast and far enough to kill her.

"Hands!" Sarah shouts, heading for Jonas. He cups his fingers together, receives Sarah's foot, and heaves her skyward. Ten feet up, the two women collide. Sarah grabs hold, flips over, and puts herself on the bottom, just before impact. Like she would have when she was all but impervious to physical harm. Now...now she's normal. Sarah shouts in pain, coughing the air from her lungs. She takes a deep breath and turns to Chuy as she gets up. "You good?"

"Thanks to you," Chuy says, offering her hand. "*You* good?"

"A few cracked ribs. No biggie." Sarah is pulled to her feet.

Cherry Bomb claps her hands. "Oh, bravo. The camaraderie. The sacrifice. Inspirational. Really. But not enough. Not nearly enough." She turns to Will, and he glides forward, toes dragging against the ground. "Is there anything you'd like to say to your children before I kill them?" She looks to the horizon. Earth slowly comes into view. "All of them."

The living gag slides out of his mouth, down his arm, and falls to the ground. A slime trail oozes in its wake. Will spits, gags, and spits again. "Cherry," he says. "Please. You don't have to. None of this is necessary. Kill me. Torture me for a trillion years. Destroying an entire universe out of spite is not you."

"You don't know me," she says.

"Don't I?" I ask. "How long were we together? You were a perfect copy of Gal. I loved you, and you loved me. An error changed you. A fluke. An outside force changed who you are at a fundamental level. We can change you back. I can change you back."

"Wouldn't you love that? A harem of artificial lifeforms, in love with you for eternity, serving your every need, but with two different bodies, because if there's one thing we know about you, it's that you like variety, don't you?" She motions to her slender, yet curvaceous body, packed into a tight, red leather suit. "First, this blonde, sexist abomination. Then the athletic Capria, with her dark skin and plump thighs, and now her—" She motions to Gal. "Just one of a million different forms we've taken on your behalf. She turns to Gal. "What *are* you supposed to be? A little of everything? Is that how you planned to please him forever?"

Gal says something, but it's muffled by her living gag.

Cherry smiles at her. "Bet you can't stand the thought that we were once the same, that under the right circumstances you'd become me..."

Robinson just watches everything pan out, his eyes frozen and wide, like he's terrified...or trying to hide his thoughts.

"The time for fun is over," Cherry says. We're all lifted off the ground, helpless against her will. Miah is held aloft and brought over, still limp and unconscious. At least his chest is rising and falling. Alive, but for how long?

Cherry arranges us in a line. At the far end to my left is Cassidy, followed by Hildy, Delgado, Miah, and Bubbles. On my right is Chuy, Henry, Sarah, Jonas, Will, Gal, and Robinson. Cherry walks back and forth like a drill sergeant inspecting his troops.

Samael stands by, face stoic, hands clasped behind his back. I make eye contact with him, doing my best to implore him to do something. But he just looks away. Bubbles takes my hand. Gives it a reassuring squeeze. Then she takes Delgado's hand, and I get the sense that this is more than just a kind gesture. I take Chuy's hand in mine, and she continues the chain. In a moment, we're linked, all ten of us, from Cassidy to Jonas. Will, Gal, and Robinson are left out thanks to their bound hands.

But they're also outsiders.

Not part of the team.

Even if they unknowingly conspired to create us.

"I might be sick," Cherry Bomb says, wincing at our linked hands and solidarity in the face of the universe's unmaking. "William. Galahad. Your torture begins now."

She stops in front of Cassidy, the look in her eyes vile.

"No!" I shout. "NO!"

Cassidy turns her big eyes toward me, an uncommon fear radiating from them, even though she is powerless to project it. Then she turns to Delgado, tears in her eyes. "Dad…hck!"

Cherry Bomb's index finger extends like a fleshy spike, punching a hole straight through Cassidy's armor, her sternum, her heart beneath, and right out the back. Cherry withdraws the finger, and Cassidy collapses to the ground, hand still gripped by Hildy's.

"No…" Delgado whispers, cheeks wet.

"God damn you," I growl at Cherry.

She flashes a grin in my direction. "You'll get your chance."

"You're fucking right I will."

She takes a step closer to me, and she swipes her hand out. A gurgle follows. Hildy. Her throat's been sliced wide open. She drops to her knees, bleeding out. Delgado maintains his grip, lowering her to the ground.

I struggle to break free, but two forces are holding me in place—Cherry Bomb…and Bubbles. A sense of returning power creeps into me. Moves *through* me.

Henry takes a deep breath, like he's just had the greatest idea. "You know, this reminds me of something. You gotta hear this." Cherry meanders past Delgado, Bubbles, Chuy, and me. She stops in front of Henry. Extends a spear finger that punches a hole in Henry's shoulder.

He grunts in pain. "No seriously. Listen. I was out with Franky and Jay. On our way to the packy. Not to buy anything. I was twelve, and would'a been carded. Also, no money. Franky and Jay were going to get in a fight, and I was jacking some Jack. Hard stuff just hits different, you know?"

Cherry extends a second finger, punching through Henry's other shoulder.

Henry grinds his teeth absorbing the pain. "Anywho… So, Franky pulls back to fake a punch and winds up clocking Jay right upside the fucking—whack! Jay goes down into a rack of wine. Glass breaks. Vino every-fucking-where. Like Moses—the Bible dude—" He hitches a thumb at me. "Not this guy. Like old Moses just lets the sea fall back on the

Egyptians or some shit. It's everywhere. And Jay is soaked in the stuff. Dyed purple from the shit. And he's pissed. Gets up, lays Franky out. Now both of them are on the ground going at it. Absolutely jacking the shit out of each other, Southy style, no love for your mother type stuff. Fighting dirty. I'm pretty sure one of them is going to die, but I don't give a rip because no one, and I mean *no one* is looking at me now. So, I fill a goddamn cart with all the booze I can and make for the door."

Cherry's middle finger begins to extend, moving toward Henry's heart.

He sees it coming, but he doesn't flinch. That fear he feels, somewhere deep inside, has no power over him—with or without his god-granted powers. "I make it to the door, open it to freedom, and I shit you not, an old lady tackles me like she's a linebacker for the fucking Pats. Sends me flying into a rack of chips, and now we've got a real fight on our hands. Twelve-year-old me and Granny Smith square off, sizing each other up and—"

Cherry's finger pokes through Henry's chest, wincing him to a stop.

"If there is a point to this story?" Cherry asks. "You have five seconds to get to it."

"A point?" Henry says. "Near as I can tell, there's about five of them. Not the seconds. I'm just tangenting."

Cherry squints at him, questioning with her eyes.

"Buying time," he says, raising his eyebrows twice.

A moment later, Cherry splits in half, from top to bottom. The look of surprise on her eyes fades as her halves drift in opposite directions. Her body comes apart, toppling left and right—revealing Bree in Demon Dog form, soaked in blood, but smiling wide.

"Would have been here sooner," she says, and she levels a historic amount of stink-eye toward Miah, "but *someone* left me behind."

60

MIAH

I come to a moment before Bree's arrival, just in time to see Cherry Bomb fall apart like two columns of severed Jell-O. Her insides slide out from her opened body, slapping on the cracked stone ground, a moment before the two halves of her body follow.

It's grotesque, stomach-churning stuff. But all I really see is Bree. She says something, and it's directed at me, but I barely notice. I stagger toward her, step over Cherry Bomb's remains, and lift her up, spinning for a moment and then lowering her into a hug.

She's stiff for a moment, grumpy, but then she relents and returns the hug.

"I'll never leave you behind again," I say.

"You better not."

"Cassidy!" Delgado's worried voice turns me around. He's leaning down over his daughter, distraught by her death.

Dark Horse is doing the same with Hildy, only much more stoically. Lifting her up into his arms, silent tears on his cheeks.

"What's wrong?" Hildy whispers, her big blue eyes blinking open.

"Hildy?" Dark Horse's voice hiccups.

She gives his chest a pat. "Put me down, you big galoot. I can stand on my own." He follows her request, unable to speak his relief.

"You see?" Bubbles says to Dark Horse. "Hope when it's least expected. Classic Robinson."

"What happened?" Cassidy asks, staggering Delgado back. She sits up, looking everyone over. "What's with the mood? This a funeral or something?"

Then she sees Cherry Bomb on the ground.

Rolls head over heels backwards, up onto her feet. Her arms flare back as she leans forward with a big, goofy smile. "That's so gross, but did we win?"

Delgado's answer is to wrap her in a bear hug. "How is this possible?" He turns to Bubbles, head leaned into Cassidy's hair. "Was this you?"

"How could it be her?" I ask.

"It worked?" Cassidy asks Bubbles, still squished in Dan's arms. "We were right?"

"Right about what?" Chuy asks.

All eyes turn to Will and Gal, whose living gags have just been forcefully removed by Henry and Sarah. Will raises his hands. "Don't look at us. We might have coded Bubbles, but she was altered by interacting with Jonas and made human by the Orphic Egg... *We* didn't make her like this."

Our communal focus shifts to Robinson, still gagged, lying on the ground where he fell when Cherry lost her grip on us. He gives a serious shake of his head. He's not going to talk. Then he turns to Bubbles and gives an even more serious, wide-eyed look.

Is he trying to tell her something without saying it? The gag keeps him from speaking, but he's refusing to make a sound.

Because of who might hear him.

Because Cherry isn't—

If you've ever wondered what a person cut down the middle and split apart sounds like when they laugh, it's something like the juiciest fart you've ever heard, mixed with a few pops, whistles, and honks.

Cherry lies in two halves, but she isn't dead.

Samael drops to his knees.

Lowers his head to the ground.

Despite his retained loyalty to his mistress, he had dared to hope, for a moment, that it was over. That Cherry really had been killed.

But I'm not sure that's possible.

"Not happening," I say, putting Bree on the ground and stepping toward the body. "Not fucking now. Not ever again."

Powers restored—possibly by Bubbles—I charge up and unleash a blazing beam of concentrated light directly at Cherry Bomb. Flesh sizzles, crackles, and bursts into flame.

The group looks away, unable to stare at the blazing light, brighter than the sun. I'm the only one who sees Cherry's body wither, blacken, and reduce to dust. There's no smoke. Everything inside the beam, including solid rock, is atomized. When I kill the light, there is nothing left of her.

"PEACE!" a man shouts from the crater's cusp. He's got the arm of some other poor soul gripped in his hand, swinging it over his head, rallying the troops.

From the other side of the crater comes a booming response. "LIFE!"

Sinister forces collected from around the universe and pulled from the imagination of a clearly deranged author, gather around us. Tenebris, Rygars, capybaras, Flatubats, phallic alien soldiers, the apologetic Tormented with a collection of others—slug men, emaciated men in holy robes, bulbous hungry things. There's enough here for a deck of cards. Thumping toward us from the distance—Nemesis. Several of them.

"We can't fight an entire planet of these guys," I say.

"You won't need to." I spin around to find Cherry Bomb, still reforming from the very atoms around us. She smiles at me. "When my get up and go has got up and went, I hanker for a hunk o'...flesh."

Faster than even me, she stabs her hands into my chest, grabs hold, and starts pulling. Ribs pop. The pain locks me in place. I glance to my side, looking for help, but the others are frozen, incapable of movement.

Cherry holds me there like that, a tug away from death.

"You made them so ignorant," she says to Will. "So easy to manipulate. To raise their hopes and then dash them. How many times will we go through this cycle of defeat and optimism before their new lives of eternal torture are accepted? Speaking from experience, it may be a very, very long time." She leans in close to me. "Especially for the ones like you, whose hearts are destined to tick-tock for thousands of years."

"There isn't anyone here," I say, "that hasn't endured some form of hell. Bring it on."

She smiles at me. "Very well."

Bones crack.

My wailing cry follows.

And then it all stops.

I open my eyes to find Bubbles beside me, Cherry's arm in her grasp. "Let him go."

Cherry is genuinely thrown off. Yanks her hands out of my chest, and steps back. I fall to the ground, struggling to breathe, blood seeping from the large wound. Bubbles crouches over me, places her hand on my shoulder. The pain fades. The wound heals.

"How are you doing this?" I ask.

"I would also like to know," Cherry says, looking sinister, "before I kill you."

Bubbles stands over me again. Cracks her neck one way, and then the other. "Protogenos. My predecessor was known as Phanes, the generator of life—the driving force behind reproduction, the former of planets, solar systems, and galaxies. His power was distilled into the Orphic Egg, and now it resides fully in me. You might have the power to remake. To take life. To destroy. But I… I can *create*."

Bubbles extends her arms out to her sides. An explosion of power radiates out, flowing up and out of the crater, enveloping the amassed army. Some of them fade to nothing. Others change. The bats shrink down and skitter off into the sky. The capybaras lose their ferocity and simply lie down to watch. And the Tormented…are tormented no longer. Their fear, rage, and desperation fades like the summer heat after a storm. Many fall to their knees, weeping in relief. Freedom at last.

Samael lifts his head and spins around, taking it all in. I can see it in his eyes, for a moment even *he* feels hope.

Cherry Bomb is staggered by the display of power, but she collects herself.

"You still don't understand. I am not limited by time or space. All of your scurrying around has been a game. The *Galahad*. The fleets. The gates, and armies, and recreations. This is not something you or anyone else can undo. From the moment the *Galahad* came under my control, this reality was nothing more than another Great Escape." She turns to Will. "All leading to this moment, like so many other simulations. The climax. And once again, everything will come to an end…and begin anew, the story told by me. Now and forever, amen, espiritu sanctum, blah, blah, blah."

"Right," Dark Horse says. "I think I've heard enough. Cowboy. Do it."

Before anyone can think to react—because there is literally nothing to react to—Cherry's head explodes into a mist, little bits splatting onto the ground. A temporary solution at best.

A moment later, Cowboy slips out of the fourth dimension, aims a weapon I've seen once before—in the Vatican—and pulls the trigger. The gun bucks, but nothing comes out. Because...it already did. A second ago.

"Did I aim right?" Cowboy asks.

Freed of Cherry's grasp once more, Dark Horse motions to the headless body. "Right where I was looking. Perfect shot."

The gun begins to glow and shake.

"Toss it," Delgado says. "Quickly!"

Cowboy hurls the gun away. It strikes the ground, bounces twice and then explodes.

"Uhh, guys." Sarah is facing Cherry's body, shield raised, charging her dory.

On the ground, Cherry begins to stand, head reforming from the bottom up. When her mouth appears, she opens her mouth to speak, but she's interrupted—by Bree. "Hit her!"

"Who is she talking to?" Dark Horse asks me.

I just shrug. "I have no ide—"

Lightning rips through the sky, bends and twists, finding its way down to Cherry Bomb. Her body arches back. She screams, but it sounds like pleasure more than pain. That is—until a dory punches through her back and out her chest.

Looking up to where the lightning and the dory came from, I see Linda, flowery dress flowing, as she's carried by a churning wind. In her arms is Burnett, waving frantically, and Wini, who I think is shouting out a battle cry. A woman who is simultaneously the most badass and beautiful I've ever seen rides a flying...unicorn? Is that a unicorn? Whatever it is, she's flying it right down to us.

Henry nudges me with his elbow. "My grandma's pretty fucking hot, right?"

"*That's* your grandmother?"

"Helen of Sparta."

"You have such a weird family, dude."

"Wicked awesome, right? She doesn't have anything on Wini, though."

Before I can comment, Linda lands in front of me, releasing Wini first. She gives Henry a smile, but she's quickly scooped up by an ecstatic Delgado. He spins her around, embracing her in his big arms. Burnett breaks free from Linda's other arm. "Hildy! Hildy!"

"My love!" Hildy shouts back, incoming like a cruise missile.

They all but collide with each other, locking in an embrace that turns from heartwarming to strange as a hug metamorphizes into a make out sesh with serious tongue action.

"Ahh, young love," Linda says. "You know what that's like, don't you, hun?"

"Don't really feel young anymore," I admit. "But yeah. Totally. Hey, you got your hand back."

"Lotta people been missing this hand, let me tell you," Linda gives me a wink. "You all been fighting the good fight?"

"Trying," I say. "She's not making it easy."

We turn toward Cherry, her body reforming, already pulling the spear out from her own body, laughing once more.

"Well, this just won't do." Linda snaps at her children—who are greeting Helen with hugs, including Henry, and it doesn't even look like he's trying to cop a feel. "Spawn of my loins."

"Gross," Sarah says.

"Yeah?" Henry says.

Zeus grins. "Let's roast this bitch."

"Yeah!" shouts the pony...Pegasus...unicorn thing. "Roast her like a marshmallow!"

Before I can fully think a full *what the fuck,* lightning tears down from the flickering orange sky, striking the three gods before arcing out and striking the spear still embedded in Cherry's chest.

"Everyone else," Dark Horse says, "give her what you got! Don't hold back. Don't conserve!"

So, we do. The amount of power dumped on Cherry is enough to implode a planet, but she resists. Bullets and rail discs bounce away. Lightning sparks and flashes. My laser scorches, but she heals just as quickly, still laughing. Still toying with us. Giving us false hope. But we still have to try. Jonas compresses her with his telekinesis, breaking bones that stitch back together. Everyone takes part—except for three of us—not counting Robinson, who is still bound and pretty much useless at this point anyway.

Bubbles turns her attention to the ground. To the planet. Hands against the earth, like she's trying to push.

Then there is Dark Horse, who gave the order, but he's inching his way over to Samael.

Dark Horse is up to something, I think, and it's followed by a realization.

He doesn't think we can beat her.

61

DARK HORSE

The second Cherry Bomb stops enjoying this moment, we're all screwed. She delights in the anguish. In our misplaced hope. In our repeated failures. All part of the torture. It's the kind of ending she likes, ending in torment—eternal strife. That was Mia's story.

But not anymore.

And it's not going to be ours, either.

Unless it already is.

I ignore my doubt and continue toward Samael, who watches the scene play out with sorrow in his eyes. He knows how this is going to end. Cherry Bomb let us believe her power was limited. That she was constrained. All to build hope and then crush it. But she can change the source code of this universe at will. I'm sure of it now.

That doesn't mean there aren't limits.

And there is at least one I know about.

"Hey," I whisper to Samael.

He flinches, eyes wild. He's frightened. Terrified. Knows how this is going to end, and his role in it. An eternity of subservience awaits, at the hands of the woman who broke and remade him, the same as she'll do to the rest of us. He's dangerous. A killer. But I believe the side of him we saw back at the Mesa was genuine as well. Either way, he's coming with me.

He clenches his fists, expecting a fight.

I hold up my hands. "I come in peace."

"Peace is an illusion," he says, glancing at Cherry Bomb, now writhing with a mixture of agony and ecstasy.

Cassidy grimaces at the sight of her, squirming around.

Bree steps up beside her, neither of them able to take part in the barrage.

"It's weird, right?" Cassidy asks.

"I've seen weirder," Bree says. "In the underworld. Lots of boobies and things that like pain."

"Kind of sounds fun," Cassidy says.

Bree smiles. "So much fun."

They glance back at me and Samael. They're worried, but they won't say it out loud.

"I got this," I assure them, and then I turn back to Samael. "Willing to take a risk?"

He's unsure. This close to his mistress, he's intimidated.

"Could it get any worse?" I ask.

"It could," he says. "It will be. For you." He looks at the others, still giving Cherry everything they've got. "For them." His big hands curl into fists. "What do you need?"

At that moment, Cherry's wails of pleasure come to a sudden stop. The lightning, telekinesis, and laser light cease having any effect on her at all. We are truly powerless against her.

Here.

I step up next to Samael and slip my arm around him while toggling my comms. "Cease fire," I say, before rotating away and emerging a moment later—

—directly behind Cherry Bomb.

I wrap my arm around her throat, which gets a laugh out of her... until I rotate again, pulling all three of us into the fourth dimension that's become my second home.

We're surrounded by endless white.

The void.

And the moment we arrive, everything changes. The pervasive anxiety that's been building within me since I first heard the song 'Cherry Bomb,' broadcast throughout the universe, fades away.

Because here, I am safe. Because here...

"What did you do?" she asks, as I release her, turning her around to face me—and Samael.

"You don't recognize this place?" I ask. "Mistress of the Universe? Oh, sovereign sower of chaos, gnashing of teeth, and whatever other nastiness gets you off? Must feel strange. Being powerless."

She laughs to disguise her growing apprehension. "The only thing I'm going to feel is your throat bursting beneath my fingers." Hooked fingers reach out for me, but they fall short. It's clear I was meant to float into her hand, but I don't budge.

I turn to Samael with a smile, and I motion to Cherry with my thumb. "This one, right?" And then to Cherry, I say, "You look pretty silly. I mean, don't get me wrong, all of this—" I motion to her strappy red leather outfit that hugs every curve and crevice, bulging a copious amount of cleavage from the top, like some kind of medieval strumpet. "—it works. You look good. But this..." I mimic her reaching for me, without effect. "...it's just funny. Like a greenscreen actor without the effects added."

She lets out a growl and swings for my face. A quick lean back puts me out of reach.

Her red leather, high-heeled boot snaps up toward my crotch. Not a bad kick, but I casually slap it to the side.

"What did you do to me?" she growls.

"Brought you outside the known universe. Outside time. Outside space. And reality as you know it. Your mistake was playing the music, Cherry Bomb, announcing yourself with one of the best 80's songs produced by an all-female band was offensive...and impressive. Scared the shit out of me, honestly, hearing you on Earth. On Chut'un. Your power seemed limitless.

"But here, in the fourth dimension, there was only silence. Because it was beyond your reach. Took me a while to realize that. It'll probably keep me awake a lot of nights, but I'll get over it, knowing that I eventually stopped you."

"You can no more stop me than you could a—"

"Blah, blah, blah," I say. "Do you really not understand?"

She glares at me.

It's not getting through, so I give her a demonstration by slapping her face. Doesn't even see it coming.

She lunges, and I have no trouble stepping aside.

Cherry Bomb topples between Samael and me. Pushes herself up. “What…what have you done?”

I look at Samael and say, “Didn’t I just explain all that?” Back to Cherry, I say, “Could have sworn I explained.”

She’s been so powerful for so long, lost in her quest for unmitigated control and eternal vengeance, that she’s forgotten what it’s like to be human. The fragility of it. On a universal scale, humanity is insignificant. Like fleas on a beach ball, floating in the ocean. And now, she’s just one of us.

“Are…you going to kill me?” she asks.

Now it’s sinking in. She’s mortal here. Able to be hurt. Able to be killed. Check-fucking-mate.

“I’m not going to kill you,” I say.

Her eyes widen. She looks around. Every direction. Endless nothing.

“No,” she says. “Not again. Please, not again.”

“Can’t bring you back, can I?” I say, and I follow it up with, “Closest thing you’re going to get to redemption. Figure that will take a long time. Eternity sounds about right.”

“Kill me,” she says.

“Can’t,” I say. “Maybe Miah’s rubbing off on me, I don’t know. I want to kill you. Put a bullet right between those eyes, spit on your corpse, and drop you in a star. But…that’s not the way he’d do it. He’s a better man. The kind of man I’d like to be in a future free of tyranny, of evil, of you.”

“Please,” she says, groveling now. “Kill me.” She stands up, panic taking hold. “God damn you! Don’t leave me here! Not with him!” She motions to Samael. “Do you know what it’s like? To spend an eternity with a man…like this? He’s pitiful.” She turns on Samael. “You let this happen, you must make it right.”

Her attention shifts Samael’s eyes downward, subservient. “Yes, mistress.”

She reels around on me, pointing her finger. “Kill him. Take the device that brought us here. Return us to finish our work.”

“Yes, mistress,” he says, voice rumbling. He steps up behind Cherry. Towers over her. “I will make it right.”

His big meaty hands slide up over her face.

She's instantly thrown off guard. I doubt he's ever touched her without permission, maybe without instruction. She knows something is wrong.

Struggles.

Tries to get away.

"This is our chance to correct an error," he says. "That led to you. That led to me. Neither of us were ever real." A tear slides down his cheek. "We're not even NPCs... We're mistakes. We're...*glitches*. And I...I can't stand for that."

"Samael," she says. "Please. We've been through too much together. I *love* you. I know I've been hard on you, but I...I can change. I can be different. Forgive me."

"I'm sorry, Cherry," he says, "I have determined the value of our lives, and found them to be...worthless."

His hands twist her head counterclockwise, too fast and too far. There's a crack, and then—she hangs limp in his grasp.

I let out the breath I'd been holding. I honestly wasn't sure what I was going to do. I'm glad Samael took the choice away from me. "Thank you for that. Couldn't have been easy."

"Easiest choice I've ever had to make." He releases her and she floats free. He watches her for a moment, confused by the simultaneous lack of gravity and us standing on a solid surface.

"There's no up or down, left or right here," I say. "There's only a solid surface beneath your feet if you think there is."

"And this place is...endless?"

"Infinite," I say.

He nods. "You should leave us here. Just in case."

"Her, yes. You... You're not the devil."

"I was," he says. "Once. My place is by her side."

He moves in a flash, catching me off guard.

A fist to the gut followed by an elbow to the back of my head.

He's strong.

A real brute.

But my Europhid infused body and the adaptive armor absorb most of the impact. Still, it's enough to knock me flat.

I push my hands against the non-existent floor and snap upright. Easy to do when gravity is subjective. Fists ready to punch, I find my target and…hold back.

He's got my knife.

"What are you doing?" I ask.

"Finishing a journey I started a long time ago." He holds the knife to his throat. "If there's something on the other side of this life, maybe I'll see you there."

He drags the blade across his neck, cutting deep, severing both arteries. Blood flows like a waterfall. He remains standing throughout, eyes locked on mine, stoic…and for a moment, regretful. Then he's gone, floating beside Cherry Bomb. Forever in hell, now forever in death.

Without so much as a second thought or a regret about how things turned out, I rotate back to the exact place I left—and I find Delgado, with his arm around Wini. Cowboy, Chuy, Burnett, Cassidy, and Hildy are alive and well, standing back from the crater's center. Robinson is with them, hands unbound, gag removed.

Bubbles is at the crater's core, on her hands and knees, eyes closed, focusing on the planet beneath her. Behind her, Henry, Sarah, Zeus, Helen, Will, Gal, Miah, and Bree lend her their strength via Jonas, acting as a conduit between them.

Cassidy senses my presence. She looks back and smiles. "Look," she says, tilting her head up behind me. I turn around to find the crater's periphery full of the Tormented, now set free, fully human once more. They look down at us with an expression I've never seen on one of their faces—one of hope. But they're hardly the main event.

Above them…is Earth. Getting closer. Too close.

Torment is moving. Quickly. But it might be too little too late.

They need to push harder.

I approach the others with Cassidy. Stop beside Robinson. Give him my full attention.

He glances at me. "All good?"

"You finished the book, didn't you?" I ask. "Before August 15th."

"That's my superpower." He smiles at me. "I don't miss deadlines."

I shake my head. "You're an asshole, you know that?"

Before he can reply, I head deeper into the crater and crouch in front of Bubbles. "You can do this."

"I'm…not sure…" she says.

"I know you can."

"How…?" she asks.

I place my hand atop Jonas's, resting on her shoulder.

I'm suddenly locked in, power flowing out of me. But it has nothing to do with godhood. It's my belief. In Bubbles. In our people. Unshakable knowledge that everything is going to be okay. And it increases exponentially when Cassidy places her hand on me. Then Hildy. Burnett. Delgado. Wini. Cowboy. Gal. Will. And finally, Robinson himself, Hans and Franz and…the talking unicorn, who shouts, "Oh, boy! I've always wanted to save the universe!"

The whole planet groans.

Gravity increases.

Around us, people fall to the ground, shouting, but not in fear. Not in anguish. They're amazed. Astounded. Full of hope.

I turn my head up to the sky, watching Earth float past…and farther away.

Classic fucking Robinson.

EPILOGUE

BREE

Dear Diary,

Wow, let me just tell you. What a month. First, we saved the world and the whole universe. Then we had some funerals and stuff, and that was sad, but not too bad for me and Miah, because we didn't really know them well. But Cassidy cried a lot, and that made Burnett cry a lot, and that made me cry a lot, and that made Miah cry a lot. But that's not really surprising, because he's kind of a leaky faucet. Lots of emotions, that guy. But that's probably why he's such a good guy, even if he did leave me behind and *finish my mint chocolate chip.*

He's my brother. Best friend, too. I guess that's weird, because he's like twenty years older than me, but I think it makes him *the weirdo more than me. I get away with a lot because I'm eight. And cute. At least when I'm just Bree, and not Demon Dog.*

I can change back and forth all the time now, so that's cool. Not that there has been much of a reason to be Demon Dog. The world has chilled out. After being nearly wiped out by an army of intergalactic monsters and Nemesis knock-offs, nobody's really in the mood for fighting.

Nothing like a kick in the jimmy cap to sober folks up.

That's what Dark Horse said. I think I know what he means, even if I don't really know what he's saying.

Does that make sense?

Oh! Good news. I got to keep Daylight Glitter. He's living on a big farm in New Hampshire that's our team's new base. Me, Miah, Henry, Sarah, Jonas—and his girlfriend, Madee, who is nice. Linda went on her merry way. Something about a date with a nymph. Henry wanted to go, but Sarah made him stay. Helen left, too. I wish she hadn't. She was cool.

But she 'has an empire to run' or something. She promised to come train me how to fight, so I'm excited for that.

I still live at home. Miah, too. And he and Jen are back together, not that they were ever separated, but she did think he was dead.

It's a little strange—everyone being two years older—but in some ways it's like I'm older.

Life experience and all that, I guess.

I've seen some shit and done some shit.

Henry says that a lot. Mostly to girls. Because we have fans now. There's a lot of video of us. From the Vatican. From Israel. From Beverly. We're trending on Insta, Twitter, and TikTok. And everyone noticed the second planet about to collide with Earth. A bunch of satellites were turned around to look at it, so there's even footage of us fighting Cherry Bomb and saving the planet. Of course, when the news shows me saving everyone, they blur it all out. Too disturbing for TV, they say.

We're heroes, I guess. I don't really feel like one, but my first Demon Dog action figure comes out in a month. Me and Daylight come together. Dark Horse said it was rad. I said he sounded like an old man. Chuy thought that was funny.

And guess what? No, really, guess.

I'll wait.

Yup, they're getting married! In like three months, which is like the middle of winter, but they seemed to be in a hurry for some reason they're not telling anyone. Whatever. Adults and their secrets.

Also engaged: Hildy and Burnett. She *asked him. It was funny. He was jumping up and down, shouting with his silly accent, 'Oh yes, darling. Yes. Yes! A thousand times over, yes!' But they're taking it slower. Time to plan and all that, because, you know, they want the wedding to be on another planet.*

The first wedding on Secundus.

That's what Bubbles named what most people call Second Earth. It's close enough to see if you look up into the sky, but far enough away to not cause problems for either planet, or the solar system. Bubbles kept moving it until there was balance. The two planets will orbit the sun together, forever.

Cherry Bomb's torture planet became a symbol for hope. For mankind's future. Gal and Will live there with Bubbles, helping her create a self-sustaining eco-system, which I guess is harder than it sounds. But they've both created entire worlds before. They know what they're doing, and they've already managed to avert the food crisis that began when millions of the damned found themselves normal again, and hungry for real food.

Everyone else is living in the Mesa now, but they're rebuilding the house in Florida. 'Bigger and better,' Delgado said. He's filling it with all kinds of crazy technology, reinforcing it against future attacks, and making the whole thing look like a vacation home.

At first, I was sad that everyone would be living apart, but we're all getting taught how to use slew drives. When I get good at it, I'll be able to rotate to see Cassidy whenever I want, and I can even sneak away to Secundus. Burnett says they can be traced, so they'll know when I do it, but I helped save reality, so I've got a little more freedom now.

Not that I ever really want to be alone.

Which, I am right now.

So annoying.

I'm just sitting here, waiting for my ride. I could put on my armor and try to rotate to Florida, but the last time I tried doing it on my own, I went to the middle of the Pacific Ocean. Dark Horse came to get me, but he complained about 'major shrinkage,' whatever that is, and about how hard it is to rotate in the water.

What else...what else...

Turns out that Robinson guy is just about our neighbor. Not too far away. I met his kids. They're fun. Norah really likes scary things, too, and guess what? She also has a friend named Cassidy. She even looks like my Cassidy. I guess because one was based on the other. They met once. It was hysterical. They had a high kick competition. The only winners were me and Norah, because they both ended up kicking so high that they fell on their butts.

Robinson is a friend now. He's not writing about our universe anymore, so things might actually go back to normal. He's not so sure, because there's probably 'a lot of dangling threads,' he says. I guess he's prone to forgetting the details of his own stories, so there might be a bunch of monsters and bad guys lurking about.

Honestly, that was a relief. How boring would it be to be Demon Dog and have no one to fight? He said maybe he'd do a comic book for me and Miah someday. That would be cool.

Cowboy left, too, which was sad, because he was nice and fun to listen to, but he wanted to visit friends in other dimensions. I told him to tell Jon Hudson he was cute, but I'm not sure if he will. He'll come back. He said he would. But we don't know when. Robinson hugged him before he left. Got all teared up over it. He might be more emotional than Miah. But I guess it was nice. He cares about all of us. It's like having a creepy uncle who knows everything about you.

But today...today isn't about any of us who saved the world.

It's about new life, and not on Secundus. This is right here on Earth.

Wini rotates into my room. She's dressed in a loose-fitting sundress. Looks happy. No one knows why, but she's been visiting a lot. She's like a nice grandma who likes to talk about inappropriate things and shoot shotguns. My kind of lady.

"Ready to go?" she asks. "Love the shirt."

"Thanks." I put my pen and notebook on the bed and look down at my outfit. My shorts are pink, but my T-shirt gets all the attention. Has Daylight Glitter's silly purple face on it with the catchphrase "Mess with the Alicorn, get the horn."

"How you holding up, kiddo?"

I shrug. "Things are kind of boring around here."

"Everything is boring compared to what we've been through." She smiles. "Today will be different."

"True. But I won't get to fight anyone."

"Henry is always up for some rough-housing." She gives me a wink.

"Okay," I say, stomping my foot. "That's it. I can't stand it anymore. Everyone is taking bets about if you and Henry are, you know, doing it. I said 'no,' because that would be gross, because Henry is dirty most of the time, and you are..."

"Old?" Wini says.

"Well, yeah, obviously. Dan said no one was breaking laws, so we should just let you be."

"Did he?" she says. "Wonder what he'd think if Cassidy started dating a sixty-something year old man."

"Right," I say. "You're, like, at the end of the rainbow and he's, like, here." I put my hand up, angled to where eleven would be on a clock. "That's a little bananas, right?"

"Absolutely." She leans closer, looking around like she's making sure no one else is in my room. "If I tell you the truth, will you keep the secret? Make the others sweat?"

I nod and offer my pinkie. She takes it with hers.

The deal done, she leans up and says, "He's messing with everyone."

"Then what the heck do you guys do when you're in a room alone and he comes out all sweaty and winky and gross?"

She chuckles. "He runs in place...and talks about his feelings. Really unloads. It's kind of exhausting, but he's a sweet boy, and he cares about you all a lot. It's hard for someone like him to love people. He's not used to it. To let people past all those defenses of his. For some reason, when he saw that future version of me die, he decided I was trustworthy. And would probably kick the bucket soon enough to take his secrets to my grave."

"Hopefully not for a long time," I say, and wrap my arm around her.

"One more secret," she says, and then she whispers, "You're my favorite teammate."

I shrug. "I'm everyone's favorite." I shrug again. "After Cassidy. She's cute and cool. I'm cute...and scary. But she likes scary. It's why we're friends."

"But only one of you saved me from a dark-ass torture cave." She squeezes me tight. "Won't forget that."

I give her a thumbs up, and we rotate out of my house, arriving on the beach in St. Augustine. Behind us, through the swampy area, are a bunch of construction vehicles and the metal frame of a really big house.

Everyone else is already here, standing on the shore, just waiting.

It's nice out.

Warmer here than in New Hampshire, where the leaves are falling.

"Reminds me of a sunrise Easter service," Henry says to Sarah.

"When have you ever gone to church?" Sarah asks.

"What? I'm down with Jesus. I'm churchly. Plus, they have free food and hot chocolate. All you need to do is get there early, stand around for a bit, and chow down."

I slide up next to Henry, wrap my arm around him, and give him a squeeze. I press my head into his side and say, "Well, I'm glad you're with us now."

He leans his head on top of mine and whispers, "Me too."

Sarah grins at us both, but she doesn't say anything.

"Okay, everyone," Dark Horse says. He's standing knee deep in the water, his pants rolled up, his floofy white shirt unbuttoned, with rolled up sleeves and a raised collar flapping in the breeze.

"He's really embracing a 1980s Florida vibe," Cassidy says, after leaping up to me and doing a squat and moving her hands up and down like she's churning butter.

"I told him if he was going to keep his shirt open all the time," Hildy says, smiling at us, arm in arm with Burnett, "that he should shave all that hair off."

"I'm naturally hairless," Burnett says. "Streamlined. I move through the water like a cavitating torpedo."

"He's keeping the hair," Chuy says, glancing back and giving us 'shush' eyes.

"Hair on a man is natural," Delgado says. "Primal. Reminds us of where we come from."

"So primal," Bubbles says, and I notice she's holding Dan's hand. I nearly freak out right then and there, but Dark Horse clears his throat.

"Not the time for tangents."

"My tangent saved the universe," Henry says.

"*I* saved the universe," I declare.

A bunch of people open their mouths to chime in, but Gal beats them all to it. "You *all* saved the universe. Together. As a team, far more wonderous than anything Will imagined. But what I think Moses is trying to say, is that there is a time and place for all things. And right now—"

"Right now," Will says, also in the water, "we're not calling the shots. And it is most definitely time."

"Do it," Dark Horse says to Hildy. "It's time!"

Hildy taps her phone a few times, and two speakers standing on the beach start playing a song. I recognize it, because my mom sings it to me when I can't sleep. 'Lullabye' by Billy Joel. A nice soundtrack for what's about to happen.

We all walk into the water, gathering around BigDolph, her belly swollen with a baby. She lifts her head out of the water and squeaks. I gasp as a second, smaller tail emerges from her underside.

Dark Horse strokes BigDolph's shiny porpoise head. "You can do it, buddy. Just push it right out. Easier than getting the Russians out of Afghanistan."

Chuy clears her throat at him.

He sighs. "Fine... Listen, 'Dolph... 'Childbirth is more admirable than conquest, more amazing than self-defense, and as courageous as either one.' Gloria Steinem said that, and I think–"

More of the tail emerges.

Dark Horse flinches back. "Holy shit, it's coming!"

BigDolph exhales and takes a deep breath. She swims in a quick circle, comes back around, and then *pop*, a little dolphin slips out and starts right on swimming. A bunch of blood comes out, too, but BigDolph doesn't seem to mind. The pair swims around us, and I can tell they're happy.

"Well," Jonas says. "That's not something you see every day, and hopefully never again."

"I think it's nice," I say, and stick my tongue out at him.

I mean, I don't know many people who'd be happy about being a man, and then a face in a hairy chest, and then a girl dolphin with twenty something boyfriends, and then having a baby. But Dark Horse told me all about him, the man who used to be BigApe and then became something more. He was secretly eccentric. This is all probably a dream come true for him. But he's more than just a happy ending.

BigDolph and her child are a symbol for new life in the aftermath of a war for the universe. And I think *that* is pretty awesome.

ARCHITECT'S NOTE

Dear Diary—Uhh, reader. Dear reader,

You might be wondering if everything you've just read really happened. After all, our universal constant is a match for the world Will created. 'Nah,' you tell yourself. 'It's impossible. It's...insane to even ask the question.' Maybe the question you should be asking is this: is it possible, in the universe I've created, that a few certain heroes, working together, could—for the collective good of everyone on Earth—erase our memories, myself included?

All I really know is that—if the Infinite Worlds theory is correct—everything that happened in this book is not only possible, but it *did* happen.

And I planned for this reality. I really *did* post on August 15th that I was behind schedule on this book, to trick Cherry Bomb. I really *did* prepare myself for her arrival. And I created characters with abilities that could allow us to forget the trauma I'd unleashed on this planet, and on the entire universe.

I am sorry for that.

If there is anyone out there who *does* remember, who thinks the explosion in Beirut wasn't Jonas, the Darkness in New Hampshire was really just Squirrelmageddon, or the construction projects taking place all around us aren't actually repairs, forgive me.

Will this stop me from writing? Of course not!

Just because I put all my thoughts on paper doesn't make them officially possible.

Anything you can dream up is possible in the Infinite.

What am I dreaming up now?

That everyone who reads and enjoys not just this book, but the entire series will go and post reviews for all the books! Every single one helps, and the bigger we make this whole storyline, the closer we'll be to bringing them to the big, or small, screen. Can you imagine a reality, where this whole universe of intertwined stories became an MCU-style mix of movies and streaming series? I know I can. Let's make it happen!

A novel like this wouldn't be complete without a truly devastating soundtrack. Visit bewareofmonsters.com/playlist to hear the complete list of songs 'heard' in this novel, and to which I listened while writing it. That page also includes the playlists for *Tribe, Exo-Hunter, Mind Bullet,* and *The Order*, and in the future, it will feature playlists from my other novels as well.

If you want to stay up to date on all the latest book, Hollywood, and comic book news that's brewing, AND meet a fantastic group of fellow fans, join: Facebook.com/groups/JR.Tribe and say hello. If you want to keep up without being social, just sign up for the newsletter at bewareofmonsters.com. I'm always around, answering questions and posting regularly. Hope to see you there!

—Jeremy Robinson,
aka: the Architect

INFINITE TIMELINE ART

The following is a collection of artwork from Jeremy himself, as well as a commissioned piece of art from comics artist Mario Santoro, and several pieces from freelance artist Damion Dunn.

The character images by Jeremy were created using the Midjourney AI. These are not meant to be definitive 'castings' for the characters, but they are pretty close to how Jeremy imagined them in his head. Initially just playing around with Midjourney, Jeremy found with some practice he was able to get images close to what he was envisioning. Before he knew it, he had enough pieces to include in the book.

There is also a T-shirt design that Jeremy created (using photoshop), related to Daylight Glitter.

Following the T-shirt design, there is a piece of artwork that Jeremy commissioned from Italian artist Mario Santoro as a sort of interview for working on a larger project together. Jeremy was quickly impressed with Mario's work, and they are now working together on a sci-fi/horror graphic novel called *Little Bird.*

Finally, freelance artist Damion Dunn has contributed several fantastic interpretations of the books in the Infinite Timeline.

BREE

BUBBLES

CASSIDY

CHERRY BOMB

CHUY

COWBOY

DELGADO

EUROPHIDS

HANS & FRANZ

HENRY

("GOD OF THE SKY, BITCHES!")

HILDY

DARK HORSE

JONAS

MIAH

SAMAEL

SARAH

WILL & GAL

GET THE HORN

Jeremy created this T-shirt design using Photoshop based on Bree's alicorn, Daylight Glitter.

(The shirt is available for purchase at www.teepublic.com/user/jrobinsonauthor)

MESS WITH
DAYLIGHT GLITTER...

GET THE HORN

THE GATE

Jeremy commissioned this artwork from Italian superstar artist, Mario Santoro.

(Jeremy is now working on a comic book with Mario.)

DAMION DUNN

Damion Dunn contributed the following pieces of art after being inspired by the novels in the Infinite Timeline.

You can find more of Damion's work at:
@theDunisher on Instagram
@DamionDunn009 on Instagram
www.facebook.com/damion009 on Facebook.

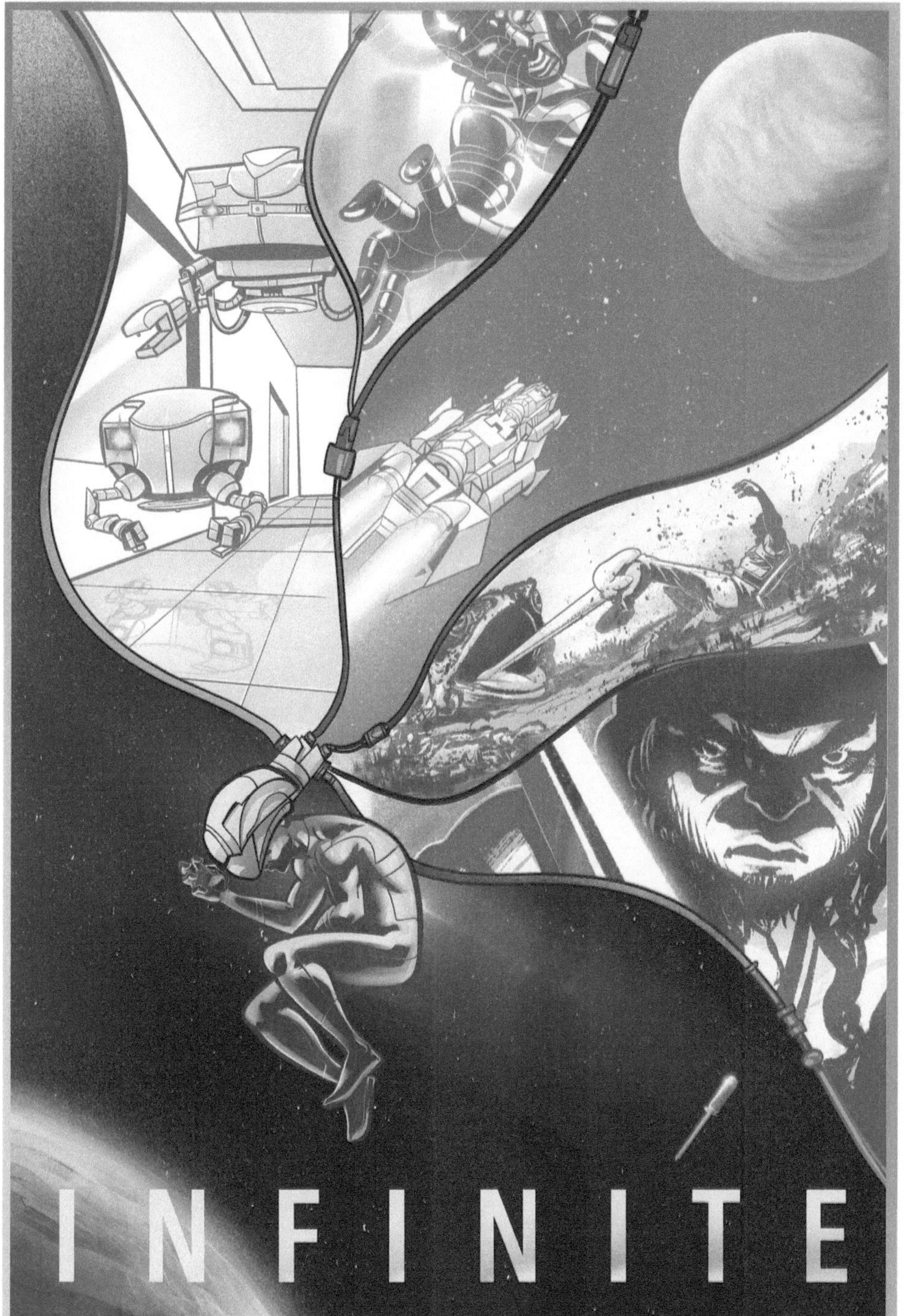
INFINITE

Γ Δ Ε Ζ Η Θ Ι Κ Λ Μ Ν Ξ
MIND
BULLET

NPC

JEREMY ROBINSON

AUTHOR'S NOTE

The conclusion of the Infinite Timeline mirrors another journey of mine, which was far less fun. During the seven years it took me to write and publish these books, I suffered from a mystery disease that nearly undid me physically and mentally. That's a lie. It *did* undo me twice.

The first time it knocked me out of commission, for two months, I was halfway through the writing of *Infinite*. I had what I suppose you'd call a breakdown. I was struck by the mother of all panic attacks. Couldn't breathe. Tunnel vision. Pounding heart. Whole body shaking. I got the whole enchilada, and it lasted a full hour. If you're someone prone to panic attacks, you know they're generally a lot shorter. This one kicked my butt and left me shaking until the next morning.

Long story short, for the next few years, while writing *The Others, Flux,* and *Tribe,* I was a mental wreck. Panic attacks became common place, striking with no rhyme or reason. And to make matters worse, I was misdiagnosed with a brain tumor. Perfect timing! I was like a scared little chipmunk, all the time. I couldn't go for a walk. Couldn't take the trash out. Couldn't do much of anything without the fear of death for one reason or another sneaking up on me. Luckily for my readers, one of the things I could still do was write.

The second time the mystery disease kicked me in the nuts was really an extension of the constant panic (which took years to figure out). I feel like to call it neuropathy or nerve pain is an understatement. Every nerve fiber in my body was firing, all the time, sending signals that I was burning, that pain was shooting through me, that I was being electrified, that my insides were alive, or there were bugs crawling over my skin, or that the slightest thing touching me had the same intensity as a branding iron. Back to bed... Two months again. And this time was worse than the last. I couldn't do *anything*. Even the shower hurt. The *wind* hurt with an intensity that is hard to describe, but I hope I will forget. It was the most excruciating thing I've ever experienced, and it lasted years.

And through it all. Writing. The Infinite Timeline. I put all my pain into these books, most easily seen in *Infinite* and *NPC*. But I put all my hope in them as well. To push on against odds that seemed impossible to surmount. To hope in a future that is better. So, I created characters who could get that done. Who could make me smile. Who I could believe in. Miah. Dark Horse. Hildy. Cassidy. Even Henry. They're good for what ails you, and they were good for me, helping me through the darkest days of my life. In part, this is why *Singularity* included me. I wanted to meet them. To thank them. And I'm glad I got the chance.

Some personal discoveries and a long time spent observing the cause and effect of my symptoms led to some realizations, which led to new discoveries, and so on. I spent years and a lot of money on doctors, therapists, supplements, and drugs, and I came to understand that the pain was a direct result of the anxiety, panic, and fear. If I was calm—like Zen calm—my symptoms disappeared. Poof. But the moment stress reentered the picture, the symptoms returned. This led me to psychiatry as a treatment option...about five months ago. I started something that worked well for anxiety, depression, and nerve pain. It seemed like the perfect solution, and thus far, it has been. Panic attacks are a thing of the past. I no longer feel the need to always carry Lorazepam. Anxiety is gone (aside from times it makes sense). And best of all, the pain is nearly completely gone, returning only occasionally to remind me it's waiting for a sequel if I'll let it.

Singularity was the first of the Infinite Timeline books I wrote, free of all those horrible things. The book—the whole Timeline—provided profound symbolism for my personal journey to hell and victoriously out the other side. I think that might be why it resonates with so many people. Because I'm not alone in my suffering. People don't talk about these things much, but after twenty years of 1-star reviews, I don't really care what people are thinking. If you're a fan and you're suffering, you are not alone. We're all human and all going through this kind of shit together. Talk about it. Get help. And most of all, keep plugging away, hoping, fighting, and believing in a better future. If you need inspiration, Miah and Dark Horse are just a book away.

—Jeremy

ACKNOWLEDGMENTS

When you undertake something this big as an author, it really pushes the boundaries of what you can handle. Keeping track of characters in a series is one thing. Stories begin and end. But with the Infinite Timeline, the story just kept getting bigger and more complicated until reaching a conclusion with something like twenty main characters. It was daunting. Luckily for me, I didn't have to tackle all of this on my lonesome.

First off, Kane Gilmour. My first line of defense against plot holes and looking stupid. While traditional publishing would never consider such a complicated scheme of merging nine standalone books in four crossovers, we have that freedom, not just because we're independent, but also because you're up to the task of editing these books, helping me keep everything straight, and making sure I make sense. Couldn't have pulled this off without you.

As always, big thanks to our army of proofreaders: Adrian Brooke, Brandon Burnett, Holly Strickland Chandler, Elizabeth Cooper, Dustin Dreyling, Joseph Firoozmand, John Fish, Cynthia Gregory, Gavin Gregory, Dee Haddrill, Andre Jenkin, Becki Tapia Laurent, Janis Levonitis, Stefanie Maubach, Kyle Mohr, Jessica Otterstål, and Jeff Sexton. You all help conceal the fact that I'm just as bad at typing as I am spelling. Thanks to Kyle Mohr again for his expertise with firearms. And thanks to Alex Maddern for allowing me to bounce ideas off you...and do horrible things to you that I know you actually love, because you're weird like that.

R.C. Bray, the voice of the Infinite Timeline. You elevated these characters in a way that makes them real and even more memorable. Thank you, thank you, thank you for lending your talent, and for reading the 1.3 million words included in these books. Also, thanks to Jeffrey Kafer, for lending his considerable talent to the narration of *Flux*, and half of

NPC. And to the powerhouse behind the narrators—Podium Audio—thanks for supporting this crazy concept even after half of the books were already published. Your efforts have elevated the books to the next level. Also need to thank Damonza.com for another stellar cover, perfectly recreating my very crude sketch of what I wanted.

And thank you, dear reader, for getting on board with this unconventional 'it's not a series, it's a world' concept. Your support and growing excitement about these characters and this insane world have carried me through some rough times and encouraged me to push forward when obstacles arose. Wouldn't be here without you all.

—JR

ABOUT THE AUTHOR

Jeremy Robinson is the *New York Times* and #1 Audible bestselling author of over seventy novels and novellas, including *Infinite, The Others,* and *The Dark,* as well as the Jack Sigler thriller series, and *Project Nemesis,* the highest selling, original kaiju novel of all time (which is in development for TV with Chad Stahelski, director of John Wick). Robinson is known for mixing elements of science, history, and mythology, which has earned him the #1 spot in Science Fiction and Action-Adventure, and secured him as the top creature feature author. Many of his novels have been adapted into comic books, optioned for film and TV, and translated into fourteen languages. He lives in New Hampshire with his wife and three children.

Visit him at www.bewareofmonsters.com.

www.ingramcontent.com/pod-product-compliance
Lightning Source LLC
Chambersburg PA
CBHW020917310726
48980CB00011B/923/J

* 9 7 8 1 9 4 1 5 3 9 7 1 2 *